2 4 AUG

D0236954

SPECIAL MESSAGE TO READERS

THE ULVERSCROFT FOUNDATION
(registered UK charity number 264873)
was established in 1972 to provide funds for
research, diagnosis and treatment of eye diseases.
Examples of major projects funded by
the Ulverscroft Foundation are:-

- The Children's Eye Unit at Moorfields Eye
  Hospital, London
- The Ulverscroft Children's Eye Unit at Great
  Ormond Street Hospital for Sick Children
- Funding research into eye diseases and
  treatment at the Department of Ophthalmology,
  University of Leicester
- The Ulverscroft Vision Research Group,
  Institute of Child Health
- Twin operating theatres at the Western
  Ophthalmic Hospital, London
- The Chair of Ophthalmology at the Royal
  Australian College of Ophthalmologists

You can help further the work of the Foundation
by making a donation or leaving a legacy.
Every contribution is gratefully received. If you
would like to help support the Foundation or
require further information, please contact:

THE ULVERSCROFT FOUNDATION
The Green, Bradgate Road, Anstey
Leicester LE7 7FU, England
Tel: (0116) 236 4325

website: www.foundation.ulverscroft.com

Tamar Cohen is a freelance journalist and writer in residence at Kingston University. She lives in north London with her partner and three (nearly) grown children, plus one badly behaved dog.

You can follow Tamar on Twitter @mstamarcohen

THE BROKEN

Two families — Josh, Hannah and their daughter Lily; and Dan, Sasha and their daughter September — have shared life and laughs since their children were babies. It is a perfect, close-knit world where friends trust each other implicitly — until one of them drops a bombshell that changes their lives forever. Best friends tell you everything: about their kitchen renovation; about their little girl's schooling. How one of them is leaving the other for a young model. Best friends don't tell lies. They don't take up residence on your couch for weeks. They don't call lawyers. They don't make you choose sides. Best friends don't keep secrets about their past. They don't put you in danger. Best friends don't always stay best friends . . .

Books by Tamar Cohen
Published by Ulverscroft:

THE MISTRESS'S REVENGE
THE WAR OF THE WIVES
SOMEONE ELSE'S WEDDING

TAMAR COHEN

THE BROKEN

Complete and Unabridged

CHARNWOOD
Leicester

First published in Great Britain in 2014 by
Doubleday
an imprint of Transworld Publishers
London

First Charnwood Edition
published 2016
by arrangement with
Transworld Publishers
A Random House Group Company
London

The moral right of the author has been asserted

Copyright © 2014 by Tamar Cohen
All rights reserved

This book is a work of fiction and, except in the case
of historical fact, any resemblance to actual persons,
living or dead, is purely coincidental.

ESSEX COUNTY COUNCIL
LIBRARIES

A catalogue record for this book is available
from the British Library.

ISBN 978–1–4448–2740–8

Published by
F. A. Thorpe (Publishing)
Anstey, Leicestershire

Set by Words & Graphics Ltd.
Anstey, Leicestershire
Printed and bound in Great Britain by
T. J. International Ltd., Padstow, Cornwall

This book is printed on acid-free paper

For Colin, with love and thanks

Lucie, aged four

I am scrunched up as small as small can be in my special place. My knees are right under my chin so that when I put out my tongue I can lick the scab on my right knee from where I fell off the swing in the playground. Scabs help you get better. You mustn't pick them. My heart is boom-booming in my chest and I have that sick feeling like when I needed to go toilet at school but didn't want to say and ended up in a warm puddle with my face hot and everyone laughing. It's not comfy sitting like this in my special place. My legs are hurting. Now I'm a big girl, nearly at big school, I don't really fit in my special place any more, but I daren't move. I must stay still as a statue. Sleeping Lions. It's dark in my special place and I'm frightened, but I mustn't make a sound. I must be quiet as a little mouse. Eek, eek, eek.

Or Mummy will find me.

1

'I'm leaving her.'

No response. Josh was fiddling with his mobile phone, trying to get it to stop autocorrecting a text he was composing to Hannah, so he wasn't really listening. He checked his texts assiduously these days before pressing Send, ever since coming back from a weekend at his parents' and unintentionally informing his mother he was homosexual instead of home. The truth was he hated texting, and was the only person he knew who still laboriously typed 'you' instead of the ubiquitous 'u'. And as for apostrophes — don't get him started. 'I thought you just said you were leaving Sash,' he chuckled, still worrying away at the keyboard, his broad fingers as unwieldy as sausages.

'I did. Look, would it kill you to pay a bit of attention?' There was something hiding in Dan's voice. A whine tucked away like a polyp under the surface of his normally cocky, over-egged Essex twang.

Josh looked up. 'You're joking, right? This is a joke.'

'Do I look like I'm fucking joking?'

Dan didn't in truth look like he was joking. His expression was strained and a little horrified.

'You can't.' It was a feeble thing to say, but Josh was too shocked to think of anything else. Dan and Sasha had been together for years.

Eight or nine. Nearly as long as him and Hannah. And then there was September. She was still only four. 'What about the new kitchen?'

Dan and Sasha had only just finished moving the kitchen up to the top level of their art deco-style house so they could take advantage of those views out across the cricket and tennis clubs towards Ally Pally, spread out along the top of the distant hill. Josh and Hannah had been at the inaugural dinner party to celebrate the end of all the months of dust and builders just a couple of weeks before, and he and Dan had ended up doing tequila slammers on the new concrete worktops.

'Sod the fucking kitchen. That was Sasha's idea anyway. I was quite happy with the old kitchen.'

'But why?'

Dan put down his pint and fixed Josh with his wide-set blue eyes — the ones Hannah had once declared, in a drunken moment, to be 'far too sexy for a man', which Josh had tried hard not to mind.

'We're just not good together any more,' Dan said, shaking his head. 'Don't get me wrong, Sasha is brilliant. I love her to bits. I'm just not *in* love with her.'

He kept his eyes trained on Josh's while the clichés spilled out of him, as if intensity was proof of sincerity. But Josh, who had accompanied Dan on two stag weekends as well as countless lads' nights out, had seen him give this look too many times before in too many less-than-sincere circumstances for it to be one hundred per cent effective. He sat back in his uncomfortable wooden chair with the saggy leather cushion, in the pub they always insisted on going to on match days, purely because it was so unappealing that they were always guaranteed a seat. Suddenly his head buzzed with adrenaline.

'You've met someone else.'

Dan's eyes widened still further, his raised eyebrows disappearing into his floppy dishwater-blond hair.

'What are you talking about? Look, mate, I know it's a shock, but sometimes people just grow apart. It doesn't mean there's someone else.'

'Cut the crap.' Josh wasn't angry — mostly because he didn't believe Dan was remotely serious. But neither was he about to let him get away with feeding him some women's magazine bullshit. 'You wouldn't leave Sasha and September unless there was someone else waiting in the wings. I know you. *Mate*,' Josh trusted that anyone listening would realize he was using the word ironically, 'you're emotionally lazy.'

'Emotionally lazy?'

Dan bristled as if gearing up to protest, but then seemed to think better of it and slumped back down again. 'OK, you're right. I have met someone.' He glanced at Josh, checking how this had gone down. 'But we haven't done anything. What I mean is we haven't slept together.'

Josh knew he was lying. 'So who is she?'

His friend's eyes suddenly brightened, and he almost fell over his words in his delight at being

4

given licence to speak of this new beloved. 'She's incredible. Amazing. Honestly, you have no idea. I met her on a shoot. Yeah, yeah, she's a model. Cliché, cliché. But she's not like all the rest. She's so smart and funny and down to earth.'

'And, don't tell me — 'gorgeous'.' Josh paused before the last word and traced exaggerated quote marks in the air with his fingers as he said it, to show he was being sardonic. But such subtleties were lost on Dan.

'No. She looks like the back end of a bus,' he grinned.

Josh struggled then to hide the wave of blind fury that swept over him out of nowhere. Anger was appropriate, wasn't it, in view of his friendship with Sasha? He refused to acknowledge, even to himself, that the anger might be overlaid with something else. Something acidic and powerful. It wasn't jealousy. Most assuredly, absolutely not. Why should he feel jealous of Dan when he was about to lob a live grenade into the heart of his family? 'Listen, Dan.' He put on the voice he used when he was talking to his pupils — reasonable, calm, but firm. 'Everyone needs an ego boost from time to time. What are you — thirty-five? Thirty-six?'

'Oi, steady on! Just because you're staring forty in the face doesn't mean the rest of us are fucking ancient as well. Actually, I'm only thirty-four.'

'Whatever.' Josh was thirty-eight. It was hardly ancient. He was fairly sure he was younger than Robbie Williams, for instance. 'Listen, Dan, most blokes our age' — he enjoyed Dan's momentary scowl at that — 'who've been with the same woman for a long time get itchy feet. Do you think I've never thought about how it would be to be with someone else apart from Hannah?' Briefly he wondered whether that was true. *Had* he ever seriously considered being with someone else? Really? 'But the thing is, I know it wouldn't be worth it. I'd be jeopardizing everything that's important to me for what? For a brief thrill?'

Dan had started shaking his head when Josh was only halfway through this speech. 'Look, I loved Sasha. That's why I married her. But she's not laid-back like Hannah. She is totally neurotic — you know that. Understandable given what happened to her as a child, but fucking wearying to live with 24/7. Stuff goes on at home that you wouldn't believe. She's always testing me, do you know what I mean? She'll say something really hurtful just to try to get me to lose my temper, and then it's all 'See, you can never trust anyone. All the people in my life who were supposed to care about me let me down.' Last week we were having a drink at our neighbours' house and suddenly Sasha announces she has a headache and gets up and leaves, telling me to stay and she'll be fine. Then when I get home she launches into me for not going with her to make sure she's OK. It's exhausting!' Dan's tone had taken on a shrill, self-justifying note. He looked up and caught Josh's raised eyebrow. 'OK, you're right,' he said in a strange, strangled voice suddenly quite unlike his own. 'I know you're right. I'd do anything rather than hurt Sasha. But what can I say, man? I've fallen in love. I realize now I was never really in love with Sasha. I wanted to look after her, but with Sienna I've found an equal. Someone who can be a real life partner. I feel alive!'

'*Sienna?*'

Dan shrugged. 'Yeah, yeah. But you can't blame her for her name.'

Josh found it hard to unstretch his eyes from their *Are you fucking kidding me?* expression. Of course. She would be called Sienna. Dan couldn't possibly have fallen for a Cathy or Melanie or Ruth. 'And how old exactly is *Sienna?*' His voice came out more sneering than he'd intended.

Dan pushed himself back from the table, dislodging the folded-up cardboard beer mat that had been wedged under one of the legs to stop it wobbling, and glanced around the pub. His guileless face, still cherubic even in his mid-thirties in that pretty-boy style that usually — Josh believed — puffs out to seed by fifty, betrayed, as ever, every emotion going on inside him just as surely as if he had subtitles running in a permanent loop along his forehead.

Josh was quietly satisfied now to recognize embarrassment in his friend's expression (not surprising) and shame (well, good). But there was something else as well, something Dan was trying very hard to hide. Triumph. That was it. On some level, Dan was *pleased* with himself.

'Don't laugh, OK, but she's twenty-four.'

'*Twenty-four!* For fuck's sake, you're a walking, talking cliché.'

'I know, I know. But she's really mature for her

age. She has an old soul.'

'Yeah, don't tell me, you were lovers in a past life.'

Dan allowed himself a quick smirk before his face crumpled again, the even, pleasant features folding in on themselves like dough. 'Oh God, I feel awful about everything. How am I going to tell Sash? And September?'

For a second Josh almost felt sorry for him. He couldn't imagine turning his back on his own wife and child, packing up his things and moving out of his family home. Just the thought of it made his heart race uncomfortably. Not waking up with Hannah's long, thick red hair tickling his face, or Lily's little hand on his arm, shaking him awake. '*Come on, Daddy, you big old sleepyhead poo-poo head.*' Not taking Toby the dachshund around the block before work, his breath coming out cloudy in the cold air, crossing paths with Janey from two doors down with her dribbling chocolate Labrador. Now *there* was a proper dog. Josh had been mortified when Hannah had first brought Toby home, a sausage on legs, a furry worm, all floppy ears and big mournful eyes. 'Just as long as you don't expect me to be seen with that thing in public,' he'd warned. Now, predictably, he doted on Toby, even more than Hannah and Lily did. Just because something started as a compromise didn't mean you couldn't end up loving it just the same.

He still couldn't believe Dan was serious about leaving it all behind — the familiar hot-water bottle of domesticity. Sure, he and

Sasha bickered a lot, but it didn't mean anything. The next minute they'd be all over each other, often nauseatingly so. It wasn't perfect, but they were happy, surely? They were all happy.

Josh started to think about what all this could potentially mean for him and Hannah. Dan and Sasha had been their best friends since they all met when the girls were newborns. They socialized together, they helped each other out with babysitting. Dan and Josh had their Saturday football, Hannah and Sasha went to art galleries or their Thursday evening bookclub (which seemed to him to be largely an excuse to drink wine and complain about their husbands). The little girls were inseparable.

'We can still hang out together,' Dan said, as if he'd read Josh's mind. 'You'll love Sienna when you get to know her.'

'Dream on, mate.'

'What?'

'If you think you can just slot another woman into Sasha's place and we'll all be like an episode of bloody *Friends*, you're living in cloud-cuckoo-land. Hannah would never stand for it. She's really loyal that way.'

'I know it wouldn't happen immediately. Just in time, that's all I meant. And don't worry, I'm going to give Sasha whatever she asks for. I don't want her or September to want for anything. I give you my word this is going to be the most civilized divorce in history.'

Josh gaped at him. 'So, let's just recap. You're leaving your wife of what — eight years? — for a

9

woman a decade younger. And you think she's going to be happy to sit down over a nice cup of tea and make arrangements about dividing up her home, her *daughter*, for God's sake. You're fucking deluded.'

Dan coloured, his skin taking on the purplish hue of under-diluted Ribena. 'I'm not leaving her for Sienna. I told you, Sasha and I haven't been right for ages. We've never really been right. Living with her is like being on eggshells the whole time. I haven't been happy in years.'

'And don't tell me, you deserve to be happy.'

'Sure. Everyone does, don't they?'

Josh shook his head. 'I'm not going to get caught up in some existential debate about the nature of happiness.' He was properly angry now. 'I just don't happen to think you can build your happiness on the back of someone else's unhappiness.' Now who was talking in clichés?

Dan looked miserable, yet defiant. Josh recognized that look from his own teenage pupils.

'I know Sasha will be in bits at first. Of course she will. But I really believe that in the long run she'll realize it's the best thing for her. This way she's free to find someone who really appreciates her.'

Josh sighed. Now that it was sinking in that Dan actually was serious, he was feeling faintly sick. Until Dan, he'd never really had a close friend, not since school anyway. He was more the type of person who got included in group outings but not intimate gatherings. And once he'd met Hannah, she was the only friend he'd

10

needed. So he'd been pleased — grateful, even — to find himself accepted so readily into Dan's inner circle. And he was fond of Sasha, too, although she could be prickly sometimes. 'When are you going to tell her?'

'Tonight. That's why it's really important you don't tell Hannah anything until I've had a chance to talk to Sash properly. I know you two can't shit without giving each other a full description, but you've got to promise me not to say anything. I don't want Sasha to hear about this from anyone except me.'

Dan's face wore a noble expression and Josh had an uncharacteristic impulse to punch him in it.

'Oh, and whatever you do, don't mention Sienna. I'm not going to tell Sasha about her until she's got used to the idea of us splitting up. It would just confuse the issue.'

'What's there to be confused about? You're leaving her for another woman. Oldest story in the book.'

Josh's anger was mounting and Dan put up both his hands in mock surrender.

'Look, Josh, I get why you're upset. I'd feel the same if our positions were reversed. And I love you for being so protective of Sash. But the fact is, I *am* leaving her. I've made up my mind.' Dan said this as though making up his mind about something was all it took to make it so. As if he had only to formulate the intent for the deed to be done. His self-assuredness stoked Josh's fury. 'And what I really need is for you to help make it as painless as possible — for Sasha's and

September's sakes. Not for mine. This thing with Sienna is still very early days. It might come to absolutely nothing. It'd be stupid to throw that into the mix now when we all need things to be as clean and simple as possible. I don't want to hurt Sash any more than necessary.'

'You're all heart.'

★ ★ ★

'*What?*'

'I'm not supposed to tell you. I was sworn to secrecy. But seeing as he's probably telling her as we speak, and there's a good chance she'll turn up on the doorstep at any moment in the throes of a nervous breakdown, I thought it was only fair to warn you.'

Hannah had her hand clapped over her mouth, above which her pale-blue eyes appeared almost completely circular. 'You've got to be kidding me. Oh my *God*. Poor Sash. What a bastard. What a complete and utter bastard.'

'To be fair, he seemed pretty cut up about it.' Josh couldn't understand why he was defending Dan to Hannah. It wasn't as if he had the slightest bit of sympathy for what he was doing. Still, some intrinsic friend-protection instinct was kicking in and he found himself trying to justify what Dan was doing. 'You know Sasha isn't the easiest person.'

'And that makes it OK, does it, to cheat on her with a twenty-four-year-old and break a little girl's heart?'

'Twenty-four isn't exactly a little girl — '

12

'Don't even joke about it, Josh. You know exactly what I mean. These are our friends, remember? How many Saturday nights have we spent round there? How many holidays have we been on together? He can't split up over some stupid affair. He just can't.'

Josh had the oddest idea that Hannah was talking about Dan splitting up with *them* rather than with Sasha. He remembered Dan's face when he'd talked about Sienna, but this clearly wasn't the time to suggest to Hannah that this might be more than a 'stupid affair'.

'I can't believe it. I really can't.'

Josh shifted along the battered wine-coloured velvet sofa Hannah had fallen in love with on eBay, which had required dismantling the door frame to get into the flat. He put a tentative arm around her, half expecting her to wriggle away, as she sometimes did these days. Now that Hannah was always so tired and their sex life had dwindled to almost nothing, all physical contact between them seemed to carry extra weight, with the result that they didn't touch each other nearly as much — or as naturally — as they used to. He felt her shoulders trembling under his hand.

'Hey.' He tilted her face up towards him so he could see her properly, taking in the freckles he adored and she claimed to despise, and the mouth with its mismatched lips — the top one so thin and well defined and the bottom one almost indecently plump. 'Don't get so upset. Of course it's horrible, but we're still OK.'

Hannah's eyes, canopied by fine, surprisingly

13

dark eyebrows, peered up at him through a glaze of tears. 'But they're our best friends. I thought they were so happy together. All those *I love yous* at the end of every phone conversation. Was that all a show? And if it can happen to them, what's to stop it happening to us?'

Josh pulled her closer, savouring the contact, and planted a kiss on the top of her head. Despite everything, he allowed himself a little smile. Trust Hannah to jump straight to the worst-case scenario. What was it that therapist had called her? A catastrophist. That's it. As if you could catch divorce from other people like the flu.

'Never,' he whispered into her hair.

After a moment, Hannah pulled away, looking utterly wretched.

'Oh, but when I think about little September, growing up without her father.'

'Not according to Dan. He thinks it will be the most amicable split in the world. He's got it all worked out. He and Sasha will sell the house and buy two flats within walking distance of each other. September will be able to see both of them whenever she wants to. She won't even notice they're not together.'

'What planet does he get this stuff from? He really thinks he's going to move in down the road with some bloody schoolgirl bimbo and everything's going to go on just as before?'

Hannah got to her feet and started angrily clearing up the remains of the Indian takeaway which were spread across the coffee table in front of them in a selection of foil containers, all

14

smeared with orange- or ochre-coloured sauce. A tell-tale pink flush was sweeping across her normally pale cheeks, and Josh felt a twinge of alarm, remembering how he'd promised not to say anything to her.

'You're not going to call Sasha, are you? Dan made me promise I wouldn't tell you about any of it, but especially not about her. About Sienna.'

He was nervous now — conscious suddenly of having gone back on a promise, of having been compromised.

Hannah made a snorting noise at the name.

'No really,' Josh went on, ignoring it. 'He doesn't want it to get out about him seeing someone else. He says it will make things nastier than they need to be.'

'He should have thought about that before he got his dick out then, shouldn't he?'

Hannah stalked out of the living room, hands full of dirty plates and silver-foil cartons. Josh heard her clattering around in the tiny kitchen next door, and he tried to still the involuntary leap his thoughts had taken hearing Hannah say the word *dick*.

'Please, Hannah. Don't say anything. I should never have told you.'

She reappeared in the doorway and flung herself back on to the sofa, curling her long legs in their black leggings up underneath her. 'OK. But I just want you to know I hate lying to Sasha. It isn't right for him to ask you to do this. She deserves to know the truth.'

'Yes, but not from us. It's not our place. We have to stay neutral.'

15

'But how am I supposed to look her in the eye? Don't forget they're coming for lunch tomorrow.'

Josh slung his arm around her once more, emboldened by his previous success, and she snuggled back against him.

'I wouldn't bank on it,' he said. 'Dan says he's telling her tonight. I can't imagine they'll be round here playing happy families tomorrow.'

2

'My head feels like there's a marching band inside it clashing cymbals and playing those big curly brass thingies and jumping up and down.'

'Why would a marching band jump up and down?'

'Don't bother trying to provoke me, Dan. I'm too ill to rise to it.'

Sasha was draped across the same sofa where Josh and Hannah had sat up far too late the previous night debating Dan's shock announcement. Her glossy black hair was fanned out across a threadbare brown faux fur cushion and one of her hands was flung across her eyes, all but obscuring her small neat features. Her legs in their skinny jeans were stretched out and she'd kicked off her Converse trainers so that she could rest her bare, brown, child-sized feet on Dan's Levi's-clad thigh. She looked a lot like someone with a hangover. She did not look like someone whose husband had just announced he was going to leave her.

'He couldn't tell her,' Josh whispered to Hannah as they were squeezed into the kitchen together preparing lunch. His cheeks, always rosy, were flushed pink by the heat fanning from the oven into the confined space, and he kept pushing his thick hair, which Hannah liked to point out was the exact colour and texture of a doormat, back from his overheated face. When he glanced at her, his greeny-brown eyes were smudged with worry. 'He was going to, but then their neighbours turned up unexpectedly.'

'Brilliant. So now we've got to sit across the table from each other pretending everything's hunky dory, while all the time there's this . . . *time bomb* waiting to go off.'

'What else can we do?'

'I can't believe he's just sitting there, stroking her feet. It's so cruel.'

'Why are you two whispering in there? Do you hate us? Do you wish we would leave?'

At the sound of Sasha's voice, Hannah glared at Josh. She could hear September and Lily playing together in Lily's bedroom, September's voice loud and clear over Lily's gentle murmur. How many lazy Sundays had they passed in this way, the six of them? The realization that this might be the last was so savagely painful that Hannah, her hand frozen in the act of chopping up some fresh basil, suddenly felt she couldn't breathe.

'Yes. Go away and take your disgusting, unsavoury hangover with you,' called Josh, making a *Pull yourself together* face at Hannah.

Lunch was, as always, a long-drawn-out affair eaten at the heavy pine dining table which was squashed into the area behind the sofa in the living room, the kitchen in Hannah and Josh's two-bedroom garden flat being far too small to eat in. The girls joined them for the start of the meal, kneeling up on cushions that they placed over the seats of the wooden chairs and chattering to each other as they tucked into their mini portions of lasagne. September, six weeks older than Lily, led the conversation as usual, lurching from subject to subject seemingly without rhyme or reason. Hannah's heart pinched a little when she saw how her daughter's face scrunched up in concentration as she struggled to follow her friend, while at the same time furtively digging out suspicious unidentified vegetable matter from her dish with her spoon and laying it carefully on one side.

'Is it me or is everyone really flat today?' Sasha was seated at the head of the table, closest to the French windows that led on to the communal garden, where the late-blooming flowers looked gaudy against the grey September day. Her eyes flickered from face to face expecting a response.

Hannah looked away. 'We're not being very good company today, are we? We're just a bit tired, that's all.' She gestured briefly towards Lily with her hand, as if blaming her for them being below par, and then immediately felt guilty. Poor Lily, she was so good. She didn't deserve to be made a scapegoat.

'Can we get down now?' September had finished her lunch and was rocking on her chair, her chocolate-brown curls quivering as she moved.

'I don't think Lily's quite finished yet. Maybe you could just wait a few — '

The rest of Hannah's gentle entreaty was drowned out by Sasha interrupting, 'Sure, poppet, you get down.'

Sasha turned to Hannah. 'Sorry, Hannah. I just didn't want Temmy to get fidgety. You know how tetchy she can be.'

Hannah smiled and hoped her irritation didn't show.

'Can I go too, Mummy? Please?'

Lily still had food on her plate, but she was already gazing after September, her lasagne forgotten, her blue eyes full of longing.

'No, Lily. You need to finish. Just that little bit on your plate.'

'But September didn't.'

'No, but September is a guest, and you're not. Which is why I'm telling you to finish up. Tell you what. If you eat four more forkfuls, you can get down.'

Hannah sighed inwardly as Lily loaded her spoon with the minimum amount of food possible and raised it to her mouth four times, counting in whispers under her breath, before throwing it down triumphantly and scooting off to find her friend. 'Thank you for the lovely dinner,' she called over her shoulder in a singsong voice.

Hannah got up and started clearing away the plates. The incident with September had done nothing to improve her mood. It wasn't the first time Sasha had talked over Hannah. Sometimes she felt as if nothing she said actually mattered. Am I here? she wanted to say. Can you even see me? She kept forgetting about what Josh had told her about Dan, and then suddenly it would come flooding back to her, as shocking now as it was when she first heard it. In the kitchen, she angrily scraped food off the plates into the plastic container they used for collecting compost, perversely enjoying the harsh, grating noise of metal on china.

'You OK there?'

Dan had appeared in the doorway carrying the big white earthenware dish that had held the lasagne and the salad bowl, still half full.

Hannah said she was fine.

She couldn't look at him, focusing instead on the chrome bin that took up half the floor space in the cramped kitchen. Josh had told her it was too big, but she'd insisted on getting it after seeing the same one in Sasha's old kitchen. She'd never admitted he'd been right.

'You just seem a bit on edge, that's all.'

'I've got a lot on my mind.'

'Like what?'

'Like what do you think, Dan?'

She looked at him then. A look that saw him react first with surprise, then, after a second's delay, anger.

'He told you. The fucker told you.'

Dan was whispering, but his voice still hissed loudly around the compact room.

'Course he told me. We're married. We don't have secrets from each other.'

'He shouldn't have. He promised.'

Dan's face, normally so open and placid, was dark with rage, but Hannah pretended not to notice.

'Look, Dan. I want to ask you, beg you, to think again. Look at everything you have to lose. Sasha, September. You'll break their hearts. And for what? For a fling.'

'It's not a fling.' Hannah had never heard

21

Dan sound so hard, despite the whispering. He was always so charming, so ready to see everyone else's point of view. 'Listen, I know how you feel, but you don't have a clue about how things are at home between me and Sash. And now I've met someone who makes me feel good about myself for the first time in years. And I'd be grateful if you and Josh would just butt out.'

'Dan!' Sasha's voice came wafting from the next room. 'Bring another bottle of red in, would you?'

Dan glared at Hannah before snatching up the bottle they'd brought round, still wrapped in its off-licence tissue paper, and stalking out.

'Coming, my little lush!'

Alone in the kitchen, Hannah leaned back against the cooker and put her head in her hands. She and Sasha had had their moments over the four years they'd been friends. She could remember a handful of times when they'd snapped at each other over one thing or another (although, if she remembered rightly, she was pretty sure most of the snapping had come from Sasha), but she'd never once had a cross word with Dan. He was always the laid-back one. Always the one to smooth out tensions with a joke or a well-placed compliment.

For the first time, Hannah allowed herself to picture how life might be dividing their time between a separated Sasha and Dan.

It didn't bear thinking about.

★   ★   ★

22

'G'way!'

Hannah had been dreaming about *that night* again for the first time in ages. Battling into consciousness, her heart racing, her mind still filled with images of Gemma's battered head and her mum's twisted, angry mouth, her airways as always stoppered up with dread, it took her a while to calm down enough to translate the indistinct noise Josh had made into proper words.

'Go away,' he said again, more distinctly this time.

Both of them raised themselves on to their elbows and listened as the doorbell of their ground-floor flat sounded a second time, prompting a half-hearted bark from the vicinity of Toby's basket in the hall.

Hannah staggered to her feet.

She had always been better at getting up than Josh. Even before her skills in that area were honed by months and years of night feeds and bad dreams and brutal dawn risings, she'd never struggled like him with that middle dimension between sleep and wakefulness. She liked to be up and getting on with things. Lying awake in that dead early morning was when you had time to think, and there were things that Hannah really didn't like to think about. Anyway, life was already so short. Why wouldn't you make the most of what time you had?

Dragging on her old purple towelling dressing gown, and regretting as she always did that she'd not yet got around to replacing it, she made her way into the hallway. At least living in such a compact space meant you were never very far from the front door if you needed to open it.

'All right already,' she muttered as the bell rang a third time, a long desperate buzz.

'Mummy?' Lily's voice from her little bedroom across the hall was still soaked in sleep. With any luck she wouldn't wake up properly.

'It's all right, Lil. Go back to sleep.'

Up until this point, Hannah had been too focused on getting up and making sure Lily wasn't disturbed to think about what a ring on the door in the middle of the night might mean. But in the split second when she pressed the buzzer on the intercom, she remembered what had happened the previous day.

'It's me. Sasha.' If Hannah hadn't already known who to expect, she'd never have recognized the voice that crackled through the intercom, deep and croaky and full of lumps.

Hannah buzzed her in and by the time she'd slid open both bolts and unchained the door that led from their flat into the communal lobby, Sasha was already there. She fell into Hannah's arms, her wraith-like body shaking violently under her thin denim jacket.

'Oh my God, Hannah,' she said in that same choked, un-Sasha-like voice.

Hannah held her friend tight. 'Come on, Sash,' she murmured, aware that they were still standing in the open doorway, letting a cool draught into the flat. 'Let's go into the living room, hey?'

Sasha allowed herself to be led through the door at the far end of the hallway, where Hannah

24

deposited her on the sofa.

'I'll make us some tea, shall I?'

If Sasha wondered why Hannah wasn't quizzing her about what had brought her to their door in the middle of the night, she didn't say. Instead she merely nodded. Her normally elfin features had puffed up so that her slanted hazel eyes, with their thick black lashes, were practically swollen shut.

Waiting for the kettle to boil, Hannah leaned her forehead against the cool fridge door, trying not to hear the gulping sobs coming from the next room. She felt guilty now for the times over the last few years when she'd wished Sasha ill. No, not ill, just for something in Sasha's Sunday-supplement life not to go to plan for once, just something to make her life slightly less shiny and bring it more in line with Hannah's own.

She'd never had a friend like Sasha before. If their babies hadn't brought them together she probably still wouldn't have a friend like Sasha. The two women led such different lives they'd never normally have crossed paths, like a Venn diagram where the two circles bobbed about completely independently with no point of intersection. Unlike Hannah, Sasha hadn't gone to university but had had a series of glamorous temporary jobs instead in small boutique galleries and country-house retreats in exotic locations. She always seemed to know someone who could fix her up with something, and if not, the trust set up by her wealthy father could usually be relied on to come to her aid. After she

25

met Dan, she'd stopped working altogether, even long before September came along, and, here's the thing, she never felt guilty about it. She spent her time on 'projects' to do with the house (a simple bathroom refit could easily turn into a four-month full-time job involving mood boards and teams of designers and builders) or arranging holidays or, after September was born, taking her daughter to art and music classes, even French classes, where young women with chunky, brightly coloured jewellery sat cross-legged on the floor and showed fractious toddlers pictures of smiley faces or suns or books and made exaggerated movements with their mouths as they pronounced each syllable. Hannah knew other women who didn't work, but none had that same sense of entitlement that Sasha did. 'Just till the kids start school,' they'd say, these other apologetic mothers. 'Childcare costs are so astronomical.' But Sasha would look at Hannah like a sleek Siamese cat and say, 'Why would I work if I don't have to?' And it would be Hannah who felt short-changed, as if something was lacking.

Hannah, on the other hand, was all about the guilt. Sometimes she wondered if it would be such an integral part of her if it hadn't been for what happened as a teenager, but at other times she felt that guilt was just woven into the thread of her DNA. She felt bad for the decisions she made, and the ones she didn't — for all the people she imagined she'd let down. An ambitious girl from a largely unambitious background, she'd worked hard to get to university in London, switching from French to Journalism in her second year when her sister Gemma finally convinced her it was OK to do a subject she liked, rather than one she thought might be useful, and had worked harder still to gain her first staff job on a magazine for teenagers. She'd always imagined she'd take the minimum maternity leave and be straight back to the nine to five (or in her case more like ten to eight), but when Lily came along she realized how unsuited babies were to be slotted in around work like superfluous padding. Reluctantly she'd resigned from the magazine and gone freelance and now spent her days wildly oscillating between feeling guilt-ridden at spending too little time on her child, and guilt-ridden at spending too little time on badly paid freelance work. Even when she *was* with her daughter, she was feeling guilty at how boring she often found it, the whole monotonous routine of feeding and washing and playing and filling in those endless hours with repetitive games that had to be played again and again, and books you'd read so many times you thought you might explode at the sight of them. Nobody ever talked about the boredom — it was as though if you admitted it, you were admitting you didn't love your child.

Until she had Lily, Hannah had never even held a baby before. When friends from the office arrived in the hospital ward on their designer heels, bearing cellophane-crinkling bouquets of flowers that failed to fit into any of the yellowing plastic water jugs on offer, they squealed with laughter and horror at the sight of Hannah attempting to change a nappy.

In a panic she'd tried to make friends with other new mothers in the neighbourhood by joining a postnatal mother-and-baby group run by the local NCT. The first meeting had been a disaster. She hadn't been able to work out how to put up Lily's new all-singing, all-dancing pushchair and had ended up, an hour and a half late, practically in tears, having run the half-mile to the hostess's house with Lily in her arms, arriving red-faced and out of breath with a screaming baby and aches in every muscle in her body. She'd had no idea a newborn could be so heavy — how had she carried this thing around inside her for the last nine months? The other women, or so it seemed at the time, had viewed her with suspicion, pulling their own babies a little bit tighter to them, smiling politely. On the second meeting, though, she'd met Sasha.

'I knew we were going to be friends for life when Hannah changed Lily's nappy right there in front of us and found a bright-red rubber band in her poo,' Sasha always liked to tell people. It was a funny story but it mortified Hannah still, the memory of that public exposure of her maternal inadequacy. The rubber-band incident, and a mutual wariness of the Proper Mums, as they soon christened the others, cemented their friendship. There's nothing like having babies of the same age to intensify and accelerate a bond. Though Hannah and Josh's two-bedroom flat could have fitted a million times into Sasha and Dan's three-storey pile it was still only a few streets away, in that

28

mad schizophrenic way of London neighbour-
hoods. Soon they were in and out of each other's
homes, introducing husbands, dogs, neighbours,
becoming intertwined in each other's lives at a
speed that would have been unthinkable in the
past pre-Lily world.

When Hannah went back into the living room,
bearing two mugs of steaming tea, she found
Sasha curled up on the sofa in a foetal position,
sobbing gently. Her tan leather bag that Hannah
had been shocked to discover cost more than she
earned in a fortnight was flung on the bottom
end of the sofa, contents strewn, leaving no room
for anyone else, so Hannah dropped a cushion
on to the floor next to the coffee table and knelt
on it, drawing her feet under her bottom to keep
them warm. Taking a sip from her scalding tea,
she surveyed her friend in silence for a moment.
She looked just like a child lying there, with her
hair all over the place. Hannah's heart
constricted as she watched Sasha's narrow
shoulders shaking. How could Dan do this?
Sasha had her moments, she could be
controlling as hell and exasperatingly over-
dramatic. But she had a huge heart and was
capable of impulsive acts of jaw-dropping
generosity. And she was the mother of his child.

'Come on,' Hannah said, when she could bear
the muffled sobbing no longer. 'Drink your tea
and tell me.'

Sasha's eyes opened — well, as much as they
could in their present puffy state. She looked a
bit startled, as if she'd forgotten Hannah was
even there. She heaved herself up into a sitting

position and brought her knees up to her chin, pulling the faded Ramones T-shirt she had on under her denim jacket down over her legs as little boys sometimes do to give themselves freakishly large fake breasts.

'Oh Hannah. He doesn't love me.'

The words were pieces of broken glass, so painful that Sasha had to spit them out one at a time.

Instinctively Hannah leaned forward and flung her arms around her friend. 'I'm sure you're wrong,' she found herself saying.

'He told me,' Sasha continued, oblivious to the lack of surprise in Hannah's voice. 'He says he doesn't think he's in love with me any more. He says he needs to go away for a while, to have some space to work out what to do.'

Hannah's hand, which had been rhythmically stroking Sasha's shoulder, froze. He hadn't told her. The cowardly shit. He hadn't told her there was someone else.

'What am I going to do? I love him so much. I can't lose him. I just can't. September is not going to come from a broken home. She is going to have a proper family.'

Sasha's voice had become increasingly shrill and Hannah felt suddenly chilled. Obviously she was upset, but there was something unnerving about her intensity. It wasn't as if they didn't know anyone else who had split up — half the kids at the nursery were from single-parent households. Besides, she was almost shouting now, and Hannah was worried the noise might wake Lily.

Too late.

'Mummy!' The little voice sounded frightened.

'I'd better go,' Hannah tried to get up, but Sasha had her hand on her arm.

'I can't live without him,' she said, staring at Hannah. Her eyes looked wild. 'He can't do this to us. I can't be divorced. I *won't* be divorced.'

'Mummy! Mummy!'

'I need to go. Lil's calling me. She needs me.'

Sasha's fingers tightened, vicelike. 'She's fine, for God's sake. She'll never stop being such a baby unless you stop mollycoddling her.'

Hannah tore herself away. Her heart was hammering. 'I'll be back in a minute.'

In Lily's room, she held her sniffling child in her arms and tried to calm her down. 'Hush now, everything's fine. I'm with Auntie Sash.' Sasha hadn't meant to be nasty about Lily, she told herself, she was just so overwrought.

By the time Lily had finally got back to sleep, Hannah had put Sasha's words from her mind and she was relieved, when she slipped back into the living room, to see that Sasha clearly had too. Her friend was sitting much straighter on the sofa, sipping from her surely stone-cold tea. She seemed more alert.

'I'm sorry, Hannah, I've been a complete idiot, haven't I?' Sasha scrunched up her face in an abject expression.

Hannah tried to insist that she hadn't.

'I have. I'm a total idiot. I'm completely overreacting, as usual. Dan's just having some kind of mid-life crisis, isn't he? All he needs to do is go whizzing around Goa on a motorbike

31

for a few weeks and he'll be sorted. Don't you think?'

Hannah looked into Sasha's hopeful, pink-rimmed eyes and found herself saying: 'Yeah, that's probably it. A mid-life crisis.'

Instantly Sasha brightened up, sniffing back the dregs of her tears and opening her eyes a little wider. 'Thanks, Hannah. I knew you'd help. You're always so good at putting things in perspective.'

Guilt tugged at Hannah's heart. 'You don't think he could have . . . found somebody else?'

Sasha's eyes narrowed. 'No.' The word practically snapped out. 'What I mean is, I asked him that. It was the very first thing I asked him, but he swore there wasn't. And one thing about me and Dan is we never, ever lie to each other. He knows that if he ever started lying to me, that'd be the end.'

For a second, Hannah almost said it. Then the moment passed.

'More tea?'

3

Josh experienced mixed feelings when he finally got to sit down during his lunch break and noticed the three 'missed call' messages. While he was relieved that Dan had got in touch after all these days of unnerving silence, he couldn't help being irritated by his friend's unfailing inability to grasp the fact that not everyone could take personal phone calls at any time of day. Some people had actual proper jobs that meant their mobile phones remained in their bags, switched to silent, and quite often weren't looked at from one end of the day to the other.

'Want to go for a coffee?'

Pat Hennessey flopped down heavily in the empty chair opposite Josh in the uninspiring staff room. The school management was forever promising to make improvements — new carpet, a decent coffee machine — but something else always came along that took priority. The five-a-side pitch needed resurfacing. The security system had to be updated. In a large inner-city state secondary, where resources were always stretched to the maximum, the state of the staff's soft furnishings was always going to come way down the shopping list.

Pat's cheeks, always flushed with colour, were looking particularly pink, as if he'd been rushing, and there was an unspoken appeal in his puppy-like brown eyes. Josh had always got on well with Pat since he'd transferred there three years before from a much smaller school in Merseyside. But since Pat had been made Head of English, things had become a little awkward. Josh always told him he didn't mind, and that he'd only gone for the promotion himself because Hannah had pushed him into it. He was glad not to have the extra responsibility, he insisted, particularly with Lily still being so young. Which was true — in fact, it was Hannah who was more upset, accusing him of 'a failure of self-belief'. But still, their friendship had never completely returned to normal.

'Love to, but I have to make a call and I think it might be quite an epic one.'

Pat looked hurt. He had one of those open faces that betray every emotion. 'Another time then.'

Outside the bottom gate, Josh pushed his way past throngs of sixth-formers and Year Elevens.

'Hi, Sir. Are you going to meet your girlfriend, Sir?'

The kids found it endlessly amusing to quiz him about his private life, as if it was an inconceivable joke that he might actually have a life outside of them and this school.

'That's right,' he humoured them. 'One of my huge harem of women.'

Before they could ask him what a harem was, he moved off across the main road and into the little park opposite. There were a few knots of school children eating crisps and swigging from cans of fizzy drinks, but he ignored them and made for an unoccupied bench under the trees.

Finally he was ready to call Dan back. Yet still he hesitated, his finger hovering over the keypad.

Josh was nervous about talking to Dan. Since Sasha had turned up in the middle of the night and had a nervous breakdown in their living room the previous weekend, things had gone eerily quiet. Hannah had tried calling a few times and left messages, but Sasha hadn't called her back. She'd been nagging him to call Dan, too, but he'd put it off. They needed a bit of time on their own to sort things out, he'd told her. Coward, she'd said. Hannah still didn't really get how men dealt with each other. Dan and Josh spoke on the phone to make arrangements for meeting up, or swapped the occasional email when they heard a joke they thought the other might enjoy. Josh would have been embarrassed to call Dan out of the blue and quiz him about his relationship. That wasn't the kind of friendship they had. It wasn't the kind of friendship he'd ever had.

There was always the chance, he supposed, that they'd patched things up, Dan and Sasha. Maybe the crisis had passed and they were holed up dealing with the aftermath. Certainly Sasha had seemed fairly positive by the time she finally left their house last Monday morning. She'd convinced herself it was some kind of phase Dan was going through. By the time Josh had got up, she'd been sitting on the sofa waiting for Hannah to bring her pancakes, only her swollen eyes signalling that anything had ever been wrong. Josh had been amazed after she'd left

35

when Hannah told him about the scene he'd missed.

'Thank God it was you who answered the door,' he'd said fervently, without thinking.

'Charming!'

He hadn't meant it to sound unsympathetic. He liked Sasha. When she was on form, there was no one more entertaining. It was just that she could be so high maintenance. So inclined to histrionics. Too much Sasha always left him feeling tired.

Still, she didn't deserve to be treated how Dan was treating her. Josh liked to think he was a fairly unjudgemental type. He knew the world wasn't black and white and that good people sometimes did bad things. But Dan was acting in a pretty shabby way.

'Dan?'

The phone had been answered on the third ring, which was unusual for Dan, who was normally dashing about, answering belatedly with a slight edge to his voice so that you always felt you were interrupting.

'Josh. Mate. Thank fuck for that!'

If Josh had been expecting to find Dan sounding subdued or chastened, he was very mistaken. The younger man sounded almost ebullient, as if he was bursting to announce some good news that he was supposed to be keeping to himself.

'Listen, I've got a favour to ask you. Can I stay at yours for a few days?'

Immediately Josh felt wrong-footed. This wasn't what he'd been expecting.

36

'Er, but we haven't got a spare — '

'Don't worry about that. I'll sleep on the sofa. It wouldn't be the first time.'

'But Sasha — '

'Sasha was the one who suggested it. She's been absolutely brilliant. Since Sunday we've been talking and talking, more than we've ever done before, and she totally gets it. About me needing some space and everything. I was talking about moving out and renting a studio flat, and she just said, 'Why don't you stay with Josh and Hannah for a little bit? Just as a first step?''

Alone on his park bench, Josh frowned. From the corner of his eye, he could see Jake Eldridge from Year Ten loitering behind a tree, smoking a cigarette.

'So what do you say?'

There was a hint of impatience in Dan's voice that grated a bit. Dan was so used to getting his way and charming everyone he met that he tended to get quite childish if things didn't immediately go to plan. Josh had noticed it before. But this wasn't an argument over whether to go to the Railway or the King's Head.

'Look, Dan, I want to help you. But you obviously haven't told Sasha that you're seeing someone else, and I just don't want to be party to it. You understand, don't you?'

A pause.

'I haven't told her because it's not an issue. I told you, the thing with Sienna is a *result* of the situation with Sasha, not a cause of it. Anyway, I've put it on hold for now. I want to put all my

37

focus on Sasha and September during this critical time.'

Dan sounded as if he was reading a prepared statement.

'So you promise you're not going to be running off to see your girlfriend as soon as Sasha's back is turned, using me and Hannah as a smokescreen?'

'What? Thanks a lot for the vote of confidence.'

Typical. Dan was the one getting outraged, and Josh was left feeling guilty.

'Listen. Breaking up a family is never easy, it's not something you do on a whim. I've really thought about this. I don't want September to be caught in the middle of two warring parents. I want her to see that it's possible for two people to go on loving and respecting each other, even if they're not together any more.'

'And Sasha sees it the same way, does she?'

'Absolutely. Like I say, she's been amazing. That's why I want to come and stay at yours. It's a kind of halfway-house thing to get us all used to the idea of being apart. It'll be easier for her. Baby steps and all that.'

You had to hand it to Dan. There he was, about to destroy two people's lives, and yet he could leave you feeling like he was the selfless one.

'Look, I'll talk to Hannah. But you'd have to promise not to be in touch with this *Sienna*, OK?'

'Sure.'

'And when would you be wanting to avail

yourself of our deluxe sofa facilities?'

'Tomorrow. It's Saturday and we could come around with September and make a big deal of me going on a sleepover at your house, and September could sort of settle me in, so it would seem like an adventure, not like me sneaking away in the night with my suitcases.'

'I'll talk to her. That's all I can do.'

★　★　★

'I still don't like it.'

Hannah was going around the living room effecting a grudging and superficial tidy-up — she'd already wiped a damp J cloth over the coffee table, going around the pile of magazines and books, leaving a narrow ring of dust around the bottom like an extra frill, and now she was picking up odd bits of jigsaw and old lidless felt pens and cramming them all into the bottom drawer of the low table where the telly sat, which had become the home for all odds and ends that didn't fit anywhere else. Josh held back from asking why she was keeping pens that clearly didn't work.

'Well, you're the one who spoke to Sasha. It's what she wants.'

'Yes, but she doesn't know the truth.'

'That's not what Dan says. I told you, he said Sienna is out of the picture.'

'For now.'

'Whatever. We can't do anything about it now. They'll be here any minute.'

Hannah sighed. 'I know, and just look at this

39

place. Dan's used to living in a house with a stay-at-home wife and a cleaner twice a week. How's he going to cope in a place where you can't even see through the shower screen because of the limescale?'

'That's not limescale, it's dirt. Anyway, who cares if Dan's appalled by our non-existent domestic hygiene? In fact, it'd be better if he was, in a way. At least it would mean he won't stay long.'

Josh was feeling very odd about the forthcoming visit. Growing up an only child of much older parents, he'd never really done the whole sleepover thing. His parents' house was the kind of place where the doors had cushioned strips of padding around them to stop them from slamming and there were three sets of slippers neatly lined up in the entrance hall ready to be stepped into the moment you came through the door. As a result he'd never been entirely easy about having people to stay, always fretting about whether they needed a glass of water or a reading light, or that he might keep them awake with his snoring, even though as far as he knew he only snored when he was extremely drunk.

Hannah was different. She came from a noisy household where just thirteen months separated her from her younger sister, Gemma. Hannah had always shared a room and was therefore accustomed to going to sleep top and tailing with someone else, waking up with a visiting friend's feet in her face, or covered in a dressing gown because someone else had filched her duvet in the night. Most of the time her mum had been the kind of parent who loved her house to be full of extra children, thinking nothing of whipping up an extra boiled egg or two in the mornings. And even when she was having one of her periodic depressive episodes where she'd confine herself to her room, the girls still invited their friends round so she knew where they were rather than risk triggering her paranoia by venturing out of the house.

Overnight guests didn't usually cause Hannah the same kind of anxiety as Josh, but today she was very definitely stressed. She'd been working until late the night before on a feature about analysing sex dreams. 'Chance would be a fine thing,' Josh had said when she told him the subject, but she hadn't risen to the bait. Their sex life, or lack of it, was too sensitive a subject for jokes. Then Lily had got up in the night and come into their bed with them, so she was tired and out of sorts, and not in the mood to host this summit meeting, which is what they'd unofficially christened this morning's visit.

'Mummy, Mummy, where's my pink dress?'

Lily appeared in the doorway of the living room wearing only a pair of flowery pants. Josh's heart turned over at the sight of her still rounded little belly. She had been such a chubby, happy little thing, sitting on his lap and leaning back so that he could blow raspberries into the soft skin of her tummy. But now she was lengthening out. Already she'd lost the dimples in her knees and elbows, and occasionally he'd seen a worried look he hated on her face in place of the usual shy smile.

'It's in the wash, Liliput,' Hannah told her. She was busy sweeping up dirt and paperclips and batteries from the remote control and old pencils from under the sofa cushions with a dustpan and brush, so she didn't see their daughter's face crumple.

'But I need it!'

'You've got lots of other lovely dresses, Lil.' Josh got up from the table where he'd been attempting to mark some essays and stood in front of her. 'Shall we go and find one?'

'No, I want that one. All my other dresses are stupid.'

'Who says that?'

' ''Tember.' Lily started crying, great, fat, round tears rolling down her pink cheeks.

Josh knelt down so that he could give her a cuddle. 'September is just jealous,' he said to her. 'Remember how she wanted your wizard outfit so much her mummy and daddy had to go out and buy her one just like it?'

Lily didn't reply, but he felt her head nodding into his shoulder.

'Well, I'm going to have words with Sasha about it.' Hannah had put down the dustpan and brush and was sitting back on her heels, looking across at them. 'September shouldn't be saying things like that. It's not kind.'

Josh turned round to her and made a face. 'I really think we could leave this to the girls to sort out, don't you, sweetheart?'

Hannah raised her eyebrows at him behind Lily's back, but merely said, 'OK, you're right. I keep forgetting Lily's a big girl now.'

Josh took Lily into her room to help her into her second-best dress — a scale that was decided, she explained solemnly, by how big a circle the skirt made when she twirled round in it. She was just demonstrating when the doorbell rang.

'Hello, strangers,' they heard Hannah say in the loud, over-bright voice she reserved for socially uncomfortable situations.

Josh was surprised by how nervous he felt suddenly, as if Dan and Sasha really were two strangers rather than their best friends.

By the time he and Lily made their way into the living room, the visitors were already installed on the sofa. Both Dan and Sasha had dark shadows under their eyes and were looking unnaturally pale, but Josh was shocked to see that they were holding hands. He shot Hannah a questioning look, but she was busy rearranging the magazines he knew for a fact she'd rearranged just minutes before.

'So this must be a bit weird for you,' Dan started.

'September, Lily. Why don't you go off into Lily's room to play?'

It wasn't like Hannah to interrupt anyone, but Josh was glad she had. If they were going to have this chat, far better the girls were out of earshot.

On her way out of the room, September paused and surveyed the sofa, with her hand on her hip and her head to one side. 'Daddy. I think this is too small to be your new bed. I think you will have to come home and sleep in your proper bed.'

'It's not too small, princess. If I bend my knees a little it'll be just cosy.'

After the girls had gone, silence settled over the four of them like the dust that Hannah had been half-heartedly sweeping up earlier.

'As I was saying,' Dan said eventually, 'this must be pretty weird for you two.'

'It's pretty weird for me too,' said Sasha. She was smiling a small, tired smile and Josh found it impossible to work out if she was being sarcastic or just honest.

Dan smiled at her and squeezed her hand in a gesture that Josh couldn't help but find a bit creepy.

'Sasha has been brilliant these last few days. We've talked about everything and I know it hasn't been easy. Things haven't been right between us for a little while and I think both of us realize we need to spend a bit of time apart while we — while I — sort out what the fuck's going on in my head. I was going to rent a room somewhere nearby, but then Sasha suggested it might be better for September if I stayed here, just as an interim step. I really can't thank you enough for agreeing to put me up.'

'Yeah, he's a horrible slob,' said Sasha. Josh felt a rush of sympathy for her suddenly. She was trying so hard to put a brave face on everything, even while her world was crumbling around her.

'Daddy!' The shout came from the next room. There was a short silence, then it came back twice as shrill. 'DADDY, I want you!'

Dan got to his feet. 'Better go.'

Once he'd left the room, Sasha seemed to

44

shrink back into the sofa cushions.

Hannah got up from the far side of the coffee table where she'd been kneeling and sat down next to her friend, putting her hand on her arm. 'Has it been hideous?'

Sasha nodded. She leaned her head on Hannah's shoulder. 'I'm just so glad he's coming here,' she said. 'I know you'll help him get things in perspective. He's been working so hard recently, doing such stupid hours. No wonder he's stressed. He just needs a bit of a break, that's all. He needs to realize just what he's got and how much he'd be losing.'

'He must be mad to even think about it,' said Josh, and he was rewarded by a flash of a smile from Sasha.

'Batshit crazy,' she said.

'Who's batshit crazy? I'm guessing it's probably me.'

Dan had reappeared in the doorway, where he stood running a hand through his long dirty-blond hair. At least he had the grace to look sheepish.

'How about a drink?' Sasha seemed not to have noticed that it was barely past midday.

Josh looked pointedly at his watch, but Hannah was already on her feet. 'Wine o'clock, is it?'

Josh followed her out to the kitchen on the pretext of helping her with the glasses. 'Bit early, isn't it?'

'I don't care,' she said, uncorking a bottle of white she'd unearthed from the back of the fridge. It was one of their many bones of contention since finances had got so tight. Josh felt they could economize by cutting down on drinking at home, while Hannah felt it was wine that would get them through the crisis.

'Dan is just doing my head in,' she hissed. 'All this *I need to sort out my head* bollocks when all he's after is a free pass to screw young models.'

'Come on, I don't think that's completely fair. Have you looked at him? The guy looks wrecked. I don't think this is easy for him.'

'Maybe not, but it's a million times worse for her.'

Hannah had a massive sense of female solidarity. Probably something to do with growing up in a female-dominated household. It was one of the things Josh loved most about her — her loyalty to her friends.

'Oi, stop talking about us and bring the wine,' called Sasha. Her voice lacked its usual confidence, but at least she was trying to keep it together.

Back in the living room, Josh reclaimed the armchair he'd been sitting in before, while Hannah knelt down at the coffee table to pour the wine.

'A toast. To you guys,' she said, raising her glass to Sasha and Dan. 'I just want you to know, whatever happens we're here for you. Both of you.'

When Josh looked over at Sasha, he saw her eyes had filled with tears.

'Thanks, Hannah,' she said. Her hand was clamped around Dan's thigh. 'I really think we'll be OK. As long as we carry on being completely honest with each other, like we have been this week, I think we'll make it. Won't we, babes?'

'Mmmm,' Dan concurred.

Leave it now, Josh urged her telepathically. *Please.* But she clearly hadn't finished.

'You know, not many couples could have said the things we've said to each other this week and still be even talking to each other, let alone loving each other,' she went on. 'But I think we've reached a new level of openness and that's what gives me the faith that we'll end up together once Dan's got past this little . . . blip. We've really laid ourselves bare, haven't we, babes?'

Dan nodded. 'We have. We really have.'

'Ha!' The sound shot like a bullet across the coffee table from where Hannah was kneeling.

'Hannah!' It was the voice Josh used in class when he was sending a clear warning to a pupil not to go any further. But it fell on deaf ears.

'No, I'm sorry. I've kept quiet up to now, but I just can't listen to that. Sasha has a right to know the truth. She has a right to expect you to be *genuinely* honest with her, Dan.'

'What are you talking about?' Sasha was looking from Hannah to Dan and back again as if waiting for a translation.

'I think you'd better shut up, Hannah.' Dan's face was the colour of liver. Josh didn't think he'd ever seen him look so angry.

'No, Dan. I love you dearly, you know that, but you're not being fair to anyone by not telling Sasha that you've been sleeping with someone else.'

Sasha moved her hand from where it had been resting in Dan's and turned to face him on the sofa. 'What's she on about?'

'It's nothing.' The purple stain on his skin made him almost ugly. In other circumstances, Josh might have quite enjoyed the transformation. 'A silly fling I had with someone at work. It was part of the process, Sash. Me trying to work out who I am and what I feel.'

Hannah exhaled loudly. Josh willed her not to say anything. 'We'll leave you two to chat, shall we?'

He was getting to his feet as he spoke, but Sasha stopped him in his tracks.

'Don't bother. You two obviously know more about my marriage than I do.'

If ever there was a voice sharp enough to cut yourself on.

'Did you fuck her? Did you? This *fling* of yours? Don't bother answering, I can see in your face that you did. Has it been going on ages? Did you all have a bloody good laugh about it behind my back?'

Josh glanced at Hannah. Hannah loathed confrontation. But then, he reminded himself, she was the one who'd caused it.

'Sasha,' Hannah began, 'I wanted to tell you. I — '

'Bitch!'

Sasha's normally delicate features were twisted into an almost demonic expression as she turned on Hannah and Josh felt suddenly cold.

'What?'

'You bloody bitch. You let me sit here sobbing

48

in your arms last weekend and all the time you *knew*! Did it make you feel powerful? Did it? Being here, all smug in your nice safe marriage, knowing my husband was fucking someone else and I didn't know anything about it?'

'No! It wasn't like — '

'Spare me!' Sasha was slipping her feet into her silver pumps and gathering up the distressed-looking leather handbag. 'September!'

No chance of the girls not hearing that — the word was so shrill it almost set the wine glasses trembling.

'Sash, don't go.'

'Fuck off, Dan.'

Josh groaned as he noticed September appear in the doorway ahead of Lily, just in time to hear that last sentence.

'Say goodbye to Daddy, darling. You might not see him for a little while.'

There was just time for the little girl's eyes to grow wide with panic before Sasha had snatched her hand and was bundling her out of the door.

'Daddy!'

The high-pitched wail was interrupted by the slamming of the communal front door, but still it continued outside, horrible and piercing, until finally the revving of Sasha's car engine cut it off completely.

In a sense, the silence that followed it within their ground-floor flat was even worse.

Finally Josh could stand it no more. 'That went well, I thought.'

No one laughed.

Lucie, aged six

Mummy loves me. This morning she let me brush her beautiful hair and my hair will be long like hers one day. It's almost at my shoulders. And she hasn't shouted at me for ages about the bad thing I did. Gobble, gobble, gobble. Eyes too big for my belly. She talks to me in French and it's like music coming from her mouth. And we don't talk about Eloise. Not ever. But out of sight isn't out of mind! Daddy is happy because Mummy is happy and we are all happy. Sometimes I'm scared to breathe in case Mummy blows away.

4

'So just call me back. Please? Even if it's just to tell me how much you hate and despise me.'

Hannah pressed 'end call', put the phone down and sat staring into space. Her laptop was set up on the dining table and she was supposed to be working on a feature for a women's weekly magazine about overprotective celebrity mums. Instead she was fretting about Sasha. That was the ninth or tenth message she'd left for her. It had been two days since that horrible scene in their living room, but Hannah could still hear the venom dripping from her friend's voice when she called her a 'bloody bitch', and September's anguished 'Daddy!' coming from outside as she was bundled into the car.

For a moment afterwards there'd been a sickening silence that Josh had tried to break with a stupid joke. Then Lily had started crying and suddenly everyone was talking at once. Dan apologizing to Hannah, Hannah apologizing to Dan, Josh apologizing to Lily.

'I shouldn't have said anything.'

Hannah couldn't remember when she'd ever felt so wretched.

'No, it's my fault.' Dan had his head in his hands, his fingers dug deep into his hair. 'I wish you hadn't told her, but I can't blame you. I should never have done it. I should have had more respect for Sash.'

'Well, now it's out there, at least you can both deal with it. Set a few ground rules, that sort of thing.'

Trust Josh to come up with a practical solution. It was his default response any time things got over-emotional. If Hannah was suddenly diagnosed with terminal cancer, Josh would probably present her with a ten-point get-well plan. It was just how he was.

Afterwards Dan had gone round to his house a couple of times, but Sasha had locked the door from the inside and wouldn't let him in. And so the three of them had sat around and got quite drunk, while Lily watched *Ice Age* over and over until Hannah finally had enough and took her to the park.

Later on they had indeed established ground rules. Dan wasn't going to be in touch with Sienna, and he was going to do everything he could to work things out with Sasha, and if they couldn't be worked out, at least to have the best break-up possible. Couples counselling, if it came to it, even if, as he said, he'd rather pull his own fingernails out. Dan had done all the right things. He'd cried, he'd appeared wracked with guilt. He'd gazed, agonized, at the photo of Sasha and September that he kept in his wallet. In short, he had not given the impression of someone who was taking the situation lightly.

After that first day, they'd hardly seen him. He had a big advertising job on that week, so he'd spent the whole of Sunday in his studio in Hoxton going over the brief, jotting down ideas and making sure he had the right equipment.

So Dan wasn't the problem. The problem was Sasha. She hadn't answered her phone the whole of yesterday, and September hadn't turned up for nursery this morning, leaving Lily inconsolable. Hannah sighed. Concentrate! She only had the three hours while Lily was at nursery to work, and this feature was due by the end of the week. Not that it was going to pay much. She'd be lucky if she ended up with £400 for something that would have taken her a week to write and research, but they really needed the money and, as Josh was always saying with a little pat of his behind, in a parody of the supermarket ad, 'every little helps'.

Sometimes she wondered if they'd done the right thing choosing to wait until January for Lily to start primary school. Most of the other four-year-olds had just started in reception, but Sasha and Dan had persuaded them that, as the girls were both summer babies, it made sense for them to defer for a few months. At the time Hannah had agreed — Lily was still so young and she adored the little nursery attached to the main school. But now she couldn't help thinking guiltily of all the extra time she'd have if Lily had started full-time school — all the extra money she could be earning.

Money. The perennial problem. When Hannah and Josh had first got together they'd both had major credit-card debts — Josh because of borrowing to fund his teacher-training course, which he'd never quite managed to repay, and Hannah because, well, when you're in your twenties and living and working in London for the first time, you start to believe you've made it and that things can only carry on getting better and better. Then they'd bought this place. They could have got a whole house if they'd moved somewhere further out, but Hannah had been sold on Crouch End, with its coffee shops and boutiques and huge red-brick houses with ornate stained-glass front doors. So they'd mortgaged themselves up to the hilt for a flat they'd already grown out of. Hannah had been banking on Josh getting that promotion. She felt silly setting so much store by it, but she still found Josh's lack of confidence infuriating. He deserved to be Head of English rather than bland old Pat Hennessey.

As always, thinking about money gave Hannah an acidic feeling in the pit of her stomach. She sat up straighter and refreshed her computer screen. *Sharon Osbourne recently sprang to the defence of daughter Kelly*, she wrote. Then she stopped. Sharon Osbourne didn't have money worries, she supposed. Sharon Osbourne didn't lie awake mentally moving money around or, more accurately, mentally moving *credit* from this place to that, borrowing from this source to pay off that bill and then from that source to pay off the first.

She wished she could talk to Sasha. She always had such a reassuringly blasé attitude to money. Of course, Hannah knew it was easy to dismiss money worries when you'd never had any yourself, but it still made her feel better hearing Sasha say, 'Pah, it's only money.' Yes, she found herself thinking, that's all it is. Anyway, what little she knew about Sasha's past put the whole

54

money thing into perspective. Sasha found her childhood too painful to talk about, but from the odd comment she and Dan had made over the years, Hannah gathered it had been beyond awful, despite her family's wealth. You could have all the money in the world, she reminded herself primly, but it still didn't buy you happiness.

The doorbell roused her from her meandering thoughts.

'Hello?'

'It's me. Open the fucking door. I've totally miscalculated on the weather front and I'm absolutely freezing.'

She couldn't remember the last time she'd been so relieved to hear someone's voice. She flung open the front door and Sasha practically fell into her arms. Hannah was shocked at how fragile her friend's shoulders felt under her fingers, as if her bones could snap like dry twigs. She'd lost weight in just two days, if that was possible. It was like holding a ghost.

'I'm sorry.' Even Sasha's voice seemed to have lost weight, sounding fainter and less robust. 'I shouldn't have turned on you.'

'No, it's my fault. I should have told you straight away. I should never have promised Josh to keep quiet.'

The two women made their way into the living room and sat down curled up at opposite ends of the sofa.

'Feels weird knowing Dan was probably right here just a few hours ago,' said Sasha. Her face, Hannah now saw, was pinched like a pastry edge and there were greasy violet smudges under her eyes.

'I can't imagine.'

'I keep thinking it's all just a dream, you know, or some kind of misunderstanding and any minute he's just going to rock up with his key in the door.'

'Well, he has tried to come round a couple of times.'

'No, he hasn't.'

'Really? I'm sure he said he — '

'The thing is, though, I've been Googling this a lot and I do think this is just a phase Dan's going through.'

'You've *Googled* it?'

'Yes, you'd be amazed how many forums and chat rooms there are for people whose husbands or wives have left them out of the blue. They call it being 'blindsided'. Anyway, they all seem to think this is a stupid phase he's going through. It's called 'being in the fog'. That's why I'm feeling a bit better about it. So he had a fling with some bimbo? He's not the first person to have a mid-life crisis. That isn't to say I wouldn't wring his bloody neck. Sometimes I feel I'd like to just . . . I don't know . . . smash his smug face in.'

Sasha pounded her little fist into the sofa in demonstration and, despite herself, Hannah stifled a smile.

'But the thing is, I miss the bastard,' Sasha went on. 'I miss him so much it's like a physical hurt. I always said I'd never forgive a man who cheated, but the truth is she probably threw

56

herself at him. Girls always do with Dan. You must have noticed that. And he was weak. So I've decided to take him back.'

Hannah's face must have betrayed her confusion because Sasha went on, 'I know you probably think I'm mad. But I've seen first hand what divorce does to families and I won't let it happen to my daughter.'

For a moment, Hannah thought Sasha was about to open up about what had happened to her as a child, after her parents split up, but instead her voice rose as she repeated, 'I won't allow our family to break apart.'

By now Sasha's dainty features had taken on an unfamiliar intensity Hannah found quite unsettling. She felt nonplussed. As far as she knew, it was Dan who'd left Sasha, and yet here was Sasha talking about forgiveness and taking him back. Had she perhaps missed something — a conversation between the two of them that neither had seen fit to disclose?

'Anyway,' said Sasha, her expression suddenly relaxing, 'he doesn't know it yet but he's going to spend the rest of his life making it up to me in exotic holidays and extortionate jewellery!'

The laugh that followed came out more like a sob, and Hannah melted, realizing with a pang how strong her friend was having to be and how much it must be costing her to hold it together.

'You're doing so well, Sash. I'd be a basketcase if it was me. Oh shit!' She had a sudden realization. 'What's the time? We're going to be late picking up the girls. September's at nursery, isn't she?'

Now it was Sasha who looked confused.

'September. You must have taken her in quite late. I waited ages to see if you'd come.'

'Oh fuck!' Sasha leapt up as if the sofa had suddenly burst into flames. 'September! She's in the car. I completely forgot. She was asleep when we left, so I carried her into the back of the car.'

Hannah held the door open while Sasha sprinted down the front path, reappearing a minute or so later carrying a very red-faced September.

'Mummy left me,' the little girl said, in the gulping voice of someone who'd been crying a long time.

'I'm so sorry, darling. I'm a naughty mummy, aren't I?' Sasha had her head buried in her daughter's neck as if she was trying to tunnel into her.

'She's a very naughty mummy,' September told Hannah, gazing directly at her.

Only later on, when Hannah was on the way home from nursery ('Seven minutes late, Lily was getting anxious,' the head of nursery reprimanded her), did she start to think how very out of character the incident with September had been. Sasha was always so in control. That was her thing. How distraught must she be to forget her own child?

★ ★ ★

Later that evening, Hannah almost jumped with shock when she heard the key in the front door

58

as she and Josh were settling down to watch *Newsnight*.

'I forgot we had a house guest.'

Seconds later Dan appeared in the doorway, holding a bottle of wine in each hand. 'I couldn't remember whether you preferred red or white, so I got both. Do I win the prize for being the best visitor or what?'

'Our best visitors always bring champagne and oysters,' said Josh, getting up to fetch glasses from the kitchen.

Hannah, who'd been thinking about going to bed before long, felt a pang of annoyance. Things had been so emotionally fraught recently, she'd been enjoying relaxing with Josh and forgetting about everything else for a bit. But then she remembered Sasha's gaunt face and September's red-rimmed eyes and felt ashamed. Trying to talk some sense into Dan was the least she could do.

'Have you spoken to Sasha?' she asked, when they were all sitting down around the coffee table with a glass of chilled Sancerre in front of them.

Dan frowned. 'I did go round there the day she found out about Sienna, but she wouldn't let me in,' he said, looking up as if seeking brownie points for effort. 'And since then I've been so busy and I kind of thought she might need a bit of cooling-off time.'

'So you haven't bothered to contact her?'

'I'm going to. Of course I am. I'm just waiting for the dust to settle before I talk to her about the next step.'

'Which is?'

'Well, me moving out on a more permanent basis.'

Dan said it as if it was the most obvious thing in the world, and Hannah felt the air going out of her as if someone had taken a pin and deflated her.

'So you haven't changed your mind then?'

Dan looked startled. 'Changed my mind? No. If anything, the last few days have made me realize I'm definitely doing the right thing. I feel lighter, like a big weight has been taken off me. Being married was suffocating, you know?'

Hannah didn't like the way he addressed that last comment to Josh, throwing up his hands as if hoping for agreement. Something occurred to her then.

'You haven't been seeing Sienna, have you?'

Dan's big blue eyes widened, as if hurt. 'No. I gave you my word. Like I said, the thing with Sienna was completely separate. I'm focusing on my marriage right now, and what's best for Sasha.'

Since when did Dan start talking like a marital self-help book?

'If you really want what's best for her, you'll go back to her. She looks absolutely awful.'

'You've seen her?'

'Yes, she turned up here today.'

'How was she?'

For a moment, Hannah thought of telling him about the shadows under Sasha's eyes and the look on September's face when she was finally rescued from the car. But something held her back. Incredible to think that less than a week

60

ago Dan would have been the first person she'd have gone to with any concerns about Sasha's wellbeing, and now she just wasn't sure. It bothered her more than she could admit, this realization that you could go from being a couple, a unit, to two individuals in the time it used to take her mother to marinate a good steak.

She shrugged. 'She's about how you'd expect her to be. The thing is though, Dan, she still thinks you're coming back.'

Dan looked pained. 'Obviously it's going to take a while to sink in. I don't expect her to accept it overnight, but you know . . . ' He gazed at Hannah with wide eyes, and she saw something in them that she'd never noticed before, a hardness glinting beneath the layers of navy and aquamarine like diamond wrapped in tissue paper. 'I'm never going back.'

5

Josh found having a house guest even harder than he'd anticipated. It wasn't that Dan was intrusive — they hardly ever saw him, and when they did he always seemed to be on the phone, long calls taken at the end of the garden, his shoulders hunched against the late-September chill. It was just that his presence in the flat was *unsettling*. Not just the physical evidence of him — the suitcase in the corner, from which faded T-shirts and jeans spilled out messily, the extra toothbrush and shaving stuff in the bathroom. It was also the change in the atmosphere, a sense of restlessness that stirred up the air in the flat, turning what used to be a relaxing environment into a place where you couldn't sit down without feeling as if there was something else you really ought to be getting on with, another world outside your living-room window that was going on without you.

It was getting to the stage where he was almost relieved to be at school, where even the giggling of the Year Eight girls and the rudeness of the Year Eleven boys felt reassuringly unchanged and familiar.

During lessons, there was little time to think about anything other than whatever set text he was attempting to drum into the largely unreceptive minds of his pupils. 'Not being funny, Sir, but why do we have to read the book when we could just go and see the film?'

Only at break times or, like now, driving home in their thirteen-year-old Golf that shuddered alarmingly up the hill towards Crouch End did his mind swing back to what was going on at home, and he'd find himself frowning as an unexplained knot formed in his stomach and his heart beat slightly faster than normal. When he tried to analyse what was making him feel so on edge, he found he couldn't put his finger on it. It wasn't that Dan ever got in the way, he was so rarely around, so why was his presence, or rather his absence, so unnerving?

'Maybe you're just jealous because he's out being single and having fun while you're stuck at home with me and Lil,' Hannah had teased him the night before.

Josh had made a joke of it, pressing his nose up against the front window as if desperate to escape, much to the delight of Lily, who insisted on climbing on to a chair to push her own plump cheeks up against the cold glass. Now, though, he was starting to wonder uncomfortably if Hannah might not have hit upon something. Not that he was jealous of Dan. Josh didn't envy his friend the late nights in crowded bars or wherever it was he was hanging out when he wasn't in their flat. No, it was more than that — something to do with the sight of that suitcase in the corner, so compact and portable, and the way Dan breezed in and out without having to give any account of himself, and the whiff of fresh starts that clung to him. It was that sense of the future opening up. Josh felt, by comparison, washed up and overburdened.

In private, Hannah griped about Dan's presence. She hated not being able to wander into the living room if she woke up during the night to sit down at the dining-room table and work in the T-shirt she wore to bed, or scroll through Twitter catching up on people's news, and she resented the pile of clumsily folded blankets on the end of the sofa whenever they sat down to watch telly. But as Josh waited by the temporary traffic lights, gently revving the accelerator and hoping against hope that this wouldn't be the day the Golf's dodgy clutch gave up the ghost altogether, he found himself trying to view Dan through Hannah's eyes. Yes, his presence might be inconvenient, but might not his new-found singledom also give him a kind of cachet, a sense of danger and alpha-maleness that had been better concealed when he was a safely married man? Josh could see how a man like Dan, clearly desired by other women, successful at work and suddenly back on the market, might be very attractive, particularly when he and Hannah were so bogged down in debt themselves. More chokingly, might not this clear evidence of Dan's healthy sex drive throw the recent deficiencies of their own into sharp relief?

This jealousy that had crept up from nowhere was like a slow-acting virus you're not even conscious of until your throat closes up and, *wham*, you find it's overtaken your entire system. It's not as if Hannah had ever expressed the slightest interest in Dan. In fact, it tended to be Josh who would leap to his friend's defence in the face of Hannah's disapproval. She'd once said, 'Dan is like cheap paint. Looks great to begin with, but give him a rub with a damp cloth and he'll come off on your hand.' Josh had argued on Dan's behalf, but inside he'd glowed with pleasure at the unspoken inference (or so he liked to imagine) that he, by contrast, was a man of substance.

Turning into their road with its mishmash of Victorian and 1920s houses, many of them converted (badly) into flats, Josh's heart sank when he noted the lack of parking places. Cruising past his house, he felt a twinge of anger when he saw Sasha's SUV parked right outside in prime position. Couldn't they have just one evening to themselves, free of drama? While Dan was the model house guest, hardly ever around and entertaining and largely discreet when he was, Sasha was the non-house guest from hell. In the ten days since she and Dan had split up, there'd hardly been a moment when Sasha hadn't been there, either curled up on the sofa sobbing into whichever of Dan's crumpled and frankly rank T-shirts she'd fished out of his suitcase, or else pacing the room on those tiny little legs that always looked to Josh as if they shouldn't even be capable of supporting an adult body, ranting about mid-life crises and responsibilities (or lack thereof) while Hannah brought her cups of tea or glasses of wine, and Josh made endless rounds of fish fingers and pasta and pesto for the girls. It wasn't that he begrudged her anything — it was just that he

65

and Hannah and Lily had developed such an easy, pleasant routine and now everything was so . . . *unsettled*.

As soon as he walked through the door of the flat, he could tell it wasn't one of Sasha's good days. Or rather, not one of her less-bad days. The tension rose up to meet him as he lingered in the hallway, taking far longer than he needed to hang his jacket on the hook and fuss over an ecstatic Toby. He could hear September's shrill voice coming from behind Lily's closed bedroom door. 'No, no. Not like that, Lileee,' she said, stretching out the last syllable of his daughter's name so that it hung gratingly in the air.

Hannah came through the living-room door bearing two empty mugs, clearly destined for the kitchen. 'Oh,' she said. 'It's you.'

Josh's heart sank. He'd had a tricky day at work. One of the Year Elevens, Kelly Kavanagh, had clearly copied her answers to a test from the girl who sat in front of her and he'd had to get quite tough, which hadn't been pleasant. Then there'd been an awkward departmental meeting where he and Pat had disagreed. It was only a trivial thing — whether to set coursework based on a production of *Macbeth* the Year Tens were going to see. Josh was in favour, but Pat thought they should encourage the kids to regard theatre as a pleasure rather than a chore. The issue had been resolved with minimum fuss, with Pat's view eventually winning over the majority, but it had left a sour taste in Josh's mouth. All afternoon he'd been looking forward to getting home and shaking off the stress of the day, but

66

here was yet more stress and his wife greeting him with a half-hearted 'Oh, it's you.'

'That's nice. You could sound a little happier to see me. I've had a shit day at work, in case you're interested.'

Hannah was banging around unnecessarily in the kitchen. 'Yes, well, at least you've done some work. I've done absolutely nothing, and I've a feature due on Monday.' She was hissing under her breath. The noise joined with the metallic whistle of their old kettle and the clanking of crockery in an unpleasant cacophony that irritated Josh's ears.

'You're just going to have to tell her you need a bit of time to yourself.'

'I can't! You can see the state she's in.'

As if on cue, Sasha appeared in the doorway. She seemed even thinner than when Josh had seen her the day before, and her small, hollowed-out face bore an expression of nervous anticipation which drained instantly when she saw him.

'Oh, hello Josh,' she said, turning away. 'I thought you might be Dan.'

In the living room, over what appeared to be yet another in a long line of cups of tea, Sasha once again returned to her favourite subject — Dan's apparently aberrant behaviour and how it was clearly symptomatic of some kind of psychological crisis he was going through, didn't Josh think? Well, Josh didn't bloody well think, actually. Josh was too exhausted to think. All he wanted was to sit down and have half an hour of silence to read the paper or listen to music, or just offload to Hannah about his crappy day.

'Why don't you just ask Dan?' Josh said.

If Sasha noticed his slightly snappish tone, she didn't let on. 'You know he's insisting we don't talk to each other until the weekend. '*We need to give each other time to breathe.*'' Sasha's imitation of her husband's laid-back drawl with its slight inflection at the end of the sentence was uncannily accurate.

'What do you think, Josh?' Sasha's hazel eyes had an unnerving yellow glint to them, like a cat's. 'Is he starting to come round yet? Does he miss us, do you think? You're his friend. He must have talked to you about it.'

'Not really.'

'Well, how does he seem then? Is he down? Subdued? Does he give you the impression he's having regrets?'

Josh had a flashback to the night before, when Dan had been entertaining them with stories of that day's shoot which had involved a particularly flatulent Great Dane and its anorak-wearing trainer. Dan was not giving the impression of a man riven by doubt. He shrugged uncomfortably. 'You know what Dan's like. He plays things pretty close to his chest.'

'Mummy!' The shout going up from Lily's room was so piercing it could only belong to one person. 'Mummy! Come here. I need you.'

Sasha stayed on the sofa, with her hands wrapped around her mug, still frowning at what Josh had just said.

'*Mummy!*'

'I think September might be calling you.'

Sasha didn't respond.

'September. She's yelling for you.'

'Oh, right. It's OK, sweetie. I'm coming.'

But still Sasha made no attempt to move off the sofa.

Josh waited for a moment and then, knowing how Lily hated raised voices, he went to investigate.

Lily's normally neat bedroom looked post-apocalyptic. Boxes of toys had been emptied out over the floor, the wardrobe door was open and clothes were spilling out in a tidal wave of pink and flowers (they'd tried to get Lily interested in less stereotypical, more androgynous clothing, but to no avail). Someone had obviously been trying to make a den out of Lily's bedcovers, which were pulled off the bed and draped haphazardly between a chair and table. Lily's prized collection of kitten stickers lay scattered like confetti over every surface.

'Is everything OK?' Josh frowned, taking in the carnage.

Lily took after him in feeling more comfortable when things were calm and orderly. Though her little round face lit up in a smile when she saw him, he could tell by her eyes that she was worried. Something in Josh constricted at the sight of her and her transparent conviction that he would make everything all right.

'I wanted Mummy,' said September, who was kneeling on the floor wearing Lily's treasured Snow White dress with lipstick smeared all over her mouth.

'Mummy's a bit busy. Won't I do?'

'No. I need her to do my hair special. You can't do that.'

Josh agreed that doing hair special probably fell outside of his area of expertise.

'I'll ask Sasha to come in when she's finished talking to Lily's mummy, shall I?'

September eyed him coolly. 'Are you coming to live with me?'

Josh was used to Lily's non-sequiturs, but this one from September caught him unawares.

'Well, my daddy has come to live with Lily, so Lily's daddy must come to live with us.'

From the corner of his eye, Josh saw Lily's eyes widen and her chin start to tremble. 'I'm sorry, September. That's not how things work, I'm afraid. I live here, with Hannah and Lily.'

'But that means Lily gets two daddies and that's not fair.'

Now both little girls looked as if they were on the edge of tears.

'This is only for a few days, September, while your mummy and daddy sort things out.'

'Then he's coming home?'

'You'd better talk to him about that, sweetheart.'

The endearment came out clumsily. While Josh had no problem being lovey dovey with Lily, he always felt awkward around other people's children, sure he sounded phoney and, even worse, creepy.

Now September started crying in earnest, her brown eyes brimming with tears.

'I want my daddy,' she wailed. '*I want my daddy!*'

Finally Sasha appeared in the doorway. 'Oh poor baby. Come here, my baby.' Throwing herself to the floor, she swept September up into a hug, crushing the little girl's head to her bony ribcage. 'You want your daddy. I know you miss your daddy.'

As she stroked her daughter's curls, Sasha gazed up at Josh, all the time keeping up a stream of whispered endearments into her daughter's shuddering ear, and he was shocked when he finally put a name to the expression on her face.

Triumph.

* * *

'Tell me again what he said.'

It was the third time Josh had been through it. He was tired. He just wanted to have dinner and slump on the sofa, but instead he was being quizzed about every single conversation he'd had with Dan, and every single conceivable nuance of every single word.

'He just said he felt like he'd been sleepwalking through the last few years of his life, and now he's waking up.'

'Yes, but that could be a good thing, couldn't it? It could mean that he's finally learning what's important to him, couldn't it?'

'It could . . . '

Josh didn't tell her about the excitement in Dan's voice when he'd talked about feeling alive for the first time in years. What would be the point?

71

'I love him so much,' Sasha said now, apropos of nothing. 'I think it took something like this to really realize it. I know it will all turn out OK in the end. You know how some things are just meant to be. Dan would never break up our family — he knows what it would do to me after everything I went through as a child. You know, I feel almost relaxed about it now, because I'm so certain he's coming back.'

Josh didn't even want to think about all the different levels on which that bothered him. The karmic *everything happens for a reason* bullshit-o-meter, the fact that for someone claiming to be so relaxed Sasha was doing a very good impression of being totally the opposite. Sitting in her usual spot on the end of the sofa with her feet tucked up underneath her, she was almost bouncing with excess energy like one of those nodding dogs people put in cars. Her eyes were like two dark glass marbles, boring into him as she waited impatiently for his response. Well, not so much a response as a confirmation.

At least it was preferable to listening to her waxing lyrical about Dan and how wonderful he was. The guy had practically been canonized over the course of the last few days. If Josh ever tried to remind her of the little matter of Dan cheating on her, she dismissed it with hardly a second thought. 'A moment of weakness' was how she'd decided to classify it. 'He was flattered. She was available. Oldest story in the book. Course I'll make him get tested for every STD under the sun before I take him back, but it'd be crazy to throw away a fantastic marriage, with all that

72

history, just because of some little slut who couldn't keep her knickers on.'

Josh would squirm with discomfort when she talked like this, glancing towards the doorway to make sure it was free of small figures with large flapping ears.

A series of loud bleeps announced the arrival of a text message. Josh glanced at his phone, which sat on the coffee table between him and Sasha, aware that her eyes too were fixed on it. Both of them knew it was Dan, texting to see if Sasha was still there. This was the pattern they'd fallen into, with Dan resolutely refusing to talk to Sasha until their Dan-imposed 'breathing time' was up. He'd already threatened to move out to an undisclosed address if Sasha accidentally-on-purpose happened to be there when he got home.

'We need to give each other this time,' he stressed. 'We owe it to each other.'

'Well?' Sasha wanted to know.

'He says he's going to be home around eleven.'

'Because he thinks that's too late for September to be out during the week. Silly man. He knows she doesn't need a lot of sleep. She's not that sort of child.'

'Yes, but Lily does,' broke in Hannah, much to Josh's relief.

Sasha frowned. 'I do think it might be good for Lily not to be quite so regimented,' she said. 'Otherwise how is she ever going to learn to cope with change? She's such a nervous little thing as it is.'

Josh opened his mouth to speak, but Hannah

glared at him and instead he counted to ten in his head, waiting for his irritation to subside.

★ ★ ★

Only after Sasha had left did Josh give vent to his annoyance.

'Just what was she implying by that 'nervous little thing' comment?' he asked, when Hannah finally surfaced from getting a completely shattered Lily to bed.

'Take no notice. She's just overwrought. She's not thinking about what she's saying.'

'Yes, but that's no excuse for — '

The doorbell cut short what he had been about to say.

'I thought Dan had a key?' Josh said.

'He must have lost it. Or maybe he's just being discreet in case we're making mad passionate love on the living-room table.'

'Chance would be a fine thing.'

An awkward pause.

Hannah went to the door and Josh listened for Dan's sing-song 'I'm ho-ome.' He was surprised to hear just Hannah, sounding fraught.

'I don't think it's a good idea,' she was saying. This was followed by an indistinct murmur of voices. Then, 'OK, OK, but I still don't think it's a good idea.'

She reappeared in the doorway with a shape slumped over her shoulder. A September-shaped shape.

'You've got to be kidding,' groaned Josh.

Hannah raised her eyebrows warningly at him

74

over the top of her charge, who was wrapped in a duvet and clearly pretending to be asleep, with just one slightly raised eyelid giving her away.

'September, poppet, I'm just going to pop you down on our bed so you can have a nice sleep,' said Hannah.

'Wanna go Lily's room.' The little girl's voice was loud, but her eyes stayed firmly shut.

'No, sweetie. Lily is asleep. You snuggle up in Auntie Hannah and Uncle Josh's bed. There's a good girl.'

'I want my mummy!'

'September, honey . . . '

'I WANT MY MUMMY!'

Hannah locked eyes with Josh over September's head and shrugged as best she could with a recumbent four-year-old on her shoulder, then she turned and walked out of the room. Josh listened to her trying to soothe the fractious child as she made her way along the hallway to their bedroom.

'I know you do, sweetie, but Mummy will be right back, just as soon as she does this important thing she has to do. And in the meantime, you're having a sleepover here with us. Isn't this fun?'

Judging by the muffled protests coming from behind the now closed bedroom door, September clearly didn't agree that this unlooked-for sleepover in any way constituted fun.

Twenty fraught minutes later, the flat finally fell silent. Twenty-one minutes later, there was the noise of a door being stealthily nudged open and then Hannah reappeared.

75

'Well?' Josh was conscious that he was using his disapproving school-teachery voice, but he was too irritated to do anything about it. Just how much of their lives were going to be taken over by Dan and Sasha and their crisis? Of course he wanted to help — they were their best friends, after all — but surely there was a line to be drawn somewhere? Surely he and Hannah were entitled to some semblance of a life of their own?

'Sasha's gone to follow Dan.'

Josh gave a questioning look.

Hannah held up her hands. 'I know, I know. I told her it was a bad idea, but she wouldn't listen. Apparently one of her friends was out for a meal in Soho and called her to say she'd just seen Dan having dinner with a woman.'

'Dan has dinner with lots of women. That's part of his job.'

'I know. I said that. Listen, you don't need to get shirty with me!'

Hannah glared at him. But rather than making him feel guilty, her defensiveness just added to Josh's sense of grievance. It was all right for her. She was at home all day. She was probably enjoying having all these people around all the time, all this activity, all this *drama*. She ought to try working in a proper job where you went out and spent all day with hundreds of people and looked forward to getting home for a bit of peace and quiet.

'Anyway,' she continued, 'this friend had no idea Sasha and Dan were splitting up. If that's what they're doing. She only made a big thing

76

about Dan and this other woman as a joke, apparently, but Sasha was straight round here to drop off September and now she's off in hot pursuit.'

'Do you think it's her? *Sienna?*'

'God knows. I'll bloody murder Dan if it is, after all his promises. Sasha says she's sure it isn't, but she wants to put her mind at rest. She promises she's just going to look through the window. She's not going to make a scene or anything.'

'Yeah, it's not as if Sasha's the making-a-scene type, after all!'

Hannah made a face. 'She promised me she wasn't going to anyway. She didn't even seem that bothered, she just said she knew she was being stupid but she just wanted to scc for herself, then she'd come straight back. She'll probably be here any minute.'

'Yeah, unless she's stabbed him through the heart. You did frisk her for sharp implements, I take it?'

'Look, like you said, Dan works with lots of women and does a lot of business over dinner. Sasha is just overreacting to everything at the moment. Bet you anything she comes through the door in the next half-hour absolutely mortified.'

'Sasha doesn't do mortified, Hannah. Sasha only does vindicated or *Now I'll make this into an amusing story to make myself look cute and quirky.*'

'Why are you so down on her suddenly? Don't you think she's having a hard enough time without her friends turning on her as well?'

Hannah rarely raised her voice, and as Josh gazed at her in surprised reproach, he noticed for the first time how tired she looked. Her blue eyes appeared almost colourless against the dark mauve shadows underneath. This situation was taking its toll on her too.

'I just wish things could go back to how they were before.' He sighed, uncomfortably aware he was sounding a bit like his own four-year-old daughter.

As if on cue, from the hallway came the sound of Lily's panicked voice. 'Mummy! Daddy!'

Glad of the distraction, he strode off into her room. Nudging open the door with its pink gingham letter 'L' interwoven with yellow and white daisies, he was thrown off guard by finding September sitting perched on the top of Lily's duvet, gazing at him impassively, while a just-woken Lily, eyes still wild and confused from sleep, cowered at the other end, rubbing her arm.

' ''Tember woke me up,' she gulped. 'She pinched me.'

September continued gazing levelly at him. 'Couldn't sleep,' she said, by way of explanation. 'Don't like your bedroom.'

'But you shouldn't have woken Lily up, should you, September? And you shouldn't have pinched her. That wasn't kind, was it?'

'*You're* not kind,' said September, her voice rising dangerously. 'You're mean and I don't like you!' Her face crumpled in on itself and she started crying.

78

'What the hell is going on in here?'

Josh had no idea how Sasha could have got in so suddenly. He hadn't been gone for more than a few seconds but here she was, appearing out of nowhere and sweeping past him into Lily's room, kneeling by the bed so her sobbing child could throw herself into her arms.

'It's all right, darling girl. Mummy's here now.'

For a second or two there was just the sound of September's noisy sobs, punctuated by soft sniffs from Lily and whines from Toby outside the bedroom door. Then, still with her back to him, Sasha said, in a cold, hard voice Josh hadn't heard before, 'I'd prefer you not to bully my daughter when I'm not here, thank you very much, Josh. Can't you see how fragile she is?'

Josh stopped himself just in time before he said something he would regret, remembering only after he'd stalked out of the door that he hadn't said goodnight to Lily.

'I've bloody well had enough,' he hissed at Hannah when he got back to the living room and saw her sitting at the table. 'This has got to stop. Do you know what she just said? She said — '

'I'm sorry. Oh God, Josh, I'm so sorry.'

Sasha had come up behind him and now flung her arms around his neck, draping herself over his back so he had the uncomfortable sensation of wearing her, like a coat. He felt her chest rising and falling rapidly and his heart sank as he realized she must be crying.

'What happened, Sasha?'

Hannah had got up from her chair and was gazing at her friend with a look of such concern that Josh felt immediately ashamed. That in turn made him irritated at having been made to feel bad, so he was relieved when Sasha finally slid off him and into a heap on the floor.

'He was with *her*.' The words sounded as if they'd been squeezed out of her.

Hannah gasped. 'No! With Sienna? But he promised us — '

Sasha's narrowed eyes flashed back pin-pricks of reflected light. 'He promised you? What about *me*? What about what he promised *me*? I'm his fucking wife!'

'Oh God, I know. Sorry, Sasha. That must have been so awful. Tell me what happened.'

Sasha put her head in her hands. 'It was a nightmare. I drove past where Shelly said she'd seen him, but there were too many people around for me to get a good look through the window, so I parked around the corner. Then I walked back and looked in the window, and there they were. The two of them. Oh shit. Oh fucking shit. This is all so fucked up.'

'But how did you know it was her?' Josh felt he ought at least to try to mount a defence of his absent friend. 'I mean, it could have been any one of the women Dan works with every day.'

Sasha's head whipped up suddenly. 'Yes, it could . . . except that he was sticking his tongue down her throat.'

Hannah's hand flew to her mouth. 'I don't believe it. Not at the table!'

'Well, maybe not tongues, but they were all over each other. I almost threw up on the spot, I swear to God.'

Sasha had pulled her knees up to her bony chest and was rocking backwards and forwards. All of a sudden, to Josh's great alarm, she started emitting a keening noise.

'Mummy?'

He'd forgotten about September and Lily. There they both were, two little figures standing in the doorway, eyes wide with shock as they stared at the rocking figure on the floor.

Instantly, Hannah was on her feet. 'It's OK, girls. Mummy's just a little tired, that's all, September. We all sometimes need a good cry when we're tired, don't we? Come on, I'll snuggle you both up together in our bedroom. How about that?'

As she led them away, Josh felt a surge of panic, tinged with resentment. Great. So she got to go off and read stories while he was left to deal with Sasha having a fully fledged meltdown on the living-room floor.

'Sorry,' she wailed, as if he'd spoken aloud. 'I just can't ... I can't ... Oh God, I can't breathe.' She was making rapid gulping noises as if she was being starved of oxygen.

Josh dropped to his knees beside her. 'Look at me,' he commanded, seizing her shoulders. 'Sasha, look at me!'

She brought her eyes up to his face, her breath still coming out in uneven gasps.

'Now breathe in,' he said in his best school-teacher's voice. 'Come on, breathe in. That's right. And out again. Good.'

'I'm sorry. I'm so sorry, Josh. I'm being a nightmare, aren't I? It's just ... it's just ... Oh

God. He was with *her*. You can't imagine what it's like, seeing the person you love, the father of your child, with someone else. Touching them. Kissing them. Oh, I feel sick.' She clapped a hand over her mouth, and for a horrible moment Josh thought she might actually vomit, right there on the rug. 'How could he? Josh, you're a man. How could he do this?'

Luckily Josh was saved from answering this unanswerable question by Hannah rushing back into the room.

'All quiet. Shit, Sasha, I don't know what to say. Did he see you? Dan, I mean?'

Sasha stared at her. 'Course he saw me. Obviously he saw me.'

'Not necessarily. It must have been dark outside and he was, erm, distracted. He could easily not have noticed you.'

'Well, seeing as I was standing five centimetres from his face, screaming at him, I think it's highly unlikely!'

Josh closed his eyes. Oh dear God. Hannah was still standing by the door, her hands on either side of her face and her mouth open in a long 'O' shape in an approximation of that Edvard Munch painting.

'Don't look so shocked, Hannah. What the fuck did you think I was going to do when I saw *my husband* feeling up some under-age slut? Turn around and walk away?'

'And what hap — '

Josh's question was cut short by the sound of a key in the door. He and Hannah locked eyes.

Dan burst through the living-room door, his

82

face grim. His slightly wild gaze flickered from Josh to Hannah and then to Sasha, still slumped on the floor. Josh felt his own indignation draining from him as he watched his friend's eyes fill with tears.

'Sash? Sash? I'm so sorry.'

'Get away from me.'

It was more of a hiss than an actual voice, and in truth Sasha had the look of an angry, feral cat crouched there on the floor, glaring at her husband with such fierce intensity, Josh half expected him to turn tail and run for the hills.

'Look . . . God, I don't know what to say.'

Dan ran his hands through his lank-looking hair as if he might find some inspiration there.

'I know that must have been an awful shock for you, but Christ, Sash, what were you thinking? I can't believe you followed me. And then screaming like that in the middle of that restaurant. It was . . . ' He closed his eyes and shook his head as if trying to shake off a memory too awful to recall. 'Horrible!'

'Was it?' Sasha had got to her feet and was looking at him with her eyes dangerously narrowed. 'Was it horrible for you? Poor Dan. We can't have that, can we? We can't have things being horrible. Not when you've done nothing to deserve it. *Apart from fucking some bimbo while your daughter is at home crying herself to sleep!*'

'I wasn't fucking her.' Dan's voice now had an unmistakeable steely edge to it. 'We were just having dinner. And unless you've left our daughter home alone, which I fucking well hope is not the case, she's right here fast asleep, so

83

don't try to play the moral card with me. Look . . . ' His tone softened. 'I know this is difficult for you. It's difficult for me. I hate not seeing September every day, but it's for the best in the long run. We're not good together any more, Sash. We need to let each other go while we're still friends.'

Feeling like a voyeur, Josh kept his eyes trained on Hannah, watching as she opened her mouth to say something, then bit down on her lip to stop whatever she had been about to blurt out. He didn't blame her. *Friends*. Jesus Christ! Two weeks ago, Sasha thought she was perfectly happily married. Did Dan really expect her to switch to being friends just like that? Clearly he did, because he was now looking at Josh, as if seeking some kind of validation. Josh shook his head, barely perceptibly, but Dan seemed to take that as a signal to press on and Sasha's silence as some kind of grudging acquiescence.

'Sash, babes, we've had eight happy years, haven't we? We've got a beautiful little girl. Let's just be thankful for that and move on with the next stage in our lives, shall we?'

He was moving towards her, his right hand slightly outstretched as if he seriously thought they might shake hands. *Stop*, Josh commanded in his head. *Stop now*. Yet at the same time as he was willing Dan to stop, there was a little part of him that was also urging him on towards the inevitable confrontation. He was so infuriatingly sure of himself, so convinced of his entitlement to happiness. So completely unaware.

Slap.

84

Sasha moved so fast, Josh hadn't even registered her getting up. One minute she was crouching on the floor and the next she'd sprung to her feet and whacked Dan around the face, the sound reverberating in the air.

'Don't you dare!' she was screeching in a voice that didn't sound quite human. 'Don't you dare imagine I'm going to make this easy for you. I am your *wife*, Dan. In there' — she gestured towards the hallway and Josh and Hannah's bedroom — 'is your *daughter*. You do not get to throw us away like so much rubbish. You do not get to slot someone else into our place the minute things get a bit difficult. You know what a divorce will do to me. You might as well take a gun and shoot us both. I won't let you do this!'

She streaked past them and straight out of the living room.

'And you do not own me!' yelled Dan after her, still holding his hand to his cheek where a livid red mark was already mapping out the shape of Sasha's hand. But his words were cut short by the slamming of the front door and the sound of Toby's upset barking.

'At least now you have some idea how fucking insane she is.' Dan was now sitting on the floor, although he kept springing up periodically to check his face, with its stinging handprint, in the mirror over the fireplace.

'For God's sake, Dan. What did you expect? Did you really think she'd just wish you luck and step aside?'

Hannah was pacing around the room. Josh hadn't seen her like this in a long time. There was a raised patch of eczema by her right temple that only ever appeared when she was stressed.

'No. Of course I didn't expect that. But Christ, you should have seen what she was like at the restaurant. Screaming her head off. So fucking embarrassing. And then hitting me like that. You have to admit that's bang out of order.'

'You lied! You told us all you weren't seeing that . . . *woman*.'

'I know. I'm sorry. But we just had dinner, that's all. We weren't *doing* anything.'

'It doesn't matter. You broke your promise. I'm sorry, Dan, but you can't carry on staying here.'

Dan's head shot up. 'Hang on. You're supposed to be neutral here. You said. How come you're siding with her all of a sudden?'

'We're not siding with anyone.' Josh's anger took him by surprise and gave his voice a pompous tone that made him cringe inwardly. 'We had a deal, Dan. You said as long as you were here you wouldn't be in contact with Sienna. So you'd have some thinking time, you said.'

'I've done nothing but think!' Dan's face was dark. 'Look, I know you guys would love for me and Sasha to get back together and for us to be a cosy little foursome again, but it ain't gonna happen. OK? I'm not about to start badmouthing my wife, but let's just say Sasha has problems, right? Big problems. You don't go through what she went through and come out the other end a completely well-balanced, sane member of society. It's not her fault and I'll do whatever I can to support her, but I am not going back to her. End of story. Fine, you want me to leave, I'll leave, but I am not going home. And the sooner you get used to that idea, the better. Now, if it's all the same to you, I'd like to go and look in on my daughter.'

'Oh, nice of him to remember he has a daughter,' snapped Hannah after Dan had stalked from the room.

'Come on, that's not really fair.' Now that his burst of anger had blown itself out, Josh felt slightly wretched. For all his faults, Dan was pretty much the best friend he had and it felt wrong to be chucking him out. 'He dotes on September, you know that. The only reason he hasn't seen her in a few days is because it would just have confused her if he'd been in and out of her life, there one minute and gone the next. It's better for her to get used to him not being around.'

'Better for *him*, you mean.'

Josh frowned. This was a side of Hannah he struggled with — the judgemental side that took a position and refused to budge from it or countenance an alternative, despite any evidence to the contrary. Josh himself was more rational — show him a persuasive argument and he was perfectly prepared to change his stance. That's what adults did, wasn't it? Listened to reason?

'We can't just throw him out. It's ten-thirty. Anyway it won't do September any good to wake up and find neither of her parents here. As it is, she's going to have to top and tail with Lily in Lily's bed, which won't exactly be comfortable.'

'Sasha will be back for her. She won't just leave her here. It's a school night. She knows September has been upset. She'll come back just as soon as she's calmed down.'

6

'How was Dan after I left? I bet he couldn't believe he had to look after September. That must have put a bit of a spanner in the works if he was planning a late-night rendezvous with the Child Bitch from Hell!'

Hannah glanced quickly around. They were standing at the classroom door waiting for story time to finish, and Sasha was talking extremely loudly. 'I assumed you'd come back, Sash. I didn't think you'd leave September at ours all night, not after she'd been so upset earlier.'

Sasha flicked her black hair out of her eyes. 'I was in no state to do anything, Hannah. After that scene at the restaurant and then seeing Dan back at yours, I just couldn't have coped with September as well. You can understand that, can't you? Anyway, I didn't think it would matter, seeing as her beloved daddy was there to sort her out. Him being so hands-on and all.'

Her voice rose dangerously as she spoke, so Hannah decided not to mention how, after they'd told Dan he had to leave, he'd insisted on going that very night, despite them then changing their minds in view of September and the lateness of the hour, so they'd ended up feeling like the bad guys. 'I don't want to put you both in an impossible position,' Dan had said as he wheeled his hastily packed suitcase across the communal hallway. 'I'll call you tomorrow and let you know where I'm crashing.'

Neither did Hannah tell Sasha about the three or four times during the night when she'd been woken by the noise of September sobbing through the wall and had gone into Lily's room to find the little girl curled up with her head on a pillow at the bottom of Lily's bed, and tears leaking from her tightly shut eyes.

'Are you awake, sweetie?' she'd asked, kneeling down next to the bed and folding one of September's clammy little hands in hers. But the tiny figure kept her eyes closed and refused to answer.

'So how was he? After I left? Dan, I mean.'

Sasha hadn't lowered her tone at all. A couple of the other mothers glanced over sharply. The children were now singing the goodbye song, where one by one they were bid a musical farewell by the group, usually the cue for their parents to gaze on misty-eyed, and any interruptions were fiercely frowned upon.

Hannah shrugged. 'You know, a bit shaken up, I suppose.'

'Did he feel guilty? What did he say?'

'Oh, you know.'

Hannah was grateful when the nursery teacher, Mrs Mackenzie, started singing 'goodbye Lily, goodbye', and her daughter got up from where she was sitting cross-legged on the carpet and cast her eyes anxiously around for her mother before making her way over to them, as pinkly self-important as if she was on a stage in front of hundreds of people, not taking leave of

90

twenty-three largely snotty-nosed three- and four-year-olds.

'Hello, Liliput.' She dropped to her knees to wrap her arms around her daughter, breathing in her hot sweet breath, nuzzling her nose into her poached-egg-soft neck, glad to escape Sasha's intensity. Sometimes when she held her daughter she felt a rush of love so overpowering she wanted to inhale her wholesale. 'How was your day?'

Lily drew back and looked at her solemnly. 'OK, I s'pose.'

Hannah's chest constricted as it always did when she thought about the things that might have happened to her daughter while she wasn't around to see, the little hurts she might have suffered, the games she might not have been invited to play, the times she might have missed her mother. Mrs Mackenzie always insisted that Lily was 'happy as Larry' when she was at nursery, but Hannah couldn't shake off the nagging doubt that there were things she wasn't told, or the fear that Lily might be putting on a brave face to mask some deeper unhappiness she didn't want them to know about.

'Hey, Hannah. Long time no see.'

The woman who'd materialized by her side, with a tousle-headed child clinging to her leg, was plump, with a doughy face and wispy brown hair. Amid the well-heeled Crouch End mothers with their expensively dressed-down labels, her baggy sweatshirt and long, shapeless skirt and the canvas bag slung over her stooped shoulder stood out. But her shy smile lit up her face,

91

making her almost pretty, and her voice was soft and warm.

'Oh hi, Marcia. I know, I've been . . . preoccupied.'

'Don't I know how that can be! I was just wondering . . . well, Sarah was just wondering,' she indicated the small child who seemed to be attempting to burrow right into her skin, 'if Lily wants to come for tea today. You as well, of course.'

'How kind. I'd love to, and I'm sure Lily would too. Lily?' Hannah felt a kind of giddy relief at the thought of spending time with someone normal, someone who wouldn't insist on making her listen while she dissected the corpse of her failed marriage. She bent her head to her daughter, who looked up at her and nodded, a closed-lipped smile making rosy apples out of her round cheeks.

'Not fair.'

Hannah hadn't noticed September coming up to join Sasha behind her.

'Lily's my friend. Not fair if she goes to Sarah's house.'

'But September . . . '

'No!' September was shouting now. 'Lily's *my* friend. I want Lily to come to *my* house.' She broke off to fling herself at her mother's legs.

'Don't you think, in view of the circumstances, it might be kinder if you and Lily came to ours?' Sasha was smiling, but her voice was tight, as if someone had pulled a thread through the middle of it.

'But I — '

'September has had a lot to deal with over the last few weeks, Hannah — as you well know — and I just think you might be a little more sensitive. Lily's her best friend. She needs her right now.'

'Oh, I'm sorry.' A vivid pink stain had spread across Marcia's pleasant face. 'We can make it another time, Hannah, if it's a problem.'

Hannah felt her own cheeks burning in sympathy. 'Sorry, Marcia,' she mumbled. 'Maybe we should leave it for today.'

'But Mummy,' Lily was tugging on her arm, 'I want to go to — '

Her words were cut short by Sasha bending down and pulling her in for a hug. 'We'll pick up jam doughnuts on the way home, and then you and September can play on her new Wii game. You know, the one you two were going on about all last week. Won't that be fun?'

She stood up and turned to Marcia, smiling at her without quite meeting her eyes. 'I didn't mean to be rude. It's just that Lily and September are so close — inseparable, really — and September is going through a bit of a hard time at the moment. I'm sure Sarah will find someone else to play with.'

As they made their way out of the classroom, past the wall of colourful self-portraits with their goggling round eyes and red, U-shaped mouths, and emerged into the playground, Sasha's mood seemed to lighten.

'You owe me,' she whispered, leaning in towards Hannah. 'I saved you from an afternoon of drinking herbal tea and swapping wholemeal-pizza recipes, followed by a nutritious tea of brown rice and veg from our own allotment.'

She did a very good imitation of Marcia's soft, tentative voice and Hannah smiled in spite of herself — and then was mortified to realize that Marcia was walking a few paces behind them.

'She's nice actually, Sasha. I like her. You really should give people a chance.'

'Oh, sorry. Didn't realize Pollyanna was in the house!'

★ ★ ★

Standing on the wooden deck in front of Sasha and Dan's dazzling white modernist house, set back from the road and up a flight of wide stone steps, Hannah for once didn't feel the usual shameful stab of resentment that Sasha, who hadn't worked in years, should have all this, while she and Josh seemed at times to be running on a hamster wheel just to hang on to a flat they'd long since outgrown. Instead she imagined how Sasha and September must rattle around in there, now it was just the two of them in those huge white rooms with their gleaming white floorboards. What would happen to the house if Sasha and Dan divorced? Hannah wondered. Dan earned good money, but he was self-employed and had a lot of outgoings, and as far as Hannah could tell he hadn't had a big job for quite a while.

'Blimey,' she said as Sasha casually threw open

the solid-oak front door, 'what's been going on in here?'

The normally pristine house was in disarray. Jackets and jumpers seemed to have been dropped wherever they were removed, lying in brightly coloured heaps on the white floors and ivory-coloured furniture, like so many exotic blooms. The glass coffee table in the cavernous living room was crowded with wine glasses and half-filled coffee cups and everywhere was littered with September's toys, including a long row of mutilated plastic dolls with toilet-paper bandages tied around them in various inventive ways.

'September was making a hospital,' said Sasha, as if that explained the empty pizza box on the arm of the sofa or the photographs strewn across the cream-coloured deep-pile rug. 'And Katia's off sick again. Honestly, that woman is ill more days than she's here. She's going to have to go.'

Sasha's inability to hold on to a cleaner for more than a few months was a running joke. Over the years Hannah had known her, she'd had cleaners who stole her underwear, cleaners who made passes at her husband and one cleaner who, when caught red-handed trying on one of Sasha's favourite dresses, looked puzzled at the furore, insisting, 'But I have alvays done zis.' Sometimes Hannah wondered whether Sasha exaggerated the stories for comic effect. A couple of times, having met and liked the pale-faced girls with their dyed-blonde hair scraped back into high ponytails and their tight stone-washed jeans and the shiny pink slippers they swapped for their towering platforms at the door, she'd found herself doubting whether they could really have committed whatever infringement Sasha was accusing them of, and worrying about how they'd make ends meet without Sasha and Dan's house to clean two days a week.

'Last week she reached up to pull a Monopoly board down from the shelf in September's room and the corner stabbed her in the eye and she reeled around the room screeching, 'I blind! I blind!''

Sasha did an imitation of the poor, afflicted Katia, staggering around with her hands clapped to her face, and Hannah giggled despite herself. But the smile died on her face as she watched Sasha collapse suddenly on to a dove-grey velvet chaise longue, shoulders sagging, face staved in by grief.

Sitting down next to her friend, grateful that September and Lily seemed to have taken themselves upstairs to September's room, Hannah put her arms around Sasha's frighteningly thin frame, feeling how the breath was being pulled out from a place deep inside her, like handkerchieves from a magician's hat.

'How could he, Han? How could he do this to me? I think I'm going crazy. I lie awake at night and it's like I've swallowed acid or something and it's burning through me, eating me alive. Oh, you wouldn't understand, but I lie there and everything hurts so much and I can't think of any way to get the pain to stop except to take a fucking axe and smash it all to bits — Dan, me, this home we built together, my stupid hurting heart, all of it, just smash it all to pieces.'

Hannah gazed at her. Did Sasha really think she had a monopoly on hurting hearts? 'You're bound to feel like this, Sasha. It's horrible, what's happened to you. But you know you have to keep strong, for September's sake. You're all she has right now.'

'I know, but it's so unfair, Hannah. How does it work out like this? How does he get to do all this damage and just move on to the next woman as if I didn't count for anything, as if I was no one? After all the things he said to me, all the promises he made me. How does that happen?'

Hannah shook her head. 'I don't know, Sash.'

Suddenly Sasha's delicate features contorted, her skin stretched out like pizza dough over her sharp cheekbones, her mouth twisting horribly at the corners. 'He won't get away with it. He thinks he will, but he won't.'

Her voice was harsh, grating, and Hannah had to stop herself from recoiling.

'I'm going to see a lawyer.' Sasha was nodding to herself, as if she'd forgotten Hannah was even there. 'I'm going to get that bastard.'

'Don't you think, for September's sake, you should hold fire a while? Far better to try to sort things out amicably . . . '

'Amicably? Really? While he's fucking some under-age bimbo? I don't think so. Do you reckon he's thinking about what's best for September, huh?'

Hannah shook her head. Glancing down, she noticed that Sasha had scraped the skin from around her thumb and was digging a sharp fingernail deep into the exposed flesh. Hannah watched transfixed as a bead of blood ballooned out from around the nail before dropping, squat and fat, on to the pale fabric of the chaise longue.

Lucie, aged seven

Yesterday it was my birthday. Daddy gave me a bike with pink glittery streamers on the handlebars and it has stabilizers but I mustn't worry about them because soon I'll be able to ride it and they'll be off quick as a flash. Mummy didn't come downstairs and Daddy said she's tired but I know it's because of Eloise. Sometimes I hate Eloise, but I can't say that because it's bad. I went creeping upstairs to see Mummy even though Daddy said I shouldn't. She was lying in her bed like a princess with her hair all around the pillow, but when she saw me she told me to go out because she couldn't bear the sight of me. It's because I had that bad thought about Eloise. Mummy knows. She knows everything.

7

'I'm going to give her whatever she wants. Anything. I know that scene last night was hideous and she hates my guts at the moment, but she adores September just as much as I do. Once she calms down a bit she'll want to do what's best for her.'

'Like having two parents living together? That'd be best, wouldn't it? Isn't that what all the studies say?'

Dan frowned over the top of his strawberry-and-passion-fruit smoothie. 'Not helpful, Josh man.'

'Sorry.'

Josh wished he didn't feel quite so awkward. They were in the café at Dan's fancy gym in the shadow of Alexandra Palace and, as always, Josh felt he was being judged. It wasn't that he was in bad shape exactly, but compared with Dan and the other blokes in there he felt flabby and poorly defined. It wasn't his fault they didn't have a spare few grand knocking about to spend on gym membership and state-of-the-art Lycra workout gear. And yes, he supposed he could do as Hannah was always suggesting and go running or cycle to work or whatever, but she had no real clue how much teaching took out of you. People always assumed it was a sedentary, physically undemanding job, but he was always on his feet to illustrate a point, or pacing around the classroom looking at individual students' work. And there was the psychological stress. It'd take more than a few pull-ups on one of those fancy weights machines they had here, followed by a sauna or a session in the jacuzzi, to sort out the knots in his brain after eight hours of teaching.

'Look,' Dan put on his sincere face just as obviously as if he were pulling on a hat, 'I don't know how many times I can apologize for last night. I know I made you and Hannah a promise, and I broke it. I feel like I abused your hospitality. But, hand on heart, it was the first time me and Sienna had met up. I just had to see her.'

'So it's serious then?'

Dan's face slackened and he cast his eyes downwards like a love-struck teenager. 'We have . . . strong feelings for each other.'

'Right. So that was all bullshit then, that stuff about Sasha not having to know about you and Sienna because it was such early days and it could go nowhere?'

Dan looked as close to shamefaced as he ever got. 'I just wanted to keep her out of it. I was being protective, I suppose.'

'Protective of who? Your wife or your mistress?'

Dan glared at him. Clearly the word 'mistress' grated. Well, good. Dan was so infuriatingly sure of himself, always bending the truth until it fitted the image he'd created of himself in his own head. He needed to see how this looked from the outside, just how grubby the whole thing was.

101

'Hey, Dan.' The woman standing by their table was the colour of a newly minted penny and dressed head to toe in electric-blue Lycra, her highlighted blonde hair pulled up into a high ponytail. 'You coming to circuit training later?'

At first Josh took her to be in her late twenties, but closer inspection put her nearer her mid-forties, the fine lines next to her eyes and the crêpey swell of her unavoidable cleavage giving her away. He watched, impressed despite himself, as Dan slipped effortlessly into flirty mode.

'Not today, doll. Things to do, people to see. You know how it is.'

She shrugged prettily. 'Well, you'd better make it next week. We can't have you going to seed now, can we? Not after all your hard work.'

Even though she was looking at Dan, Josh couldn't shake off the feeling that she was referring to him when she said 'going to seed'. It was always like this when he went out with Dan, that feeling of suffering from comparison.

'*Doll?*' Josh enquired as the woman moved off, her ponytail swinging behind her.

Dan smirked. 'I'm using it in a post-ironic way, naturally.'

'Course you are. So go on. Back to your *mistress*. I don't suppose you slept at her place last night?'

Dan pressed his lips together. 'No offence, but I think the less you and Hannah know about where I am, the better. I don't want to put you two in an awkward position.'

'Bit late for that! So you are with her then?'

'I didn't say that. I just think it's best Sasha doesn't know where I am at the moment, and if I tell you you'll either feel obliged to tell her, or you'll feel bad about not telling her. Either way it's shit.'

Josh had to agree it was shit. 'I still can't believe you're splitting up. I always thought you were so together, you and Sasha. All those *I love yous.*'

'Yeah, well, that was Sasha's doing really. She is very needy emotionally, if you know what I mean. If I texted her and didn't put a kiss or a *love you*, she'd act like it was the end of the fucking world.'

'Aren't you worried, then, about what this is going to do to her?'

Dan shook his head. 'Underneath the neediness and that fragile *Touch me and I'll break* exterior, Sasha has a rod of steel running through her. I'm not even joking. She's the hardest person I know.'

Seeing Josh's expression, he held up his hand defensively. 'That's not a criticism. I'm still really fond of her.'

'*Fond?* She's your wife, for God's sake, not your granny!'

The whole conversation was making Josh feel uncomfortable. How was it possible to go from love to fond in just two weeks? And if it could happen to Dan and Sasha, couldn't it also happen to him and Hannah?

'Well, she's not going to be my wife for much longer,' Dan pointed out matter-of-factly.

'You've already seen a lawyer?'

'No. Course I haven't. We don't need lawyers, Josh. It's not going to be that sort of break-up. I'm not out to shaft Sasha. She's the mother of my daughter, for fuck's sake. I'm going to be more than generous. She can have half the money from the house, even though I put up most of the deposit and have paid the entire mortgage and every single bill since we got it. If we split the equity, she'll have more than enough to buy a two-bedroom garden flat in the same area — the same street even — without a mortgage. Something like you've got, only a bit flashier, if you know what I mean.'

'Thanks.'

'I didn't mean it like that. It's just, you know what Sasha's like, everything has to be perfect. Then I could buy my own place nearby so that when she's a bit older September can walk between the two. I was even thinking I might get somewhere near that new secondary school, so that she'd definitely be in the catchment.'

'Blimey, Dan, they're not even at primary school yet. Anyway, you know Sasha will insist on private school.'

'Yeah, well, whatever, but I just want you to see I'm thinking long term about this.'

'And what about custody?'

Dan looked blank.

'Of September. Are you going to ask for half and half?'

Josh took savage enjoyment from the expression of horror that flickered across Dan's face. 'Well, that wouldn't make any sense, would it, seeing as I'm the one who has to go out to work to fund everything? No, I think it'll be a much less formal arrangement — when I'm not working I'll have September 24/7, other times less. We'll have to come to some sort of flexible agreement.'

'Good luck with that.'

Dan sighed deeply and rubbed a hand across his eyes. The whites were pinkish in the corners, which Josh had at first attributed to Dan being fresh from fifty lengths of the gym's ozone-cleaned pool, but now he wondered if it might just be stress. Dan was putting up a good front, but it couldn't be easy, breaking up a family. Josh wondered how much he was sleeping — with or without the added complication of a twenty-four-year-old model in his bed. The sudden mental image that accompanied this thought left him feeling momentarily hot with guilt.

'Look, I know this initial bit is going to be difficult,' said Dan, still rubbing his eyes. 'Sasha's furious and she has every right to be. I've been a fucking twat. But once she realizes it really is over and I'm not about to be a complete bastard about money and stuff, she'll have to accept it, won't she?'

'Whatever you say.'

8

'I want the house, full custody of our daughter, of course, and at least £50,000 a year.'

'Um, I did ask for the bottom line of what you'd be prepared to accept, Mrs Fisher.'

'That *is* the bottom line.'

Sasha was dressed in full executive gear — fitted black jacket, black trousers and soft suede high-heeled black boots — and was clearly not about to be cowed either by the lawyer with her silk shirt and thick-framed Prada glasses, or by the plush wood-panelled office in High Holborn.

'I can quite see why you'd be tempted to go for the jugular, Mrs Fisher, but in cases like this a certain degree of compromise is inevitable, and if you could just indicate in which areas you're prepared to be flexible I — '

'No compromises.'

Hannah winced. This was what she'd been afraid of when Sasha asked her to accompany her to her first meeting with Caroline Briscoe, the highly recommended divorce lawyer whose hourly fee had made Hannah choke on her digestive biscuit when Sasha dropped it casually into the conversation over tea the day before.

'Blimey, Sasha. Does she charge by the breath?'

'What do I care? I won't be paying for it.'

Useless to point out that even if the money

came from Dan, it was still part of the same pot she'd be relying on to live. Now Sasha was glaring at Caroline Briscoe with unblinking intensity and it was the hardened lawyer who looked away first.

'Very well, Mrs Fisher. In that case you're going to need to give me everything you have on your husband — every annoying thing he did, every argument, every grievance. Did he smack your daughter? Was he unreasonably possessive? Was he mean with money? Were you frightened of his moods?'

Hannah couldn't help exclaiming, 'Dan's not like that.'

Instantly Sasha swung around, her face contorted with fury. 'Shut up, Hannah. You know nothing about our life together. You don't know what he was really like, when no one else was around. You don't know how he treated me.'

Hannah stared at her friend, her mouth still open to form the words she had been about to say. She knew Sasha was angry. She had the right to be angry. But surely she wasn't going to start making stuff up about Dan? Anxiety prickled as another possibility occurred to her. Could there be a chance she wasn't making it up? Might there be a side to Dan that she and Josh had never seen?

'And will you be seeking the usual custody arrangement in cases like this? Every other weekend and one night during the week?'

Caroline Briscoe had taken a black Moleskine notepad from the top drawer of her imposing desk and was jotting things down with an expensive-looking pen. Hannah noticed that her nails with their clear varnish were impeccably shaped, with perfect white crescents at the base, as if she'd come straight from a manicure. Her heart sank. How was it possible to be a top lawyer, with all the work pressures that entailed, and still have time to stay groomed? Hannah barely had time to shower these days — how did other women manage it?

'I'd only allow that on the condition *she* won't be there. That bitch is not coming anywhere near my child.'

'Of course, that's something you could agree privately with your husband, Mrs Fisher. It's not something that would become part of any legal contract. Unless, of course, you have reason to believe this woman would present a threat to your daughter's wellbeing in some way.'

'She's breaking up my daughter's fucking family. Don't you think that might present some threat to her wellbeing?'

Hannah felt her face burning, although why she should be embarrassed by her friend's behaviour, she couldn't have said. It was always the same — guilt tugging like muscle cramp inside her. 'It's not your fault,' Josh was always reminding her, if friends had a dud meal at a restaurant she'd recommended or the supermarket delivery van couldn't find a parking space in their road.

Hannah would never know if she'd have been this way anyway, regardless of what had happened when she was seventeen — taking responsibility for things that weren't her fault, feeling bad for people she'd never met or about situations totally outside of her control. Like Sasha being rude to the lawyer she was overpaying to take her husband to the cleaner's. That was the actual phrase she'd used, seemingly unaware that it was something said only in bad Hollywood films. 'I'm going to take that bastard to the cleaner's.'

Afterwards, Sasha insisted on going out for lunch.

'How often do we do this?' she asked, when Hannah muttered about having work to do. 'How often do we go to town and enjoy ourselves?'

She had a new way of talking at the moment — high and bright, as if someone had Shellacked her real voice. Hannah swung between sympathy and exasperation. Sasha seemed so alone. She hardly spoke to any of her family — not surprising, in light of all the murky secrets that surrounded them — and for someone with hundreds of acquaintances she seemed to have very few real friends.

'Funny, that,' Josh said drily when she'd pointed it out over dinner the night before.

They'd argued then, about Hannah accompanying Sasha to the lawyer.

'It's taking sides. We're supposed to be neutral.'

'I'm just going to support her. I won't be taking part in any discussions. I'd do the same for Dan.'

'Yeah, well Dan doesn't seem to think he'll need a lawyer. He thinks they can sort it all out like reasonable people.'

Hannah made a snorting noise at that phrase *reasonable people*.

Now she and Sasha sat in an upmarket noodle bar in a part of the East End that had been practically a no-go zone when Hannah first moved to London, but was now achingly trendy. How quickly things changed. The noodle bar was part of a converted warehouse building with soaring ceilings painted white and supported by giant steel beams. They sat on high chrome stools, from which Hannah's legs dangled weightlessly, and ate at a white counter that ran the length of the huge plate-glass window.

'He isn't going to know what hit him,' Sasha said with unconcealed relish.

Hannah was alarmed by the slightly fanatical look in her friend's feline eyes, but she tried to ignore it.

'If he thinks I'm just going to roll over and accept whatever crumbs he deigns to throw me, he has got another thing coming.'

Hannah nodded. They'd had this conversation so many times she was getting sick of it. Anyway, she'd long since realized that Sasha wasn't actually expecting her to contribute anything to the discussion.

'If you knew what Dan was really like, you'd run a mile.'

Sasha was waving her chopsticks around in the air like castanets. Hannah noticed she had hardly touched her stir fry, for all the fuss she'd made sending it back because the first one contained coriander and if there was one food she couldn't stand it was coriander, and if they were going to include coriander they ought to say so clearly on the menu. (Meanwhile, Hannah's face burned, her eyes glued to the table, unable to look at the poor young waitress whose fault the menu wording was not.)

'I've already told you, Sash, I don't want to know. We've all done things we're not particularly proud of.'

'Not like this.'

'Oh, I wouldn't be so sure.'

'Really? So you're a wife-beater, are you, Hannah?'

Hannah looked up sharply. 'What do you mean?'

'Domestic violence. What's the matter? You don't think Dan's the type? Haven't you seen all those campaigns? You can never tell what goes on behind closed doors.'

'I don't believe you. He wouldn't.'

'Wouldn't he? Want to read my medical files?'

Hannah felt sick. She knew, of course she did, that you could never judge a relationship from the outside. She'd done enough features over the years on people who had turned out to be hiding secrets — child abuse, bigamy, cross-dressing, you name it. People were rarely what they seemed. But this? Dan? She just couldn't, wouldn't believe it.

'When? Why didn't you do something about it, in that case? Why did you stay with him?'

Sasha pushed her largely untouched bowl aside crossly. 'I don't want to talk about it. I just

111

thought you ought to know, before you start defending him. Just remember, you don't know the half of it.'

★ ★ ★

'She's making it up.'

Josh swivelled round on the bench until he was facing Hannah straight on. She registered for the first time the lines around his soft greeny-brown eyes — puddle-coloured, she used to tease him. When had they appeared? Had they sprung up overnight, or was it just that she hadn't noticed them before? She remembered a time when she would study his face for hours, as if trying to commit it to memory: every mole, every gentle hollow, the faint scars from a long ago bout of chickenpox. But lots of people in long-term relationships got out of the habit of seeing each other properly. There was nothing sinister about it. She just hadn't imagined it would happen to them, that's all.

'Dan has many faults, but he's not a wife-beater. That's absurd.'

'Shh!'

Even though Lily was on the climbing frame several metres from the bench where they were sitting, Hannah still worried that she might hear something. And this was definitely one conversation she didn't want her daughter to repeat. She'd asked Josh to meet them at the park on his way home from work so that they could chat privately while Lily was preoccupied, but their daughter had a habit of picking up on things,

112

even when you thought she wasn't within earshot.

'I know it's absurd. That's what I said to her. Then she said something about showing me her medical records. She says her GP measured her bruises and photographed them. Would she make that up?'

'She's hurt, that's all. And so she's getting back at Dan any way she can. What's that phrase my mother uses? *Hurt people hurt people.*'

'Mummy! Look at me!'

Lily was standing near the top of the climbing frame, gripping tightly to the bars, her chubby legs stiffly rooted to the spot.

'Wow, Liliput! You're so high! Be careful up there!'

Hannah turned back to Josh. 'You have to talk to him.'

'Me? Why?'

'Because you're his friend. You have to let him know what's being said about him.'

'Oh what, I'm just supposed to sit down over a pint and say, 'By the way, mate, your wife says you hit her. Mine's a bitter!''

'Don't be so facetious. But yes, you have to tell him straight.'

'I can't. No way. I couldn't accuse him of that.'

'You're not accusing him, you're just letting him know what Sasha said. You're warning him, that's all.'

'Uh-uh. Not doing it. He'll find out soon enough without me sticking my oar in. Ever hear the phrase *shooting the messenger?* No way am I getting mixed up in this.'

Hannah glared at him. There were times when she could find Josh's emotional awkwardness endearing, but this was not one of them. 'I don't believe you,' she said hotly. 'What kind of friend are you?'

'The kind that wants to stay friends.'

Josh had turned around so he was resolutely facing away from her, watching the climbing frame where Lily was slowly inching her way down. Hannah's chest tightened at the sight of her.

'So you'd rather not find out the truth, and leave Dan completely in the dark just because it might be a bit awkward to bring it up? Is that right?'

'Yes. That's about the size of it. Now can we just drop it, please?'

On the way home in the car, Hannah nursed her resentment. Conversation between her and Josh was minimal and to the point. Had she got anything in for dinner? Should they stop off at Tesco Express to pick up some dog food for Toby? Was there a cake sale at nursery the next day that they should be providing something for? Yes. No. Shrug.

Back at the flat, Hannah keenly felt the lack of a separate living space. Josh and Lily positioned themselves on the sofa — Lily to watch some incomprehensible cartoon she'd recently fallen in love with, and Josh to start on a pile of marking. Sitting at the table with her back to them, Hannah couldn't concentrate on the feature she was supposed to be writing. Josh kept

114

pressing the top of his plastic biro in and out, click, click, click, while a cartoon character on the television burst into raucous song. She found herself flicking to Twitter, where she had an account she had set up to promote herself as a freelancer.

Her fingers jabbed at the keyboard.

My OH is being a wankerpricktosspot

She stared at the words in the box for a few seconds as Josh clicked his pen maddeningly in and out behind her. Then she pressed Delete.

9

'I know it was her. It has to be.'

Dan jumped up from the sofa to stand in front of the living-room window staring out at his car, hands on hips, as if it might somehow look different from the last time he had jumped up to check, just minutes before.

'She knows how much that car means to me. It's just the kind of thing she'd do.'

Josh joined him at the window. As usual, Dan had parked his bright-red vintage Alfa Romeo Spider convertible across next door's driveway, blocking them in. Josh had asked him not to do so on a couple of occasions, after the neighbour had arrived at the door, tight-lipped, baby in arms, muttering about the difference between communal and private rights of way. But the problem with Dan was that he'd be all affability and apologies at the time, and then do exactly the same thing the next time he couldn't find anywhere immediate to park.

'It doesn't look *too* bad, not from a distance anyway.'

Dan turned to face him, incredulous. 'What the hell are you talking about? There's a fucking great crater running around the whole car where she's scratched it with her keys. How can you say it doesn't look too bad?'

'Come on, Dan. You can't be sure it was Sasha. How could she have known where your

116

car was in the first place?'

'Didn't she follow me the other night and practically assault me in a restaurant? How hard would it have been to find out where I've been staying? All she'd need to do is ring the agency and pretend to be biking something over to Sienna.'

Josh's eyes swung to face Dan. 'I don't believe it. You really have been staying at Sienna's? Bloody hell, Dan. You're supposed to be trying to make this transition as smooth as possible.'

Dan looked shifty. 'Where else was I supposed to stay? You and Hannah threw me out, and I can't afford to go shelling out on a hotel now I've got two households to support. Anyway, it's traumatic not seeing September. I hate it and obviously I feel guilty as fuck. Sienna's been helping me through it. I don't think I could have survived the last few days without her.'

Josh shook his head slowly, as if trying to dislodge what he'd just heard. Couldn't Dan see what an idiot he was being?

For a few seconds, the two men stood side by side in silence, studying the mutilated car.

'So where does she live then, Sienna? Don't tell me, Notting Hill?'

Dan looked surprised. 'How did you know that?'

'Because every aspiring model, creative type or newly separated man trying to run away from his mid-life crisis heads for Notting Hill.'

Dan grimaced at the phrase 'mid-life crisis', as if Josh had said something offensive. 'Yeah, well, don't make too many assumptions. It's only a stopgap. Anyway, Sienna's flat is tiny. It's not like we're shacked up in some swanky Hugh Grant-style townhouse or anything. As soon as my house is sold I'll get something around here, big enough for September to have her own room when she stays with me.'

'Your house?'

'OK, our house, although I did pay for the whole thing practically single-handed.'

'That's not the point.'

'I know, I know. Look, I've already said I'm going to be fair, haven't I? Although after what she's done to my car, I feel like taking the whole fucking lot.'

They sat down again, Josh in the armchair and Dan on the sofa. Josh couldn't help eyeing up the pile of exercise books on the coffee table that he'd been in the middle of marking when Dan turned up out of the blue. It was Sunday afternoon, and his Monday-morning GCSE class would be expecting their essays back the next day. He hoped Dan wasn't planning on staying too long.

'I went round to pick up September,' Dan had explained when he arrived. 'I left Sasha a long voicemail explaining exactly what time I'd be getting there, and she was fucking well out. Can you believe that? I didn't even say anything about the car in the message — I was going to bring that up in person so I could see her reaction. I can read Sasha like a book. I can't believe she'd just go out like that.'

'She's out with Hannah. They've taken Lily and September to one of those soft-play places.'

118

'Brilliant. I spend forty minutes sitting in traffic in my banged-up car just to see our daughter, and Sasha is out having fun with her mates.'

'I wouldn't exactly call it fun. Have you ever been to one of those places?'

'That's not the fucking point, Josh.'

'No, I know, but I was very relieved to give it a miss. Especially as I've got so much marking to do.'

If Dan had noticed Josh's pointed tone, he hadn't let on, and an hour later he still showed no sign of moving. Josh had sudden inspiration.

'It might not be a bad idea if you kind of weren't here when Hannah gets back,' he said awkwardly. 'She's still pretty angry about you breaking your promise about seeing Sienna. And obviously she feels very loyal to Sasha.'

This was the perfect opportunity to throw in a mention of Sasha's wild allegation. Josh could feel the words on his tongue, sitting there like lumps of meat. Yet he couldn't bring himself to say them. Josh was certainly no expert in communication, but even he knew that there are some things that, once said, cannot ever be unsaid. Dan was his friend. Josh knew there was no way he would ever have hit his wife, so why risk inflaming things by passing on what Sasha had said?

'Yeah, well, that's exactly why I'm going to stick around for a bit — so I can show Hannah the damage to my car. She needs to realize there are two sides to this story. I know I'm the one who walked out, but Sasha is not the innocent you think she is, believe me. Shit, do you know it's only since I've been with Sienna that I've realized just how fucked up Sasha really is? You have no idea how good it feels to be with someone who isn't testing me the whole time, and who actually treats me with a bit of respect and wants to hear how my day's been and genuinely cares how I'm feeling.'

Josh felt a twinge of resentment. When was the last time Hannah had asked him how he was in a way that made him feel she was really interested? These days she seemed so impatient with him, as if everything he said irritated her.

He wondered again whether Hannah might be making unfavourable comparisons between him and Dan. Wasn't he always hearing that women are attracted to bastards, not nice guys who take out the rubbish without being asked? And if anyone was acting like a bastard at the moment, it was Dan.

At school and university, Josh had always been the quiet one who girls spoke to if they wanted to know why their boyfriends were acting like dickheads, or whether Nick or Jason or Finn was seeing anyone at the moment. The role of Friend to Someone More Dynamic was one he'd been playing all his life, it seemed to him. Why should things be any different now, just because he was older and the person he was playing that role to was his own wife?

'What if Sasha comes back here with Hannah?'

'Good. That's absolutely fine with me. I've got a couple of questions I'd like to put to my ex-wife.'

'Ex? Last time I checked, you're married until you're divorced.'

'Not married. Separated. Sasha and I are separated.'

Josh felt another jolt of unease at how quickly it was possible to pass from couple to single, from lover to enemy.

When Hannah walked in with Lily an hour and a half later, Josh couldn't help feeling relieved at the cool reception she gave Dan.

'Hi, Dan. Thought it was your car outside.'

'Oh, you noticed it, did you? Did you also notice the fucking great scratch all around it, courtesy of my darling ex-wife?'

Hannah gave him a look of exasperated disbelief. Josh noticed she seemed strained. There was that little patch of eczema again, up near her hairline, the skin pink and raised with tiny flakes like grains of sand.

'Oh, really. And you know that for a fact, do you? You know it was Sasha who crept out in the middle of the night, leaving her four-year-old daughter behind, and somehow tracked down your car and risked being arrested in order to scratch it with her keys? You know it was her, not some mindless vandal? Where was it, anyway?'

'What does it matter where it was?'

'It matters because how would she have known where to find your sodding car?'

'He was at Sienna's.'

Josh couldn't help himself. But as soon as he'd spoken he wished he hadn't. He sounded so eager — as if he couldn't wait to dob in his mate.

121

He saw Dan shaking his head silently and felt a stab of shame.

'Oh, Dan. You can't seriously be staying with that woman?'

Dan looked as if he was about to protest.

'I know how it must look to you, Hannah,' he said eventually.

'Do you? I don't think so. I think if you had the first idea how shitty this looks to me, you'd never have done it in the first place.'

'I didn't have much choice. I had nowhere to go after you threw me out, and I just wanted to be with someone who doesn't treat me like the devil incarnate just because I'm finally being honest for the first time in years.'

'Oh I see, so now it's us who drove you to it, is that it?'

The patch of dry skin on Hannah's face looked red and angry now against her pale forehead, clashing with the burgundy sweatshirt she was wearing. The sweatshirt was an old one of Josh's, faded and shapeless, and he secretly wished she wouldn't wear it. She had such a beautiful body, he couldn't understand her need to cover it up all the time. Not that he'd say as much to her. He'd tried that at the start of their relationship but she'd become defensive, sure he was either being controlling or trying to flatter her, so he'd given up.

'I'm not saying that, Hannah.'

Josh turned his attention sharply to Dan. Surely there wasn't a catch in his voice just now? The prospect of Dan being overcome with emotion was vaguely horrifying.

'I'm just trying to explain things to you.' His voice was definitely wobbling. 'I know what I'm doing seems really brutal, and you have no idea how much I hate hurting my family. But I was dying in that relationship. That's how it felt. Sasha has such fixed ideas about how she thinks a couple should be, and what image of us she wanted to present to the world. Sienna allows me to be *me*. Do you know how amazing that feels after ten years of trying to fit into someone else's picture of me?'

Josh felt strangely embarrassed. Dan and he didn't talk about this kind of stuff. That was part of the reason Josh felt so comfortable with him. He'd heard him open up to other people about emotional stuff at the dreg-end of a dinner party. How a cousin he was really close to had dropped dead at a football match when they were teenagers, something about an irregular heart-beat, and how ever since then he'd felt a spiritual connection, as if part of his cousin was always with him. Freaky stuff like that. But as if by unspoken agreement, when they were on their own they never strayed into emotional territory.

If Hannah was moved by Dan's display of vulnerability, she wasn't showing it.

'Look, no one disputes your right to leave if you're unhappy. But not like this — dumping your wife for a model ten years younger. It's so tacky, so demeaning.'

'I didn't dump her for Sienna. Sienna might have been the catalyst, but I'd been looking for a way out for years. Sasha just wasn't listening to me. Nothing I said got through to her.'

123

'Is that why you hit her?'

There was a pause.

Josh had heard the expression *the colour drained from his face*, but this was the first time he'd ever seen it happen. Dan's head whipped backwards as if he'd been struck and he stared at Hannah, wide-eyed. 'What?'

'You heard.'

'What the fuck are you talking about? Hang on, is that what she's saying? The crazy bitch is saying I hit her? You have got to be kidding me.'

Hannah was the first to drop her gaze, looking down at the fingers of her right hand, which were worrying at the skin around her thumb. Josh could tell she was regretting bringing the subject up. A bit late for regrets now!

'She says it's in her medical notes.'

Dan was on his feet now, pacing around with both hands clasped over his head. 'This has got to be a joke. Please tell me you're joking.'

Hannah glanced at Josh.

'She is crazier than I thought. Oh, fuck. Why would she say something like that? You don't believe her, right? You don't think I would actually do that, do you?' Dan's eyes flicked from Hannah to Josh and then back again, under the cradle of his clasped hands.

'Course we don't think you'd do that. We're your friends.'

Josh felt compelled to jump in with his support, to stave off whatever scene Dan was heading towards. Anyway, it was the truth. He didn't think Dan would do that.

'Jesus!' Dan dropped back heavily on to the

sofa, his face grey and suddenly saggy, like someone decades older. 'When did it come to this? We loved each other. We had a beautiful little girl together, and now she's claiming I'm a *wife-beater*? How does that happen?'

'It was just something she said on the spur of the moment when she was really angry and really hurt,' said Josh. 'She probably doesn't even remember saying it now.'

'I hope so. I really hope so. It's all so fucked up.'

Dan's voice cracked, and Josh shut his eyes so he wouldn't have to watch the single tear trickling down his friend's face.

Opening his eyes just a fraction, he saw Hannah, pinkly overheated now in the thick sweatshirt she still hadn't taken off, dropping down next to Dan, all the fight now gone, and resting a hand on his leg.

'You're right there, Dan. Totally fucked up.'

Lucie, aged eight

I am going away to school. Daddy says I must be brave and not mind and Mummy just needs a rest, but I know it's really because of the bad thing I did. Sometimes I talk to myself in French and say really bad words. I know they're really bad because one time when Mummy was well and not resting I said them to her and she was shocked and she said a dirty mouth is a dirty mind. But she didn't go all cold and stare at me and make her eyes like little daggers to stab me with, so I didn't really mind. I'm scared of going to school, but sometimes I'm scared of Mummy, too. I hope I will have some friends there and we can have midnight feasts under the covers and maybe it will be like a holiday camp, Daddy says.

10

'You can't keep doing this.'

'Doing what? I'm not doing anything, Hannah.'

'You know what I mean. You have to let Dan see September. Whatever you think of him, she needs her daddy.'

'I'm not stopping him seeing her. It's not my fault things keep getting in the way.'

Sasha took a swig from her plastic cup of vending-machine coffee, spilling some on to the Formica table top as she replaced it. The sludge-brown liquid pooled on the white surface, which was already littered with empty cups and juice cartons, their straws sucked virtually flat, the detritus of ninety minutes in the hell that was the soft-play area at the local leisure centre. To their left, behind a curtain of netting, throngs of small children frolicked in a sea of brightly coloured balls, or clambered up netting or crawled on hands and knees through giant plastic pipes. Everywhere you looked there were children, hyped up on E-numbers from the vending machine, crying in corners or hitting each other over the head or pushing each other down slides. There were children shrieking with laughter or shouting to each other or to their parents, insisting they witness some death-defying feat. The noise level in the huge room was almost unbearable. Shell-shocked parents and dead-eyed au pairs sat at tables that were bolted to the floor, or else stood by the netting, dutifully calling out encouragement to their less adventurous charges. It was Hannah's third visit in ten days and she felt as if the place was slowly sucking the soul out of her. She'd only come because Sasha had begged her. Now they were here, she found herself growing more and more frustrated with her friend.

'Yes, but the things that keep getting in the way are things mostly manufactured by you.'

'That's not true. It's not my fault September was invited to Molly's for tea yesterday. It's really important for her to maintain a normal routine at a time like this, that's what all the books say. September needs her friends around her at the moment, she needs continuity. God knows she hasn't got much of that at home.'

'Oh, come off it, Sash. You could have rearranged that playdate. You're punishing Dan, that's all. I know he flew off the handle about that ridiculous car thing — as if you're petty enough to go around vandalizing people's things! I don't blame you for being furious with him. But you're also punishing September, who's done nothing wrong.'

Looking furious, Sasha tried to push herself back from the table, clearly forgetting that the bench she was sitting on was firmly bolted to the floor. For a second she appeared confused, then, to Hannah's consternation, her face crumpled and she began to cry.

'Sash, I'm sorry. I know how hard this is for you.'

128

These days Hannah felt she was trapped in some endless groundhog day, repeating the same routines over and over — the soft-play centre, coffee, Sasha's tears, her apologies, more coffee, wine, more wine, more tears. Over and over. She couldn't remember the last time she had got any proper work done. There always seemed to be some emergency — could she pick up September and bring her home, because Sasha was meeting her lawyer? Could she drop everything and come round, because Sasha couldn't bear to be on her own? She wanted to support Sasha, but worry about the money she wasn't earning was starting to eat away at her. At night she lay awake counting up her debts. She and Josh had already remortgaged once to release equity for a new boiler plus a foolishly extravagant holiday in Majorca a couple of years before. Their monthly outgoings on the flat now topped £1,500, and with half of Josh's salary going on their credit-card debt they needed her earnings just to break even.

'Want to see something funny?'

The sudden brisk tone, coming hard on the tears of a moment ago, left Hannah nonplussed. She'd barely replied before Sasha had whipped her iPhone out of her bag and was jabbing at it with her delicate fingers so savagely Hannah worried they might break.

'Here. Look.'

She thrust the handset under Hannah's nose abruptly, so that it took a moment for Hannah's eyes to focus on the screen. It was a Facebook page. But the people on it all seemed very young.

129

'What exactly am I looking at?'

'Her. It's her. The Child Bitch from Hell.'

Hannah scrolled up to the profile photograph. *Sienna Sinclair*. Oh shit. Well, at least now she knew what Dan saw in her. The picture was black and white and looked professionally done. It was a close-up of a natural-looking girl wearing a cowboy hat and smiling into the camera as if sharing an intimate joke with the photographer. There was a dimple in one of her cheeks, just by the corner of her mouth, and a strand of her long darkish hair was blowing across her face. She looked like someone you wanted to be with, someone you might see with a group of friends at a neighbouring table in a restaurant and wish you could join, someone fun.

'Have you seen?' Sasha wanted to know. '*In a relationship*. That's what she's put. No prizes who with. And look at this.' She snatched the phone from Hannah and began jabbing at it again before pushing it back across the table with a tight smile of triumph. 'It's them. Together. Her and my husband.'

Sasha had called up a photograph which showed a couple at a party, clearly taken by surprise, spontaneously mugging for the camera, the girl (her hair toffee-coloured in this photo, with some lighter sun-kissed streaks) turned towards Dan and holding on to his arm, with one leg bent up behind her at the knee, her face raised to his in a gesture of mock adoration, while he pretended to look bored without quite managing to wipe the pleasure from his face. A golden couple. If she'd seen them herself on the other side of the room, she'd have envied them.

'I don't understand,' Hannah said now. 'How come you have access to her photos?'

Sasha's eyes lit up as if she'd been waiting for Hannah to ask this very question. 'Because the stupid bitch has no privacy settings, that's why. She *wants* me to see. She's taunting me.'

'Oh, come off it, Sasha. If she was taunting you she'd have made it much more obvious than that, surely. She probably just doesn't know that everyone can see her pictures.'

'Don't be stupid, Hannah.' Sasha grabbed the phone back as if Hannah had failed some sort of test and had lost the right to look at it any more. 'Everyone knows about privacy nowadays. They have it practically drummed into them at school, which, don't forget, she's barely out of. She's done it deliberately. She writes things too. On her friends' walls. Things like *D and I absolutely loved that film.*' Sasha had put on a high-pitched, girlish voice. 'Or *Will pop into the launch with D later.* She practically lists every boring shitty detail of their life.'

'Then don't look at it, Sasha. I mean it. It's going to really mess with your head. Please tell me you don't sit at home obsessively checking that woman's Facebook page.'

'Course I don't.'

Sasha's shoulders slumped.

'That's a lie. I check it all the time. Wouldn't you? It's like an addiction. Last night I was up till four, going through photo after photo. I even looked up the friends who were tagged in her

131

photos and started checking through their albums. Complete fucking strangers, and I was looking at their parents' silver-wedding anniversary parties and their boyfriends and their cats.'

'Sasha, you're going to drive yourself mad.'

'I know, but I just can't help it. I just can't bear that he's with her, Hannah. I can't bear thinking that September will grow up in a broken home. I can't bear that I'll have to wear that *divorced* label for the rest of my life, like there was something wrong with me, like I've been returned to the shop.' Sasha's hand in Hannah's felt like a nub of bone, something impossibly small and unyielding. 'I get what you said before about September needing to see her dad. But Dan has got to see there are consequences to what he's done. If he's allowed to have free access to her whenever he wants, he's won, hasn't he? He's got everything he wants. And what have I got? Nothing. Absolutely nothing.'

Hannah thought about reminding Sasha that it wasn't a contest, that nobody could win, but decided against it. She was so tired of the drama now. She longed to go back to the routine they'd had before. At the time she'd complained about it, about there not being enough hours in the day, but now she looked back on her life before Sasha and Dan's split as a golden age, a comforting and orderly progression of hours, one after the other, all organized and calmly executed. She hadn't wasted time she didn't have in overheated soft-play areas, going over and over the same ground with a woman who

132

seemed incapable of hearing anything other than what she wanted to hear. Even when she got home, it was impossible to escape the whole thing. Dan had taken to calling all the time to complain about Sasha keeping him from September and to plead with Hannah to intervene, and Josh seemed constantly to be in a weird mood.

Increasingly her sleep was plagued with flashbacks to *that night*, which always happened when she got stressed. In her dreams she once again felt fear thudding against her ribcage as her mother's face swam in front of her, contorted in fury, her beloved features twisted into something unrecognizable. Hannah's heart was racing, her mouth sandpaper dry as she stared down at the hole in her sister's head, magnified by her subconscious to crater-like proportions.

'I couldn't stop it,' she'd plead with her sister in her dream while the blood oozed from the hole, thick and tarry. 'I'm so sorry, I couldn't stop it.'

Once, she woke up to find Josh gently shaking her shoulder. 'What couldn't you stop?' he asked. But her blood was pounding in her ears and she didn't reply.

At least Gemma was coming to stay for the weekend. With her demonstrably alive-and-well sister right there in front of her, maybe she'd finally get a break from it all.

'Listen, Sash.' She leaned across the table, realizing too late that the ends of her hair were trailing in the puddle of coffee. 'Why don't you

133

go away for a couple of days this weekend? If you don't want Dan to look after September, you could take her with you.'

'Where would I go?'

Sasha's eyes were suddenly pebble-hard and Hannah felt uncomfortable, wishing she wasn't still holding Sasha's hand in hers, not sure how to take it away without seeming awkward.

'I don't know — a friend, maybe? You need a break, and I'm not going to be around much because Gemma will be here.'

Abruptly Sasha withdrew her hand, sitting back so that Hannah was left leaning into empty space.

'I didn't realize your sister being here would rule out you spending time with me.' Sasha's voice was thin and reedy. 'Doesn't she like me or something?'

Hannah felt herself blushing. The one time they'd met, Gemma hadn't much taken to Sasha, pronouncing her the spoilt-princess type. Her heart sank when she saw tears welling up once more in Sasha's eyes.

'I understand. It must be so wonderful to have a supportive family. You're so lucky, Hannah. Don't worry about me. I know I've been a burden these last few weeks. I'm sure you can't wait to spend some time away from me.'

'Don't be silly. It's not like that.'

'I just don't know what I'd have done without you. Sometimes I feel I'm going completely crazy. You're the only one I can talk to.'

Hannah watched, stricken, as a fat tear made its way down Sasha's gaunt face, until she

134

couldn't stand it any more.

'Of course you can still come round when Gemma's here. She'd love to see you,' she lied. 'The three of us will have a laugh together. She's great fun.'

★ ★ ★

'It just came out. I felt so sorry for her.'

'Hans, how many times have we been through this? There's a little word you need to learn. It starts with n and ends with o and it's got two letters. Can you think what it might be?'

'I know, I know. But with any luck she won't take me up on it. She could tell I wasn't that keen.'

'That woman is so self-obsessed she wouldn't notice if you're keen or not.'

'Give her a break, Gem. You only met her once. She's had a really hard time.'

'Ah, bless. Tell you what though, if her husband's back on the market, send him my way. He was fit.'

'He's already got another woman. Anyway, where's your solidarity?'

'Same place as my desire to spend my weekend listening to your friend crying into her designer handbag about how hard done by she is.'

Hannah sighed, tilting her phone so the noise didn't carry down the line. Gemma could be very judgemental sometimes, taking against people for no better reason than a limp handshake or a single questionable joke. It had

135

taken years for Josh to overcome the unfavourable first impression he'd created when, seized by nerves at meeting Hannah's family, he'd drunk too much and ended up droning on loudly and (though she wouldn't admit it at the time) boringly about the perilous state of secondary education. And Gemma had been even more scathing about Sasha. Hannah could hardly bear to think how hurt Sasha would be if she could hear their conversation. She knew she ought to mount a more vigorous defence of her friend, but as always she found herself swaying in the wind of her sister's forceful opinion. Though Gemma was a year younger, Hannah couldn't remember a time when her judgements hadn't coloured her own. It had been like that even before the thing that happened when they were teenagers, from which none of them — Gemma, Hannah nor their mother — had ever quite recovered. But there was a small part of Hannah that was enjoying not having to be understanding and sympathetic for once. She seemed to spend her entire life tiptoeing around other people at the moment. It felt good to be having a normal conversation — even if it was on the phone to her sister, sixty miles away in Oxford — without having to worry about saying the wrong thing, or upsetting someone by mistake.

'I still don't understand how you're managing to stay friends with both of them,' Gemma continued. 'I'm surprised Sasha hasn't issued an ultimatum yet — him or me. I know I would have.'

Gemma's own divorce had been finalized four

years earlier, and she'd made no secret of the fact that she didn't want any of her family or friends to keep in touch with her ex, or 'that wanker I married', as she insisted on calling Sam at the time.

'It's different though, because Josh and Dan are such good mates. And Sasha says she feels better knowing we're in touch with Dan. At least she knows what's going on in his life.'

There was a pause on the other end of the phone.

'Hans,' Gemma said eventually, and her voice was suddenly serious, 'you need to be careful. Divorces are toxic things. You don't want to be pulled into someone else's mess. Be nice, but keep your distance. Understand?'

11

'She's here.'

'What? I can't hear you.'

'She's here!'

'What? Now?'

'Yes. Look, Dan, I really don't feel comfortable about this.'

'I know. It's a fucking shit situation to put you in, but I've been going so crazy. I owe you. I really owe you.'

'I've got to go. Remember, not a word of this to Hannah.' After clicking off the phone, Josh flushed the toilet, just for authenticity. Something was twanging sharply in his chest, making him doubt whether he'd done the right thing. Not that he didn't believe Dan had the right to see his daughter, whatever he'd done. And September had the right to see her father. Fathers were important. Still, Hannah would be furious if she knew he'd called Dan. They had to make it look like a coincidence — that Dan had just happened to turn up at their house unexpectedly while September was round playing with Lily.

Emerging from the bathroom, Josh heard the increasingly unfamiliar sound of Hannah shrieking with laughter. Good, he thought. She'd been so stressed recently, restlessly shifting position in bed throughout the night, moving her pillow forward, backwards, to the side, over her head, until they were both wide awake.

Josh hadn't been thrilled at first when Hannah told him Gemma was coming to stay. Not that there was any animosity between them any more. They'd long since come to a tacit understanding — or rather a mutual acceptance of their lack of understanding. But he had been hoping for a bit of down time at home, his first chance to think properly about the awful thing that had happened at school — the thing he still half believed he must have invented. No sooner had the memory flitted across his mind than Josh pushed it away again, his heart racing. Not now. He couldn't deal with that now.

Gemma was full-on and she brought out a loud, reckless side of Hannah that was normally hidden and that Josh found uncomfortable. Though they never talked about it, Josh suspected that Hannah was still compensating for what happened when they were teenagers — going along with whatever Gemma wanted, even when it went against her nature. Plus there was that usual thing of having someone staying in their tiny flat. Josh had never mastered the art of hosting. He was one of those men who spent half an hour in the toilet straight after breakfast with a coffee and last weekend's colour supplement, but with only one bathroom even that simple pleasure seemed selfish and unbearably intimate when there were guests in the flat. He'd rush through it and emerge, flame-faced, hoping not to bump into anyone. On Gemma's last visit he'd been mortified to find her waiting outside the bathroom door in her dressing gown.

'Thank God, I'm bursting,' she'd said, darting in after him and locking the door. All day his cheeks had burned when he'd imagined her sitting down on the still-warm seat, breathing in the fetid air.

'He said *and it fits exactly into the contours of the rug*,' came Gemma's voice, followed by another burst of appreciative laughter from her sister.

'Josh, you've got to hear Gemma's latest dating disaster story,' Hannah said as he walked through the door. 'It's too funny.'

'Funny for *you*!' Gemma put on a mock pout. 'She went out with a guy who was so boring all he talked about was this coffee table he'd made himself to fit the rectangles on the living-room rug.'

It was one of those awkward moments where everyone present knows a story that might have been funny first time round hasn't stood up to repetition.

'It also fitted exactly into the boot of the car,' Gemma threw in pointlessly.

'We were thinking we might go for a quick potter around the shops,' said Hannah. 'You don't mind, do you? Lily and September are playing really quietly.'

'Not at all. Go for it.'

Josh tried to disguise his relief. With any luck, Dan could nip round to see September without Hannah even knowing he'd been. Not that he was doing anything wrong by reuniting a father with his child, but he didn't want Hannah to feel — what was the right word? — compromised.

That's it. Sasha was her friend, after all.

But Josh had forgotten how long it could take Hannah to put any plan into action when she was with her sister. Though it was early afternoon, they were still in their dressing gowns. Hannah hadn't even bothered to get dressed when Sasha dropped September off an hour earlier. That had been a prickly half-hour, with Sasha and Gemma eyeing each other warily and Sasha talking way too brightly to try to cover up her nerves, brittle as a dried reed, while Gemma smiled politely in an unconvincing way. Sasha had tried to be funny. 'Remember me? I'm the Tragic Friend,' she'd introduced herself. It sounded like a line she'd been rehearsing in the car. 'I'm the person to come to if you want to feel better about your own life.'

Sasha had been vague about where she was going. Josh got the feeling Hannah knew but had been sworn to secrecy. He hated this new development — he and Hannah keeping secrets from each other. He guessed Sasha was going on a huge shopping splurge or something like that. She was one of those shopping-therapy kind of people, plus her spending money was a way of winding Dan up. Thankfully Hannah didn't have that particular gene. It seemed as if Sasha would be gone a while. Long enough for Dan to drop by and spend a little bit of time with September. 'Ten minutes — five, even,' he'd pleaded. 'I just need to see her.'

Having brought up the possibility of an outing, Hannah and Gemma seemed in no hurry to get going. They wandered in and out of the bathroom and loitered by the table, flicking through the Saturday papers. Hannah decided she couldn't leave without one more cup of tea, and then, to his dismay, Josh heard Gemma joining in a game of vets with Lily and September. 'Bring in the patient, Nurse Lily,' he heard her say. 'No time to lose. We must operate immediately!'

Josh grew increasingly anxious, glancing out of the window on the lookout for Dan's distinctive red car. Why didn't they just leave? When Dan did arrive, he was driving a powder-blue VW Beetle, which is why Josh didn't notice him until the doorbell had already rung.

'Dan?' he heard Hannah exclaim as his heart sank. 'What are you doing here?'

'Just passing and saw your car and thought I'd drop in for a cup of tea. Josh home?'

Josh wandered nonchalantly into the hall, wishing he didn't have one of those faces that broadcast every lie.

'Nice motor,' he said, attempting a jocular tone that fell immediately flat to his ears.

'I've borrowed it.'

Josh didn't need to ask whom he'd borrowed it from.

A shout went up from behind Lily's closed door.

''Mergency, 'mergency,' came September's unmistakeable strident shrill. 'I have to chop off his leg 'mediately.'

Dan's face broke into a broad grin. 'I recognize that voice!'

Josh was impressed and a little bit discomfited

by how genuine Dan's surprise seemed. His friend was exceedingly good at pretending, it occurred to him.

'We must amputate, we must amputate,' came Gemma's Dalek impression from behind the door.

'Princess!' Dan was moving towards Lily's room. 'Where are you?'

'Daddy!' The door flew open and September, plastic stethoscope around her neck, rushed out and flung herself at Dan. In spite of his anxiety about the situation and his part in engineering it, Josh couldn't help feeling a rush of warmth as he watched the two embrace, clutching each other as if they'd been apart for months.

'My God, you've grown a foot at least!' murmured Dan, showering his daughter with kisses. 'You must be at least as big as me now. If not bigger!'

'I'm not big as you. Silly Daddy!'

Behind September, Lily appeared in the doorway of her bedroom, twiddling her hair shyly as she watched Dan and September.

'Oi, girls, we've a patient with half a leg off on the operating table,' came Gemma's voice from inside the room. Seconds later she, too, appeared at the door, clutching a tissue blotted with fake felt-pen blood.

'Oh, hi,' she said as Dan straightened up, September still clinging to his legs. 'Remember me? I'm Gemma, aka Dr Death.'

Dan smiled his charming smile. 'Course I remember you, Gemma. What a stroke of luck that you're all here. I must drive past more often!'

Josh glanced over and noticed that Hannah was frowning.

'Funny that you saw our car, seeing as I had to park it round the corner after picking Gemma up from the station last night.'

Dan's smile didn't falter. 'Weird. Must be one just like it then.'

'Yeah, very weird.' Hannah glared at Josh until he looked away.

* * *

'I really think Sasha is losing it.'

'Can you blame her?'

'No, I'm serious. You should see the emails she writes. Pages and pages of bile. Some of the stuff is scary, I'm telling you.'

Josh shot a glance towards the living-room door to make sure there were no small figures lurking there, then he heard September laughing in Lily's room and relaxed a little. Hannah and Gemma had been gone about an hour, but it was only ten minutes since September had finally slid off Dan's lap and gone to play, leaving the two men free to talk.

'What kind of stuff?'

'Like she sent me a whole load of links to newspaper articles about gonorrhoea and really sick photographs of syphilitic dicks. She says Sienna has all these disgusting sexual diseases and that basically my dick is going to fall off in a very painful way.'

Josh grimaced, but really it didn't sound so outrageous to him. Of course Sasha was going to

144

be vitriolic. Hurt people hurt people, wasn't that what he and Hannah had been discussing?

'And she's spending a ton of money. You should see my bank statements. Clothes, shoes . . . Do you know she spent £250 at the White Company the other day? Two hundred and fifty quid on fucking *sheets*! And the garden. Remember how she insisted on getting it decked a couple of years ago — top-grade Indonesian teak decking, no less? Well, now she's hired a garden designer to come up with plans for re-landscaping. What the fuck? I've tried to get her to meet up so we can talk about selling the house, but she hasn't replied to any of my calls or emails. Jesus, Josh, I don't want to get heavy with her, but she's going to leave me little option.'

Josh's stomach gave an uncomfortable lurch at that word *heavy*. He thought about what Sasha had said to Hannah about the measuring of the bruises.

'Heavy, how?'

'You know, go the legal route.' Dan looked at Josh's face and his expression darkened. 'Fuck me, you thought I meant physically heavy, didn't you? You thought I was going to beat her up?'

'No, of course I didn't. I know you wouldn't do that.'

'Fucking right I wouldn't. Jesus, Josh. You're supposed to be my mate.'

'I am. Course I am.'

Dan was silent for a moment.

'In that case, as you're my mate, I've got

145

something to ask you. Well, you and Hannah, really.'

Josh didn't like the sound of that. The muscles along the tops of his legs clenched as Dan spoke.

'I want you to meet Sienna.'

'Are you crazy? No way, Dan. Not happening.'

'Hear me out. I know I've been downplaying this thing with her, but the fact is I'm serious about her. She's important to me, and you two are important to me. I want you to get to know each other.'

Josh was shaking his head, but deep down in some shallow, ignoble part of himself, he was also feeling flattered. They were important to Dan, he and Hannah. They mattered. He imagined how Dan might have talked about them to Sienna. *You're going to love these guys,* he might have said. *They have such integrity.*

'I can't, Dan. We can't. It would be so unfair to Sasha. Try to see it from her perspective.'

'OK, OK, I'm not asking you to go against your principles, but do me a favour and just think about it. Sienna isn't going to go away. Sooner or later you're going to have to meet her.'

Josh looked down at his hands, broad and fleshy as they'd always seemed to him, with those thick fingers spiked with stubby black hairs. His thumbnails were bitten right down and he felt a flash of annoyance with himself — he thought he'd beaten that childhood habit. He glanced again at the doorway to make sure they were alone. For a second he baulked at asking the question on his tongue. It felt too intrusive, too intimate, as if it might take his relationship with

146

Dan to a level neither of them felt comfortable with. But the words were too big to swallow back down.

'Has it been worth it?' he blurted out, his face hot. 'All the misery? What I mean is, do you ever regret it?'

For a moment, as Dan blinked at him in surprise, Josh worried he had gone too far. Then his friend's face split open like a pea pod in a smile he didn't seem able to control.

'Not for one minute,' he said. 'If it wasn't for not being able to see September, I'd be the happiest man alive.'

* * *

Hannah and Gemma were in high spirits when they arrived home. Josh eyed their collection of shopping bags. Some of them were those thick paper ones with the cord handles that came from the more expensive clothes shops. He tried to work out the distribution ratio of bags per woman, but it proved impossible as they dropped them all in a collective heap as they came through the door.

'You've been busy,' he said, attempting jocularity but falling well flat.

Hannah's smile shrivelled on her face. 'Don't start,' she snapped.

'I didn't say anything!'

He had a right to be concerned about what Hannah was spending. They were only hanging on by a thread, and he knew for a fact that she hadn't been doing much work recently. No chance of that with Sasha round all the time. It was all right for Gemma, with her secure hospital-administrator job and no dependants. Hannah needed to realize she couldn't compete.

'How long did Dan stay?' asked Hannah as she retreated to the kitchen. He heard the tap going on and the kettle being filled.

'Not long. September was so thrilled to see him.'

'Yeah, funny that he should happen to drop by when she's here.'

Josh felt disgruntled. Since when was Hannah so quick to jump to conclusions, especially ones that cast him in a negative light?

'Ta-da! What do you think?' Gemma held up a dress which she'd unfolded from tissue paper in one of the bags.

Josh eyed the wisp of black and red fabric, which looked altogether too insubstantial to contain the contours of his slightly chubby — sorry, *curvy* — sister-in-law. 'Lovely.'

'Josh, would it kill you to sound a bit more enthusiastic?' asked Hannah, coming through the door bearing two mugs of tea.

'Thanks for asking. I'd love one,' he said, as she handed one to Gemma and kept the other for herself.

Gemma looked from one to the other with raised eyebrows, but said nothing. Her curly hair was pushed back from her face and Josh found his eyes gravitating towards the slight indentation in her forehead, outlined by that curved, raised, silvery scar. He glanced away quickly in embarrassment, hoping she hadn't noticed.

A ring on the doorbell broke the tension.

'Got to be Sasha,' said Hannah. 'She's going to flip when she hears Dan was here. Let me tell her, OK?'

But as she was moving towards the door, they heard September squealing 'Mummy!' and the sound of the flat door flying open.

'Guess who was here?' came the little girl's excited high-pitched voice. '*Daddy!*'

Seconds later, Sasha appeared in the doorway with September hanging off her arm. Her face looked as if it had set in plaster.

'Dan was here?'

She was addressing Hannah, fixing her with hard, unblinking eyes.

'Yeah, it was just one of those things. He was driving past and saw the car and dropped in.'

'Driving past from where?'

Hannah looked helplessly at Josh. 'I assumed he'd been to your house. I don't know. I didn't really talk to him. Gemma and I went out. We left Dan here with Josh.'

'And with Lily and September?'

'Come on, Sasha.' Josh felt compelled to intervene. 'We always said we were going to remain neutral. What were we supposed to do? Refuse to let him in?'

'I just wish you'd called me to tell me he was here. It's very confusing for September, having her father waft in and out of her life like this.'

'What's waft, Mummy? Why was Daddy wafting?'

Sasha switched her attention to Josh. 'Dan never just happens to be driving past. And he

149

wouldn't have been at my house — my solicitor
has sent him a letter warning him to keep away.'

'That's a bit extreme, isn't it?'

'Don't tell me how to behave!'

The room fell silent. Then September started
to cry.

'It's OK, poppet.' Sasha dropped to her knees
to take her daughter in her arms. 'Don't be
scared. Mummy just got a little cross, that's all.
Silly Mummy!'

'Silly Mummy!' sniffed the little girl.

Sasha straightened up. 'Sorry,' she said in a
soft voice. 'I know it's not your fault.' She
glanced over at Gemma, as if only just taking in
her presence. 'You must think I'm completely
batshit.'

Gemma shrugged. 'You're not the only one
who discovered the husband she married was
abducted and replaced by an alien. I get it.'

'It happened to you, too?'

'Sadly, yes. There ought to be a universal
signal so that we can recognize each other,
shouldn't there, like a weird Masonic handshake.'

Sasha smiled weakly, but Josh got the distinct
impression she didn't relish the idea of being
lumped in some weird kinship with Gemma.

'No bags?' he asked in a clumsy attempt to
change the subject.

Sasha looked questioning.

'I thought you might have been shopping or
something.'

'I do actually have other things in my life apart
from shopping, you know. I was at the doctor's.'

150

'On a Saturday?'

Sasha made a face at him. 'The benefits of being private, darling!'

Hannah, who had been observing, intervened. 'Did you get them?'

Sasha shot her a weary look, and Josh was shocked to see how old she seemed suddenly, her skin shrunken around her cheekbones.

'Yep, I'm officially a junkie.' She picked up her handbag and shook it vigorously. 'Can you hear that rattle?'

'Antidepressants,' Hannah mouthed to her sister, with a nervous side glance at September.

'I was on the happy pills for years,' Gemma replied airily. 'Don't think I'd have survived without them.'

'Yes, but I'm not that sort of person.' Sasha didn't seem aware of how that sounded. Not surprising, Josh thought. He'd never met a less self-aware person than Sasha. 'I like to be in control of myself and my life. I can't bear that this is what he's done to me — turned me into yet another lobotomized housewife!'

'Charming.' Gemma didn't look best pleased and Josh couldn't help feeling she wouldn't be swapping any secret handshakes with Sasha, after all.

'Sometimes I wake up in the morning and I don't recognize myself.' Sasha seemed now to be in a kind of trance, talking only to herself. 'I look in the mirror and I think, *Who is that little person, that nobody? Waste of space.*' Suddenly she contorted her mouth and made her voice deep and snarly. '*Little Miss Nobody.*'

151

'Mummy!' September's eyes were wide and frightened, her upper lip pressing down urgently on the lower one. 'You musn't talk in that voice.'

Sasha looked down, as if surprised to find her daughter there. 'Sorry, darling.' She swooped down and crushed September to her in a smothering embrace.

'Get off,' cried the child.

Lily, who'd been leaning against Hannah, detached herself from her mother to seek Josh out. As always he felt himself soften all over at the feel of her small hand in his. He looked down at her and smiled, stroking her cheek gently with his free hand. Glancing up again, he was startled to find September staring at him and Lily with a fierce concentration that sent a chill through him, despite the crowded, stuffy room.

12

'I'm sorry, Madam, your card has been declined.'

'Pardon?'

The waitress, who didn't look old enough to count, let alone work an electronic till, blushed, but the smile remained bravely fixed to her face. 'Your bank has declined your card.'

Sasha blinked at the girl. 'I don't understand.'

'Perhaps a different card, Madam?'

'Oh, honestly!' Sasha dug angrily around in her purse, the one that matched her bag, before pulling out a second card.

Still smiling, the waitress ran it through the machine. The smile slipped gradually as she shook her head. 'Terribly sorry, but that one doesn't work either.'

'Don't worry, Sash. I'll pay.' Hannah fumbled for her bank card, hoping against hope there was enough left on her overdraft to cover the brunch Sasha had generously invited her out for.

'But I don't understand,' said Sasha. Then she stopped still. 'That bastard. That fucking bastard.'

The waitress's pale, downy cheeks turned a vivid shade of puce as she pretended to busy herself with the card machine.

'He's frozen my cards.' Sasha was gaping at Hannah, her eyes wide. 'I don't bloody believe it.'

'I'm sure he wouldn't . . . '

Hannah tailed off because, really, she wasn't sure of any such thing. In fact, it was a possibility that had crossed her mind more than once since Josh had told her about his conversation with Dan about Sasha's out-of-control spending and her continuing refusal to talk to him about the house or anything to do with money. It was a joint account, so he had the right to freeze it. And, of course, Dan had his own separate bank account for his business that he could take money from.

'Bank card and credit card. How could he? How am I supposed to feed September without access to any cash? What does he expect us to do — grow our own food?'

'Pin please, Madam.' The waitress slid the machine in front of Hannah and gazed off into the middle distance, trying to make it seem as if she wasn't listening.

'I guess he must be using it as some sort of leverage to get you to talk about the house and money.'

'Leverage? Blackmail, more like. Well, he's not getting away with it. Imagine, freezing my bank account while he swanks around in fucking Notting Hill with that *tart*! She lives in a massive big villa, you know.'

'Just a converted flat in a villa, surely? Anyway, how do you know where she lives?'

'He's still my husband, Hannah. I'm entitled to know where he is.'

As the waitress scurried gratefully away, Hannah pocketed the bill, feeling slightly sick at

154

the amount. Sasha had always treated her to lavish meals out, claiming Hannah was doing her a favour as otherwise she'd have to eat alone like a pathetic saddo with no mates. She knew Hannah and Josh struggled for money and she liked being able to treat them. Her generosity was just one of the things that had drawn Hannah to her in the first place.

Glancing at her phone, Hannah noticed the time. Shit, almost the whole morning gone, and she'd done nothing. She'd tried to resist brunch, but Sasha had been so insistent, and Hannah hadn't needed much persuasion to bunk off with her instead of going home to work after morning drop-off. Now guilt lodged inside her like something heavy and undigested. Not only had she not earned any money, but she'd actually ended up spending money they didn't have. She gathered her things together hurriedly, only noticing as she stood up that Sasha hadn't moved. Instead she was sitting very still, staring fixedly at the single red rose in a slim vase in the middle of the table. Something about her expression and the way she kept opening and closing her hand, rhythmically splaying out the fingers then clenching them together in a tight fist, made Hannah uneasy.

'Come on, Sash, I've got to get going.'

Still Sasha didn't respond, just kept on doing the hand thing. She had already confessed that the antidepressants were doing bizarre things to her body, making her jittery and strung out, liable to jump to her feet late at night to drag the Hoover over the floor or clean out the enormous

American-style fridge-freezer. Now it was as if her hand belonged to someone else entirely, doing its own thing while the rest of her stayed staring rigidly ahead.

Hannah shivered. 'Sasha, please?'

By the time they reached the car, parked on an exorbitant meter in one of the wide leafy roads behind Hampstead High Street, where they'd been eating, Sasha's mood had flipped from taciturn to hyper. Installed behind the wheel of her Toyota RAV4, she now wanted to talk. And what she wanted to talk about was Gemma.

'I know Gemma's your sister, and of course she's lovely and everything, but it must be a bit awkward sometimes.'

'What must?'

'Oh, you know, being around someone who's so jealous of you.'

Hannah swung around to face Sasha, her mouth stretched back in a shocked smile.

'Oh, Hannah, it's obvious. You're tall and slim and gorgeous, with a husband who adores you and a beautiful daughter and an exciting job and a flat in a lovely part of London. She's overweight, divorced and working as a hospital administrator in the provinces.'

'Don't be ridiculous!' Hannah didn't know whether to be angry or to laugh. 'She's my sister. She's not jealous. She's not like that. And Oxford is hardly some boring provincial hick town.'

'I'm not saying she doesn't love you. I'm just saying she's a little bit . . . well, resentful. You can't blame her.'

156

'How on earth do you come to that conclusion?'

'It shows in everything she says. Have you noticed how much she puts you down?'

'That's what sisters do!'

Sasha made a face. 'Not like that. Not all the time. And there was something . . . No, never mind.'

'What?'

'It doesn't matter, Han. I'm sure it's nothing.'

'If it doesn't matter, then there's no harm in saying it.'

Hannah was getting irritated. If Sasha had something to say, better she came out with it, so that Hannah could dismiss it, rather than let it fester out of control in her imagination.

'I think she's . . . well . . . overly interested in your husband.'

'In Josh?'

'Do you have another husband?'

'Sasha, this is getting preposterous now.'

'Haven't you seen the way she looks at him? And there's the photograph.'

'Photograph?'

'When September was there, she saw Gemma take a photograph of Josh from that bookcase in the living room and slip it into her bag.'

Hannah couldn't help it, she actually laughed out loud. 'That's the most absurd thing I've ever heard. Sash, you know perfectly well four-year-old girls are on a different planet most of the time. Half the stuff they come out with is complete rubbish.'

'Right.'

'What do you mean, *right*? Why do you say it like that?'

'You believe whatever you want to believe, Hannah. It's none of my business.'

They sat in silence for the rest of the journey, except for Sasha's fingers drumming on the leather steering wheel. Hannah didn't trust herself to speak. After all the support she'd given to Sasha, it seemed such a slap in the face for her to drive a wedge between her and Gemma. This was such a transparent, pathetic attempt to stir up bad feeling, it really rankled.

After driving around the block several times, Sasha parked near the nursery and turned the engine off. They sat still for a few seconds, each gazing out of the window.

Sasha reached out her hand. 'Sorry,' she said, feeling around for Hannah's fingers. 'I shouldn't have said anything. I was angry about the bank cards and took it out on you. Erase it from your mind. Forgive me?'

Hannah nodded and smiled, although she wasn't sure she really could forgive so quickly. But they were at school now, and she didn't want there to be a bad atmosphere between them when they picked up the girls. They got out of the car and made their way through the gates. Marcia Verney nodded to them, but didn't come over.

As they hovered by the doorway, watching the children singing the goodbye song, Hannah was uncomfortably aware that things were still not quite right between her and Sasha. There was a certain prickliness in the air. One by one the

158

children were sung out of the classroom. September was one of the first.

'You go ahead, I'll walk home with Lily,' Hannah urged Sasha.

'Don't be silly, I'll drop you home.'

'No, really. I want the exercise.'

Sasha eyed her uncertainly. 'Well, if you're sure . . . '

Lily was the last child left on the carpet. Hannah saw her casting her eyes around, checking she was there. She waved from the doorway and was rewarded with a huge smile that warmed her insides.

'Mrs Hetherington? Could I have a quick word?'

Mrs Mackenzie, the nursery teacher, was beckoning her over to a little yellow-painted octagonal table in the corner, strewn with playdough models of animals with giant legs and pea-sized heads or trunks longer than their entire bodies.

Hannah pulled up one of the tiny red chairs and sat down gingerly, her knees coming up almost to her chin. The other woman eyed her sharply and then smiled, revealing a gold filling hidden away at the back of her mouth.

'Nothing to worry about, Mrs Hetherington. I just wanted to have a wee word about Lily.'

'Is she OK?'

'Oh yes, absolutely fine. It's just she's been a wee bit quiet lately. I just wondered if anything was bothering her.'

Hannah frowned. 'When you say 'quiet', what do you mean?'

'Just that she's a bit more reluctant than usual to speak up in carpet time. More and more, September seems to be answering on her behalf, and I'm not altogether sure if that's the healthiest thing for her. I do wonder sometimes if September can be a little bit, well, overprotective.'

Overprotective? Surely that was a positive thing, quite sweet if you thought about it. Yet, reading between the lines, which is something you always had to do at the nursery, as Hannah was finding out, it sounded more sinister than that.

'Do you mean like domineering?'

Mrs Mackenzie maintained her smile. 'No, no, I wouldn't say that. It's just that September can be a forceful character and your Lily is such a shy wee girl sometimes.'

Hannah gazed into the nursery teacher's eyes, trying to read her expression. It seemed that everyone she'd come across who worked with young children was so scared to say anything that could be deemed negative they all spoke in these euphemisms that you were expected to somehow translate. She thought she saw something flicker across the other woman's face, like a warning, but it was gone almost as soon as it arrived, and Hannah wondered if she might have imagined it.

'Hello, Mummy.' Lily had materialized by her shoulder and was burrowing her face into Hannah's neck.

'Hello, pumpkin.'

Hannah felt a rush of love for her daughter so

powerful it was almost overwhelming. She put her arms around the sturdy little body she knew so well, feeling a stab of nostalgia at the realization that it was noticeably less rotund than it used to be. How did other women cope, she wondered, with this terrible, primeval need to prevent anything bad happening to your child? How did they manage the fear that came out of nowhere and caught you round the throat and left you breathless at the possibility — no, the certainty — that sooner or later, when you took your eye off the ball or when you weren't around to see, it would come — that scary thing, that angry, mean thing. And all of your love and your precautions and your safeguards would be for nothing.

'Did you have a lovely day?' she whispered into Lily's soft ear, brushing her lips against the wispy, silk-fine hair that, to her daughter's heartbreak, refused to grow more than a couple of centimetres a year.

Lily nodded. 'Me and 'Tember were angels.'

Hannah glanced up at Mrs Mackenzie, who was watching them intently. For a moment it looked as if she was going to say something, then she changed her mind.

'I'll see you and Mummy tomorrow,' she said.

Lucie/Eloise, aged eight and a half

I like school. It is called Archminster and I have three best friends and one of them is called Juliette and she has long hair down to her waist and I am going to have hair just like hers. I am absolutely determined! When I came here, Juliette asked me if I had a nickname and I told her it was Eloise and now everyone calls me Eloise and I am nice and funny and very, very kind and I am not the person who did that Bad Thing. A leopard can change its spots! Mummy will be proud of me and call me Purty Cushion, which is her special name for me. Purty is how she says Pretty, I think, but I don't know why she calls me a cushion.

13

'Look! Just look!'

Dan's phone was thrust so close to Josh's face that he could hardly make out the letters looming up from the screen.

'What am I looking at?'

'I'll read it to you. 'Bet you think you are a big stud, lounging round half naked in your shabby-chic shag pad with that slut. Just 'cos there are shutters on the windows doesn't mean no one can see you.''

Dan glared at Josh expectantly, with the air of someone awaiting vindication.

'What am I supposed to say?'

'Don't you get it? She's fucking stalking me, Josh. I could have her arrested.'

Josh shrugged. 'Or it could be just a lucky guess. I mean, how many people who live in Notting Hill have shutters on their windows? It's got to be about ninety per cent. I think there might even be a law about it.'

'And the shabby-chic bit?' Dan wasn't in the mood for joking.

Josh held his hands up. 'Find me a house in that neighbourhood that *isn't* done out in shabby chic.'

Dan shook his head, as if he couldn't believe what he was hearing. 'Why the fuck are you defending her? You know this is bang out of order.'

'I'm not defending her.'

But in reality, Josh supposed, that was exactly what he was doing. There was an outside chance Sasha could be guessing about Sienna's apartment, but he had to admit it wasn't likely. And there was something a little creepy about the idea of her sneaking around outside Sienna's window spying on them. But then, Dan wasn't exactly trying to smooth things over between them — cutting off Sasha's bank cards without warning had been seriously underhand. And even though he'd unfrozen the current account soon after, Sasha swore most of the money that had been in there had already disappeared. Siphoned off into a secret offshore account, Sasha had insisted in her usual hyperbolic way. It had only been weeks since Dan had sat down opposite him in this very same pub, at this very same table, and told him that he was leaving his wife. Now everything had changed. Sasha and Dan were at each other's throats. Hannah walked around the flat sighing heavily and whenever he asked her what was wrong she gave him that *are you a complete idiot?* look and said 'Nothing' in a very pointed way. She complained about Sasha monopolizing her time, but then she'd agreed to accompany her clubbing next week. When was the last time she went out clubbing? Even Lily seemed subdued. Hannah had told him what Mrs Mackenzie had said, and while she was clearly exaggerating the sinister aspect, Josh couldn't help agreeing that maybe it would be a good thing for Lily and September to spend some time apart. And overshadowing it all was that horrible thing that had happened at school, which he still couldn't bear to think about, let alone share with Hannah.

If only Sasha wasn't round there all the time they might have a chance of getting back to normal. But he could hardly ban her from coming to see them. Even this regular post-match drink with Dan wasn't like it used to be. On the surface, everything was normal. They'd sat in their usual seats at the match, surrounded by the same characters they saw week after week. There was the middle-aged couple to their right, the normally softly spoken woman with her pearl earrings and pastel-coloured cashmere cardigan, yelling streams of expletives throughout the game, and the two brothers behind them who never spoke to each other, just watched side by side in companionable silence. Josh's particular favourite was the old guy who came with his young granddaughter. He'd hear them chatting at half-time about formations and goal point averages. 'Life doesn't get much better than this,' the old man had once beamed at Josh, his arm around his granddaughter, after Arsenal had just snatched a last-minute victory at the tail end of a nail-biting game. Josh remembered it because for once the sun was out, and they weren't all shivering in their scarves and hats and layers of T-shirts and jumpers (*The secret of staying warm is layering*, his mother had always told him). And it had struck Josh that he was absolutely right. Life didn't get much better than that.

But already those were coming to seem like

halcyon days, when everything was simple, straightforward. Now that there was this undercurrent with Dan, this misalignment in the natural order of things, Josh couldn't seem to find his way back to that easy mateyness he and Dan had enjoyed.

Dan was still fiddling with his phone, and Josh found himself staring at Dan's hands with their long, slightly feminine fingers. Could those hands have inflicted damage on his own wife, so much so that she'd had bruises worthy of measuring? It was impossible, of course. And yet, and yet . . . Wasn't the news full of people saying, 'He was the last person you'd suspect,' after yet another father went crazy and strangled his wife, or gassed his kids?

Dan looked up and caught Josh staring. Suddenly his expression changed, a bright smile playing out across his rugged face. 'Do you want to see her?'

Josh felt himself floundering. 'Who?'

'Sienna, of course. I've got a photo of her here on my phone.'

Dan's eyes had taken on the rapt fervour you sometimes saw in fundamentalists on the television talking about their faith. Josh felt a disagreeable prickling sensation in the pit of his stomach and realized suddenly that he really, really didn't want to see a photograph of the famous Sienna. At the same time, he acknowledged that on a completely different level he had a desperate hunger to see what she looked like.

Maybe she wouldn't be as gorgeous as Dan had made out. Maybe he'd look at her and think,

Really? You left your family for that? And feel relieved to think of what he still had: his intact, safe domestic life.

'I suppose so,' he said. Before he'd even finished the sentence, Dan had thrust the phone in front of him, eyes fixed on his face, waiting for his reaction.

Josh looked down reluctantly and, *oh*, such a visceral reaction, that blow to the lower abdomen, that punch of jealousy. A lightly tanned, heart-shaped face with a neat, pointy chin, wide-set green eyes with thick dark eyelashes, silky, sun-streaked, honey-coloured hair hooked over one shoulder and hanging loosely down over the front of her white T-shirt. Faded denim shorts revealing coltish brown legs that went on for ever. Bare feet, one rubbing the top of the other endearingly as though she was finding the experience of being photographed something of an ordeal. Smiling shyly up at the camera, the sun reflecting amber in her eyes.

Beautiful.

'Well?' Eagerness lit up Dan's face as he scoured Josh's expression, looking for clues. 'What do you think?'

Josh swallowed, giving himself time to corral his feelings. 'Yeah, nice enough. Too young for me, though. Reminds me too much of the girls at school.'

That was a lie. Most of the girls at Josh's school either had spots and braces and refused to meet his eye, or were hard-faced and confrontational, their hair scraped up into ponytails that pulled the skin of their faces taut

167

over their cheekbones, taking every off-the-cuff comment as a personal attack, always on the lookout for imagined slights.

He was gratified to notice Dan's smile dimming a notch.

'She's twenty-four. Hardly a child.' Dan snatched his phone back as if to protect the picture from Josh's critical appraisal and gazed at it again. 'I gotta tell you, mate, she's so soft and gentle, but she's got a steely side to her, too. People think that because of how she looks they can get away with being somehow patronizing, but she won't take shit from anyone.'

'Steady on, Dan. You'll be declaring undying love next.'

Dan stared at him. 'I *do* love her. Of course I love her. What's wrong with that?'

Josh felt another terrible punch to his stomach. He waited for it to pass. 'It's just so quick. You've only been apart from Sasha for a few weeks. It's too soon to go falling in love again.'

'Come on, Josh. You can't timetable love. It comes along whenever it wants to.'

Josh's insides were churning. People like him tried and tried to do the right thing. They honoured their commitments, they stuck with their marriages, even through the tough times. Dan walked out on his wife and child and not only was he unscathed, he was *ecstatic*. If it was that easy, what was to stop everyone giving up the minute things got a bit difficult?

Dan, not normally the most intuitive of men, seemed nevertheless to guess something of what

168

was going on in Josh's head because he said, 'Don't get me wrong. It's not all perfect, I know that. It kills me to think of September missing me and not being able to see me, with only that crazy bitch for comfort.'

Josh frowned. 'Steady on.'

'No, I'm serious. I'm not saying Sasha hasn't got a right to be angry, but sneaking around outside my house, *spying* on me and freaking out my girlfriend? Listen, can't you talk to her for me, about letting me have access to September? You must admit it's wrong, what she's doing.'

'Yes, but whenever you talk to Sasha, she's always got some reason why she can't let you see her.'

Dan snorted. 'Yeah, the reason is she's a vindictive cow.'

He registered Josh's disapproval.

'OK, OK, I didn't mean that. It's just . . . you have no idea how much it kills me not to know what September had for her tea, or who her friends are at the moment, or what bedtime story she's reading at night.'

Josh stared at his friend. Dan had always been so wrapped up in his own career, he'd never been around for the day-to-day domestic stuff. As far as Josh knew, he'd never once picked September up from nursery, and Sasha always used to complain that on the rare occasions when he was ever home in time to read September a story, he'd fall asleep before she did! But Dan seemed really to believe this image of himself as the devoted hands-on father torn apart from the child he'd single-handedly raised.

His eyes were full of hurt.

'I'll talk to her. I don't think it'll make that much difference, but I'll try. And . . . ' Josh paused, knowing Hannah would go mad if he finished what he was about to say. 'September is coming to spend the afternoon at ours tomorrow while Sasha . . . well, while she does something. Maybe you could drop by again.'

He was expecting Dan to break into one of his warm smiles. Instead, he looked suddenly shifty, glancing around the pub, not meeting Josh's eyes. Immediately Josh regretted his generous gesture.

'Oh, that's really good of you, Josh. I appreciate it, I really do. And I'd give anything to spend some time with September, you know that, only Sienna and I are going to Rome tomorrow for a couple of days.'

Before Josh could stop it, there burst into his head an image of Dan and the beautiful Sienna, who now had a face and a body and was real, in a rumpled bed in a hotel with French doors thrown wide open to the faraway buzzing of scooters in busy Italian streets. Naked in the middle of the afternoon, with no small child clamouring to be let in, no need to go out and eat in child-friendly places where you could ask for ketchup without being frowned upon, no need to spend the afternoon in garishly lit rooms painted in primary colours where the sound of children screaming bounced off the walls and the only thing to do was eat orange artificially flavoured crisps from the vending machine and keep checking the clock until it was the time you'd said you'd leave, knowing there'd be a scene and hot tears when you tried to call it a day.

It wasn't fair.

'Right.' He didn't care how huffy he sounded. 'Never mind, then. Wouldn't want you to miss out on a shagfest just to see your daughter.'

Dan looked shocked. 'I'm sorry. It's just it's already booked. Sienna has taken time off.'

'Oh well, then that definitely takes priority over your four-year-old.'

'Why are you being so judgemental all of a sudden?'

Josh couldn't explain it. Couldn't tell Dan about the image that was now seared across his brain of the naked couple in the messed-up sheets. Couldn't let on how Hannah hadn't let him go near her in weeks, how dirty it made him feel to even try to initiate something. Couldn't confess that jealousy was burning a path through his gut.

He looked at Dan and forced himself to smile. 'Your round,' he said.

14

'Told you this would be fun, didn't I? Well? Didn't I?'

Sasha was standing so close that every time she spoke, Hannah felt a fine spray of spittle on her cheek that she had to refrain from wiping off. Sasha was swaying while she talked, and her hazel eyes were hard and bright and glinted under the overhead lights. At first, Hannah had wondered if Sasha could be on something. That is, something more than the four or five vodka tonics she'd already downed. Then she'd remembered the antidepressants. Weren't you supposed to avoid alcohol when you were taking those?

The evening hadn't started well when Sasha had turned up at the flat, dressed for their night out in a black, skin-tight bodycon dress with soaring heels and more make-up than Hannah had ever seen her wear. Josh had been noticeably taken aback when she arrived. He'd started talking really loudly and fast, which he always did when he was nervous. Normally, Hannah found it endearing, but this evening it just irritated her. 'No need to shout,' she'd said. 'We're not deaf.'

Sasha looked incredible. She made Hannah, in jeans and boots and a newish, loose white top with no egg stains down it — which had seemed charmingly boho chic when she'd put it on,

172

standing with her back to the full-length mirror in their bedroom, craning her neck over her shoulder to check how it looked from the back — feel frumpy and middle-aged by comparison. 'You look nice,' Josh had told her when she came out of the bedroom, and she'd instantly deflated. *Nice?* Really?

Hannah hadn't been able to stop staring at Sasha. Yes, she was wearing more make-up than usual, but there was something else as well. She seemed luminous.

'Have you done something to your hair?' she asked, head cocked to the side. 'Eyebrows?'

In the end Sasha cracked. 'Botox,' she squealed delightedly. 'I wasn't going to tell anyone, but isn't it fab?'

Hannah felt a sharp pang then, which she'd put down to concern for Sasha and for the heartbreaking insecurity that would make a beautiful thirty-four-year-old woman pay to have bacteria injected into her own face. Only much later would she admit to herself that the concern was tinged with resentment. Not that she'd ever put herself through that kind of invasive cosmetic procedure, but it seemed so unfair that she'd been working ever since she left uni and still couldn't afford to get her legs waxed. Yet Sasha, who'd earned no money of her own for years, could splash out hundreds on making herself look better without even thinking about it. Hannah felt like Sasha's frumpier older sister, even though Sasha would turn thirty-five six months before she did. It was not a comfortable feeling. She was going to be left behind, she

173

suddenly realized. She would be the drab, tired-looking woman wearing yesterday's fashions, while women like Sasha with their fortnightly hairdresser appointments and weekly facials would stay just the same.

Sasha had insisted on a drink before they set off, and the change in her behaviour had been marked. Her voice had become loud and strident, her laugh piercing and false. She had put on the dance playlist Hannah had made for a party the year before, and immediately started undulating suggestively in front of Josh.

'Come on, big guy, let's see you throw some shapes,' she said, attempting to haul him to his feet.

Josh looked so appalled, Hannah couldn't help laughing. Even his ears were blushing.

When they eventually called a cab, he didn't even bother to hide his relief.

'Have fun,' he said gamely as they left, and she wished suddenly, desperately, that she wasn't going out at all, but was settling down with him on the sofa with a glass of wine and the *Breaking Bad* box set. At the very same time, the thought of yet another Saturday night in, watching Josh marking his interminable pile of exercise books, and listening to other people, people with lives, walking past the window on their way out to wherever it was people with lives went on a Saturday, made her want to scream.

Sasha had been in a bizarre mood in the taxi, flirting with the Somalian cab driver, then nearly causing him to crash by leaning through the gap in the front seats to crank up the volume on the tinny car radio when a song came on that she liked. And ever since they'd arrived at the club, her behaviour had become increasingly erratic. She and Hannah had found themselves a table near the bar, but Sasha couldn't sit for more than a few minutes before she was up, throwing herself around the dance floor, or just standing next to the table, drumming her fingers and swaying, while her eyes darted around the room looking for available men.

And it seemed there were *plenty* of available men.

Practically from the second they arrived, they'd been attracting male attention. By *they*, of course, Hannah actually meant Sasha. Flicking back her silky black hair and rubbing one brown foot in her unfeasibly high shoes up the calf of the other brown leg, Sasha was like a man magnet.

'God, I'm on fire tonight. What's going on?' she laughed, after a man with hair cropped close to his head to disguise his premature baldness had come over expressly to inform her that she was the most beautiful woman in the room.

But Hannah had seen how she did it, holding a man's gaze across the room just that fraction longer than was strictly acceptable, drawing him in with a playful half-smile, then looking away after he'd committed himself to coming over, glancing up as he arrived as if surprised to find him there.

'I told you this would be fun, didn't I? Well? Didn't I?'

They moved from the table to the bar, and

Sasha was swaying and standing too near, and Hannah was feeling cross and out of place. Most people in here were five or ten years younger than they were, cool, confident types who didn't need to keep glancing at their phones in case of child-related emergencies, women whose cropped tops and cut-away dresses revealed taut abdominals that had never seen a pregnancy.

'You look like you're in the waiting room at the dentist, not out enjoying yourself.'

The man had appeared from nowhere, materializing by her shoulder and speaking from the side of his mouth. She glanced up sharply and was surprised to find herself looking into a pair of shockingly blue, clearly amused eyes set into a ruggedly chiselled face.

'It's not really my scene,' she said.

'Mine neither. I was dragged along by a group of mates. We're on a stag night. You can't imagine the hell.'

Hannah smiled, the grumpiness of just a few moments ago miraculously melting away.

'Who's this?'

Hannah had been vaguely aware of Sasha's intense gaze flicking between her and the unknown stranger during the course of this brief exchange.

'I'm Ed.' The man whose name was Ed nodded at Sasha, without making any attempt to move closer to her. Sasha's lip-glossed smile spread like a stain over her face.

'And you came all the way over here because you thought Hannah was about to top herself! That's so sweet. But don't worry, that's just her

176

regular default expression, although she can also do bored and indifferent. Don't be alarmed, she can't help it. Inside, she's positively beaming!'

Hannah felt a wave of anger, sudden and ferocious. How dare Sasha try to score points by putting her down? She hadn't wanted to come in the first place. Was it any wonder she wasn't exactly dancing a happy jig in this overloud, overheated place?

Ed smiled at her, and she was conscious of his arm brushing hers and a burning sensation where their skin touched.

'I don't know,' he said. 'I rather like Hannah's default expression.'

Sasha's features seemed to freeze. Through her flattered embarrassment, Hannah had a flash of insight. Sasha was jealous.

Of her.

Meanwhile, she'd moved her arm so that it was no longer quite touching Ed's, but in a way this was even worse because now the hairs on both their arms seemed to be reaching out to make contact, creating an unsettling tingling effect.

'Do you want to dance?'

For a moment, Hannah allowed herself the fantasy. It had been so long since she'd felt anything like this, what harm could it do? She would step forward with this charismatic stranger with his pale-blue T-shirt that set off his tan, and his eagle tattoo, and his jeans loosely hanging off his narrow hips, and the faint whiff of nicotine that hugged him close, reminding her of boys she had lusted after in her youth. And he would take her hand as they pushed through the sea of bodies to find a space and she would feel once again that particular thrill of closing your fingers around an unknown hand, the shocking vulnerability of another person's soft palm in yours. And when they arrived on the dance floor the force of the crowd would push them together until they had no choice but to —

'Oi-oi!'

Sasha thrust herself between Hannah and her fantasy suitor, shattering the daydream.

'Hands off my mate. She's a happily married woman, I'll have you know.' Sasha was speaking in a loud, faux-jolly voice Hannah had never heard before. 'If you're after a dance, I'm afraid you're going to have to make do with me — the sad, single friend.' She pouted, tilting her head down and gazing up at him through her lashes. Then, with a final flick of her hair, she grabbed his hand, the very one Hannah had just been fantasizing about, thrust her bag at Sasha to look after, and pulled him off in the direction of the dance floor. He turned his head to Hannah as he was led away and gave her a helpless *What can you do?* look. She smiled and shrugged, hoping her face didn't betray the ugly feeling that gushed, acidic and corrosive, through her gut.

She didn't have a leg to stand on, she knew. She *was* married. And she couldn't blame Sasha for wanting to snaffle the first attractive man they'd seen all night. This evening was supposed to be about her, after all. But all the rationalizing in the world couldn't stop the rage that swept through her as she stood on the edge of the

178

dance floor watching Sasha and Ed weaving their way through the crowd until they disappeared from sight. Her fingers gripped her glass of rum and Coke tightly until her knuckles were four pale splodges under the dimmed lights. She set her face into a 'good-sport' expression, ignoring the ache where her half-smile felt heavy and started to sag. A red mist swirled around her brain, but she forced herself to stay very still, concentrating her anger into the pressure of her hand around the glass. The music changed, and then changed again, a relentless bass beat that rattled her insides. Where *were* they?

'You on your own?'

A cloud of beery breath engulfed her, almost making her gag. The man who stood swaying next to her was shorter than she was, with hard gelled black hair and fleshy red cheeks.

'You on your own?' he repeated more loudly, as if she might turn out to be foreign.

'No, I'm with a friend.'

'And she's left you? That's not very nice.'

'It's fine. I'm fine.'

Hannah kept her eyes fixed on the dance floor, willing Sasha and Ed to reappear.

'Lemme buy you a drink.'

The man was leaning in close towards her, so the brittle spikes of his hair prickled her cheek.

'No, thanks.'

She scoured the room again, standing on tiptoe, hoping for a glimpse of Sasha's black silky head. But nothing.

'Come on. Let's go somewhere quieter. Have a chat.'

179

He put a meaty, clammy hand on her arm, and she jumped back as if burned.

'No! Look, I'm sorry, I've got to go to the loo. I'll see you later.'

She hurried off without a backward glance, lugging Sasha's bag as well as her own. In the ladies' toilets there was the usual queue for the cubicles. Women stood in a straggly line, peering into the mirrors as they waited, touching up their make-up and brushing their hair in the over-bright, greenish light.

'Could take a while,' the woman in front of Hannah muttered to her. 'There's three of 'em in there.' She indicated the middle cubicle, from which was coming a variety of shrieks and giggles. The woman in front of Hannah put her finger to the side of her nose and inhaled deeply to indicate what might be taking place. 'And in *that* one,' she pointed to the cubicle at the far end, 'there's a couple. A bloke and a bird. No prizes for what *they*'re doing.'

If the woman's thin tattooed eyebrows had arched any higher they'd have come clean off her forehead. Just then there came the noise of a bolt being unlocked. The women waiting wearily in the queue suddenly shot to attention as the door to the far cubicle was flung open. Hannah's idle curiosity about the occupants turned to shock as a figure in a tight black dress came lurching out. Sasha's lipstick was smudged across her mouth and she was missing an earring. Behind her followed a sheepish-looking Ed, whose expression turned to horror when he caught sight of Hannah.

Sasha, on the other hand, looked triumphant.

'Hannah! Where've you been? I've been looking for you all over,' she giggled.

'Slag,' Hannah heard someone hiss behind her.

'Er, I think I'd better be off,' said Ed, sidling towards the door.

'Good idea,' snapped Hannah.

A woman in the queue behind them called out, 'Typical man — gets what he wants then buggers off.'

'What the fuck are you doing?' Hannah turned on Sasha, not caring that the entire queue was listening. 'You have no idea who that man is or who he's been with.'

'You're just jealous,' sang Sasha.

Hannah, who was only holding it together by a thread, was relieved when another door opened and she was able to push past Sasha and lock herself away in a cubicle, leaning her head back against the wall, only now aware that she was trembling, her calves visibly shaking through those stupid frumpy jeans. Why had she agreed to come? Sasha was a liability, a joke. Why had she ever thought they had anything in common? Only now could Hannah see the truth about their friendship, that it had been based solely upon convenience and desperation, and a simple need for company. They had different values, different politics (Hannah would never forget Sasha's shrieks of derision when she told her she'd voted Green in the local elections. Sasha hadn't even bothered to vote at all), even a different sense of humour.

Hannah emerged from the cubicle resolved to tell Sasha that she was going home. After that she'd begin the process of disentangling herself from their relationship. Her resolve lasted just as long as it took to catch sight of Sasha sitting in a crumpled heap on the filthy toilet floor, her dress hitched up her thighs, black mascara streaking down her cheeks, her face a mess of tears and snot.

'Oi, you need to get your friend home, you do,' said a disapproving girl, frozen in the act of reapplying her lipstick by the cracked sink, her hair pulled up into a ponytail so tight it gave her eyes an oriental appearance. 'You should never have let her get into this state. It's a fucking disgrace. What kind of friend are you?'

'She's my best friend,' sobbed Sasha from the floor. 'Leave her alone.'

Hannah felt something tugging at her insides. What was happening to her lately? She'd always prided herself on her loyalty. At school she'd always been the one the other girls would confide in when they had a problem they didn't want anyone else to know about, yet she'd been about to turn her back on Sasha just because she was having a tough time.

'Come on,' she said softly, bending to put an arm around the still-weeping Sasha. 'Let's get you home.'

'I should think so an' all,' remarked the girl with the ponytail.

Hannah, who had hauled Sasha to her feet and was supporting her on one side, turned to glare at her. 'How dare you judge her? You don't

182

know anything about her life and what she's going through. You should be fucking ashamed.' The expletive came out sounding prissy, as if she were a child trying out swearing for the first time.

The girl shook her head, unmoved, the ponytail swinging vigorously from side to side. 'We've all got our problems, sweetheart. But some of us have got a bit of pride as well.'

Outside the club, Sasha was sick into a bin, her bony shoulder blades jutting pale and sharp in the semi-darkness. Hannah held back her hair and stroked her back, and tried not to meet the bouncers' eyes. Two cabs pulled up, saw the state of Sasha and sped off again, and the third only agreed to take them when Hannah offered to pay for the car to be valeted if Sasha threw up in it.

On the way back to Crouch End, through streets lined with scantily clad women, many in a similar state to Sasha, and groups of men laughing over-loudly to compensate for not having pulled, Hannah kept her hand on Sasha's and willed the night to be over.

'Sash,' she ventured at one time, sneaking a glance at her friend, who was compressed into a corner of the backseat of the cab like a cornered cat. 'You know that guy . . . Ed?'

Hannah shot a nervous look at the driver, a squat, bearded man, who was fiddling impatiently with his radio, trying to find a station that didn't offend him.

Sasha made a non-committal noise in reply.

'You were . . . you know . . . *careful*, weren't you?'

183

Sasha groaned, shrinking still further into the grubby upholstery of the car. Hannah decided not to pursue the subject, but she couldn't stop thoughts of Sasha and Ed and what had happened in the toilet from surging around her head. It was disgusting. So distasteful and seedy. Like animals mating in public. No self-control. No pride — that awful girl had been right about that. Where was Sasha's self-respect? To let that man reach out his knotted muscly arms with that stupid tattoo and put his hand up her tiny dress and slide those loose jeans down over his hips. Did they do it standing up, pressed together in that minuscule cubicle, stifling breaths and moans in each other's skin and hair? Or maybe he was sitting down on the toilet seat — no lid, mind, probably to discourage drug-taking — and she astride him. Hannah pictured Sasha lowering herself on to his thighs, his tanned arms reaching round to guide her down as her dress rode up her thighs. Obscene. That's what it was.

And yet . . . oh God.

'You don't have to come in. Just drop me off.'

It was the first time Sasha had spoken properly since they'd left the toilets, and her words sounded slurred and heavy, as if they were being dragged from her against her will.

'Don't be stupid. I'm seeing you home.'

'No. I . . . '

'Forget it, Sasha. I'm not letting you go in on your own. Anyway, I'm desperate for the loo. I'll come in and walk home from here. It's only a few minutes.'

She wasn't desperate for the loo, but it was the

only way she could stop Sasha arguing with her. Not that she particularly wanted to go to Sasha's house, but she knew she'd feel bad if she left her to deal with a babysitter in this state. It would be so humiliating.

'Who've you got babysitting?'

Sasha looked blank.

'Your babysitter? Who is it?'

Sasha shrugged. 'Katia.'

The word was so indistinctly spoken as to almost not be a word at all, just a sludge of sound.

'Katia?' Hannah frowned. 'That's weird, isn't it? She never normally babysits.'

Sasha shrugged again, and retreated into silence as the cab driver drew bad-temperedly up outside her house. Hannah rifled through her purse for cash, baulking at the twenty-five pounds he demanded.

'Can't find the key.' Sasha sat down on her doorstep, practically inhaling the contents of her handbag.

'Oh, give it here.'

Hannah snatched the bag from her, eventually locating the doorkey in an inside pocket and letting them in.

'Katia!' she called as she helped Sasha into the hallway.

No answer. She walked into the living room. Nothing, although the television was on — a re-run of a news quiz show, it looked like. A strange choice for a woman with a very limited grasp of English.

'No sign of her,' Hannah remarked as Sasha

lurched into the room and flopped down heavily on the chaise longue.

'She's staying the night. I told her to go to bed.'

Hannah was taken aback. Sasha never had people staying the night. She was so particular about everything, so controlling. Although she had her own en suite, she'd confessed to Hannah once that even the sight of other people's toothbrushes in the guest bathroom made her gag. 'It defiles it. Do you know what I mean?'

'I'll be off then. I'll just go to the loo.'

Hannah went to the bathroom on the ground floor. She was surprised to find the door to the guest room wide open and the room quite empty. She gazed around at its grey Farrow & Ball painted walls, as if she might find Katia hiding there, somehow camouflaged against them.

'Where did you say Katia was sleeping?' she asked, re-entering the living room.

Sasha, who had kicked off her inhospitable shoes and was lying back on the chaise longue, put one hand up over her face. She had her eyes shut, but Hannah had the distinct impression that she was far from asleep.

'Sasha!' she prompted, loudly. 'Where's Katia?'

'Hmm . . . ?' Sasha murmured, as if she'd just woken up.

'Katia!' Hannah snapped.

Sasha opened her eyes just a fraction. 'She's upstairs in Dan's office. Or rather, Dan's *former* office,' she said languorously. 'I told her to sleep

186

on the sofa there, so she could be nearer September.'

'Oh.'

But something still didn't feel right.

'I'll just pop up and check, shall I? Make sure September is OK.'

That woke her up all right. Sasha sat up with such alacrity her head seemed to jerk backwards. 'Leave her alone. She's fine.'

Hannah, who was already halfway across the room, stopped, stunned at the sudden ferocity in the other woman's voice.

'Didn't mean to jump at you,' said Sasha, not getting up. 'September's been so tired. I don't want to risk her waking up. That's all.'

As Hannah made her way down the outside steps, she couldn't shake off a sense of misgiving. It was so unlikely that Sasha should have asked Katia to babysit in the first place, let alone to stay over upstairs in what had previously been Dan's office, a hallowed space that Dan had always fiercely guarded. Of course, no one could blame Sasha now that Dan had left her for letting anyone she wanted sleep there. And yet it seemed so strange, so out of character. But then again, why would she lie about it? Unless . . .

But no. Hannah wouldn't allow herself to go any further. People like her and Sasha, they put their kids first. Always. She was allowing the weirdness of the evening to play tricks on her imagination. Sasha might have been a complete liability tonight, but she was a good mother. She'd never do anything to put September at risk.

It was a moonless night and the street was deserted, the huge houses looming monstrous out of the darkness on both sides. Hannah's stupid going-out boots made a clicking noise on the pavement as she walked, the echo shockingly loud in the silent urban landscape. A shape appeared from between two parked cars up ahead and Hannah's heart lurched painfully in her chest. A large fox, its white breast luminous under a dim street light, blocked the path. It stared out at her impassive, unmoving. Hannah stopped, holding her breath. For what seemed like minutes, but could only really have been a few seconds, Hannah and the fox stared at each other in the still early-morning air. Then it turned and disappeared from view as noiselessly as it had arrived.

Hannah carried on her way, her hand curled tightly around her mobile phone, the sound of her own blood deafening in her ears.

15

'No way. Absolutely not.'

'I didn't say we were doing it, I just said maybe we should think about it.'

'OK. I've thought about it, and the answer is no way.'

Josh frowned, his hands gripping the steering wheel in the way Hannah seemed to find irrationally offensive (*'the ten-to-two position is for learners, Josh,'* she'd *once berated him during an argument, 'not for proper grown-ups'*). Had Hannah always been so dogmatic? He tried to remember. But as so often these days, he found it next to impossible to think back to a time when things were uncomplicated and his relationship with Hannah wasn't refracted through the prism of Dan and Sasha's separation.

'Look, I don't like the way Dan has behaved any more than you. But what's done is done. He's obviously not going to change his mind about this woman, so either we accept that, or we tell him to piss off altogether.'

'We can accept it without having to become best friends with them.'

'He just asked if he could bring her round for a coffee or if we'd pop round there. Why must you always overreact?'

They continued in silence, both gazing out fixedly through the windscreen, the weight of

189

their resentment causing the little car to feel like a pressure cooker. One wrong word and the whole thing could explode.

'Look,' Josh tried again, 'we're in a really difficult position here. We're not only friends of Sasha and Dan, we're also very fond of September, and we've got to think of what's best for her. Sasha has still only let Dan see her a couple of times, in return for unfreezing the bank card, and even then it was only on the condition that they stayed at their house. I mean, how easy can it be to repair bridges with your daughter when your ex-wife is standing right there rolling her eyes at everything you say? September needs to spend time on her own with her father, especially since, as you've said yourself, you're concerned about how Sasha is behaving towards her.'

'That isn't what I said.'

'Yes, you did, you said you were worried Sasha might have gone out and left her without a babysitter.'

'I was tired. I wasn't thinking properly. Of course she wouldn't do that.'

'Yeah, but the fact that it even crossed your mind means there's something not right. Sasha is not prioritizing September at the moment.'

Hannah swung her head towards him, mouth open. '*Prioritizing?* This is not some business strategy meeting, Josh. These are our friends' lives we're talking about. God, sometimes you sound just like someone off *The Apprentice.*'

'Failure is not an option.' Josh meant to lighten the atmosphere by quoting a line from

190

the TV show, but it fell flat, like practically everything he said to his wife at the moment. Of course, it didn't help that they were on their way to visit his parents, which always made Hannah tense. Not that they were ever anything less than lovely to her. And of course they adored Lily — currently fast asleep in the back with Toby the dachshund's head cradled on her lap. But he knew Hannah found the neat, quiet suburban house near Leicester oppressive, and was secretly convinced she found his parents, with their fixed habits and their felt-pen-ticked copy of the *Radio Times*, depressingly dull.

Hannah sighed loudly, setting Josh's teeth on edge.

'OK,' she said, her tone more conciliatory. 'I know Sasha has been distracted recently. Who wouldn't be? But I take your point about September needing a bit of continuity and stability. She needs to see her father. Which doesn't mean to say she needs to meet his new girlfriend as well. But I suppose we will have to meet her at some stage, if he's really serious about her.'

Josh felt a curious mixture of vindication and fear. He was glad that she'd seen things his way (for once!). But at the same time, the thought that they might actually get to meet the woman he'd seen in the photo on Dan's phone, with her carelessly tousled hair and her endless brown legs, made him feel strangely anxious.

At his parents' house, everything was much the same as it had been the last time they'd visited, and the time before that. The hedge at the front was kept trimmed to the same height at all times, its corners as sharp as if they'd been drawn with a ruler; the beige furnishings never altered. There was nothing to mark the passage of time: no new ornaments, because his mother couldn't stand clutter; no birthday cards stacked up on the mantelpiece; no post sitting on the perfectly clear kitchen worktop; no postcards tucked under the mirror. Instead there were three silver-framed photographs in the living room — his parents on their wedding day, Josh's own graduation photograph, and a picture of Lily as a baby — each displayed on the deep windowsill at exactly the same angle, so as to be perfectly parallel to its companions.

'You'll be hungry,' said his mother. And though that was just her way when she was tense, to phrase a question as if it was a statement of fact, in the way German and Dutch people sometimes do when speaking English, Josh knew it would wind Hannah up. 'I wish she'd ask me how I feel, instead of telling me,' she'd complained to him in the past.

And once they were installed in the semi-detached house he'd grown up in, with its neatly shelved box-room and its pink-tiled bathroom and all its unspoken rules — dinner at six-thirty; a glass of wine with dinner, but rarely more and never taken with you to the living room or, God forbid, upstairs; no television before seven o'clock — it was as if he'd never left it. The smell of home — Flash cleaner underlaid with stale, unstirred air. The memory of interminable Sunday afternoons spent gazing at the road through the pristine net curtains, wondering when life would begin. Sandwich suppers before bed, card games on the dining-room table, long hours spent lying on his bed listening to Radio One and dreaming of a different kind of future.

'Is Lily OK?' asked his mother that first evening, as they sat down in the immaculate living room with its cream-coloured sofa stuffed so tightly it was like sitting on a bus seat.

'Of course.' Hannah gave a tight-lipped smile. 'She's absolutely fine, Judy. Why do you ask?'

Josh was always surprised when he heard his mother's name used. Growing up, she'd always been 'love' (his dad) or 'Mum' (him), or 'Mrs Hetherington' (callers on the phone) and they'd so rarely had friends round, he must have been at least ten before it occurred to him that she even *had* a first name.

'Oh, nothing. It's just she seems a little quieter than usual.'

'She's just a bit shy until she gets used to people, that's all.'

'Shy! She's never been shy around us, has she, love?' Josh's mum turned to his father for back-up.

'No, never,' came the dutiful reply.

'See, dear? She's normally a little chatterbox the minute she gets here. We can't shut her up, can we, love? It's Grandma this and Grandpa that. That's why I thought something must be up.'

Hannah's little patch of eczema was flaring up again. Josh watched the angry red rash as if it were something alive that might move at any second.

'Lily was just tired, Mum. It's a long journey when you're only four.'

'Course it is, love. Wish it wasn't sometimes.'

Her words hung in the stuffy living-room air, their subtext obvious. Josh felt Hannah stiffen on the sofa beside him.

'And how are those friends of yours, the ones with the child with that strange name. November, was it?'

'September, actually,' Hannah said. 'And when you think about it, it's no stranger than calling a child June or May, which I'm sure you'd consider perfectly normal.'

Josh felt a tinge of impatience. Why did Hannah have to be so contrary? She'd often expressed doubts about September's name in private, worrying that it was a lot to saddle a small child with. Yet here she was defending it, just because his mother had dared to criticize.

'Sasha and Dan? They're not doing too well actually, Mum. They're splitting up.'

'Oh dear.'

Josh's mum had on her pained expression. Josh knew that if she started on the *People don't work hard enough at marriage* speech, Hannah was liable to explode. Luckily she kept quiet.

'Mind you, I did think she was a little bit . . . what's the expression? . . . high-maintenance. He was very charming though, and the little girl was very . . . lively.'

His parents had met Dan and Sasha the last time they made the trip down to London, which was mercifully, as far as Hannah was concerned, a rare occurrence. Josh's dad hated leaving the house unattended, convinced it became a Mecca for thieves for miles around as soon as they'd driven off. And his mum claimed the pollution in London made her allergies worse. 'I don't know how you breathe here,' she said. Sasha had been hungover and irritable, unwilling to be drawn out by his mother's nervous chatter. Dan, to make up for it, had gone straight into charm offensive, questioning Josh's father about the journey and the route they'd taken, and listening to his mother hold forth about the parlous state of the NHS and how they were all paying the price for decades of unchecked immigration.

'It's always sad though, isn't it, when marriages don't work out?' his mother said now. 'It's so hard on the children.'

Was he imagining things, or did Hannah just glance sideways at him? He felt a cold hand suddenly grip his insides and squeeze tightly. That was the problem when your friends split up, you started seeing divorce and separation everywhere you looked.

As they settled down to watch *Masterchef* on catch-up, Hannah's ringtone sounded, a quirky birdsong alert she had uploaded. Instantly Josh's father shot out of his seat.

'What the . . . '

'Relax, Dad, it's just a mobile.'

Josh was constantly amazed at his parents' wilful ignorance where technology was concerned. They seemed so determined to resist change, so content to confine their world to this house. He found himself glancing again at Hannah as she left the room to answer her phone, wondering whether she ever looked at his father and secretly despaired that this was what was in store for her — waking up one day to find herself married to a man who held strong views on garden trellising.

'Hannah seems a bit stressed,' his mother remarked as soon as she was out of earshot, tucking her feet underneath her as she had since she was a coy young newlywed. 'Is she OK, love?'

'She's taking it quite hard, I think, this split,' Josh replied, feeling disloyal as he always did when he discussed his wife with his parents. 'Sasha's one of her best friends and she's been very needy recently. It's not easy to be around someone who is falling apart.'

His mother, who regarded psychological illness as something of a lifestyle choice, frowned. 'I'm sure we'd all like to fall apart sometimes,' she said briskly. 'But you can't afford to be indulgent like that, not when you've a young child to look after.'

Josh made a face. 'You're all heart, Mum,' he smiled. Inside though, he couldn't help feeling his mother had a point. It would be easy for him to lose it, with that awful business going on at school, but you just had to get through it. Instantly he wished he hadn't thought about school. He closed his eyes as a wave of nausea swept over him.

Toby waddled in from the kitchen on his unfeasibly short legs and Josh's mother sighed. These days, after numerous heated discussions, she forbore from saying anything about the dog,

196

but her antipathy towards having a four-legged creature shedding hair in her house was so tangible it was like an extra person in the room. The first time they'd brought Toby with them, his mother had followed the dog around the house with a hand-held vacuum cleaner. 'I'm afraid I just don't see the point of pets,' she'd said, leading Hannah to hiss, when they were alone, that never mind women being from Venus and men from Mars, it was dog people and non-dog people that really split the population.

There was silence then in the square, low-ceilinged living room — not awkward, but familiar, the calm hush of Josh's childhood, and for a wild moment he thought he might open up to his parents about what had been happening at school — the unthinkable thing he'd been accused of, and the way he felt guilty even though he knew he hadn't done anything. The words sat on the end of his tongue like boiled sweets, but he just couldn't find a way to let them out.

'I'll just go and see what Hannah's up to,' he said finally, heading off to the kitchen. Through the window, next to the small white table on which were laid the placemats his father had cut out of the remnants of beige lino from when they had the floor done, he could just about make out the outline of Hannah striding about in the dark back garden. He wondered if she was cold. The autumn nights had started to carry a definite chill. There would soon be frost on the ground. Then he reflected that this was precisely the sort of thing his father would worry about, and this made him feel anxious again. Whoever she was on the phone to, Hannah seemed to be having an animated conversation. Josh couldn't remember the last time the two of them had had one of those — apart from when they were snapping at each other. He felt a twinge of jealousy towards the unidentified caller.

When she finally came in, he was still waiting for her in the kitchen.

'Sasha,' she said, holding up the phone and shaking her head.

'What now?'

'She's in a right state. She says things have gone missing from the house. That weird little limestone statue they had on the windowsill, a painting from the bedroom, a couple of rings that Dan's mother gave her.'

'So they've been robbed?'

'Well, no. Or rather, yes, but . . . Well, she thinks Dan is responsible.'

Josh stared at her. 'Dan? But he wouldn't . . . '

Or would he? It was still technically Dan's house. He was still paying for it. His stuff was still all over the place. Presumably he still had keys. Why shouldn't he let himself in while the place was empty and help himself to a few things?

'Anyway, could you really blame him?' he asked out loud.

Now it was Hannah's turn to stare. 'You're joking, right? Dan *left* Sasha and September. He *chose* to go. No one forced him. He should have thought about money before he walked out on his family. And to sneak into the house while

198

Sasha was out, stealing stuff . . . It's just creepy.'

'Come on. It's hardly stealing if it was his in the first place.'

'Josh! It was a complete invasion of her privacy. Surely you're not trying to defend him? Sasha is in pieces. She says she doesn't feel safe in the house any more, thinking he could just let himself in at any time. She's had all the locks changed — and that wasn't cheap, let me tell you — but she still says she feels violated.'

'Is she going to report it to the police?'

'Too right. Apparently her lawyer said it would be great for her case because — ' Hannah stopped short. 'I shouldn't tell you. It'll get straight back to Dan.'

'Don't be ridiculous.'

'No. Forget it. I'm not saying anything more.'

A sense of injustice flared within him. Just where did Hannah's loyalties lie these days? It was supposed to be the two of them who were the team, who didn't have secrets from each other, yet increasingly he found himself locked out from what was going on in her head. The other night when she'd come home from that club with Sasha, he'd got the definite sense that something had happened, something bad, but she hadn't wanted to talk about it and had fobbed off his enquiries with vague answers. Anyway, he soon stopped quizzing her when she made it obvious that she was in the mood for sex for the first time in months. He'd been so surprised, so pathetically grateful, he hadn't attempted to find out what lay behind this sudden and, it turned out, short-lived change of heart, and after that the moment had passed. And now she wouldn't even talk to him about this legal stuff.

'Right, if you're going to hold out on me, I'm going to ring Dan right now to find out what's going on.'

Hannah glared at him, calling his bluff. 'Fine. Call him. Just don't mention lawyers.'

He had expected her to back down and open up about what Sasha had told her, so they could discuss things between them the way they used to, but now he was left in the position of having to follow through and put in a call to Dan, right there and then, which he had no inclination at all to do.

'Mate! How you doing?'

Shit. He hadn't imagined Dan would pick up, not on a Friday evening. Oughtn't he to be lying in bed drinking champagne with his hot new girlfriend? Wasn't that the whole point of having left his wife and child?

'Fine. Listen, I'm at my parents' and Hannah just got a call from Sasha to say someone's been in the house and taken stuff. I know it's your house and everything, but it's not clever to — '

'What? They've been robbed? Why didn't she tell me? Are they both OK?'

Josh was wrong-footed. Dan sounded genuinely concerned. Either he was doing some very convincing acting, or he truly didn't know anything about it.

'Yeah, they're fine. I don't think much went missing — a bit of art, some jewellery. It's just that — well, she thinks it was you.'

Dan went silent.

'She thinks you let yourself into the house when she was out and nicked a load of stuff.'

Dan's exclamation was so loud Hannah looked up, eyebrows raised, from the kitchen table, where she'd been digging grooves with a fingernail in one of the lino placemats.

'I don't believe it! She's trying to make me out to be a fucking thief as well as a wife-beater. The woman is totally insane. Do you know what? I wouldn't be surprised if there was no break-in at all, and she's just making the whole thing up. Did that ever occur to you?'

It hadn't occurred to him, but now the idea had been put into his head, Josh couldn't help feeling it made sense. Sasha was totally unhinged at the moment. Just thinking back to last weekend, when she'd come round before she and Hannah went out to the club and had been all over him like a horrible rash, made him feel mortified all over again. He hadn't responded to her. He was sure he hadn't. But there'd been a moment when she was rubbing her hands all over him when he'd found himself thinking about Hannah and how rarely she touched him these days, and how much he longed for her to be doing what Sasha was doing, and he couldn't help it, he'd become ... No, no, no. He couldn't, wouldn't think about that. The point was that Sasha wasn't stable. But was she really crazy enough to invent a break-in, just to get back at Dan?

'This is getting serious, you know, mate,' Dan was continuing. 'This is getting fucking serious.

I'm beginning to really worry about her state of mind, and whether September is safe with her. Do you know, we've been getting a stream of pizza deliveries and cabs turning up at the door that we never ordered. Yesterday, get this, a guy turned up to quote for a conservatory we'd apparently expressed an interest in. We don't even have a fucking garden.'

'Yeah, but just because she orders a couple of prank pizzas it doesn't make her a bad mum. She dotes on September, you know that.'

But even as he was saying it, Josh was remembering what Hannah had said about the guest room being empty and no sign of a babysitter.

'Look, Dan, I've been talking to Hannah.' Josh wasn't looking at his wife, who was sitting at the kitchen table, but he felt her stir to attention at the mention of her name. 'Anyway,' he pushed ahead, 'we both feel like maybe it would be a good idea for us to meet Sienna now. I mean, she's clearly a part of your life that isn't going away.'

'Oh mate, that's — '

'But that doesn't mean we're in favour of what you did or anything, and just because we're ready to meet her, it doesn't mean you should introduce her to September or anything.'

'No. Absolutely. I wouldn't. Not yet, anyway.'

From the corner of his eye, Josh could see Hannah gesturing angrily, but he ignored it.

'I'll tell Sienna. She can't wait to meet you guys. Maybe you could come over for dinner. She makes a wicked Thai curry.'

After he ended the call, Josh remained staring out into the dark back garden where in a previous life he'd stood for hours alone with a swingball set, hitting the ball backwards and forwards through the dragging afternoons, imagining he was two separate people.

'I can't believe you just did that.' Hannah looked up accusingly, her pink cheeks clashing with her red hair.

'Hang on a minute. You said — '

'Yes, I said *eventually*. I said we'd meet her *eventually*. Not right now. What am I going to tell Sasha?

'Don't tell her anything. She doesn't need to know.' Josh put out a conciliatory hand to touch Hannah's arm. 'Look, Hans, I know Sasha is our friend, but this *our* life. Yours and mine. We don't have to place her at the centre of everything we say and do. We're entitled to be friends with who we want.'

A shriek went up from the living room.

'Josh!' came his mother's agitated voice. 'Your dog's just weed on the Flokati!'

Hannah pulled away. 'Our life,' she repeated, as if he'd said something amusing. And again, softly, in a tone he didn't altogether like, 'Our life.'

Lucie/Eloise, aged nine

Sometimes I miss Mummy so much it gives me a tummy ache. I don't miss her being cross or making gobbling noises and looking at me with her cold-fish eyes, but I miss the way her voice sounds when she tries to learn all the funny English sayings from her book. When I told her on the phone that I miss her, she said 'fiddlesticks'. (Except it sounds like this when she says it: feed-el-steecks.) She was in a good mood when I spoke to her on the phone, and I almost told her about being Eloise, but didn't dare. When we said goodbye and I was crying she told me, 'Don't be silly!' (seeley) and said, 'Onnyva,' which I asked Madame LeFeuvre about and she said means 'Let's go!'

16

Hannah was finally getting down to work. That endless weekend at Josh's parents' house, where she'd got no work done at all, had left her really behind and it was such a relief to have a proper child-free stretch to really focus her mind on the feature that was already two days overdue. Lily had jumped at the chance of going to Sarah's house for lunch, and Marcia had seemed genuinely pleased when Hannah accepted her offer of picking up the two girls from nursery and taking them home for a couple of hours. It would make a refreshing change for both her and Lily to spend a bit of time with people who weren't in the middle of a domestic crisis.

She'd been nervous about broaching it with Sasha and had tried to be as casual as she could when explaining why they wouldn't be able to join her and September in the park straight after school, but in the event Sasha hadn't seemed bothered. In fact, she hadn't reacted at all, which was a relief. Sasha's moods were so hard to judge these days. Hannah didn't think she could have spent time with Sasha, not without giving herself away. The invitation to dinner at Sienna's flat this evening was looming so large in her conscience, she was surprised she didn't have it tattooed across her forehead.

It was incredible how much you could get done if you knew you had a clear run of time.

Hannah had done three phone interviews and sorted out the basic structure of her latest piece. She'd even nailed the introduction, which was always the hardest part. Petra, the features editor on the magazine Hannah wrote for most regularly, was an ambitious, go-getting twenty-nine-year-old who wore Louboutins in the office and worked through lunch eating quinoa salads from little plastic pots. She didn't understand about childcare or how you felt after a few sleepless nights, or why it was impossible to get anything done if your toddler was at home sick. Hannah had had to blame the lateness of the feature on the fact that one of the interviewees was being difficult, rather than saying she just didn't have enough hours in the day. With any luck, now she'd got going, she could finish the article before they had to leave for dinner with Sienna and Dan, and it would be in Petra's inbox first thing in the morning. Just as well — she'd had so little work lately, she and Josh really needed the cash. As it was, it'd be at least a month before her invoice was paid. Most magazines clearly imagined their journalists wrote for love, not money.

The other thing about burying herself in work was that Hannah hadn't had time to think about what was hidden in the wardrobe in her bedroom. And as long as she didn't think about it, she could pretend it wasn't there and keep that gnawing low-level worry at bay.

Damn. Twenty past three. She ought to be getting off to Marcia's now to pick up Lily. Lily was still so young, if Hannah left her too long in a new place she'd be totally exhausted, particularly on a Monday when she was still tired from the weekend.

Marcia lived a few streets away, in a road where the Victorian terraces on one side had been bombed during the war and replaced by social housing. Most of the houses were now privately owned, but a few still had the council-regulation front doors and the neglected appearance of long-term tenanted properties. On the way there, Hannah rehearsed in her mind the shape the rest of the feature would take, remembering an argument she hadn't included in her plan and making a note to herself to scribble it down as soon as she got home.

Marcia's was one of the former council houses that had been lovingly cared for — the front garden was a cheerful mass of greenery and gravel, with painted window boxes on every sill. Inside the little glassed-in porch, Hannah could make out Sarah's and her two older sisters' flowery wellies lined up in a haphazard row beneath three pegs accommodating an assortment of brightly coloured raincoats and stripy woollen scarves. The effect was one of happy chaos, and Hannah found herself looking forward to going inside and having a cup of tea and a chat with the ever-calm Marcia about subjects that for once didn't involve cheating husbands and their money-grabbing girlfriends.

But when Marcia came to the door, she looked uncharacteristically po-faced. Behind her, Hannah could hear the sound of a small girl in the throes of a crying fit.

'Sounds like you've got your hands full. Is everything OK? That's not Lily, is it?'

She was smiling, but uncomfortably aware Marcia wasn't following suit. In fact, the other woman was frowning at her, seemingly confused.

'Lily's not here. Surely you knew?'

Hannah froze. 'What do you mean, not here? Where is she?'

'When I got to school to pick them up, Mrs Mackenzie said Lily had already left with Sasha. Apparently she turned up early. Said she was collecting both Lily and September.'

'But I told her — '

'Sarah's pretty upset — as you can probably hear.' Marcia opened the door wider so Hannah could hear more clearly the steady wailing coming from inside the house.

'Oh, Marcia, I'm so sorry. I don't know what to say.'

Hannah felt hot with embarrassment, even though she had no idea how the mix-up could have happened. Hurrying away down the street, her cheeks burning, she rang Sasha's numbers — mobile and landline — without success. Both went straight to voicemail. Where was she? Hannah knew she'd told Sasha about the arrangement with Marcia, and even if Sasha hadn't been paying attention, she knew better than to take Lily without consulting Hannah. They'd always been so respectful of each other like that, never presuming something was OK without checking it out first.

Not knowing what else to do, she went round to Sasha's house and leaned heavily on the buzzer. No answer. By now Hannah was out of breath and sweaty, her stomach churning uncomfortably. Worry nipped at her insides.

She rang Josh, letting out a groan of frustration when his phone also went straight to voicemail.

'I can't find Lily,' she snapped, deliberately omitting to mention that she was with Sasha. 'Call me back.'

Hurrying back home, she tried to ignore the painful stitch in her side, convincing herself that when she turned the corner she'd see Sasha and the girls waiting outside the front door. There'd be some easy explanation. Yet she could see right away that there was no one there and no sign of Sasha's car outside.

She started to feel afraid. Sasha had been so erratic recently. If Hannah was honest with herself, she knew Sasha wasn't really fit to be looking after her own daughter. What had she done with Lily? All sorts of terrifying scenarios passed through her head. Sasha queueing for the ferry with the girls strapped into the back seats of the car, or going out somewhere and forgetting she had them with her, or leaving them on the tube, or in a supermarket car park.

At home, she paced the floor, phone in hand. No sooner had she ended one futile call to Sasha than she was redialling her number. '*Please pick up,*' she muttered. '*Come on, for Christ's sake, pick up.*'

'Sasha, it's me again. Call me,' she repeated for the millionth time.

When her phone finally did ring, she was

unreasonably furious to see Josh's name flashing up on the screen.

'I thought you'd be Sasha.'

'Well, sorry,' he said. 'You did call *me*, don't forget. I was in a staff meeting.'

Cutting the conversation short, she checked her phone for missed calls, even though she knew it always made a beeping sound if someone had tried to ring while she was talking. She glanced at the time. Half past four. In just two hours, they were supposed to be making the trek across town to Notting Hill, and in between now and then, she was supposed to be finishing her feature, getting Lily fed and bathed and ready for bed and settling in the babysitter — a sixth-former from three doors down with waist-length hair and eyelashes so weighted with mascara Hannah wondered how she could possibly open her eyes, who always came lugging a backpack full of textbooks and whom Lily quietly idolized. And that was to say nothing of getting herself ready. Ever since Josh made the dinner arrangement, Hannah had been agonizing about what to wear. She'd been feeling so washed out and tired lately, and nothing seemed to fit her properly. The thought of meeting up with a fresh-faced, twenty-four-year-old model was just depressing.

Hannah had never really been someone who compared herself to other women, getting a boost when the balance swung in her favour and despairing when it didn't. She was what she was, she had always believed, and no amount of fretting was going to change that, so she might

210

just as well accept it and move on. Besides, you only really noticed the way people looked in the early stages of meeting them; as soon as you got to know them, looks ceased to matter. Her boyfriend before Josh had been, in her mother's words, 'very quirky-looking', but from the moment he'd first made her laugh, she'd ceased to see his large, hooked nose, or the criss-crossing front teeth.

Yet something about this meeting with Sienna had got to her. Maybe it was just that she was feeling generally so insecure. She knew things weren't right with Josh. She couldn't remember the last time they'd gone so long without having sex, apart from that drunken, frenzied coupling the night she'd come home from the nightclub with the image of Sasha and Ed in that grubby toilet cubicle playing across her mind. But she didn't have the energy to address the problem. Easier to ignore it than to have to start thinking about what lay at the heart of it. Funny how the lack of a physical relationship made one feel so insubstantial, so un-vital. A sexless, sapless husk of a person. And she was dreading being around a couple who were so overtly at the honeymoon stage. She couldn't bear the idea of her and Josh sitting side by side like maiden aunts, while Dan and this woman — this girl, really (in her imagination she was getting younger and younger by the minute) — were all over each other.

She'd been planning on having a shower before they went and washing her hair, maybe applying a treatment from the hugely expensive tub she'd been persuaded into buying the last time she'd visited the hairdresser. But now all thoughts of clothes and make-up had been swept aside by worry for Lily. Even her anxiety about the thing hidden away in the wardrobe, which had been like a constant buzzing in her ears over the last couple of days, ever since she'd brought it into the house — was pushed out of her head by this new crisis.

It was nearly six when the doorbell went. Hannah had been standing at the table going through the class list, trying desperately to think of anyone else she could ring for information.

'Hi.' Sasha stood with an arm around both Lily and September, a broad smile cracking her face. 'Aren't I the best friend you ever had? Kept her out of your hair for five and a half hours! Hope you got masses of work done, or I might just have to kill you.'

Hannah grabbed Lily's shoulders and pulled her towards her, almost crushing her in her need to feel her warm, solid little body again. She glared at Sasha over the top of Lily's head. 'Where the hell have you been?'

Sasha's smile evaporated.

'You knew Lily was supposed to be going to Marcia's for lunch. Since when do you take her out of school without telling me?'

'Now hang on a minute. I had no idea Lily was supposed to be going to Marcia's. And I did tell you. I sent you a text before I picked her up.'

'No you didn't. That's a bare-faced lie.'

Sasha's face was pinched and dark. 'Don't you

dare call me a liar. Check your phone. Go on. Check it.'

'I don't need to check it. I've been checking it all afternoon, while I've been trying to get hold of you.'

Even so, Hannah couldn't help glancing at her phone. Sure enough, there was an alert, showing that a text message had come through.

'I don't believe this.'

Clicking on it, she saw it was indeed from Sasha.

Am picking up Lil so you can get your head down x.

'But you've only just sent this. You must have done. What use is that when I've been frantic with worry all afternoon?'

'Hannah, I don't believe this. First of all, I sent that text hours ago. I don't know why it took so long to get through — maybe because we were in the park when I sent it and you know how dodgy the signal is there. Secondly, I don't know why you were so frantic — Mrs Mackenzie would have told you Lily was with me. All I wanted was to do you a bloody favour.'

Sasha's face, tilted sharply towards Hannah, was a scrunched-up scowl of indignation. September, meanwhile, looked as if she was about to cry, moving her eyes from one woman to the other and back again, and Hannah felt the anger drain from her like dirty bath water.

'Sorry,' she grunted. 'I just panicked, that's all.'

213

'Get a grip. This is me, OK? I love Lily like my own daughter, you know that. Anyway, now I'm here, any chance of some tea?'

'Yes, *please*,' begged September.

Hannah froze. She was already so behind schedule. There was no way she could get everything done if Sasha came in.

'Um, it's not really a terribly good time, Sash. Josh and I are going out tonight and the babysitter is due any minute really.'

'Babysitter? On a school night? You *are* a dark horse. Going anywhere nice?'

'Not really. We'll probably just go to a movie or something.'

Once it was out, she wished she hadn't said it. It was one thing not to tell Sasha that they were going to meet Sienna, but another entirely to invent an outright lie. For a second she thought about taking it back and telling her the truth, but now she'd missed the chance of dropping it in casually, it would become even more of a big deal.

Sasha shrugged. 'Oh well. Have fun,' she said, turning away.

'But Mummy . . . ' September was resisting being steered in the direction of the car, and Hannah felt even more wretched.

'Come on.' Sasha was practically dragging her daughter along now. 'Home time.'

'Sorry,' Hannah called after them. Her voice sounded tinny and false in her own ears.

Lily, her chubby arms clasped firmly around Hannah's waist, watched them go without saying a word.

17

Now that they were finally about to meet her, Josh wished he'd never agreed to go to Sienna's flat. It wasn't just because Hannah was so clearly guilt-ridden, although that didn't help. Trust Sasha to choose today of all days to try to do her a favour. There was also this horrible, anxious, rushing feeling that wouldn't leave him alone, as if he was about to open a door he ought to have left closed.

'Maybe we shouldn't have agreed to go,' he said.

Hannah, who'd been gazing glumly through the car window as they circumnavigated Regent's Park, swung around to face him.

'You're kidding, right? You were the one who pushed this through. I told you it was too soon. Don't tell me you're having second thoughts now.'

Josh sighed. 'Sorry.'

He put his hand out to squeeze her thigh, just as he had always done when driving back from friends' houses or boring dinner parties where he'd spent the evening sneaking glances at Hannah and wondering what underwear she had on, or through the French countryside on one of the trips they used to do before they'd had Lily, getting in the car and driving from one town to the next, stopping whenever they saw a chateau they liked the look of, or a village square, or a bar. 'Here!' Hannah would cry out, the guidebook open on her lap, as they passed a signpost to a cluster of white houses on a rocky outcrop. 'This is the one with that restaurant in someone's living room. Let's take a look.'

How many times had they sat like this in pubs or trains or (less cheerfully) hospital waiting rooms — his hand unconsciously resting on the top of her leg, absorbing the heat through her jeans or skirt? Yet now it felt wrong, awkward. His hand felt like it didn't belong to him, a grotesque prosthetic clumsily planted and now difficult to remove without drawing attention to it. Was it his imagination or had she stiffened her leg muscles, as if desperate for his hand to be gone?

Somewhere around Westbourne Park Road, they got lost. Hannah hadn't brought the reading glasses she'd only recently been prescribed and was too vain to wear, and the street names on the *A-Z* were too small for her to see.

'Why don't you get a sat nav, like everyone else?' she complained, as they drove past the same deli for a second time.

They were so snappy with each other, it seemed impossible that just weeks ago they'd made love — urgent, passionate and, in Hannah's case, drunken love. Now they were once again miles apart. Josh knew he was partly to blame — he still couldn't bring himself to talk to his wife about the nightmare going on at school, even thinking about it brought on a rush of nausea. The shameful secret was like a boulder between them.

By the time they pulled up outside an ivy-clad, four-storey white stucco villa in a square of similar houses looking out on to a gated garden in the middle, they were coated in a thick, bad-tempered silence. While Hannah scrabbled on the back seat for her handbag, somehow contriving to grab it the wrong way up so that the contents tipped out in the footwell and had to be painstakingly gathered up, Josh reached for the wine he'd bought on his way home from school. In the shop he'd dithered over what to choose, not wanting to seem either cheap, or ostentatious. In the end he'd plumped for an £8 bottle of French white, but now, standing outside the glossy black-painted railings, gazing up at the high Georgian windows with their antique wooden shutters opening on to pale airy interiors, he wished he'd spent more. When Hannah finally appeared, flushed, around the side of the car, he noticed for the first time what she was wearing. It had all been such a rush when he got home, with both of them struggling to get Lily ready in time and Hannah locked away in the bathroom until the last minute, that he hadn't noticed her outfit, but now he could see there was something peculiar about it. Normally Hannah was such a straightforward dresser — jeans for the most part, or for smarter occasions plain dresses, usually black, with striking jewellery. But today she had clearly dressed in a hurry, teaming a pair of dark, wide-legged trousers she hardly ever wore with a long, baggy, smock-style top. The effect was to make her look several

217

sizes larger than she actually was.

Dan came to the door, looking as if he had swallowed a smile too big for his mouth so it bulged out of his cheeks. 'You made it out of north London. Did you have to show your passports?'

He was talking loudly, like a child projecting his words in a school assembly. Josh could see he was nervous and wanted to tell him to relax, but he didn't quite trust himself to speak. The flat, which took up the entire raised ground floor, had high ceilings and dark-wood floors. The furnishings were an eclectic mix. A shocking-pink sofa smothered in mismatched cushions was complemented by a battered leather armchair and a couple of threadbare kelim rugs. On the chalky white walls, oil paintings in ornate gilt frames vied for space with modern silkscreen prints and arty black-and-white photographs, many of them showing the same long-limbed, high-cheekboned figure Josh recognized from the picture he'd seen on Dan's phone.

'Oh my God!' The voice coming from the inner hallway of the flat was surprisingly deep and had the kind of husky tone that comes from a nicotine-based diet. 'I'm such a total div, I've forgotten the ginger!'

Dan threw back his head and laughed.

'Never mind,' he called, once he'd composed himself. 'We'll just have to imagine the ginger. Now come in and say hello.'

There was the sound of a metal implement being banged down and then a blur of movement like butterfly wings flapping as Sienna

218

appeared in the doorway, wiping her hands down the legs of her baggy grey sweatpants. Her caramel-coloured skin, glistening under a tight black vest, and the damp tendrils escaping from the tortoiseshell clip with which the rest of her hair was messily held up gave some indication of the heat in the kitchen from which she'd just emerged.

Her make-up-free face was wide across the cheekbones, and when she smiled the smattering of freckles across the bridge of her neat, wrinkled-up nose joined together into one solid brown splodge.

'I'm so happy you're here,' she said simply, and Josh got the impression she was holding herself back from hugging them, perhaps out of deference to the delicacy of the situation. He tried not to look at the wide strip of flat brown stomach visible between the bottom of her vest and the waistband of her sweatpants, set so low her hip bones jutted from them like knuckles.

Dan was looking expectantly from them to her and back again, like a cookery-show contestant waiting for the verdict on his signature dish.

'Lovely to meet you,' said Hannah, in that voice she used when she was stressed, the one that sounded as if she'd clipped it on top of her real voice like an extra pair of lenses. Next to Sienna's casual informality, Hannah seemed stuffily overdressed.

For a second or two there was silence. Then Dan grabbed the bottle from Josh's hand. 'A situation this awkward calls for alcohol. Plenty of it.'

Dan was wearing a pair of faded jeans and a nondescript T-shirt. On his feet he had a pair of black flip-flops, from which his toes protruded, long and shockingly white. Josh found himself focusing on the flip-flops. Last night they'd had the first winter frost. When he'd taken Toby for his late-night walk, his breath had come out in puffs of white cloud, yet here was Dan padding around with his pale, bony feet, the subtext obvious in every soft slapping step: *This is where I live, I inhabit this space, and this woman.* Josh looked down at his brown suede lace-ups and felt like his own father, jarringly out of step.

They sat around the low coffee table piled with books and magazines and old coffee cups and phone-chargers. Josh wondered if Sienna was in any of the magazines, but he didn't want to ask. There was a part of him that felt asking would draw attention to Sienna's beauty, which would somehow count as a win for Dan. How Dan would have won or what the competition was, he couldn't have said.

'Lovely flat,' Hannah said to Sienna, her eyes travelling over the ceiling mouldings and the vast white marble fireplace with its cast-iron insert and white plaster Roman-style bust on the hearth.

'Thank you! It's a hideous mess, I know. I'm such a housework slut. But it scrubs up well, doesn't it, baby?'

Baby? To Josh's amazement, Dan looked pleased rather than embarrassed. In fact, he was practically basking in the glow of Sienna's attention. The two of them had positioned themselves so that they weren't touching (was that deliberate?), but they kept stealing glances at various parts of one another — forearm, knee, ankle, the inside of an elbow — as if trying to commit each one to memory, as if they could caress each other with their eyes only.

'Listen, you two.' Dan had a serious voice on suddenly. 'I just want you to know I really appreciate you coming. I know it can't have been easy for you, and I really respect how much you've been supporting Sasha. But this means so much to me. Because you guys mean so much to me. And so does she.'

Here he snatched up Sienna's delicate hand in his, and they gazed damply at each other for what seemed like aeons but in reality could only have been a second or two.

Josh felt himself squirming on his tapestry-covered floor cushion. *Please don't let them start stroking each other.*

Sienna slipped off the sofa and knelt on the floor in front of the fire, which had already been expertly laid. Grabbing hold of a box of long matches, she bent forward to light the newspaper, her bottom in the air. Josh felt suddenly suffocated. It had been a mistake to come here, he realized now. They ought not to be endorsing Dan's shitty choices.

'The thing is, Dan,' said Hannah, who was nestled into the leather armchair, 'it *is* awkward for us to be here, and that's no reflection on you, Sienna. It's just the situation that's tricky. But I really would feel more comfortable if we didn't talk about . . . well, you know, about Sasha. It feels like a double betrayal. Do you know what I mean?'

'Absolutely. No, we absolutely understand, don't we, baby?'

By this time, Sienna had thankfully leaned back and was sitting at Dan's feet, the newly lit flames reflecting orange in the faint sheen of her cheeks as she nodded in agreement.

'But I do just have to say one thing,' Dan continued. 'This latest claim of Sasha's — that I burgled my own house! It's a complete pack of lies. You do know that, don't you?'

Josh stared down at his wine glass, as if he'd spotted something unusual there.

'She was very upset.' Hannah sounded as if the words were being dragged from her. 'Something obviously happened. And she went to the expense of changing the locks.'

Dan had been waiting for this.

'And guess who paid for that? Can you imagine — paying to be locked out of my own house? You know, it can't go on, all of this. I'm completely skint, and Sasha is just out of control.'

Josh gazed around pointedly at their surroundings — the flat in one of the best parts of town, the oil paintings, the rugs, the smell of old money wafting up from the cracked leather chair.

Dan followed his gaze. 'I know what you're thinking, but you're wrong. This is Sienna's place.'

'Anyway,' Sienna cut in, 'I'm pretty much broke myself since I went back to college.'

'You're not modelling any more?' Hannah asked.

'Just the odd thing. But to be honest, I was never going to make a career of modelling. I haven't got the look they're after. I get the odd advert or fashion spread, but no more. And I need to do something with my brain now. It's been too long in the wilderness.'

'What are you studying?'

'History of Art, at Goldsmiths.'

Josh couldn't help being impressed. She was obviously no slouch intellectually.

'But the thing is,' said Dan, 'I need to be able to support myself. And I need to be able to offer September a stable home. She doesn't seem to have that at the moment. I thought we could sort the money thing out through mediation, but Sasha refuses. If it carries on like this we'll end up in court and the fucking lawyers will take everything. Tell me how that makes any sense?'

'Well, maybe if you hadn't taken your money out of the joint account she would have been more amenable to mediation.' Hannah's voice was measured, but the sharp undertone gave her away.

Dan's face flushed deep wine-red. 'What choice did I have? I have to get her to be reasonable. She can't expect to stay in that house and not even think about getting a job.'

'She can if she's the main caregiver.'

'Well, she's not going to be. She's proved she's not up to it. Fuck it, you two, I'm seriously worried about September. I'm going for fifty-fifty custody.'

Hannah could hardly hide her shock. 'You've never done the childcare, Dan! Who's going to look after her when you're off shooting in Morocco or South Africa? Who's going to pick her up from school when you're working a fourteen-hour day?'

'I've thought about all that. I'll get an au pair.'

Josh snorted with laughter. 'You're joking, aren't you? You're going to hire a complete stranger, even though Sasha is right there with nothing to do?'

'I don't trust her any more.'

'Let's not talk about this.' Hannah sounded dangerously close to tears. 'Josh and I are in an impossible situation. I didn't come hear to listen to you badmouthing Sasha. She's my friend, remember?'

For a moment it looked as if Dan would continue, but Sienna squeezed his knee and he sat back, resigned.

'Let's talk about something else,' said Sienna brightly. 'Let's talk about . . . I don't know . . . bagels. What's your favourite type of bagel?'

'Cinnamon and raisin, without a doubt,' Dan countered instantly. 'Josh? Where do you stand on the bagel issue?'

'The fruit-flavoured bagel is an abomination, in my opinion. I put it to you that a bagel with fruit bits in it is nothing more than a jumped-up teacake.'

They were all trying so hard to make this work, to keep things bright and breezy and reassuringly superficial, painting a hard shell over the things that weren't being said. And for a while it worked. They chatted about work, about the latest viral dance craze, about whether Toby the dachshund had Munchausen's Syndrome because he kept limping for no reason. They sat around the long dark-wood Gothic dinner table and ate the gingerless stir fry and declared it a triumph nevertheless. They drank the mid-price white wine Josh had brought, and Hannah made them all laugh with a story about doing a phone interview with a television personality while Lily was at home ill — the rising hysteria as she fed biscuit after biscuit into the surprised child's mouth to keep her from making a sound. Sienna countered with an amusing anecdote about arriving to shoot a skincare commercial sporting 'a spot the size of Brazil' on her forehead, stylists squealing in horror and attacking the monster with paints and potions.

Josh concentrated on the food and the chatter, and tried not to look at Sienna's hand resting in Dan's lap or notice the way his eyes followed her greedily when she got up and left the room.

They were drinking coffee from the most enormous cafetière Josh had ever seen when the crash came. One minute he was sitting with both hands around a chipped mug that read 'I love New York', feeling absurdly rebellious to be drinking coffee so late in the evening, and the next there came a noise so violent he thought someone had been shot. When he turned his head, one of the panes in the enormous sash window in the living room had been smashed, a jagged crack running from the bottom left-hand corner up to a hole in the middle, framed by the still-open wooden shutters. Josh was too stunned to move, but Dan jumped up and ran for the front door, wrenching it open. They heard the creaking of the heavy communal door just as an engine started up outside and a car pulled away.

'Can you see anyone?' Sienna sounded like a small, frightened child and Josh fought back an insane urge to pull her on to his lap and hold her and stroke her hair.

Dan, reappearing in the living room, shook his head. His face was noticeably paler than when they had arrived, and Josh realized just how much of a shock they had all had. He glanced over at Hannah. She was sitting stiffly upright, not saying anything. One of her long fingers worried away at the eczema patch which stood out raw and red on her forehead.

'She's gone too far this time.' Dan was staring down at the large pebble that he'd picked up from among the shards of glass on the wooden floor.

'Who?' Hannah's voice was sharp.

Dan looked up, frowning. A dark groove ran from his forehead down between his eyes. 'Sasha, of course. Who else would throw a fucking great rock through the window? How many other psychos do we know?'

'That psycho is still your wife.' Hannah was half standing, as if unsure whether to walk out. 'There is nothing at all to say that was Sasha. It could easily have been local kids.'

'Local kids? In Notting Hill?' Josh wasn't sure if he was trying to make a joke, but it was obvious it didn't go down well.

Hannah turned on him. 'Don't *you* start. I can't believe you're jumping to conclusions about Sasha. She had no idea we were coming here tonight. There'd be no reason for her to turn up.'

'Oh don't be naive, Hannah.' Dan sounded angry. 'You know she's been spying on us. What about that text she sent?'

'That text didn't prove anything — except that you're totally paranoid!'

'Hannah's right.' Sienna had crossed the room and looped her brown, toned arm around Dan's waist. 'We don't know it's Sasha. It could be anyone.'

Dan shook his head. 'Too much of a coincidence,' he muttered.

Sienna put up a gentle hand to his cheek to hold his head still. Eventually he shrugged and held up his hands. 'OK, OK. We'll chalk it up to coincidence, if you insist.'

For a second or two they stayed like that, eyes closed, gently swaying. Josh knew he should look at Hannah, maybe share a complicit *What are they like?* raising of the eyebrows, but he couldn't, for fear of what she would see written on his face.

'I feel sick,' Hannah announced on the way home. They'd left soon after the window incident. Even though they'd bolted the wooden shutters, the awareness of that terrible jagged hole in the pane stifled their attempts at conversation. But now Hannah wanted to talk, to tell him how awful she felt. What if it *had* been Sasha? She knew it wasn't, of course. Yet what if

227

it was? Should she say something to her? Admit they'd been to Sienna's flat, just in case?

Josh didn't know what to say. He didn't want to think about the possibility of Sasha outside in the dark square, looking in on the four of them cosying up together in that comfortable, fire-warmed living room. He could just imagine how she might have felt. But then again, if it was her, shouldn't they be more worried about her state of mind than about her feelings? If she'd come out in the night, perhaps even bringing September with her, to spy through the windows, and then picked up a rock and hurled it at the glass, wasn't that dangerously unhinged?

'I think we should back off from both of them for a while,' he said finally, as they waited at a traffic light by Tufnell Park tube. 'This whole situation is getting too intense. I think we should leave them to it for a bit.'

'Oh, that's right. The tried-and-tested Josh formula for when things get tough — walk away.'

'Hey, that's not fair. Whose idea was it to go tonight and show some solidarity?'

'Yeah, and look where that got us!'

The lights changed and Josh pulled away, gears grating. How had this suddenly become his fault, he'd like to know.

'Oh God, I hate this,' said Hannah. 'I hate that we've ended up in this position. I'd be mortified if Sasha found out where we've been. But you know the worst thing?'

Josh shook his head.

'I actually quite liked Sienna! I wanted to hate

her, but I couldn't. What did you think?'

Josh batted away the image of Sienna leaning forward into the fireplace.

'She was OK,' he shrugged.

18

Hannah held her breath, waiting for Sasha's response. She'd hardly slept, worrying about whether to say anything about their dinner at Sienna's the night before, and having decided that she would, she'd blurted it out as soon as they were alone together.

'I'm sorry,' she said. 'I didn't really want to, but you know, Dan is still Josh's best friend. His *only* friend, in many ways.'

She'd expected Sasha to explode, and would even have half welcomed a scene, if only to offload some of the guilt she'd been feeling ever since they accepted Dan's invitation. But in the event, Sasha seemed curiously unconcerned.

'I'm not exactly thrilled, but there's nothing I can do about it, is there? Just don't tell me about it. The less I know about that woman, the better.'

Hannah studied her face. They were in the café on the high street. Well, one of the hundreds of cafés, to be accurate. Sometimes it seemed Crouch End was just one big café full of women with buggies and baby-carriers and expensive tote bags stuffed with crayons and rice crackers. Women in many respects just like the two of them.

Hannah hadn't really wanted to come. She was all too aware of the unfinished feature on her laptop, but the scene last night with the smashed window kept coming back to her — the sickening crack, the glass, that awful jagged hole.

'Something weird happened while we were there.'

'I told you.' Sasha was drinking her cappuccino from a bowl, as all the customers were, and it had given her a ring of froth around her mouth like a clown. 'I don't want to hear about it.'

'Yes, but this was odd. Someone threw a rock at the window. Smashed the whole thing.'

Sasha's clown mouth turned up at the corners. 'Ha! That's brilliant. Serves you all right.'

Hannah smiled tightly, but in her head she heard that cracking sound, and something cold shifted inside her.

'We even wondered for a moment if it could have been you!'

Now Sasha's face set hard, the smile fading to a fissure. 'What do you mean, you thought it was me?'

'Oh, don't take it like that, we didn't really think — '

'No. I don't believe this. Not only do you go behind my back to cosy up with the woman who has destroyed my life, but then when some yob lobs a brick through the window, you try to blame it on me.'

'No, it wasn't like that. Sit down, Sash. Please?'

Sasha had half risen, propelled by her fury.

'I was joking. Please sit down.'

Hannah's voice wobbled as she reached out to detain her friend, and after a brief pause, Sasha slumped back down in her seat. Seemingly unable or unwilling to look at Hannah, she sat forward with her elbow on the table, one hand up to her head. The nub of her wrist bone jutted through her paper-thin skin and Hannah found herself thinking how easily it would snap clean in two.

'Sorry,' Sasha mumbled. 'I know I'm over-sensitive, it's just that this is so hard. Parents shouldn't split up. Parents should stay together. Terrible things happen when parents separate. It's not right.'

'I know.'

Sasha now raised the other hand to her temple, so that her head was resting in her hands. As she did so, the sleeve of her mushroom-coloured cashmere jumper rode up, and Hannah was horrified to see a long, deep, red scratch scored widthways into her flesh. Another similar scratch intersected it halfway up, but disappeared under the jumper's cuff. The dried blood had beaded in places, thick and dark. She tried to think of an innocent explanation, but there was none.

Hannah knew she ought to say something. Yet the words lodged in her mouth like boiled eggs, impossible to get out.

Sasha put her hands down, and instantly the scratches were gone — and with them the opportunity to raise concerns, to be a good friend. Hannah sipped her coffee and tried to forget. Perhaps she hadn't seen what she thought she'd seen. She was prone to exaggerate things in her head — wasn't Josh always telling her that? — liable to leap to wrong conclusions.

'It's Dan's night to see September, isn't it?' She was deliberately changing the subject, trying to get things back to normal.

'Yeah. We're meeting at the pizza place at seven.'

'Why won't you let him see her on their own?'

Sasha put down her coffee so heavily that some of it sloshed over the side of the bowl and on to the weathered wooden table. 'I've told you before. He's violent. And he's a thief. He's not to be trusted.'

★ ★ ★

All the way home, Hannah kept thinking about the coincidence that both Dan and Sasha should use the same phrase — that the other was not to be trusted. Impossible to believe that just weeks ago they were living together, sleeping in the same bed.

Back in her flat, she struggled to concentrate. The conversation with Sasha had unnerved her, not to mention the ugly red cut in Sasha's childlike arm. She tried to focus on her article, on what pay-off she could use to end it, but nothing came. Instead her head was full of Sasha and Dan and Sienna — and the thing hidden away in the back of her wardrobe.

She should leave it alone. She should just forget about it. But once she'd let it into her mind, she couldn't get rid of it.

Abandoning the dining table, she made her way through the hallway and into the bedroom she and Josh shared at the rear of the flat. Once it would have been a dining room — in the days before the houses were all carved up into poky, badly soundproofed conversions. There was a big window looking out on to their section of garden and a plain cast-iron fireplace through which a pigeon had fallen the winter before last, arriving dazed and sheepish in the grate. Hannah didn't look at the bed, with its white duvet cover and four white pillows. She was always trying to re-create the beds in the Sunday supplements with their plumped-up covers and scattering of welcoming cushions and throws, but instead the duvet was bunched up at one end, leaving the other end limp and flat like an empty sac, and the pillowcase on Josh's side had a faint yellowish stain in the middle. By her side of the bed was a teetering pile of books, some abandoned halfway through, others long since finished but unable to be accommodated on the already over-stuffed shelves.

She opened the door of the old pine wardrobe, taken aback as always by the jumble of clothes and shoes and bags and general junk that was crammed inside. Where was it that other people, with their lovely minimalist flats, managed to store old bottles of suntan lotion and beach towels and winter hats and scarves?

Feeling around behind a box of photographs, she withdrew the small plastic bag. Kneeling on the floor with the bag in her hand, something unpleasant and bitter came up inside her and jumped clear into her throat. She fought it down.

Clutching the bag to her chest, she crossed the hallway with purpose into the bathroom, bolting

234

the door behind her, even though she was alone in the flat.

The bathroom was the one room they'd never got around to decorating. Long and narrow, with a bath running along the side and a sink crammed down the far end, it resembled a dingy corridor and normally she couldn't go in there without feeling depressed. Now she sat down, oblivious, on the toilet and took out the package from its plastic bag. She and Josh had had sex just once in the last four months, after that night out with Sasha, and though she'd been far too drunk to think clearly about contraception it had been nearly time for her next period so she'd assumed it was safe. But her period had never come. For days, weeks even, she'd been ignoring the tenderness in her breasts and the great weariness that made her limbs feel leaden and her bed so inviting at two or three in the afternoon. She couldn't have another baby. Everything was so weird at the moment. Things weren't right between her and Josh. They didn't have enough money. She needed to keep working. Lily was still such a baby herself. Sure, they'd talked about giving their daughter a brother or sister, but only in abstract terms. Not as an actual thing. Not now.

If not now, when? The phrase came back to her as she held the white plastic stick in her hand and stared at the window, watching with a growing feeling of nausea as the blue line worked its way slowly across, as she'd known, deep down, it would.

The sound of her stupid birdsong ringtone

caught her by surprise. Stick in hand, she burst out of the bathroom. Picking up her phone from the dining table, her heart still hammering from shock, she was surprised to see Dan's name flashing up. Dan always rang Josh, that was the way it worked, and Sasha rang her. She supposed that was just one more thing that would be different from now on.

'Why didn't you tell me?'

For one surreal moment Hannah thought he was talking about the baby, and stared at the plastic stick as if it might turn out to have supernatural powers.

'Tell you what?'

'That Sasha has lost her fucking mind. That she's on mega doses of happy pills?'

'I didn't think I needed to.'

Hannah couldn't understand where this sudden outburst had come from.

'Don't give me that, Hannah. That woman is in sole charge of my daughter. She's been acting totally fucking insane lately — the spying, the keying of the car, the smashing of the window. Don't tell me that's normal. And now I find out she's sufficiently nuts to be put on major medication — and no one thought that maybe I had the right to know?'

Hannah's head was churning. She hadn't even started to absorb the shock of the baby thing, and now here she was being harangued about something that wasn't anything to do with her. She thought about the angry red cut on Sasha's arm and doubt wound itself like wire around her heart. Could she really be putting September at

236

risk by remaining loyal to Sasha?

'Who told you?' Her voice was uncharacteristically combative to mask the doubt.

'What does it matter?'

'I think Sasha deserves to know who has been passing on private information.' How prissy she sounded. How prim. 'Have you stopped to think it might be someone with an axe to grind? Sasha's a bit like Marmite — you know that. People either love her or hate her.'

'It wasn't like that. I found out from Josh.'

Hannah fell silent.

'Don't be so shocked. We do speak to each other. And email too. At least one person believes fathers should have rights, at least one person has got September's best interests at heart. Hannah, if Sasha is having some sort of nervous breakdown, don't you think I need to know about it?'

'She's not having a breakdown.' Hannah, her emotions already churned up by the pregnancy test, felt herself quivering with rage. 'She's just trying to cope with having been thrown to the kerb by her own husband. Dumped for a younger model — literally, in this case — the oldest story in the book. You have no right to use this against her, Dan. And Josh had no right to tell you.'

'I have every right. My daughter needs a stable home life. I'm going to go for full custody.'

Hannah was so surprised that for a moment she doubted she had heard correctly. 'What? You can't. Where would September live? In your little love nest with you and Sienna?'

'No. She can stay in the house for now. She needs stability and consistency. I'll move back there. I fucking pay enough for it. And Sasha can rent a place nearby until she sorts herself out and becomes a fit mother again.'

Hannah shook her head. Dan was totally unlike his normal, laid-back self. He seemed almost possessed. 'I don't want to talk to you about this any longer, Dan,' she said, trying to force her voice to be neutral. 'It challenges . . . my integrity.'

'Your *integrity*?' Dan barked. 'Tell you what, Hannah. If anything happens to September because you withhold information I need to know in order to protect my daughter, I'm holding you and your integrity responsible.'

After the phone went dead, Hannah remained at the table, fighting a wave of nausea that came out of nowhere. What was happening to her life? A few months ago, everything had seemed so . . . under control. Sure, she and Josh had had their differences, but they were manageable, predictable even for pressurized working parents of a young child. But recently she seemed to exist in a permanent state of tension, out of sync with everyone, including her own husband. And now there was to be a baby.

Hannah put her head in her hands and cried until the tears and snot formed a mask that dried on her face.

And then she cried some more.

Lucie/Eloise, aged thirteen

Maman came to school today for the prizegiving. I was so excited because the prize for All-Round Excellence is pretty much the biggest deal EVER and Juliette said her parents would literally drop dead from pride if she ever won anything like that. And at first it was great. Maman looked amazing and Binky from the year above actually asked if she was on telly because she thought she'd seen her in Casualty or something. And Daddy was so pleased with me. And we all had lunch in the dining room and Maman was being very funny and had lots more silly English phrases that she'd learned from her book. Like Lickety-split. And we kept saying 'Lickety-split' and laughing and laughing. And I could see the other girls were looking at me and wishing they had parents like mine and my heart was just EXPLODING, but at the same time I couldn't eat because my tummy was churning like something bad was about to happen. And later on, when Mrs Winn-Parry gave the speech to introduce my prize and said, 'This is for Lucie, or as she's known to us in our Archminster family, Eloise,' I knew what that something bad was. I was sitting on the stage in a row of chairs with the other prizewinners and I heard the scream and I stayed in my chair as if my bum had been superglued to it while there was a big commotion in the audience. And when Mrs Winn-Parry started talking again and gave me my prize, I didn't look at the empty seats where Maman and Daddy had been sitting. I already knew they were long gone. Lickety-split.

19

Josh gazed at the white plastic stick on the table as if it might turn out to be some sort of trick. While he gazed, neither of them spoke, their silence a concrete presence in the room. He reached out and picked it up, turning it over in his hands as if looking for some other meaning.

'You're not going to find any answers hidden on the back, you know.' Hannah snatched it back from him and threw it to the other end of the table. 'Well?' she said.

Shock had wiped Josh's mind clean. He blinked at her, opening his mouth and then closing it again when he realized there were no words to come out.

'I knew it. It's a disaster, isn't it?'

Josh now became conscious of thoughts returning to his brain as if back from a minibreak. He probed them cautiously. Another baby. How did he feel? Slowly the thoughts took shape and he was astounded to find he felt . . . *ecstatic*.

Let Pat Hennessey keep the promotion, let Dan keep his gorgeous new girlfriend. This would show them both. Josh had what they didn't. He was virile, dynamic, the founder of a dynasty. Babies were something Josh could do. They were something he was good at. And a new baby would sort out whatever had been going wrong between him and Hannah. He wouldn't need to worry about her going off him — or secretly lusting after Dan. A new baby, he couldn't help but feel, would restore him to himself. It was something clean and pure to counterbalance that ugly business at school.

He got up and walked around the table so he could put his arms around Hannah. 'I'm thrilled,' he whispered. For a moment, she slumped into him and they swayed together wordlessly. Then she pulled away.

'We can't afford it,' she said flatly.

'Sod the money.'

Hannah made a strange noise then, halfway between a sob and a snort, and Josh tried to pull her back towards him.

'We'll make it work. I'll look for another job if you want, with more money. Come on, Hannah. We never wanted Lily to be an only child, and isn't it better to do this now, while they can still play together and enjoy each other? Can you imagine how excited Lily is going to be?'

Hannah nodded slowly. Lily had been begging them for a little brother or sister practically from as soon as she learned to talk. She and September were always pretending to be sisters, desperate for entry into what they fondly imagined to be a twenty-four-hour-a-day sleepover-and-midnight-feast club. 'We're like you and Auntie Gemma,' Lily would tell Hannah happily as she and September were tucked up into her single bed.

'I just can't help feeling it's the wrong time though,' Hannah said. 'Not just the money, but also this thing with Sasha and Dan, which — thanks to you — has just got a lot worse!'

Josh sighed. They'd been through all this. He'd acknowledged he shouldn't have told Dan about the happy pills. He'd tacked it on the end of an email when he'd been feeling particularly fed up with Sasha. He hadn't thought it through. He didn't know how many times he could say sorry.

'We've become way too caught up in their shit, and it's not been healthy,' he said. 'This is something that's just about us — about our little family. It'll help us get a little bit of distance, re-prioritize.'

Hannah nodded again, but still she didn't seem convinced, and later that night when he snuggled up to her in bed and laid the flat of his hand on her gently rounded belly, he could have sworn that, just for a second, she flinched.

★　★　★

'It's the last fucking straw. I'm not kidding, Josh. This is it. I'm finished with being Mr Nice Guy.'

Dan's face was so disfigured by his outrage that, for the first time, Josh wondered whether his friend might actually be quite ugly. They were, once more, at the odious gym café, but Dan was a long way from his normal relaxed self. His shoulder-length hair looked unwashed and slightly greasy in the bright downlighters, and the shadows under his eyes were the colour of red onion.

'It's got to be crossed wires, Dan. Sasha wouldn't do that to September deliberately.'

'Know what? I'm beginning to realize there's nothing Sasha wouldn't do. She told me seven

243

o'clock. I wrote it down. I've been looking forward to it all week.'

'Well, maybe she got her times mixed up.'

'She did it on purpose, Josh. She deliberately got there an hour early, just to make me look bad, and then left before I arrived. How do you think it feels getting a voicemail from your daughter, crying hysterically because she thinks you stood her up? I was in the car, on my way to meet them. At the time we'd agreed.'

'Didn't you try to go round to sort it out?'

'Course I did. Sasha refused to come to the door. I completely lost it, shouting through the letterbox. I think I even threatened to kill her. Then she sent me a text saying I'd upset our daughter enough for one day, and if I didn't go away she'd call the police and tell them what I'd said.'

Indignation caused Dan's voice to rise until he was almost shouting, and the woman sitting on the table behind him turned around to frown.

Josh felt his skin prickling with irritation. He'd only agreed to meet Dan here because he couldn't wait to share his news, and now Dan had hijacked the whole thing with yet more vitriol about Sasha.

'Well, like I said, it's the last straw. I've already called my lawyers about this, and they're going to take her to the fucking cleaners.'

'Lawyers? What lawyers?'

Josh was sure he hadn't heard Dan mention lawyers before. In fact, last thing he knew, Dan was still hoping Sasha would change her mind about mediation and there wouldn't be any need

244

for lawyers. Hadn't he talked about the most amicable divorce in history?

'Piers Butler. Sienna put me on to him. He's a fucking Rottweiler.'

'But do you really think — '

'Look, I've tried to play fair, but now she's started using September as a pawn, fairness has gone out of the window. I've got to do what's best for my daughter.'

Dan had a glass of something green in front of him that looked like the stuff that came out of Toby's mouth when he'd eaten too much grass. Josh took a sip of his coffee and tried not to look at it.

'Anyway,' Dan went on after a short silence, 'that's enough about me. What did you want to talk about? Your text said you had news.'

Josh hesitated.

'Hannah's pregnant,' he said. 'We're having another baby!'

Dan's mouth froze, his lips ringed with green sludge. *Yes*, thought Josh jubilantly. *Gotcha*. All that gut-twisting speculation about Dan's sex life with Sienna, the feelings of inferiority. Well, now he had something better. A family. Stability.

Josh watched as the news sank in and a smile slowly spread over the other man's face, until it looked as if it would burst clean off his cheeks.

'That's fantastic. So pleased for you both.'

Still that smile, stretching his skin clingfilm tight. *No*, thought Josh, before he'd even recognized what the smile meant. *Don't let him say it*.

'I've got to tell you something.'

245

No, no, no, no, no.

'We weren't going to say anything, but I can't keep it secret now.'

No, no, no, no, no.

'Sienna's pregnant too! Isn't that the weirdest thing? We're going to be new dads together!'

'Yeah, that is weird. But isn't it a bit soon?' Josh knew he should try to sound more enthusiastic, but he could hardly speak.

Dan was nodding, even before Josh had finished his question. 'We didn't plan it. It's a total fluke. Sienna was on the pill, but she was doing these all-night shoots and someone gave her this stuff — you can only get it on prescription in the States, apparently — that makes you stay awake, and she took it for a few days. And only after she got pregnant did she find out it totally reacts with the pill. She's going to make the most fantastic mum. I can't wait. Just think, Josh, our babies can grow up together just like September and Lily.'

Josh struggled to find something to say. 'Who'd have thought it, eh?'

Dan suddenly looked serious. 'Listen, mate. I'm sure I don't need to tell you that I don't want Sasha finding out. I'll tell her and September when the time's right. But now you can see how important it is that I push the divorce through as soon as possible, and sort out money and custody and all that.'

'And you really intend to take the house and September? Don't you know what that'll do to Sasha?'

'Just in the short term, until everything gets

246

sorted and Sasha gets her head together. Of course I'm going to make sure she's well looked after in the long term, but for now September needs stability, and it'll be good for us all to get used to living together as a family, especially now there's a baby on the way.'

Josh couldn't believe what he was hearing. What kind of rock had Dan been living under that he really believed he could just slot Sienna into Sasha's place without messing up his daughter for life?

'Look.' Dan leaned across the table to put a hand on Josh's arm. Josh froze, muscles tensed, feeling his skin itch where Dan touched it. 'I know Sasha is a good mum, or at least she has been up until now. But she's not herself, and frankly I'm afraid of what she might do. Of course I feel guilty as fuck about what's happened to her, but I need to look after my daughter. That has to be my priority.'

Dan was saying all this as though if he could just explain things properly, Josh would agree that he was right, that everything he was saying was reasonable. When Josh didn't reply, he sat back, nodding to himself, clearly taking the silence as tacit endorsement.

'You know,' he said after a while, 'I still can't get over this joint pregnancy. Sometimes the world is in-fucking-sane.'

Josh stared long and hard at the disgusting green mulch in Dan's glass.

In-fucking-sane.

★   ★   ★

247

Hannah had agreed to wait until Josh got home before they broke the news to Lily about the baby. They both knew it was still early days, but Hannah had sailed through the first pregnancy and Lily could really do with a lift. She'd seemed so down recently. All day at school, he'd been thinking about the look on Lily's face when they told her and having to stifle a smile, but by the time he came through the door his pleasure had dissipated, leaving only a lingering, stale taste.

Trust Dan to ruin it. Did he have to compete on everything?

When he walked into the living room, Lily hurled herself at his legs.

'Daddy! I made an angel in school and Mrs 'Kenzie said it was the best angel and can we get a puppy 'cos I think Toby is sad because he has nobody to play with?'

Hannah, sitting at the table with one of Lily's reading books open in front of her, shrugged. She looked tired, Josh thought. Her lovely hair was scraped back and knotted on the top of her head with a rubber band, giving her face a vulnerable, exposed look. Her shoulders slumped as if weights were resting on them. If she'd just wear something other than that old black jumper all the time, she might not look so peaky.

'You OK?'

'Yeah, fine,' she said, in a voice that suggested she wasn't fine at all. 'You?'

'Good. Well, I was until I stopped off for a coffee with a certain person at a certain gym not far from here.'

Her eyebrows shot up. 'And?'

248

He sighed. 'I'll tell you about it later.'

Hannah had made pasta with tomato sauce again. Josh tried not to mind. It wasn't as if Lily was the most adventurous eater in the world. They were both constrained in what they cooked by her conservative palate. But it would be so nice to have something different — just for a change.

Once the food had been served up and they were sitting down, Hannah took a deep breath. 'Lily, Daddy and I have something very important to talk to you about.'

Lily's round blue eyes flicked between the two of them and something jolted painfully in Josh when he recognized the fear in them.

'I don't want Daddy to move away,' she said, her bottom lip trembling. 'I don't want you to be 'vorced like 'Tember's mummy and daddy.'

'Oh, darling.' Hannah got up and threw her arms around their daughter. 'Daddy and I aren't getting divorced, I promise you. This is nice news. Exciting news.'

She glanced at Josh over the top of Lily's head, and he nodded encouragingly before getting up and coming round to kneel in front of Lily's chair.

'What do you want most in the world, Lily?'

She thought carefully, her blue eyes cloudy with the effort of it.

'A Baby Born?' she said hopefully, naming a doll Hannah had always refused to buy.

'No,' Hannah smiled. 'Much better than a Baby Born.'

Lily looked at her wonderingly. 'It's not a

puppy though, is it?' she said, every word sending the message *Please let it be a puppy*.

Hannah shook her head. 'Darling girl, you're going to have a little brother or a sister.'

Lily's eyes seemed to grow bigger, like a cartoon character's. Josh felt a dissolving somewhere at the heart of him as he watched the news sink in, the smile spreading like sunlight across his daughter's face. He felt a weight lift off him and was hit by a sudden conviction that things would turn out all right.

But first he had to tell Hannah about the conversation with Dan.

* * *

'You are joking. Tell me you're joking.'

They'd only just managed to get Lily to bed after a long, protracted bedtime where she'd made them promise again and again that she could help choose the baby's name and when it was old enough it could sleep in her bed. Now Hannah, who a minute ago had looked like she was asleep on her feet, was sitting bolt upright on the end of the sofa, staring at him.

'I know. Crazy, isn't it? I don't think he meant to tell me, he just blurted it out when I told him our news.'

'Which I wish you hadn't. I haven't even told Sasha yet. Couldn't think of how to broach it. Shit, Josh. I don't believe it. What's Sienna doing getting pregnant by a married man who's old enough to be her father?'

'Oh, come on. That's a bit much. And they

250

didn't intend to. You see, Sienna was taking these pills and — '

'What a bastard! What an utter bastard! This is going to destroy Sasha.'

'Yes, well, you can't tell her. You must promise, OK?'

Hannah said nothing, just continued gazing at Josh without seeing him, shaking her head softly from side to side.

'Hans? We have to stay out of this now. We've let ourselves get far too drawn into Dan and Sasha's stuff,' he said. 'This is where we have to lay down a bit of distance. You've got to start focusing on yourself now. Surely there are other friends who can rally round to give Sasha some support. Other mums at school?'

Hannah slowly shook her head. 'You know what Sasha's like. She always said she wasn't a woman's woman and she's right. The other mums don't really get her. And she doesn't seem to have many other friends. I think the people they hung out with tended mostly to be people who knew Dan.'

'You're going to have to pull back, Hannah. It's not healthy. For you, I mean. And I wouldn't mind having a break from Dan as well. How about we go up to see my parents again next weekend and break the news? They'll be made up.'

'Your parents? We've only just been up there. How about we go and see *my* family for a change. It's been ages since I visited Mum.'

Josh swallowed. 'Do you really think you're up to it?'

'Course I'm up to it. She's my mum.'

'OK, whatever you like.'

Later, Josh lay next to Hannah in the dark, listening to the sounds of her sleeping, the little snuffling noises she made just before she changed position that never failed to move him. He tried to think himself back to how he'd felt earlier, when he'd been so sure of the inviolability of their little unit, to that sense of well-being he'd experienced for the first time in weeks. But it eluded him, and in the end he fell asleep thinking of the forthcoming visit to Hannah's mother and wishing there was something, anything, he could do to stop it happening.

20

'I came as quickly as I could. Where is she? How is she?'

Hannah was so out of breath the words tore from her in great painful bursts. She'd run all the way to the school, cursing herself the whole way for allowing herself to get so out of condition. She would start jogging. Everyone was doing it these days.

'Please don't worry yourself, Mrs Hetherington, Lily's fine now, playing in the sandpit, happy as a . . . well, a sandboy!'

'But you said she was hurt.'

Mrs Mackenzie breathed in heavily as if weighing up her words. Her eyes seemed to be drawn to Hannah's clothes and, following the direction of her gaze, Hannah was mortified to see she'd come out in what she'd been wearing when she got the call — namely her nightdress, night T-shirt really, over an old pair of jeans, with one of Josh's fleece-lined hoodies pulled over the top. She hastily pulled the bottom edges of the hoodie together and zipped it up.

'There's been an *incident.*'

'What kind of incident? What's happened?'

'It's nothing to get concerned about. It involved Lily and September. September . . . well, perhaps you'd better see for yourself.'

Hannah's heart was hammering under her T-shirt as they made their way into the play corner of the nursery. There she was. How little she looked, standing there on her own, concentrating on pouring sand from a small bucket to a larger one, the tip of her pink tongue protruding from between her lips.

'Liliput? Darling?'

'Mummy!'

Lily ran to Hannah and flung her arms around her, burying her face in her mother's dirty jeans.

'Lil? Are you all right? Let's look at you.'

Hannah crouched down in front of her daughter, taking in her swollen red face and pink-tinged eyes.

Mrs Mackenzie bent down too. 'Lily,' she said gently. 'Do you want to show Mummy your poorly arm?'

Lily looked stricken, but she nodded very deeply and very solemnly.

Mrs Mackenzie took hold of Lily's pink cardigan and carefully slid the left sleeve off. Underneath she was wearing her favourite T-shirt with the yellow and orange flowers. Mrs Mackenzie turned Lily away from Hannah, and Hannah let out a gasp of horror. There, in the sweet pink flesh of Lily's upper arm, just above her plump elbow, was a perfect purple bite mark.

'It looks worse than it is, Mrs Hetherington. The nurse from the big school has had a look at it and luckily the skin isn't broken, though there's obviously some bruising. She doesn't think there's any need to take her to hospital, though that's completely up to you.'

Hannah pulled her daughter to her, almost crushing her in a sudden need to feel that warm little body safe in her arms. When she finally pulled away, Mrs Mackenzie was gazing at them, her head to one side, her eyes full of sympathy.

'Are you all right to play here for a few minutes longer, Lily, while I just talk to Mummy in the quiet room?'

Lily nodded, stepping obediently back to the sandpit.

Back in the other room, which was really little more than a corridor, with one side devoted to coat pegs, each marked by a different sticker, Mrs Mackenzie filled Hannah in. There had been some tension between the girls in the last few weeks, September becoming overpossessive and Lily seeming nervous. But today they seemed to have been playing fine.

'Lily was so happy,' Mrs Mackenzie reported. 'She told the whole class she was going to have a new brother or sister.'

Hannah felt herself blushing.

'She and September were in the dressing-up area, where there's the castle where they play kings and queens. They both disappeared in there, which they do all the time. And the next thing, there was this scream, and Lily came out with that on her arm. September has been taken home by her mother, and we called her father in, too. He'd already asked to be kept independently informed of everything that concerns his daughter. I gather the relationship between the parents is a wee bit strained at the moment.'

'Sasha told you that?'

Mrs Mackenzie shook her head vigorously, setting her black curls trembling. 'Not Mrs

Fisher, no. Mr Fisher was the one who let us know. And he came in today, with his new friend. After September had gone home, of course.'

'His new friend? You can't mean he brought her here?'

Mrs Mackenzie pressed her lips together discreetly. 'Like I said, September wasn't on the premises, so there was never any question of any awkward meetings. I imagine he just wanted the support.'

Hannah was conscious that her mouth was still hanging open, but she was struggling to take this in. Could Dan really be so insensitive? Did he imagine that now Sienna was pregnant, they could present themselves at school as a new family unit and no one would object? Josh was absolutely right. They needed to distance themselves from Sasha and Dan. Not only for their sake, but clearly for Lily's as well.

On the way home, she held Lily's hand so tightly the little girl eventually wriggled her hand loose. 'Ouch, Mummy,' she scolded. 'That's too hard.'

As they walked, she could feel her phone vibrating inside the pocket of the hoodie she was wearing. *Sasha*, said the caller display. She put it back. Almost immediately it started vibrating again. She ignored it.

Back in the flat, Lily was unusually clingy, asking Hannah to cut up her food for her and even feed her — something she hadn't done for a while.

'Were you and September fighting?' Hannah asked her. 'Was that why she bit you?'

Lily fixed her round blue eyes on her mother and shook her head.

'But September must have been cross about something.'

Again Lily shook her head. Afterwards she lay on her bed listening to a CD of her favourite story, and fell asleep with her thumb in her mouth.

By this time, Sasha had left more than ten messages.

'What shall I do?' Hannah asked a shocked Josh, when she finally got through to him between classes and explained what had happened.

'Call her back, but be firm, no matter how much she grovels. Tell her the girls need a break from each other. And so do we. We're not blaming her, or September, but we need to step back.'

Afterwards, Hannah knelt on the floor of Lily's bedroom for a long time, watching her sleeping. Then she took a deep breath and picked up the phone.

'Finally!' Sasha didn't sound like someone about to grovel. If anything her tone was combative. 'I've been calling you all day!'

'Yes, well, I've been busy. Lily has been very upset, as you can imagine.'

'That's what I wanted to talk to you about. How is Lil? Hope she's over it now.'

When Hannah finally responded, her voice cracked with indignation. 'Over it? Sasha, did you see Lily's arm?'

Sasha made a noise that sounded dangerously

dismissive. 'Oh, it was just a little bruise, that's all. You know how Lily likes to play up an injury. Remember how she was when she had that MMR vaccine. You'd have thought the nurse was trying to kill her!'

Hannah's fingers gripped the phone so tightly she wondered it didn't shatter into millions of tiny pieces. *Shut up*, she urged Sasha silently. *Be quiet now*.

Sasha, clearly failing to intuit what Hannah was telling her, continued, 'But what I really want to talk about is how we're going to tackle the issue of why September reacted how she did.'

'What do you mean?'

Hannah's words were shards of glass, sharp enough to sever an artery, sharp enough to rip open the scab on Sasha's arm.

'What I mean, Hannah, is that September would never have done what she did if Lily hadn't been taunting her about having a new baby sister or brother. Lily knows September has just seen her own family ripped apart, she didn't need to rub her nose in it, telling her she'll never have a brother or sister because her daddy doesn't love her or her mummy any more.'

'Lily would *never* say anything like that!'

'Hannah, Lily's no angel, as you well know. None of them are. I'm not *blaming* her, I'm just saying it would have been so much better if you'd told me you were pregnant first, so that we could have agreed a strategy for the girls.'

'I don't *fucking* believe you!' Hannah was so choked up with bile, she could hardly get the words out. 'How dare you criticize my daughter,

258

when she's lying here with your daughter's teeth marks in her arm? She could have been scarred for life.'

'Oh, don't be so ridiculous, Hannah.'

'This conversation is over, Sasha. If it goes on any longer, we'll both say things we regret. I think the best thing is that we take a breather from each other. You and September and Dan have things you need to sort out by yourselves. And me and Josh and Lily need time to get used to the idea of a new baby, and really solidify our family unit.'

Did she use that phrase deliberately? Because she knew it would cause the maximum hurt? Well, good. For a moment she savoured a vicious stab of triumph, visualizing Sasha's stricken expression, September's crumpled face.

'I'm sorry, Sash,' she said, and her voice was softer now. 'I know you're going through hell at the moment, but I need to concentrate on my f — On things at home.'

She pressed the End Call button gently, hoping Sasha would somehow be able to tell that she hadn't cut her off in anger. Then she went to look once more at her sleeping daughter, her sandy lashes resting on the still-rounded curve of her cheek, her thumb firmly clamped in her mouth. Could Lily really have said those things to September? Might she be just another blinkered parent, unwilling to admit that her child was capable of wrongdoing? Suddenly Hannah felt swamped by a crushing tiredness. She picked up the edge of the blanket covering Lily and slid in underneath, curling herself

259

around her sleeping child. Then, with one hand over her belly, where, incredibly, new life was stirring, whether or not she wanted it to, and the other arm wrapped around her daughter, she too fell asleep.

* * *

She woke to the sound of the doorbell. A long, persistent buzzing, as if someone was leaning against the bell. Outside the window, the sky was caught in that no man's land of an English late-autumn afternoon where the greyness of the incoming night met the greyness of the outgoing day and it could be any time at all.

To her surprise, she heard Josh talking into the intercom. She hadn't even heard him come home. She sat up, trying not to wake Lily, and made her way out of the bedroom.

She could hear raised voices in the communal hallway. 'You can't,' she heard Josh say loudly. Then a woman shouting. Seconds later, Sasha burst through the door, closely followed by Josh. Her skin was sallow in the gloomy half-light, her eyes huge and wild in her shrunken face, and her chest was juddering as if there was some living thing loose in there, slamming itself against the ribcage, desperate to be free.

'Someone tried to kill me!'

'For heaven's sake!' Beyond exasperated, Hannah put a hand on Sasha's shoulder and steered her roughly into the living room, where she was less likely to wake Lily.

'Hannah, I'm not joking. Look!' Sasha wrested

off her coat and threw it to the floor before rolling up the leg of her jeans, revealing a distinct red mark on her tiny calf at least five inches long, which was already starting to bruise. Hannah couldn't help noticing that, breakdown or no breakdown, Sasha had had time to wax her legs.

'I was in Brent Cross. I'd gone to start Christmas shopping and because I was so upset about the argument with you, and the thing with the girls. I left September with Katia. She wanted to come with me, but I told her it was her punishment for what she'd done to Lily.'

Sasha shot a sly glance at Hannah, as if seeking approval, but Hannah didn't react.

'All the time I was there, I felt like someone was watching me. You know that creepy feeling you get sometimes? There was this one time I was in Gap — you know that bit where the knickers are? — and I swear to God there was someone right behind me, kind of breathing on to my neck. I was so freaked out I just froze, and by the time I turned round they'd gone.

'I was going down those escalators — the ones outside Marks and Spencer — and the next thing I knew . . . ' Sasha stopped to gulp down a sob. 'The next thing I knew, I felt this shove from behind and I went tumbling down. If there hadn't been a man a few steps further down who broke my fall, I'd have gone right to the bottom. Hannah, I thought I was going to die. You know how they say your whole life passes through your head? Well, the only thing going through mine was *Brent Cross? Really? I'm going to die in Brent Cross?*'

261

She was trying to smile, but tears were leaking from her eyes.

'But there must have been loads of people around.' Trust Josh to get straight down to practicalities. 'If you'd been pushed someone would have seen something.'

'That's precisely it,' Sasha said. 'The place was packed, and after I fell it was just pandemonium. Can you imagine? At the top I'd pushed in front of a group of women who looked like they were on some sort of wedding mission — to pick bridesmaids' dresses or something. They were moving so slowly, I made sure I nipped on to the escalator ahead of them. There was only that one man ahead of me and when I fell I knocked him over and we both lay at the bottom with a crowd around us. Whoever did it would have been able to just saunter away. And apparently no one noticed who was directly behind me.'

'Maybe someone just accidentally bumped into you.'

Josh had his teacher's voice on, Hannah recognized.

'No, Josh. I was there, it wasn't an accident.' Sasha's voice caught.

'And this 'someone' who tried to kill you. I'm guessing you think it's Dan?'

Sasha glared at Josh as if calling his bluff. 'How many other people have threatened to kill me recently?'

'And you told the police, I take it?' Hannah kept her voice neutral. She was still furious with Sasha over what she'd said about Lily earlier, but on the other hand her friend was clearly distressed.

'I told the security guards,' Sasha said. 'They wanted me to wait until the police arrived, but I just wanted to come home. They took a statement though, and they said they're going to look at the CCTV footage, so maybe they'll catch someone.'

Hannah glanced over at Josh to see what he was making of it all. Their eyes met, and he gave a slight, almost imperceptible shake of the head.

'I think I'd better take you home, Sasha,' he said gently.

'But I don't want to go home. I'm scared.'

'You must go home, for September's sake,' said Hannah. 'Today can't have been easy for her either.'

'Let's not get into that again, please,' Sasha begged. 'The school totally overreacted. You know what they're like.'

Hannah dug her nails into her palm and forced herself to take a deep breath.

'I'm taking you home, Sasha,' Josh repeated, and this time there was no hint of a question.

'Hans?' Sasha appealed directly to Hannah now. 'You've got to help me. I feel like I'm going crazy. Someone pushed me on that escalator, I swear. Please believe me.'

Hannah dropped her gaze. 'Sasha, I'm sorry, but I'm really tired. It's been an emotional day. Why don't you go home and be with September? I'll call you when I've had a bit of time to think about things. Maybe after we've been away.'

'Away?'

'We're going to Oxford for a couple of days. At the end of next week, probably. To tell my mum about the baby.'

Sasha stared at her as if she'd been slapped. 'Why are you doing this?' she said. 'Why are you cutting me out? Is it because I'm not a family any more? Am I no use to you now I'm not part of a cosy couple?'

'Let's go, Sasha.' Josh put a hand under Sasha's elbow and manoeuvred her out through the door, picking up her coat as they went.

Hannah listened as Sasha's sobs outside the window grew fainter and then died away altogether.

Then she listened to the silence.

Eloise, aged fifteen

Daddy's funeral is the first time I've seen Maman in nearly two years. I can't believe I ever used to think her beautiful. Her skin is yellow and seems to have shrivelled up, wrapping itself around her bones like old clingfilm. One of Juliette's dogs got ill last summer and its eyes were covered over in a disgusting kind of milky stuff and that's what Maman's are like, too. Like she is staring out through a film of cack. Auntie Valerie and Uncle Michel are with her, supporting her between them as if she were made of glass. Fiona and Hugh, Juliette's mum and dad, dropped me off at the church. They've been so nice to me — looking after me in the holidays and telling me to treat their house like my own home. Of course, you can never really feel at home in someone else's family. But it's good of them to say it. Sometimes I wonder what they would say if they found out what I'm really like — if they reached a hand deep inside me, inside Eloise, and scooped out a handful of Lucie instead.

Maman comes over and kisses me on both cheeks. Her lips feel dry, like toast. Juliette's older sister is on a raw-food diet and puts her food in a dehumidifier to take out all the water. I think Maman has been dehumidified, all her moisture sucked out. The service is long and dull. I wonder if Eloise will be mentioned, but the vicar only talks vaguely about 'family tragedies'.

Afterwards we go back to the house. I haven't been here in so long I've forgotten how it feels, even though it used to be home. Home is where the heart is, hey Maman? Daddy used to come to school to see me, or sometimes to Juliette's home. Twice we went away, just the two of us — once to Paris, once to Barcelona. Daddy didn't like talking about feelings. He once told me that's why they're called feelings, because you feel them, not because you speak them or hear them or see them. I think I know what he meant. He told me that what happened to Eloise sent something skew-whiff in Maman's brain. Well, not just that, but that was the thing that pushed her over the edge. The straw that broke the camel's back. He said she loved me really, but we both knew he was lying.

I sit at a table with Maman and Auntie Valerie and Uncle Michel and she asks me about my school and my life and which subjects I like, and every now and then she breaks off to talk in French with the others and it's so RUDE my blood BOILS (see, Maman, how good I've become at those clichéd British sayings you always loved?). She tells me I look well, but she doesn't quite look at me while she says it. Instead her eyes slide off my face as if it's made from ice.

I look at her, though. Her face is so thin it makes her blue eyes look huge, the irises round like water balloons. I imagine taking a pin and popping them.

266

21

The head had assured him he had everyone's support, but still as he walked about the school, Josh felt as if he was being judged. He'd stopped going into the staff room, imagining what the other teachers and admin staff might be thinking. *Mud sticks*, as his mother had often said. Most days now, he brought sandwiches to school, hastily prepared affairs soggy with mayo, and spent lunch-time at his desk in his form room as he was doing now, pretending to plan lessons but often just staring out of the window.

After his initial euphoria about the new baby, he now found himself beset by doubt. If Hannah had to take time off, the financial pressure would fall completely on him. Was he up to it? And what if the disciplinary hearing went against him? His insides turned to liquid as they always did when he thought about what had happened.

It was weeks now since he'd been called out of one of his classes and ushered in to see the head. The only other time he'd been summoned like this was to be told he hadn't got the Head of Department promotion, and for a wild moment he'd thought maybe the head was going to say he'd made a mistake and Josh really was the best candidate for the job. But when the head's PA wouldn't meet his eyes, he knew it was bad news.

'I'm sorry to tell you there's been an allegation made against you, Josh.' The head hadn't bothered with small talk. 'A very serious allegation.'

The head wasn't allowed to give him the details of the allegation, only to say it involved 'inappropriate behaviour'. Only later would he find out through the school grapevine that one of his Year Eleven pupils, Kelly Kavanagh, had accused him of 'touching' her while they were alone in the classroom between the end of one class and the start of the next. But even just the sketchy details the head was able to provide were enough to make him feel he might be sick, right there on the head's orderly desk.

Afterwards everyone had privately rallied around him. It was well known that Kelly Kavanagh would say anything for attention; she had form on making accusations against staff. There was that teaching assistant and the allegation of a slap around the face, the other staff members reminded him. Kelly had later withdrawn her allegation, but by then the teaching assistant had been so traumatized she'd had to go on long-term sick leave, and had never returned. Josh had had a recent run-in with Kelly over a test where he knew she'd copied her answers from the person in front, so she had clear motivation. He knew that was why the decision had been made not to suspend him while the investigation into the allegation was underway, although the head had warned him never to put himself in a position where he was on his own in a classroom with a pupil. But still,

268

there was always that faint chance, wasn't there, that he wouldn't be believed? Since the Jimmy Savile scandal, everyone was scared of missing something, scared of being the one who failed to listen.

Josh had been intending to tell Hannah about the allegation and the investigation for ages, but it had never been the right time. It seemed at the moment that she was perpetually disappointed in him. He longed to bring her some good news, something to make her proud of him the way she used to be, not more shit to heap on top of all the other shit that was going on. And now that she was pregnant, coming clean seemed more impossible still. He was supposed to be the provider, and yet all he was providing was yet more problems.

Weirdly, the only person he'd really confided in was Sienna. He hadn't intended to at all. He'd called Dan about football one evening, and Sienna had answered. Dan was at the gym and had left his phone on charge. Josh still couldn't quite work out how it had happened, but Sienna had been so easy to talk to, and suddenly he'd been telling her about what was going on — opening up to her in a way he wasn't able to do with his own wife. She had a way of listening without passing judgement as Hannah would have done, or trying to minimize what he was going through as Dan might have attempted.

'Hello, stranger.'

Pat Hennessey's ginger hair seemed more orange than ever today. Funny how other days it could seem almost blond. Unlike Hannah's, which was always red.

Josh was relieved to see him. It seemed like years since he'd talked to someone who wasn't having some sort of crisis. Pat was so reassuringly uncomplicated.

'I'm lying low, as you can see,' he admitted.

'Not because of that thing with Kelly Kavanagh, surely? You know none of us believes a word of it.'

Josh nodded. 'Thanks. I do know that, but it's still good to hear. It's just my own stupid paranoia. I hate this bit of the job. Plus we've got this situation going on at home where a couple we're very good friends with have split up and it's all got very messy very quickly and we're kind of caught in the middle, even Lily.'

He had a brief vision of Lily's arm, teethmarks stamped into the flesh like branding on a piece of steak.

'Ouch,' said Pat, who had by now come into the room and was leaning against a table at the front of the classroom. 'That's tough. The same thing happened when one of my sisters got divorced from the guy who'd been her childhood sweetheart. We'd all known him for years — he was like another brother to us. When they first split up we were all so sure we could stay friends with him, but you know, you can't reason with love, and you especially can't reason with love gone wrong.'

Josh sighed. 'The problem is, we're so involved now, it's proving really hard to extricate ourselves. We just wish — '

His sentence was interrupted by the sound of

270

his own ringtone. He'd switched his phone on for once at the beginning of the lunch break, just in case Hannah had been trying to call him. She'd been so down last night, hardly able to raise her head up when he'd come back through the door after taking Sasha home. Now that had been an awkward journey. Sasha had been hysterical, sobbing about how no one believed her and she had no one and she didn't understand why everyone had deserted her. He'd been so relieved when Katia came to the door of the house, he'd practically thrust Sasha at her and scuttled straight back to the car, calling something over his shoulder about needing to get back. When he'd arrived back home, desperate to talk over the bizarre events of the day, he'd found Hannah droop-headed and uncommunicative.

He snatched up his phone without looking at the caller display, mouthing 'Sorry' to Pat as he did so. But instead of Hannah's voice, it was Dan, in a belligerent mood.

'Right, Josh. This has gone too far now. First September and Lily have that set-to.' Josh winced. 'And now Sasha's fucking bitch of a solicitor has got on to my solicitor to say *her client* has been assaulted and is considering pressing charges. Against *me!* She has totally lost it now, and I can't stand by and see September suffer any more. I need you and Hannah to make a written statement for my lawyer.'

'What?' Josh glanced up and was startled to meet Pat Hennessey's eyes. He hadn't realized the other man was still in the room. He put his hand over his phone and angled it away from his mouth. 'Sorry, Pat,' he whispered. 'This is going to take a while.'

The other man blushed, turning the skin around his freckles pink. 'No problem,' he mouthed, heading for the door with a brief wave.

Josh felt a tug of guilt. He liked Pat, but it seemed as if he was constantly turning him away. He turned back to the phone. 'What do you mean, written statement? Written statement saying what?'

'What do you think? That Sasha is unfit to be in charge of a young child. Just the stuff you already said in that email where you told me about the happy pills. I'm not asking you to lie, just tell the truth about what's been going on. I need written evidence so that I can start looking after September properly. Come on, you know it's the right thing to do. How would you feel if it was Hannah out of control and Lily at risk?'

But Josh couldn't imagine Hannah out of control, although he couldn't say that to Dan. His stomach felt tight and uncomfortable. He wished he'd checked who was calling before taking the call.

'We can't put anything in writing,' he said, and his added *mate* sounded contrived and false — which it was. 'We told you right at the start that we wouldn't take sides.'

'Yes, but that was before. Look, Josh, you have to help me. I'd do it for you in a heartbeat.'

The tightness in his stomach worsened. There was something in Dan's voice he didn't like, a

272

kind of wildness or desperation he hadn't heard before.

'I can't, Dan. You're putting me in an impossible position. I want to help you, but I just can't.'

There was a silence then. The kind of loaded silence that makes you dig your fingers into the palms of your hands and pray for it to be over.

'Thanks, Josh. Thanks a lot.'

'Look, I'm sorry.'

'Yeah, sure. We're all fucking sorry.'

After the phone clicked off, Josh sat with it in his hand, until the Year Tens started trickling in for afternoon registration.

'You trying to hatch that, Sir?' asked Jake Eldridge.

Josh swallowed hard and got on with the afternoon.

★   ★   ★

When Josh got home, Hannah was finally in the mood to talk. She was sitting at the table sorting through Lily's school bag, which she did every Friday. Amazing the amount of stuff one small girl could accumulate over the course of a week — drawings on rough paper with printed writing on the back, collages made from dried pasta covered with glitter and glue, notes from the nursery staff about the upcoming inset day. While she sifted through, Hannah quizzed him about what he thought of Sasha's bizarre claims yesterday. Josh was surprised to find he'd almost forgotten about the whole escalator story.

273

'It's typical Sasha,' he said. 'She couldn't deal with the fact that someone else was in the limelight for once, that it wasn't all about her. Think about it: not only are you pregnant and she didn't even know about it, but your daughter had just been badly hurt. She was looking for attention.'

'And how do you explain that mark on her leg?'

'That could be anything. Or maybe she really did trip on the escalator and decided to concoct this whole story around it. Maybe she really is crazy enough to think we'll believe that Dan is following her around Brent Cross, trying to bump her off.'

Hannah sighed. She was looking through a pile of rough paper with scribbles on she'd taken from Lily's bag, and started smoothing out a picture Lily had drawn of a house, complete with chimney and smoke and a neat front path. 'Well, what do we do? If she really is cracking up, shouldn't we talk to someone about it? Mrs Mackenzie, maybe?'

Josh shook his head. 'We don't get involved, remember? Neutral? . . . Hannah?' Now he was staring at her with concern. 'What's up? Darling?'

But Hannah didn't answer him. She was staring down at the piece of paper in front of her, one from the stack she'd removed from Lily's bag, and all the colour seemed to leach out of her face as he watched. Josh went over to stand next to her and followed her gaze.

In place of the normal childish drawings on

the other sheets of rough paper, there was a message scrawled across the page in capital letters in angry red felt pen.

YOU ARE NOT IMMUNE

Long after Hannah had gone to bed, Josh remained in the living room looking at the note on his lap. They'd asked Lily if she knew how it had got there, but she didn't understand what they were talking about. 'What's it say?' she'd wanted to know. 'Oh, nothing really.' And in truth, what *did* it say?

Hannah had wanted to call the police. The fact that someone had put a note in their daughter's backpack felt grotesque. If they could get to Lily's backpack while she was supposedly safe at school, didn't it stand to reason that they could get to her, too?

And yet, really, what did the note say? It wasn't threatening. It didn't mention anyone by name. It might even have been meant for someone else, or have been brought in by mistake by whoever had donated the rough paper to school. Josh was sure the police wouldn't be able to do much.

Hannah said she'd go into school first thing on Monday to quiz the staff about how the note could have got into Lily's bag. The trouble was that as the grand sorting-out of the bag was only done weekly, there was no way of knowing what day it had been put in there.

Josh felt a tidal wave of inadequacy sweep over him at his failure to keep his family safe. His wife was walking around like a ghost, and now his daughter was exposed to God knew what potential danger. What was wrong with him that he couldn't provide the security they both needed?

Hannah had been unnerved when he told her about the conversation with Dan about writing a formal statement for his lawyer, and said that Sasha had asked her a similar favour just a few days before. 'But we have to keep neutral. We can't get drawn in.'

'Don't worry, that's what I told him.'

But still she'd seemed anxious, and when he'd tried to put his arms around her to comfort her, she'd jumped up almost immediately. Later, while they were watching a mindless Friday-night chat show, she'd asked him, 'Are we doing the right thing by keeping this baby? Maybe it's not the right time.'

'Don't say that. This is the most positive thing to happen in our lives for ages. It's a fresh start. This is about us, and Lily. Our family.'

But now he found the weight of responsibility hanging on him very heavily indeed. How could he protect this new life if he couldn't even protect himself from the likes of Kelly Kavanagh? Just thinking about her and her allegation brought a sick taste to his mouth. He ought to tell Hannah. He knew that the secret he was keeping was a part of the barrier that was building between them. But he couldn't find the words. He'd wait until the investigation was over and he'd been formally cleared, and then he'd let her know.

Now Kelly Kavanagh was in his head, he couldn't get her out. She was a heavy-set girl of fifteen. One of those — and there were a few in every year group — who'd developed months, even years ahead of her peers, and had spent the first few years of secondary school sitting in assembly looking like a freakish adult in a sea of children, her back rounded, her arms permanently wrapped around her well-developed chest. There'd been older siblings before her — three or four as far as he could remember — all with that same slack-jawed stare. It was ludicrous, what she was suggesting he had done in a thirty-second gap between the end of one class and the beginning of the next, while he kept her behind to explain that she would have to stay in one lunch hour to retake the test she'd cheated on. That he would put his hand . . . there . . . with people passing the classroom and the door ajar . . . A kind of nauseous excitement stirred inside him as he allowed his mind to play out the malicious fantasy Kelly Kavanagh had invented to try to ruin his life. He knew even thinking about it was wrong. It was disgusting. She was a child. He wasn't remotely attracted to her. But it had been so long since he'd had any kind of sexual activity. He blurred her face in his mind so she could be anyone, put his hand to his groin and let out a groan.

Afterwards he felt grubby and sticky with shame. As he mopped himself up in the bathroom, he couldn't meet his own eyes in the mirror. A dull dread cramped inside him. Who on earth was he? A father who couldn't protect his child. A teacher who fantasized about his own pupils. He rested his head against the cool bathroom tiles and, with the tap running full blast, he cried for the first time in years.

22

'I'm not being funny, but there's no way one of us put that there.'

Nikki, one of the nursery helpers, flicked her straggly platinum-blonde hair extensions out of her eyes and glared at Hannah as if she was being accused of something. Hannah tried not to look at the metal stud in her nose that seemed to have gone septic, the flesh around it puckered and purple.

'No, I'm not saying that it came from anyone who worked here.'

Hannah wished she didn't always feel as if she had to be so over-friendly, even obsequious to the nursery staff, some of whom looked hardly more than children themselves. It was as if their role as guardians of her daughter put her helplessly in their debt, as if any bad feeling between them and her might somehow affect their treatment of Lily.

'I'm just wondering who else might have been in the nursery during the week, who might have been able to slip something into one of the kids' bags.'

As soon as she said it, she realized the futility of it. The cloakroom area was in almost constant use. Hadn't she been there just a couple of days ago herself, talking to Mrs Mackenzie?

Nikki gave her a blank stare. 'No disrespect, but if we was to keep tabs on everyone who goes in and out of the cloakroom, we wouldn't be able to do our job. Practically everyone who works here or has a child here is there at some time in the day.'

'Yes, I see that,' Hannah said, feeling hopeless. She sent her daughter, the most precious person in her world, to nursery believing her to be safe, but it seemed anyone could gain access to her.

'Anyway, how is Lily after that little ding-dong with September?'

Hannah felt herself prickling. *Little ding-dong?*

'She was a bit shaken, as you'd expect.' Her tone was cold and hard. 'It's always a bit of a shock when something like that happens out of the blue.'

'Yes, I can imagine. Though I wouldn't exactly say *out of the blue.*'

'Really? What do you mean?'

Nikki caught the ends of her hair extensions between the second and third fingers of her right hand and started absently combing her fingers through them, her long, electric-blue nails shimmering like beetle shells in the sun.

'Well, you know how kids are. She was laying it on a bit thick about having a new baby sister. In't it funny how she's already decided it's a girl? I'm not defending September or nothing, but it can't have been easy to hear all that, not with things as they are at home.'

Here Nikki shot Hannah a glance that was half complicit, half hopeful, as if Hannah might take this opportunity to discuss the salacious details of September's home life.

'I'm sure Lily didn't mean to be unkind,' said Hannah. 'She's not that sort of girl. She was just excited. It's only natural.'

Hannah was expecting Nikki to jump straight in to reinforce her defence of her daughter, but to her surprise, she hesitated.

'It's not unkind though, is it, at that age?' she said eventually. 'They don't know any better.'

'But I know my daughter.' Hannah didn't even try to disguise her outrage. 'She's the last person to ever want to hurt anyone's feelings.'

Nikki went back to examining her hair extensions and her ham-fisted efforts at tact enraged Hannah even further.

'Isn't she?' she prompted, determined to get some kind of confirmation.

Nikki sighed. 'Lily's just a normal little girl,' she said, and all of a sudden Hannah found herself loathing the way she pronounced girl as *gel*. 'And unfortunately little girls can be quite mean sometimes. It doesn't mean they're not lovely on the whole. And of course they're different here to at home — they're learning to be their own little people. You know, some parents would be quite shocked at the way their kids act when they're not around.'

★ ★ ★

After Nikki had gone, Hannah stood by the door waiting for the session to be over, churning with rage. She was realistic about Lily, it was just that she knew her daughter wouldn't have taunted September like that. She *knew* it.

While she waited, trying to calm down, she watched the kids playing. Lily was at one of the nearby tables, her head bent over some colouring, concentrating intently to make sure she stayed within the lines. A shout from the Wendy house in the far corner was followed by a squeal of laughter and September's head poked out, making a funny face, with her eyes crossed and her tongue out. Mrs Mackenzie had called Hannah yesterday to tell her they'd talked to September and she recognized that what she'd done was wrong, and they were happy to take her back into the nursery if Hannah was OK with that. Well, what could she say apart from 'Fine'? September caught Hannah's eye and smiled. Hannah tried not to stare at her teeth, imagining them pressed into Lily's skin like tiny stones set into a pebbledashed wall.

'How are you holding up?'

Marcia had appeared at her elbow. Hannah felt her face grow hotter. She hadn't really spoken to Marcia since the mix-up on the day when Sasha had picked Lily up when she was supposed to be having lunch with Marcia's daughter, Sarah.

'Oh, you know.' Hannah rolled her eyes and made the kind of face you make when you want to imply that unpleasant things have been happening, without actually spelling them out.

'I still feel awful about the other day, Marcia. I had no idea Sasha was planning to pick Lily up.'

'Don't worry about it. These things happen.'

Marcia was so solid, so calming. Hannah almost told her what Nikki had just said about

Lily, so that they could laugh about it together, but something held her back. What if Marcia didn't jump in to defend Lily? What if she shifted about and looked uncomfortable? Anyway, Marcia had moved on to talking about the snowflakes the children had been making which had just been stuck up on the windows, even though Christmas was still weeks away, and the moment had passed.

Hannah was hoping that as she was so early, she could collect Lily before Sasha got there. Sasha was always late, arriving in a whirr of motion and excuses. With any luck, Hannah wouldn't have to see her at all. Josh was right. She needed to start putting her family first, particularly now there was a new baby to think of.

The thought of the new baby was like a punch to the stomach. She ought to be excited about it, but all she could think of was the tiredness and not having room to think and that sour-milk smell permanently wafting off her clothes.

All the way home from school, Hannah fought off a creeping feeling of despondency. She fretted about the baby and what it would mean. Doubt had been building up inside her like plaque. During the daytime she'd drag her body around like an oversized bag, hardly able to lift her head, but at night she'd be awake, lying in the dark counting worries instead of sheep. Money, work, Josh, Lily, Sasha and Dan — all churning around in her brain, adding to the low-level nausea that now permeated everything she did. And when she did eventually drop off, her sleep was patchy and restless, punctuated by stumbling trips to the toilet or dreams so vivid that when she awoke she had the disquieting sense of being unable to tell which was the dream world and which the real.

Too often, she dreamed of that night when she was a teenager. She saw her mother's face once again, purple and ugly with rage, and Gemma's swollen, bashed-in head, felt fear ripping through her body. And always, mingling with the fear, there was the guilt. She should have stopped it. Why didn't she stop it?

Later, of course, her mum had dissolved in a puddle of self-loathing. 'What have I done?' she'd sobbed, hitting her own head again and again. 'I'll never forgive myself.' And her distress had been harder to bear than her anger.

For years after it had happened, Hannah had dreamed of it regularly. But after Lily was born, it had stopped for a while. She was always so exhausted, so burned out with childcare and work, she hadn't time to get caught up in the nightmares of her past. She'd even started to think that Lily had somehow wiped the slate clean. Her daughter was so pure, so utterly blameless, perhaps that had mitigated against what had gone before?

But now she was waking up drenched in sweat and panic once again, with her mother's twisted face etched on her eyelids and the horrible, leaden, guilt-soaked reality of it all lodged in her gut.

'It's just a dream,' Josh would tell her, his eyes still half shut, his body clinging to sleep even while his hand absently stroked her back. 'Be better in the morning.'

But Josh didn't understand how some dreams come from the inside, not the outside, how they hunker down in the darkness and wait.

'Can we go to the park, Mummy?'

Usually Hannah was in such a hurry to get home, back to whatever deadline she was racing against, counting the seconds until she could stick Lily in front of a DVD and get back to work, that she'd have dismissed Lily's habitual request to go to the playground out of hand, but today something stopped her. Though she didn't like to admit it, the conversation with Nikki had got to her. She didn't believe for a minute that Lily had been deliberately mean to September, but still she felt a nagging worry that she'd let her daughter somehow slip out of her grasp. When was the last time she had spent proper quality one-on-one time with Lily, without secretly calculating how much longer before she could break away and get on with whatever was more pressing instead?

What was more pressing than her own child?

'Why not?' she said, and her daughter's wide beam of surprise brought a lump to her throat.

In the playground, Lily wanted to play 'cafés'. She climbed the ladder up to the little wooden house attached to the climbing frame, her eyes doggedly fixed on the top, her hands clutching tight to the sides as if she were scaling a great height, rather than just six or seven feet above the ground.

At the top, she peered through the bars of the

285

fence. 'What would you like, Madam?'

Hannah pretended to consider an invisible menu. 'Do you have any hot chocolate?'

Lily smiled. 'Yes.'

'Well, I'll have one hot chocolate, please.'

Lily pretended to write the order down. It tugged at Hannah's heart to see how she held her invisible pencil so carefully. 'With swirly cream?' she asked shyly.

Hannah thought for a moment, as if deliberating. 'Yes. And I'd like chocolate sprinkles on it, please.'

'Of course, Madam.'

'And a banana.'

Lily exploded into giggles. 'You can't have a banana in your hot chocolate, silly!'

Hannah looked mock-stern. 'Yes, I can, because I'm the customer, and the customer is always right.'

While Lily disappeared into the wooden house to make the hot chocolate, Hannah looked around the playground. There were a couple of other younger mothers sitting on a bench by the sandpit, their heads bent together, oblivious to their two boys, who were having a sand fight in the corner that was bound to end in tears. From nowhere, Hannah was seized by a wrenching sense of loss. How many times had she and Sasha sat on that very bench over the years? Winter mornings when their breath came out in clouds of white steam and they warmed their hands on take-out cappuccinos from the organic café next to the now empty paddling pool; summer evenings when it was too nice to go home, and they'd buy the girls mini portions of pasta and pesto and let them play out until their shadows were long ribbons of darkness against the grass, and one or other of them fell over and lay slumped on the ground, crying with exhaustion.

They'd been so close then, she and Sasha, swapping complaints about broken nights and temper tantrums, about Dan's antisocial work hours and Josh's lack of direction. Or had they? Had they really been close? Maybe it was just convenience that threw them together, a shared need for company during those lonely baby-and-toddler years, for someone with whom to navigate the perplexing new world of routines and naps and a life suddenly lived in miniature, within the stunted and claustrophobic triangle of home, park and school?

One of the women threw back her head and roared with laughter, her hand on her friend's arm as if to stop her rolling clean off the bench with mirth. Hannah watched. It *was* real, her friendship with Sasha. They had sat like that too. She remembered now, how Sasha could laugh at herself, making a joke of her own need to be in control. 'Have you disinfected in there?' she'd call up to September and Lily, ensconced in the little house. 'Have you brought the Marigolds? Are you wearing hair nets? I'll be up to inspect.'

She missed her, Hannah realized suddenly. With Sasha around all the time, it hadn't been necessary to make any other close friends among the playground parents. Sasha was inclined to monopolize, to demand your complete and undivided attention. Now Hannah regretted having put all her eggs in one basket. Now there was no one to go to for advice about what had happened between Lily and September, no one to roll their eyes and say *Don't you hate it when that happens?* and make it normalized and all right.

'Here you are, Mummy. I mean, Madam.' Lily had appeared on the platform and was holding out an invisible cup through the wooden bars.

Hannah reached up and took it, her heart inflating with love at the mixture of pride and anxiety on her daughter's face. As if this was a real drink she was waiting to hear the verdict on.

It was an hour or so later when she finally let them in through the door of the flat. By this time, her pleasure at having spent proper time with her daughter was already vying with her guilt at having neglected her work. As usual, the guilt was winning. The first sign of everything not being as it should was the small pink-and-yellow flowery backpack in the hallway. Not Lily's. The second sign was a stifled giggle from the living room.

'Thank God you've arrived. We can stop posing. My arm has practically fallen off.'

Sasha and September were sitting on the sofa, beaming, September holding an extravagant bouquet of flowers so large it practically obscured her face, and her mother proffering a bag of cakes from that expensive bakery on the Broadway.

'But how . . . ?'

'We waited outside for ages. Practically days. Then I remembered that you'd given me your spare key, so we let ourselves in to wait. We thought you'd spontaneously combusted or something, you took so long.'

Hannah was too surprised to react. True, she did remember giving Sasha and Dan a set of keys before they went away on holiday a couple of years back, in that nonsensical way you do, as if having a keyholder a few streets away rather than a time zone away will somehow guard against anything bad happening. But surely they'd asked for the keys back afterwards? She tried to think, to reach back in time to pluck the memory from the air — the act of reclaiming the spare keys. But it eluded her. Maybe they'd forgotten to ask for them. Maybe by the time they needed them again they could no longer remember who they'd left them with and went to get another set cut, Josh complaining — as he was bound to do — about the cost. It was possible. But this? Letting herself in? Taking possession of the sofa? Hannah noticed that September was wearing a daisy-chain headband of Lily's. Then she remembered how bereft she'd felt in the playground, wishing Sasha was there, and her anger stalled.

'Don't be cross, Hans.' Sasha had dropped the brittle frosted-on smile and was gazing at her anxiously as if everything depended on her reaction. Her eyes seemed sunken into her head, as if they were drowning. 'Please let's not fall out. I can't bear it. Look, I brought you these peace offerings.' She made a sweeping gesture with her tiny hand, indicating the cakes and the flowers.

Hannah tried to smile at September, whose pretty little face was poking out between the blooms.

'Why don't you two girls go into the kitchen and get a biscuit?' she suggested over-brightly. 'I think there are some of those chocolate dinosaurs.'

There was a pause while Lily and September eyed each other cautiously. Hannah could almost see the teeth-shaped bruise on Lily's arm burning through the wool of her jumper. Then September laid the flowers on the table and jumped up, grinning at Lily, and they made their way out of the room.

They'd hardly set foot through the door before Sasha started.

'I'm sorry I upset you the other day. I know it sounded like I wasn't taking it seriously, what September did, but I was. It's just I was so freaked out by what happened at Brent Cross. And finding out you were pregnant came as such a shock.'

Again that instinctive blow to the guts. *Pregnant*.

'I'm happy for you, don't get me wrong. It's just that it brought home to me how disastrously wrong everything has gone in my life. I mean, we used to talk about doing it together, do you remember? We'd get pregnant at the same time so that our younger kids could grow up together, just like Lil and September. And now here you are going ahead and having another baby, while my husband is living with someone else and may well be trying to fucking kill me.'

Her voice wavered on the last two words, but she visibly fought against crying. 'I promised myself I wasn't going to get upset. I know I'm like a stuck record and it must be so boring to be around me.' Hannah could hardly bring herself to look at Sasha. Clearly she didn't know yet about Sienna being pregnant. She imagined how it must feel for her, having her future yanked out from under her like a magician's tablecloth. The family she thought she'd have, the home she imagined she'd built.

'Did you talk to the police again?' she asked, to change the subject. 'About what happened on the escalator? Did they look at the CCTV footage?'

Sasha gave a dismissive snort. 'The police made it pretty obvious they think I'm some mad rich bitch with an overactive imagination. They came round to the house, two of them, and they didn't stop staring at my things. They kept saying things like, 'Nice sofa. Could fit my whole flat into that sofa,' and, 'Lovely views. I look out on to the Dixi Chicken.' You know, it was like they were judging my suitability as a victim based on all the *stuff* I have.'

Sasha's violet-shadowed eyes were momentarily wide with remembered outrage. Hannah could imagine it all too clearly. The police officers silently noting the velvet chaise longue, the French crystal chandelier, the Bang & Olufsen sound system. Sasha brittle enough to snap.

'Do you know something, Hannah? They

291

hated me. No, really, they did. I suddenly realized it, and it was such a shock, I can't tell you. Do you remember after 9/11 when Americans were saying, *But we didn't realize anyone hated us?*' Here Sasha put on a fake American drawl. 'Do you remember how thunderstruck they were? Well, that's how I felt when those policemen were there. They were very polite, but I knew they hated me. And they knew I knew. When I asked about the CCTV, they almost laughed. They asked me how many people I thought went up and down those escalators every day. They said even if they could find me on the camera, all we'd see would be a crowd of people, and then one of them tripping over. That was their exact phrase. *Tripping over.*'

Hannah sighed. Behind Sasha's head, she could see her laptop open on the table, surrounded by papers and newspaper cuttings and notebooks. The work she wasn't doing formed a tight ligature around her chest. And still she couldn't shake off the uneasy feeling she'd had since coming in and finding Sasha installed in her home. She couldn't help feeling *violated*.

'Shall I make us some tea?' she asked, realizing that the chances of getting back to work were non-existent.

Sasha didn't reply. She looked so frail, dwarfed by the huge sofa, gazing intently off into space as if listening to some inner voice.

'Sasha? Tea?'

Sasha turned her newly dulled eyes towards Hannah. 'Haven't you got anything stronger?

292

Gin and tonic? Wine? Oh, come on, Hans, don't look so disapproving. Remember when the girls were little and we used to reward ourselves with a drink at teatime, just because it was all so fucking stressful? Don't you think I deserve it now?'

Hannah smiled, although uneasiness still prickled at the back of her neck. Even though she'd been reminiscing herself just an hour before, she couldn't help feeling manipulated by Sasha reminding her of their shared past, forcing intimacy on her like a once-favourite jumper now shrunk in the wash.

She was surprised to find the kitchen empty. Stepping back into the hall, she heard muffled voices coming from behind Lily's emphatically closed bedroom door. *Good*, she told herself. *It's all behind them.* Amazing how quickly children could move on from things, rifts that had seemed irreparable forgotten in the blink of an eye. But still she hesitated, not liking that flat expanse of white wood door. Even the gaily decorated letter 'L' seemed somehow forbidding.

Back in the kitchen, she opened the fridge, her heart sinking as ever with the knowledge that somehow, in a couple of hours, she was going to have to concoct some semblance of dinner from the sad assortment of aged vegetables and half-empty tins — they'd stopped telling you not to keep tins in the fridge, hadn't they? — messily arranged on the smudged plastic shelves. The endless repetition of domestic life seemed suddenly overwhelming. There was an open bottle of white Sauvignon in the fridge door.

Thank God for screw tops. What did people *do* when it was all corks — wine turning vinegary overnight? She poured a glass for Sasha and, after a momentary hesitation, a tiny one for herself, too.

Back in the living room, Sasha took a long gulp from her glass, then leaned forward, her eyes intense, the fingers of her left hand plucking savagely at the skin of the right. She clearly had something she wanted to say, and Hannah knew with complete certainty that whatever it was, she wasn't going to like it.

'I've got to talk to you, Hans. I don't know who else to turn to. Something awful has happened. I don't even know how to say it.'

'What, more awful than someone trying to kill you?'

Hannah was trying to make a joke of it, to lighten the atmosphere and head off whatever it was Sasha was about to tell her, but Sasha didn't smile. Instead her eyes filmed over with tears.

'In a way, yes. Hannah, I found porn on the family computer.'

Hannah tried to maintain a concerned expression, but her stomach was fizzing with relief. Porn. That was distasteful, but manageable.

'I know it's horrible, Sash. But Dan wouldn't be the first man to download porn. You've got to keep it in persp — '

'This is hardcore porn, Hannah! Obscene pictures of women doing the most degrading things. Disgusting, sado-masochistic violent stuff. Rape, even. Oh Hannah, I can't tell you.'

294

The tears were spilling out now. Hannah's head was reeling. She didn't believe it, not really. She knew you could never tell what turned people on, but even so, if someone was into something like that you'd know, wouldn't you? There'd be something that gave it away. Yet Sasha seemed genuinely distraught. If she was making it up, she was a lot more damaged than Hannah thought. A hard lump formed in her stomach. Then she had a thought.

'If these are saved images, they'll be dated, won't they?'

If for any twisted reason Sasha had planted those pictures there herself, the dates wouldn't tally. They'd be after Dan left home.

Sasha was staring at her as if she had gone crazy.

'I didn't *leave* them on there, Hannah! Christ, you've got to be joking. September uses that computer. What if she'd found them? They were *vile*, you need to understand. Disgusting. I deleted them and then I emptied the trash and then I went and had a shower because I felt so grubby.'

Hannah shook her head. 'I'm sorry, Sasha, but this is enough now. You need to see someone. Surely you can see how insane this all is. This is Dan we're talking about, the man you loved, September's father. I know he's hurt you horribly, but he's not this monster you're trying to turn him into.'

'You think I'm making this up? You think I'd actually want people to know my husband is secretly a sick pervert?'

Hannah's certainty started to waver.

'Could you have misinterpreted what you saw? Might the pictures have been to do with some photographic assignment Dan was doing? You know how blurry the line is between art and porn sometimes.'

Sasha was shaking her head vehemently. 'No way. I know what I saw, Hannah. This was porn, and the very worst kind of porn.'

The two women exchanged a long look and it was Hannah who broke away first, taking a gulp of her wine, trying to make sense of the thoughts flying around her head.

Sasha's ringtone — a customized recording of September shouting, 'Mummy — pick up your phone!' — eventually broke the silence.

'Oh God,' muttered Sasha, taking it out of her bag and glancing at the screen. 'I'd better take this. Hello?'

Hannah was relieved to have a break from the conversation they'd just been having, even if it was only momentary.

'I don't understand,' Sasha was saying into her phone. 'I don't understand what you're saying.'

Whatever the other person was saying, it was clearly nothing Sasha wanted to hear.

When the call had ended, she cradled the phone in her hand, as if unwilling to believe the conversation was over. Then she lifted her eyes to Hannah.

'That was Caroline, my lawyer,' she said. 'She says Dan is going for full custody. Apparently Josh has made a written statement confirming I'm an unfit mother.'

23

'It's not my fault.'

Josh was well aware that a whine had crept into his voice, but he was just so sick of justifying himself. And why did he have to do that anyway? Hannah should automatically be on his side.

'That email was private. I had no idea he'd give it to his lawyer.'

'Yes, but why were you saying things like that to him in the first place? You know we said we'd stay neutral.'

'Yes, but that was before Sasha went off the rails so spectacularly. You know perfectly well she's not capable of looking after September in the state she's in. No wonder the poor child is going around biting people. She's all over the place.'

'Yeah, well, thanks to you, Sasha will probably never speak to us again.'

'You know, I'm starting to think that might actually be a relief.'

Hannah's nostrils flared. She picked up her fork to spear the last new potato on her plate, then thought better of it. 'That's typical. It might be a relief for you, but what about me? She's my friend, Josh. She helps me out. Don't forget all the times she's looked after Lily when I've had to go off and do an interview and you're at work. I need that support. It's OK for you — you just swan into school in the morning and come home at night and there's never any question of it being any different, whereas I'm the one who has to sort out all the childcare and make excuses if I miss deadlines because Lily's sick or there's an inset day.'

Josh stifled a sigh. So this too would turn out to be his fault? If he didn't have a full-time job he'd be able to help with the childcare and maybe Hannah wouldn't be so reliant on Sasha. Was that the subtext here? That old unwinnable argument. If he earned more, she wouldn't need to work or scrabble around for childcare, or conversely, if he had a worse job, she'd be the main breadwinner and he'd have to go part-time to take up the slack in looking after Lily. But this middle-of-the-road job, neither one thing nor the other, was somehow a failing. Shouldn't she just be happy that he worked at all? Plenty of women would jump at the chance of having a partner with a steady, reliable income. He pushed his chair violently back from the dinner table, the legs making a grating sound on the wooden floorboards. Hannah flashed a warning look at him. Lily hadn't long gone to bed.

'Well, that's it with Dan,' he said. 'I told him very clearly that I wouldn't put anything in writing for his solicitor. He knew how I felt. Then he goes and takes something I wrote in a private email to use against Sasha. It's really underhand.'

The more he thought about it, the more furious he was. Such a violation of their friendship. But there was something else as well. Something that made him feel cold. Hadn't he also mentioned Hannah in that email? Said something about her going off sex? Hadn't he made a comment about Siberia, even used the word 'frigid'? He'd been joking, of course. But she'd never forgive him if she found out — not for sharing something so personal. Surely Dan wouldn't have given that bit to the lawyer? Or might he have had to provide the entire email intact, just to prove it hadn't been edited?

'Dan's changed,' Hannah said. 'The old Dan would never have done anything like this. Do you think it's her doing? Sienna?'

Josh felt a ridiculous surge of protectiveness. Sienna had been so nice about that whole Kelly Kavanagh thing, so understanding. Hannah oughtn't to be criticizing her. She didn't even know her!

'It seems to me,' Hannah went on, 'we don't know the first thing about Dan any more or what he would or wouldn't do.'

'Oh come off it, Hans. You're not talking about that allegation of Sasha's, are you? You know she'll say anything to get back at him. It's such a cheap shot. You can't seriously be considering it?'

They looked at each other, then immediately looked away.

But still Josh was uneasy. This was all too close to home. Since Kelly Kavanagh had made her allegation against him at school, he'd felt sick with fear at the thought of Hannah finding out. Of course, he told himself, she wouldn't believe it for a second. But now, seeing her face, he wondered whether his confidence was misplaced.

299

He could see that she didn't really believe Dan was capable of what Sasha was saying — Dan wasn't the sort to get his kicks from seeing hideous things done to women, the idea was preposterous — and yet there was that awful, infinitesimal wisp of doubt. And once doubt entered into your head, did it ever really go away?

'Dan's always been such an open book, I just don't think he would have shared our private emails with his lawyer without someone pressurizing him. I think Sienna must have something to do with it. Ever since he's been with her he's been different — probably because he's been thinking with his dick.'

The sound of Hannah's familiar clipped voice enunciating the word *dick* echoed around Josh's head, thrilling and disturbing him in equal measure.

'I just *hate* all this, you know?'

To Josh's consternation, Hannah's eyes filmed over with tears as she spoke. He remembered then about her being pregnant. Here he was, thinking about himself and what this all meant to him, while she was having to cope with a pregnancy as well. He got up from his seat and moved around the table so he was sitting next to Hannah and put his arm around her. He was surprised at the shape of her shoulders under his fingers. How long had it been since they had properly held each other? Wasn't there some-thing terribly wrong, that his wife's body should feel like a stranger's?

She leaned against him, her forehead nuzzling

against the hollow at the base of his throat. 'What's happening to us, Josh?'

He tightened his grip around her shoulders. 'Nothing's happening to us, darling. It's everyone around us who is falling apart. We're fine. We're strong. You and me and Lily and now this new little person. We'll be OK.'

Was he imagining the way she stiffened when he referred to the new baby?

'Look. This thing with Dan and Sasha has been a nightmare, but it's over now — at least our part of it. Sasha says she can't be in contact with you now that my bloody email is being used against her, and Dan must know he's burned his bridges with me by doing that. I mean, he asked me to make a statement and I refused. He knew exactly where I stood, but he went ahead and involved me anyway. I can't stay friends with someone who'd do that. So now it's just us, which is a massive relief, to be frank. Let's have the weekend to ourselves and stay in the flat, just the three of us, and eat lovely food and drink fine wine and watch telly. Doesn't that sound perfect?'

But Hannah had pulled away from him and was glaring at him. 'I don't believe you. You've forgotten, haven't you?'

'Forgotten what?'

'Forgotten that we're going to see Mum this weekend.'

Josh's heart plummeted. He hadn't really forgotten what she'd said about visiting her mother; rather, he'd been hoping that if he didn't mention it, she might just lose interest in the whole thing. These visits to her mother always took their toll on Hannah, leaving her in a strange, distracted mood. At the best of times, she'd be hard to reach afterwards, and the way things stood between them at that moment, that was the last thing they needed.

'Are you sure?'

Hannah was shaking her head. 'Don't try to wriggle out of it now. I had to put up with *your* parents for a weekend, with your mum insinuating that there was something up with Lily, like I was a neglectful mother for not noticing.'

'I don't think she — '

'So don't you try to get out of going to Oxford.'

Josh stared at the flaming pink patch of dry skin on Hannah's forehead and swallowed back the words he had been about to say, aware that this had now passed beyond being about what made sense and moved into that hazy territory of loyalty and love and duty and doing what the other person wants just because it's what they want.

'Fine. We'll go.'

★   ★   ★

The thought of the trip to Oxford and about what had happened with the lawyer sat heavily in Josh's stomach overnight like undigested meat, making sleep almost impossible. At one point he even got up and dashed off an angry email to Dan, asking what he thought he was playing at.

302

Thinking about it in the cold light of day, he probably shouldn't have sent it, or at least should have tempered it. He couldn't remember exactly what he'd said, but he knew he'd let rip about friendship and betrayal and — the memory came into his head with a sickening thud — even threatened to write a statement for Sasha instead, a formal one this time.

He shouldn't have sent it.

The thought made him uncomfortable as he drove to school the next morning, shifting around in the driving seat. He'd ring Dan at lunchtime, he decided, in a total U-turn from yesterday's adamant position of non-communication. He'd clear the air, give Dan a chance to explain himself. And then he'd tell him that he and Hannah were stepping back from the whole mess, before they got swallowed up in it themselves.

The heaviness of Josh's mood transferred itself to his surroundings. Despite the half-hearted Christmas decorations, north London had never looked so gloomy. The normally leafy streets appeared grey and barren in the dim light of a November morning, bare branches clutching at the air like gnarled fingers. The bin men — or 'waste-management technicians' as he'd read you had to call them now — hadn't been in a while. Since collections had gone from weekly to fortnightly, rubbish seemed to be constantly piling up outside shops and blocks of flats, black plastic bags spilling out of wheelie bins. The cold made everyone appear hunched and awkward in their uniformly dark overcoats, their pale faces

303

pinched and serious.

There was a giant billboard next to the traffic lights where Josh waited irritatedly, his feet determinedly balancing between clutch and accelerator, refusing to admit defeat and go into neutral as if this small act of defiance could force the lights to change faster. The billboard featured an advert for perfume — all the adverts seemed to be for perfume at this time of year, celebrities in gold body paint spouting nonsensical snatches of poetry as they rolled around on satin sheets. The model — one of those who seemed to have become a celebrity in her own right, as if she had some other gift apart from taking off clothes and putting others on and staring into a camera lens with blank eyes — was wearing a long string of beads and high heels and very little else. He wondered if Sienna had ever posed like that.

Pulling into the staff car park, his depression deepened. With the exception of a gleaming 4×4 belonging to one of the receptionists who was married to a property developer and worked part-time to 'keep herself busy', the rest of the cars were similar to his — ten years old, self-consciously low-key. Golfs, Renaults, Hondas, Toyotas in silver, navy and black. Dan was the only person he knew who didn't see an inherent ethical dilemma in having a statement car, a car that said, 'Look at me, I'm happy to be defined by my car.'

He was late, so the cramped car park was already nearly full, apart from the corner spaces which were notoriously difficult to manoeuvre into and next to impossible to get out of.

Rushing into school, having spent a long time inching his way into the space, Josh hoped no one had been watching from the classroom windows on the first floor. When it came to all things motor-related there was no more critical audience than a class full of Year Elevens who had yet to take a driving lesson and still believed there was nothing to it.

The bell was already sounding as he hurried along the corridor to his first class and he was mentally rehearsing the lesson he was about to take, so at first he didn't hear the head calling softly to him from the open door to his office. When Josh finally turned and retraced his steps, he struggled to hide his irritation. Now he would be late, and as any teacher knew, being late meant you'd immediately relinquished the upper hand and had to spend half the lesson trying to recover it.

'Josh, will you come in for a minute, please?'

The head had sandy hair and almost non-existent eyelashes, against which his severe black glasses frames appeared cartoonishly over-exaggerated.

'I've actually got a class . . . ' Josh gave an apologetic shrug and made as if to walk off.

'Ah, yes. Well that's the thing, Josh. You've been relieved of the particular joy of drumming *Macbeth* into 9E.'

The head smiled at his little joke, but the smile was forced and awkward, and a pink stain was appearing on his neck above the collar of his pale-blue shirt.

'I don't understand.'

'Well, Miss Stokes — Marisa — has kindly stepped in to cover so that you and I can have a little chat.'

The pink stain had crawled up over his jaw now, and Josh's heart began to hammer. This had to be about Kelly Kavanagh. What had she been saying now? Suddenly the unfairness of it all hit him like a slap to the face and he thought for a horrible moment that he might burst into tears. The head, whose name was Ian, although no one ever referred to him as anything except 'the head', indicated a padded chair across the L-shaped desk from him, and Josh sank heavily down into it, only now becoming aware that there was another person in the room — one of the PE teachers, Sean Silverman, a broad, compact man with a swarthy complexion and thick black hair protruding from the top of his white T-shirt. Sean was leaning against the wall and gave Josh an apologetic shrug. Josh was mystified. What on earth was Sean Silverman doing here? He hardly knew the guy.

Then all of a sudden it came to him with a sickening jolt of realization. Sean was the school union representative. This was a disciplinary matter.

'Josh, there are times when I really hate my job.' The head gave Josh a rueful smile, and for one wild instant Josh imagined he might be about to confess something, as if getting someone in to cover Josh's class might turn out to be an elaborate way of facilitating an unburdening that only he could possibly understand.

'And this is one of them,' the head continued, and Josh knew without doubt that this was a prelude to something bad.

'I've asked Sean to come here in his capacity as union rep, because I'm sorry to tell you there's been another allegation of inappropriate behaviour made against you. As you know, I'm not at liberty to go into details, but suffice to say this was an anonymous phone allegation from a former female pupil.'

And there it was. The Something Bad that had, he now realized, been hanging in the air all morning. Under the desk, his legs were shaking.

Struggling to hold back the panic he could feel building inside him, Josh fixed his gaze on the photos displayed on the windowsill, showing Ian on holiday with his wife and two small children, all of them pale-fleshed and beaming up from under a huge beach umbrella. He felt strangely embarrassed, as if he was spying on something private.

'"Former"? Why wouldn't she have said something at the time?'

Ian, who had made a steeple out of his hands, which he was pressing against his mouth, sighed. 'Josh, you know I can't go into any more detail about the allegation — as much for your sake as for . . . the other party's.'

Josh was aware of his head shaking from side to side as if on a fulcrum. If he just closed his eyes and pretended he hadn't heard, this would surely turn out to be a mistake — a manifestation of his own crappy mood. But when he opened his eyes, and saw the head's

307

pale eyes peering at him from over the top of that steeple of fingers, waiting for his reaction, he knew it was real. He glanced over his shoulder at Sean Silverman, who gave him a weak smile that was probably meant to be supportive but somehow made him feel even worse.

'She's lying.'

His voice lacked conviction, even to his own ears, going up slightly on the last syllable in that American way.

'Any idea why anyone would want to make something like that up?'

Josh once again felt his head shaking from side to side, even while he realized that, yes, there were people with an axe to grind against him. Kelly Kavanagh, for one. She'd probably expected him to be suspended after her original allegation. Who was to say this wasn't her determinedly sticking in the boot?

'I should tell you at this moment we are treating this as completely separate from the earlier allegation.'

For a second, Josh thought he must have been voicing his thoughts out loud, before he realized that, of course, it was the obvious conclusion.

But the head seemed to want to make it very clear he didn't think the two allegations were linked. So who then? Who would want to do him harm? It came to him like a body blow, knocking the breath clear out of his chest.

Sasha.

She wouldn't.

Would she?

He remembered Hannah's face as she

308

described Sasha's reaction to the phone call from her lawyer. 'She was actually shaking,' Hannah had said. 'She kept saying, over and over again, how she couldn't believe you'd done that to her.'

Josh had seen Sasha turn on people enough times over the years to know what she was capable of. Once on a joint holiday in Spain, she'd taken exception to another British tourist and buried her clothes in the sand while she was swimming late one afternoon. When the woman had emerged from the sea and started hunting around for her clothes, Sasha had pretended not to know anything about them. He and Hannah had sat there, rigid with embarrassment, waiting for Sasha to give them back, but she hadn't. In the end the two of them had slunk away, unable to watch any longer.

But that was a total stranger. They were her friends. Was it really conceivable that Sasha could have phoned his head teacher and made an allegation like that, knowing it might cost him his job? No sooner had the thought formed than he experienced a bolt of nausea. It was true — this was the kind of thing that ended careers. How many times had he heard about it happening?

'Josh?'

There was a concerned expression on Ian's pale face, but Josh thought he detected a wariness that hadn't been there earlier, as if he was already trying to distance himself from this teacher with the question mark swinging over his head.

'There is one possibility. Some good friends of

ours are in the process of splitting up and we've somehow become embroiled in their battle. I think at least one of them might feel like I've sided with the other one. You know how that can happen. Maybe even both.'

The head was looking at him faintly disapprovingly. 'You know you should never get mixed up in other people's break-ups, Josh. I wouldn't have thought I'd have to tell you that.'

For a moment there was silence while Josh's stomach churned and the head looked increasingly pained, as if he was in physical discomfort.

'I want you to know, Josh, that you have my complete confidence,' he said at last. 'Personally speaking, that is. But I'm sure you'll appreciate I'm now in a very tricky situation. Normally I might be able to use my discretion over one anonymous call, but taken together with the previous allegation — well, you can see my hands are tied. There are procedures to be followed, governors to be appeased.'

'You're suspending me?'

Josh swung around to face Sean, looking for outrage — *Did you hear what he said?* — but the other man was staring straight ahead.

'Just while we make some investigations. You'll be on full pay, of course.'

'Mud sticks, Ian.' Josh's voice came out louder and harsher than he'd intended. 'You know that. Even if I can prove these two ridiculous claims are malicious rubbish, which they are, some people will still believe there's no smoke without fire. If you suspend me, there'll always be a cloud hanging over me.'

The head leaned back in his chair and removed his glasses, then rubbed them absently with a small pale-blue cloth he picked up from his desk. His eyes, when they looked up at Josh, seemed genuinely sorrowful, although maybe that was just how they looked without the lenses to give them focus.

'I really wish there was another option, Josh, but I'm afraid we have to follow a strict protocol in cases like this.'

Cases like this.

Sexual abuse, paedophilia — that's what *cases like this* meant.

'You know Hannah is pregnant again?'

The note of accusation in Josh's voice was undisguisable and he felt gratified when the head's eyes widened in shock.

Ian put his glasses back on slowly.

'I'm really terribly sorry,' he said. 'All I can do is reassure you that we'll be carrying out our investigations just as quickly as we can, and hopefully we'll have you back at work before anyone even notices you're gone. Maybe you and Hannah can use it as an opportunity to spend a bit of time together before the baby comes.'

'Oh yeah, every cloud's got a silver lining, right?'

'I don't blame you for being angry, Josh, but my hands are completely tied on this.' The head clasped his hands together as if to demonstrate.

It was clear the interview was now over, but still Josh stayed in his padded chair, as if by staying he could delay making this real, keep the nightmare confined to this room. Once he'd left, it would spread in the wind like pollen.

'Go home, Josh,' Ian said eventually. 'Kiss your wife. Hug your daughter. Remind yourself of all the good things you have.'

⋆　⋆　⋆

Josh drove home in a daze. Though he'd navigated this same route just over an hour before, everything looked as different as if it was a foreign country. In fact, that's just what he felt like — a tourist who'd got lost somewhere he didn't know, but knew he didn't want to be.

Somewhere dangerous.

'This isn't happening,' he told his own reflection in the rear-view mirror.

He was possessed by an overwhelming fear. Someone was trying to end his career — maybe two people even. Everything he'd done and worked for throughout his adult life could be ripped to shreds, and there wasn't a thing he could do about it.

Hannah.

How was he going to tell Hannah? He'd have to admit that he'd kept the Kelly Kavanagh allegation from her these past weeks. She wouldn't forgive him for that, especially if she knew he'd confided in Sienna instead. At the thought of Sienna, he felt a pang that was almost like grief. He longed to get out his phone and call her now and tell her what had happened, feel that curious release he always got from talking to her, but how could he after Dan had shared his private emails with his lawyer?

Once again his thoughts swung back to Hannah. She deserved to know everything — but what if she thought his not telling her about Kelly Kavanagh meant he had something to hide? Everywhere he looked, it seemed, there were dead ends and risks.

Josh swerved over to the kerb, earning a long beep from the car behind. The driver, a middle-aged man with headphones in his ears, glared at Josh as he overtook him and shook his head slowly from side to side.

Josh put his forehead on the wheel, aware he was hyperventilating but not sure what to do about it. He wondered if he was in a bus lane, but couldn't face looking to find out. All he needed was to get a ticket on top of everything else. Hannah had got one recently just for pulling in momentarily opposite the post office while he flew out to post a letter. She'd only stopped for a few seconds, but a couple of weeks later a letter had arrived with a photograph of their car. CCTV. It was everywhere. No doubt there was a camera trained on him right this moment. Well, good. Let him be captured like this for posterity — a man slowly falling apart in his car.

Now he was shaking, his whole body convulsing. He wondered if he was having a breakdown, right here by the side of the road. Pulling away into the traffic, all he could think about was having Hannah's arms around him. He felt weak suddenly. He supposed it was shock. And cold. He was so cold. As he drove, his leg quivered on the accelerator pedal as if in spasm. Hannah was the only woman apart from his mum who'd ever been able to comfort him. He remembered one weekend morning, early in their relationship, lying in her bed in that flat in Maida Vale she'd shared with so many housemates that the galley kitchen had had to double as a living room, people perched on stools at the breakfast bar watching the portable TV on the worktop. She was asleep, her head on his chest, and he remembered trying to work out what it was that felt so good about being there and realizing, with amazement and a huge rush of gratitude, that he felt completely safe. A strange thing for a man to think, but that was the truth. She made him feel safe.

But letting himself into their flat now, he felt neither safe nor comforted.

'Josh? Why are you home early?'

He hesitated in the doorway, his back to the still-open door. Hannah's voice was tight, as if it had been wound up too much. He fumbled for the words he'd been rehearsing in his head, but they evaporated, leaving him gasping for air.

'I'm not feeling well.'

He felt Hannah's sigh as much as heard it. A gust of breath that whispered through the flat, blowing disaffection like dust into his eyes and ears.

'What's up?' She was trying to sound sympathetic, but the strain of it was threaded through the question.

'Headache,' he mumbled.

Another sigh. Louder this time.

'Wish someone would give *me* a day off,' she said, but when he came through the doorway into the living room, something in his face made her soften. 'Actually, you don't look too good.'

'I feel like shit.'

'Have you spoken to Dan? He's rung here three times leaving messages for you.'

Josh took out his phone, as always set to silent. There were six missed calls from Dan and a voicemail.

'Josh, mate. I've been trying to get hold of you. My lawyer told me what happened. I swear to god, mate, I never gave him permission to use that email. It was just part of a whole load of background stuff I sent to the legal team to help them make their case. It was never intended to be quoted. I told him straight off to take it off the official documents. I read him the fucking riot act, actually. Please don't think it had anything to do with me. Call me back. OK?'

'He says he didn't give his lawyer permission to use my email.'

Hannah didn't even look up from her laptop. 'Yeah, I gathered that. Doesn't change the fact that he should never have given it to them in the first place though, does it?'

'No. I know. You're right.'

'God knows what Sasha is going to do now. I'm pretty sure she's going to insist I write a statement in her favour, just to counterbalance that email.'

'Well, you can't. You know she's not stable.'

'And Dan is? With pictures of women being raped on his computer?'

315

'Oh, Hannah, you know you don't believe all that crap.'

'I don't know what to believe. All I know is Dan isn't going to provide a stable home for September any more than Sasha is. He's so loved up he probably wouldn't even notice she was there half the time. God, I'm so glad we're getting away tomorrow.'

Josh's stomach lurched, an unpleasant sensation that left him instantly sweating and short of breath. On top of everything that had happened, he had this to look forward to — a visit to Oxford with all that entailed.

Hannah looked up, eyeing him watchfully as if waiting for him to object. The moment stretched out between them, each of them painfully aware of the things the other was not saying. Josh was the first to turn away. He didn't have the energy left for a fight. All thoughts of Hannah comforting him had now been banished so thoroughly it was as though they had occurred to someone else entirely. He couldn't remember ever feeling so weak, as if those minutes in the head's office had opened up a hole inside him through which all life force had drained away, leaving him hollow and empty.

'I'm going to go and lie down,' he said.

In their bedroom, he drew the curtains and lay fully clothed on top of the duvet. Closing his eyes, he probed the newly empty space inside him, looking for something. Eventually he found it: a lump of hatred, hard as a cyst.

Sasha.

24

'OK, prepare for a shock, Mum. Prepare to be amazed. I'm pregnant. Yes, again!'

Hannah smiled, and for the first time in what seemed like months, she felt herself relaxing. This was exactly what she needed. She felt a powerful sense of release and calm.

'Don't go too far, Lil,' Josh called from his position a few feet away.

Lily was playing in the grass in the wintery sunshine, picking at the weeds that grew around the low stone walls. She was making a bouquet, Hannah saw now. From the way she kept stealing sly glances in her mother's direction, Hannah could tell the posy was intended for her, and she felt a rush of tenderness for her daughter. It would be all right, she thought suddenly. All of it. The new baby would cement them together as a family.

'Bet you never thought I'd be able to look after myself, let alone two children!' She laughed, leaning back to give her mother a better view of her still non-existent bump under her thick jumper.

Josh was looking uncomfortable, as he always did. Would it really kill him to chill out for once? Sometimes when she thought about how much she put up with from his mother, with her endless underhand digs that only Hannah ever seemed to notice, she felt like screaming at him to make an effort for her, too.

'Shall we go, darling?'

Despite the watery sunshine, the wind was biting and Josh was looking cold and underdressed in his thin leather jacket. Hannah frowned, desperately wanting to stay, but aware it was unfair to expect Lily and Josh to hang around for too much longer. On summer days the graveyard was a joyful place to be, full of wildflowers and people carefully tending the graves. But in the depths of winter, it was damp and grey and eerily still.

Yet still she lingered, loath to tear herself away, nervously rearranging the flowers she'd brought to replace the ones her sister had left when she'd been there the weekend before. She knew Josh thought it was creepy, the way she and Gemma kept gravitating back to their mother's grave, but he'd never understood how close they had been. By the time Josh met her mum, she was already ill with the cancer that would eventually kill her, so he'd never known her in the days when she could throw her arms around you and hold you in an embrace so warm and heartfelt that you felt nothing bad could ever happen to you. He didn't get it, of course. He'd accused her before of 'sanctifying' her mother, reminding her that things hadn't always been easy between them.

'What about those episodes?' he'd demanded, referring to the bouts of black depression her mother had been prone to throughout her life. Not many, but intense and terrifying, even so. A quick flashback to her mother's venomous face at the hospital — no, she wouldn't think of that

318

now. That's why their father had eventually walked out on them — because he couldn't handle the downs. He'd stayed in periodic contact, but Hannah and Gemma had little respect for him. There was a Marilyn Monroe quote Hannah had once read — *If you can't handle me at my worst, then you sure as hell don't deserve me at my best* — and it had made her think of her parents. Her father was long gone by the time Gemma was injured and their mother was finally properly diagnosed and given medication to keep her moods stable. Maybe he'd have stayed if he'd known, but having turned his back on her at her worst, he certainly didn't deserve her at her best, when she could make you feel like the most loved, cherished person in the world.

But Josh had never really seen that side of her mother, which is why he'd accused Hannah of being 'ghoulish' more than once, for insisting on coming here to talk to her. He'd been supportive at first, but his enthusiasm had quickly waned in the face of the long tedious hours he'd spent here waiting for her to finish. 'You're always so moody afterwards,' he complained. 'It's not helpful for you.' As if he had the first clue how to help her! She was being unfair. She knew it. But they had drifted so far apart, she struggled sometimes to imagine them ever being close again. Maybe it was the pregnancy hormones, but everything he did at the moment irritated her. Yesterday he'd come home from work feigning illness and, after disrupting her work, had just taken himself off to bed, leaving her sitting at the table fuming and unable to focus on the feature she was writing. She was sure he wasn't really ill at all. In fact, she half suspected it was a ruse to try to get her to drop her plans to come here this weekend. She couldn't imagine Dan doing that. Dan would just come straight out and say if there was something bothering him, not sneak around inventing illnesses that didn't exist.

But why was she thinking about Dan all of a sudden?

She knew exactly why she was thinking about Dan. Since their conversation yesterday morning, he'd hardly been off her mind. He'd been so concerned about her, so worried that she'd hold him accountable for his lawyer using Josh's email. 'You're one of my favourite people in the whole world, Hannah, I couldn't bear you to think badly of me,' he'd said. She'd got the definite impression the honeymoon might be coming to an end for him and Sienna, now that she was pregnant. 'She doesn't really like me leaving her on her own,' he said. 'It's cute in a way, but it makes it a bit difficult to earn any money.'

'Maybe I should have chosen someone like you, Hannah,' he said later. 'Someone used to being independent.'

Lily had stopped picking weeds now and was wandering around aimlessly, running her hands along the tops of the newer headstones with their smooth, shiny marble surfaces. Josh had a face like a wet weekend, as her mother would have said. He'd been in a vile mood since yesterday.

Again Hannah found herself comparing him to Dan, whose moods were famously writ large on his open face, impossible to misinterpret. For a second she weakened, allowing herself to remember the thing she'd promised herself to forget.

After listening to what he had said about choosing someone like her next time, Hannah had made some self-deprecating comment, comparing herself unfavourably to Sienna, and he'd said, 'She's jealous of you, you know. She knows you mean a lot to me and she's jealous.' Hannah had laughed it off, but when she came off the phone her cheeks were burning.

Now Josh had gathered their things together — Lily's colouring book that she'd been entertaining herself with, the canvas holdall in which Hannah had brought the trowel and secateurs she used to tend her mother's grave — and was standing waiting, shuffling the bags from hand to hand in a pointed manner. Meanwhile Toby, who had to be kept on his lead in the graveyard for fear that he would start indiscriminately digging, had grown tired of lying at Hannah's feet and was sitting by a neighbouring grave plaintively whining.

'I'm sorry, Mum, it's time to go.'

Even as she said the words, her eyes were filling with tears. It never got any easier. Even all these years after her mother's death, Hannah still was no closer to coming to terms with losing her.

'You rushed me,' she said, once they were in the car and on the way to Gemma's house. 'You know how much I was looking forward to seeing

Mum, and you just couldn't let me have that time with her, could you?'

Josh, who was driving, swung around to look at her, then immediately turned his head back, shaking it from side to side as if he couldn't believe what he'd just heard. 'We drive for an hour and a half so I can spend a day freezing in a graveyard and it's still not enough for you.'

'It wasn't a day. It wasn't even a couple of hours. Admit it, you just don't like me coming here.'

Josh slapped his hand down loudly on the steering wheel. 'All right, I admit it. I don't like you coming here. I don't think it's healthy for you to spend hours talking to your dead mother. I think you need to move on, Hannah, and maybe start paying a bit more attention to the people around you who are still alive.'

'What's that supposed to mean?'

'Me. Lily. You're so wrapped up in yourself and your grief and bloody Sasha, you don't care if your family is falling apart around you.'

Hannah turned to face him. 'What do you mean, *falling apart*?'

'Nothing.'

'No, come on, you must have meant something.'

'Forget it. We're here now.'

'Yes, here now,' sang a little voice from the back seat. Hannah had completely forgotten Lily was even there. She shaped her features into a smile before turning around.

'Come on, baby. Let's go and see Auntie Gemma.'

Gemma's flat was as chaotic as ever. Shoes, bags, clothes, books, ashtrays, all seemed to live in a permanent state of homelessness, migrating their way in piles and clusters around the three cramped rooms.

'I miss Gem like crazy,' Hannah's ex-brother-in-law Sam had said the last time they saw each other, just before the divorce was finalized. 'But I don't miss her stuff everywhere, or her last-minute panics, or always being late because she's left something essential behind.'

Hannah knew what he meant. It was tiring being around so much disorder. She was disorganized, but her sister took clutter to a whole new level. In the end, Sam was effectively saying, it had only been a matter of time before the mess in their lives became the mess of their lives.

'How was Mum?'

Despite it being mid-afternoon, Gemma was wearing a pair of pyjama bottoms with an old grey T-shirt that looked as if it had shrunk in the wash. No bra, Hannah couldn't help noticing. And Gemma was not a petite girl.

'Oh, you know,' said Hannah uselessly, horrified to find her eyes filling with hot tears.

Josh glanced at her sharply, then looked away. She could read the expression on his face as clearly as if he'd spoken. *I knew it. I knew we shouldn't have come.*

'What's up?' Gemma was lying on the sofa with Lily wrapped around her middle, so she couldn't move, but she had missed neither the tears nor Josh's reaction.

'Nothing,' said Hannah over-brightly. Gemma's hair was scraped back with an old, rather grubby pink hairband, and the scar on her forehead that she usually kept hidden was exposed, curved and raised like a fossil under her skin. Hannah's stomach turned and she quickly looked away. 'I'm just over-emotional. It's the hormones, I expect.'

She allowed a moment for the implications of what she'd just said to sink in.

'Oh my God,' said Gemma, eventually twigging. 'You're not?'

Hannah nodded.

Gemma exclaimed in surprise. Was it Hannah's imagination or did Gemma sound a little flat when she said 'congratulations'?

'You going to have a little baby brother, sweetpea?' Gemma asked Lily, nuzzling her face into her hair.

'Not brother, silly. Sister. But I'm the big girl so I'll have to look after her.'

Gemma's face remained buried in her niece's hair, so Hannah couldn't see her expression.

'Actually, I've got a bit of a headache,' Hannah said eventually. 'Have you got any paracetamol?'

'Next to the bed,' said Gemma, waving towards a door that led directly off the living room.

Gemma's bedroom was in as great a state of disarray as the rest of the flat. Hannah winced as she recognized her own slovenliness magnified in that of her sister. Was this what it was like for Josh, she wondered, sharing a home with her, this sinking feeling walking into a room where nothing was calm?

The bed looked like that Tracey Emin art exhibit — all rumpled sheets and overflowing ashtrays and old screwed-up tissues.

'Gemma, when was the last time you changed this duvet cover? And what's this gross stain? Eugh — it *stinks!*'

Hannah thrust the offending cover away from her. Her sister was a slob, no doubt about it. It was quite disgusting how she lived, and yet looking around at the chaos, a part of Hannah felt jealous of Gemma's freedom to leave yesterday's knickers on the floor, knowing that no one would notch it up against her in some unspoken war of attrition you didn't even know you were taking part in until your transgressions were flung at you all at once during some late-night row.

There was no sign of the paracetamol on the crowded bedside table. Hannah nudged aside a teetering pile of books, sending them all crashing down on the wooden floor next to the bed. As she picked them up, she noticed a photograph tucked inside one of them — that giant tome *Wolf Hall* that, to her shame, Hannah had never managed to finish, having become confused about who was who and who was talking. The photograph was of Josh. She suddenly remembered Sasha's remark about September seeing Gemma take a photo from her flat, which she'd instantly dismissed as troublemaking. She sat on the edge of the unmade bed with the picture in her hand, her mind blank, until there was a squeal from Lily, followed by the thud of something hitting the floor, and then Gemma appeared in the doorway.

'Did you find them?'

Hannah didn't look up, just carried on gazing down at the photo of Josh. It was one she'd always loved, slightly over-exposed so his skin was bleached and his smile seemed dazzlingly white as he squinted up into the sun. He was wearing the mustard-coloured jumper he'd owned when they first got together and she'd spent ten years persuading him out of. Funny how she missed it now she saw it again, like seeing a picture of an old friend she'd lost touch with.

'What's that?'

Gemma picked her way towards Hannah over the discarded clothes and books that littered the floorboards.

'It's a photo,' said Hannah eventually. 'Of Josh.'

Gemma, now standing next to her, glanced down at it as she pulled off the pink hairband and shook out her unruly curly hair — brown not red, to Hannah's lifelong jealousy.

'Oh, yes, I found that in my stuff the last time I came back from yours. I've been using it as a bookmark. You can have it back if you like, but don't lose my page or I might have to kill you.'

Gemma sounded so casual, totally unperturbed. Immediately Hannah was wrong-footed. Could it have been an accident? Such things did happen. Particularly to her disorganized sister. One time she'd come back from the airport with someone else's bag. Hannah remembered shrieking with laughter when Gemma opened the case and withdrew a pair of men's boxers emblazoned with the slogan *Lucky Pants*.

She dropped the photo on to the creased sheet and put her head in her hands. Instantly Gemma was next to her, arms around her.

'Hey, hey! What's up, Hans? What's going on?'

Hannah couldn't look at her, knowing that if she did she'd be completely lost. Now that the hairband had gone, Gemma's scar was covered up, but Hannah was as aware of it as if it was lit up in neon. So she stared at her hands instead, the bitten nails still bearing the flaky blue varnish from Lily's last beauty session. Would she ever be the kind of woman who had properly shaped nails with pared-down cuticles and glossy, hard surfaces that shone like the inside of a shell?

'Is it the pregnancy? Aren't you happy about the new baby?'

'Yes! ... No! ... Oh, I don't know. Everything's so weird.'

Gemma tightened her arms around her sister's shoulders. 'What's weird? What's going on, Hans?'

Hannah tried to think how to explain it all. The wall that had come up between her and Josh, the situation with Dan and Sasha, and how despite all their good intentions they'd got caught up in the middle of it and sucked right down with them. And Lily? The bruises on her arm were now fading to green, but Hannah could still hear Nikki's words in her head. Could there be a chance she didn't know her own daughter as well as she thought she did? In which case, what kind of mother was she? And how could she even contemplate having another baby?

Her shoulders slumped under the weight of Gemma's arm. 'Oh God,' she sobbed. 'I miss Mum!'

For a moment, the two sisters sat side by side, holding each other without speaking, each lost in their own thoughts. Then Gemma spoke.

'You know, I miss her too, but you mustn't let your rose-tinted glasses make her something she wasn't, you know. You mustn't forget that she could be awful sometimes. Don't you remember when — '

Her speech was cut short by a blast of birdsong. Hannah had forgotten she'd turned the volume on her phone up to high. She darted out of the bedroom to retrieve it from her bag, still on the floor where she'd dropped it.

'Sasha,' she announced, reading the screen.

'Can't that bloody woman ever leave you alone?' Gemma had followed her out of the bedroom and was standing in the doorway.

'You tell her,' said Josh from his position on the sofa, watching cartoons with Lily curled up next to him.

Hannah made a face. 'She wouldn't be trying to get hold of me if it wasn't for you,' she said.

Then, of course, she had to fill Gemma in on what had been happening, and about Josh's email being appropriated by Dan's lawyer and used against Sasha.

'She shakes all the time, and she's convinced people are robbing her and trying to kill her. And I think — '

She hesitated, remembering that Lily was in the room. But her daughter was engrossed in the television, laughing at *SpongeBob* — a programme Hannah had never managed to understand.

'You think what?' Gemma was looking at her expectantly, so Hannah went on, keeping her voice low.

'I think she's self-harming. She has all these awful scratches on her arm. I haven't seen them properly — she pulls her sleeve down when she sees me looking — but they look pretty bad.'

'Sounds like Dan's right then, Hans. However sorry you feel for Sasha, it doesn't seem like she's in any state to look after a child. More likely she needs help herself. You can't let yourself get drawn into her shit.'

Hannah thought about those scratches, and Sasha's tear-stained face on the floor of the nightclub toilets, and something tightened inside her painfully as if it was about to snap.

'That's just it though. I'm already drawn in.'

Not Lucie/Not Eloise, aged eighteen

Now that Mother is dead, Lucie is dead too. RIP Lucie! RIP Mother! And Eloise? Well, survival never was Eloise's forte. RIP Eloise! That has meant drawing a line under some friendships. Juliette and her family, who were so kind. Lucie was the one who drew that line. They'd never met Lucie before. I don't think they'll want to meet her again. I'm feeling kind of bad about that.

I don't think anyone was surprised when Mother died. As far as I know, her little book of sayings never taught her to say, 'I'll never make old bones,' which is a shame. I think she'd have enjoyed that one. When she hanged herself, just eighteen months after Daddy died and six months after I left school to look after her, Valerie and Michel tried to make a fuss. They said she'd never have done anything so violent. I had a good laugh about that. About their definition of violent. But they're wrong. She wanted to go, all right. Her number was up. She couldn't do it on her own, of course. She couldn't do much on her own by the end, but what else are daughters for?

And things will be different now. I feel lighter. I sense new beginnings. I'm looking for a new name. I think it might help to think of myself as a brand. Like a tin of beans or a washing powder. What's the best name for Brand Me? Plus I'm loaded. Well, not loaded, but I've got some money. Money can't buy you love, isn't that right, Mother? But it can buy you a home. A place to call your own. And that'll be a novelty enough!

25

Pat Hennessey couldn't have looked less at ease. His wet brown eyes were wide and unblinking as he gazed around the crowded gastropub. Not for the first time that evening, Josh wished he'd chosen somewhere else. He'd only picked this place because he'd been here before with Hannah and Sasha and Dan and because, being in Archway, it was convenient for both him in Crouch End and Pat in Holloway, but he could tell Pat felt intimidated by the prices and the trendy staff — the barman with his waxed 'tache and pointed beard and sideburns — and the fact that the pork scratchings they had ordered were home cooked and came piled like entrails in a large bowl.

'Will you gentlemen be eating?' asked a waitress with dyed red hair which was long on one side and shaved on the other with a Maori-type tattoo etched into the scalp. 'I can recommend the jellied pig's head.'

Josh couldn't look at his companion for fear of the horror he'd see on his face.

'Sorry,' he mumbled when the waitress had left, jamming her pencil behind her multi-pierced ear. 'We should have gone somewhere else.'

'No, no, this is grand. All the pubs around my way have great big TV screens everywhere and you can't hear yourself think, so this is a real treat.'

'But you won't be trying the jellied pig's head, I'm guessing.'

'No, probably not.'

They sat for a few seconds in silence, squinting at the blackboard where the menu was chalked in curly letters.

'Should have brought my specs,' said Pat. 'I keep forgetting that I'm now a person who wears glasses. I wonder how old I'll have to be before I come to terms with it. What does that third one say, under the rabbit dish?'

'Beer-battered cod with thick-cut skin-on potato wedges.'

Pat's face relaxed. 'Fish and chips,' he said.

While they waited for their food, the headache that had been thrumming in Josh's brain all day started to build. He knew it was stress, but knowing that didn't help him deal with it any better. He turned over in his mind ways to broach the subject of Kelly Kavanagh and his suspension to Pat. He assumed that's why Pat had called to suggest a drink, but now they were here, his erstwhile colleague seemed in no rush to get to the point. And the longer they went without talking about it, the more nervous Josh became. It wasn't so much the elephant in the room as the great blue whale.

At last Pat pressed his lips together as if considering what he was about to say, and then opened his mouth. 'I can't tell you how sorry I am, Josh, about what's happened to you.'

There. It was out. Josh felt some of the pressure that had been building up inside his head escape like a mini gas leak. *Pffff*.

'It's what we're all afraid of, isn't it? All of us men. There but for the grace of God and all that. How are you bearing up?'

Josh thought about telling Pat about the pressure in his head, and the way his heart occasionally raced for no reason, convincing him that he was about to go into cardiac arrest, or how he lay awake during the early hours of the morning, listening to Hannah's rhythmic breathing and the second hand of the alarm clock softly ticking away, while panic burned through him like acid until it was all he could do not to cling on to her like a drowning man grabbing a piece of driftwood. He could tell him about the walks he took with Toby through the dark streets when lying in bed became too unbearable, his footsteps echoing on the deserted pavements, how whenever he saw another person going about their business in the dim light he was seized by a mad impulse to tell them who he was — a man accused of paedophilia, an abuser of innocence — just to watch their expression change. How it felt to be on the outside of life, when he'd always done everything he could to fit snugly in. He could tell him how, more often than not, those walks led him to Sasha's road, where he stood looking up at her house, his thoughts poisoned darts, each one aimed at her.

'Oh, you know. It's pretty shit really, as you might expect.'

Pat nodded, his Adam's apple bobbing furiously in his throat. Josh noticed he was wearing exactly the same sort of clothes he wore to school — a checked shirt under a pale-blue

334

crew-neck jumper, a pair of brown cords. It was as if Pat didn't have a private side — he was 'Sir' in his personal life, just like at school.

'How has Hannah taken it? It must be a big worry for her, especially with her being pregnant.'

Josh stared into his pint, concentrating on the surface where the bubbles popped. There was a dog on the floor by the next table, a little grey shaggy thing, lying on its side with a look of resignation. He always forgot there were places you could bring dogs, and had a momentary pang of remorse for Toby, cooped up in the flat.

'I haven't told her.'

Pat, who'd been making a chequerboard pattern out of square coasters, looked up then, his mouth open, eyes wide. Then he sucked the air in through his teeth in a long, loud inward breath. 'Wow. I mean, I can see why you wouldn't want to say anything, but Josh, it's been nearly a week. You don't want to be carrying this on your own. It's too much.'

Josh pressed his lips together, enjoying the sharp pressure of teeth against flesh. 'I keep meaning to tell her, but I lose my nerve. And then I convince myself that it won't last long, this suspension. They'll finish their investigation — which has to be cursory at best, I mean, what evidence do they have? — and then I'll be back at work and Hannah need never know anything about it.'

Pat was still staring at him, stricken, so he added, 'Maybe I'll tell her later on, when everything isn't so stressful.'

335

The red-haired waitress materialized by his side, balancing out-sized white plates on her skinny, bird-like arms. He'd asked for his steak medium rare and it was bleeding watery pink across the expanse of white china. Revulsion heaved suddenly inside him, and he swallowed it back down.

'So what have you been doing during the day, while Hannah thinks you're at work?'

Josh sighed. 'Just hanging out with friends mostly. Outstaying my welcome probably.'

This was almost true. He had been hanging out with one friend in particular. Dan. Or rather, not Dan, as Dan was almost always at work. Sienna. He'd been hanging out with Sienna. He hadn't intended to, he told himself. It had just kind of happened organically.

He'd started off on the first day of his enforced leave driving around aimlessly, circumventing the congestion-charge zone, then on the second day, he had found himself in west London and decided to call in on impulse. He still hadn't completely forgiven Dan for sending his email to the lawyer, but he could understand how it had happened. So he'd called in, and found Sienna home alone, and bored. And again he'd ended up telling her everything — about the new allegation at work, about Hannah, even Lily. She had a way of listening with her whole body, leaning towards him, fixing him with those green-flecked eyes, that made him feel as if he was actually being heard for the first time in a long time. He'd left feeling lighter, less like he was being crushed slowly in one of those

336

car-cubing machines. Since then they'd met a few times, mostly at the Notting Hill flat, but once in Regent's Park and a couple of times, when it was too cold to be outdoors, at Tate Modern. Josh would drive off as if heading to work and park the car a few streets away, catching the bus to Finsbury Park and then the tube on from there. Sometimes he felt a twinge of guilt about these meetings, since obviously he couldn't mention them to Hannah. It didn't help either that Sienna was gorgeous — he'd seen the way men looked at him when they were out together. *What has he got?* was what those looks were saying. Mostly, though, he justified it to himself. They were keeping each other company. And Sienna was keeping him sane. She was so refreshingly unjudgemental, so unfazed by things. He'd found himself confiding stuff he'd never even verbalized to himself, let alone anyone else — things about his childhood, about his disappointment that the two women he loved most in the world — his mother and his wife — had never bonded, about how moody Hannah was now she was pregnant.

Sienna, on the other hand, seemed to be taking pregnancy completely in her stride, hardly registering it at all. He knew it was unfair to compare a twenty-four-year-old to a woman ten years older who'd already given birth before, but Sienna seemed to have none of the problems Hannah was always complaining about — the tiredness, the floods of tears for no reason, the way her favourite food suddenly tasted all wrong. Sometimes he thought Hannah was actually

337

losing it a bit. Like when she'd suddenly started quizzing him about Gemma and whether he'd ever fancied her. Where had that come from?

In her turn, Sienna had opened up to him. Dan was taking it very badly, she told him. About not being able to see September. He was tearing his hair out with worry. Sasha wasn't stable. Something ought to be done — for her sake as much as anything. Sienna felt awful about what had happened to Sasha, and couldn't sleep some nights for the guilt of having taken Dan away. It seemed wrong to build your happiness on someone else's unhappiness, she told Josh (weren't those the exact words he'd used himself?). But then equally you couldn't help who you fell in love with. Sasha was still relatively young — and quite attractive, Sienna said earnestly. She could find someone else. But she had to move on with her life — it had been three months, for God's sake — and to do that she had to get some help. And while she was getting that help, they were all going to have to accept there'd have to be some changes. She and Dan couldn't possibly look after a child in Sienna's one-bedroom flat, so they'd have to move into the house, at least until it could be sold. It wasn't what *she* wanted. Sienna was scathing about Crouch End with its yummy mummies and artisan bread shops and supermarkets which grew their own vegetables on the roof. She called it suburbia until she remembered Josh lived there too. But Josh thought she was probably right. It *was* pretty suburban. It didn't even have a tube. It had been Hannah who'd wanted to live there in the first place, if he remembered rightly. He would have been happy somewhere cheaper and more convenient.

'I just wish things hadn't got so bitter,' Sienna said to him, as they sat huddled on a bench outside the Tate, watching the muddy river churn past and the crowds surge over the steel ribbon that was the Millennium Bridge. 'I'm absolutely hopeless at confrontation, but when I see what she's doing to him, keeping him from his daughter, it makes me so angry.'

Josh had smiled then, he couldn't help it — the notion of this girl with her soft eyes and the freckles over the bridge of her nose getting angry.

Across the table, Pat was gingerly probing the emerald-green mushy peas that had arrived in a small bowl of their own. He kept clearing his throat as though he were about to say something. Eventually he lowered his fork. 'Listen, Josh, I have to tell you, I think it might take longer than you're imagining. The investigation, I mean.'

'What do you mean?'

'Just that everyone seems to be taking it very seriously. It's bad timing, that's all. With all those high-profile cases that have been in the news, I think they're using you to prove how tough they are on any kind of . . . impropriety, and how willing they are to listen to supposed victims.'

'But I haven't done anything!' The lump of meat on his tongue felt suddenly monstrous.

'I know that, Josh. I think everyone knows it really. It's just that they've got to be seen to be taking action. It would help if you could find whoever made that anonymous call and get them to withdraw it. Any ideas?'

Josh swallowed the unchewed meat and felt it lodge painfully in his throat before sliding down to his stomach, where it sat uneasily. Sasha had done this. He was convinced of it. His whole life reduced to nothing. His marriage hanging by a thread. Killing time during the day when he ought to be at work, hours lost that would never come back.

Hatred spread black as ink through his bloodstream.

* * *

Sasha's house loomed up at the side of the road. It was one of a short terrace of three wide three-storey white modernist houses that had been built in the 1950s, on the road that joined Crouch End to its more established neighbour Highgate. This road was cut into what originally would have been a hill; the houses on one side dropped down towards the allotments and cricket club and, way down below, a secondary school, while the houses on Sasha's side were set up from the road, accessed by steep steps. Their width made them extra imposing from pavement level, which is where Josh was standing. He'd driven here straight from the pub, imagining Sasha inside her beautiful house, with her white floorboards and her distressed furniture, getting on with her life.

Anger tightened like a band around his chest, leaving him short of breath.

340

The steps were in full view of the road, but one side, out of range of the light by the front door, was in darkness. That was the side Josh kept to. That was the side he always used now, even in daylight when there was little differentiation in shade. He'd been here a few times over the past week. Standing in these very shadows, keeping an eye on things. Watching. Waiting.

On either side of the steps were terraces of Japanese plants, staggered down to the road like the neatest of green waterfalls. Josh fought the urge to seize them by the stems and rip them from the earth.

He wanted to do damage.

At the top of the steps there was a polished-hardwood decked terrace running the entire width of the house. In the middle was the front door, and on either side were wide windows that made the most of the light, one from the room Sasha referred to as her 'office', although as far as Josh could tell she'd never done a day's work in her life, the other the guest bedroom. When they'd moved into the house, the entire ground floor had been the kitchen, but they'd recently changed all that with the help of a team of architects, switching the kitchen to the top floor, along with Dan's office and September's bedroom, and dividing up the lower space. Dan had confided that the renovations — or Sasha's kitchen project, as it became known — had cost almost as much as the actual house. He'd looked a little sick when he said that, Josh remembered.

It was the office Josh was interested in tonight.

He could see Sasha sitting at the vast desk that the designer had had made from concrete poured into a giant mould and then polished to a sheen. Dan had said it must be like working on the hard shoulder of the M25, but Sasha had been exultant because it was unique. Sitting on her own at the far end of the concrete runway, staring intently at her iPad, Sasha looked dwarfed by the monolithic surroundings she'd created and for a moment Josh felt sorry for her. Alone in this huge gallery of a house. Then he remembered what she'd done, and his hatred returned, sliding down over the pity like a shop shutter.

He didn't know how long he watched her. Nor could he have said why. Only that something was drawing him here to lurk in the darkness outside someone else's house. While his own wife and child waited at home, he drew some sort of perverse satisfaction from watching someone else's family like a peeping Tom, feeling something inside him crystallizing, becoming hard and blade-sharp. He had no idea what it was, but was content to bide his time until it all became clearer. After all, time was one thing he had plenty of.

26

Could Josh be having an affair?

The idea had never crossed Hannah's mind before. Not because she felt their relationship to be inviolable, but because she'd always felt she held the balance of power in their marriage. He had so often told her he was lucky to have her that she had long since accepted it as fact. Not that she'd ever put it into so many words, but if it came right down to it, which thankfully it never had, she felt sure she was the beloved in the relationship and Josh the one who loved. Or rather, she always had felt sure of it — until now.

Suddenly, nothing felt certain any more. Josh, a man who normally relished routine to an almost compulsive degree, was acting inconsistently. Since that afternoon when he'd come home early from school with a headache — unusual in itself — there'd been a couple of occasions where he'd arrived back from work late without any real reason. Another time he'd been there when she got home from picking Lily up from school, saying it was an inset afternoon, although previously the staff had always been required to stay on school premises during inset days. Then there were the nights where she'd wake to find him staring glassily at the ceiling or else vanished altogether. 'I couldn't sleep,' he'd whisper, sliding back into bed later. 'I took the dog out for a walk.'

Often after these disruptions she'd fall back into a light, fitful sleep and find herself a teenager again, standing in the hospital, looking down on Gemma's grotesquely swollen face, trying to ignore the large white pad on her forehead that Hannah knew hid a gaping hole, a horrible, black oozing space where there used to be bone, tissue and skin. And always playing in the background on an endless loop, the image of her mother, her features at first distorted by anger, then later by self-reproach. 'What have I done?' this dream mother wailed, clutching the metal rail that ran along the side of Gemma's bed, so her knuckles pressed up white through her skin like teeth through babies' gums.

Occasionally, in these dreams, Gemma wouldn't be in bed. Instead she'd be climbing out of the passenger seat of the car and limping down the road towards Hannah, her bleeding head dangling from her neck like a flower on a broken stalk. 'I'm sorry,' Hannah would call to her. 'I couldn't stop it. It wasn't my fault.' But she knew she was lying and would wake up bathed in sweat that, in her panicked, bleary state, she mistook for blood.

She stopped working. Or rather she continued sitting at the table attempting to work, but she stopped producing anything worthwhile. Instead she doodled spirals on the lined paper of her notebook and wrote her name in jagged writing over and over again until the pen tore clear through the page. She made so many excuses to so many people she stopped recognizing what was true and what fiction.

344

The baby expanded inside her like a balloon. Sometimes she felt it might never stop growing until one or other of them popped like a piñata.

The disrupted sleep and the ongoing worry about unmet deadlines and unpaid bills that buzzed constantly in her head like white noise on a radio made Hannah feel increasingly as if her mind was detaching from her body and floating formlessly above it. Strange memories of her mother's depressive illness and the devastating effect on their childhood began to surface in her mind for the first time in years.

Even Lily didn't provide the usual comfort. Now when Hannah looked at her she felt weighed down by the inadequacy of her parenting and the many ways she failed her daughter daily. She looked at other children at the school being whisked off to ballet and gymnastics and private French lessons — all the things she'd always insisted that her tight work schedule wouldn't allow. She knew other mothers who picked up their children, handbags bulging with magazines and books to fill the long hours that would have to be spent loitering outside piano teachers' houses and church halls given over twice a week to the teaching of Kumon Maths. Hannah used to eye those mothers, laden with half-size guitars and trumpets, with amusement, but now the sight of those misshapen black cases was like a reproach. When she walked past open windows on Saturday mornings and listened to the tortuous sounds of a child practising scales, sawing away on a violin, she no longer felt relief, but a stabbing guilt. If only she'd been a more attentive mother, would Lily now be less reticent, more confident in social situations? That was the thing no one ever told you about being a parent. How you were constantly getting glimpses of your child's alternate, idealized selves — which they could have achieved if only you'd been happier, more consistent, less prone to doubt. Better.

For the hundredth time in the last few days, Hannah found herself longing to speak to Sasha. From the little she knew, Sasha had had the very worst example in her own mother, and after the last few weeks could herself hardly qualify for Mother of the Year, but nevertheless she had a way of minimizing Hannah's maternal neuroses without dismissing them or trivializing them. She had issues with control when it came to how she parented September, but she was always full of praise for how Hannah managed to earn a living as well as look after a young child. In the end you just had to do your best, didn't you?

Well, didn't you?

Hannah had covered every inch of her open notebook in biro doodles, so that the scant writing she'd done was all but lost. She pushed it away in disgust and desultorily clicked her laptop into life. Her Twitter account popped up on screen. As usual, she automatically went first to her notifications, to find out if anyone had tweeted her directly. She did this more out of habit and hope than for any other reason. She hardly ever seemed to get any direct interaction

346

these days. Perhaps that was due to her own patchy online attendance, her tendency to lurk rather than to post. She'd originally set up her account for work reasons, because everyone else was doing it, and as a way to publicize pieces she'd written and to promote herself as a freelancer, but some days Twitter made her feel like the loneliest person in the world. So many busy, productive people leading busy, productive lives, going to parties, to book clubs, climbing mountains for charity, winning awards, while she sat at home mired in inactivity, drawing spirals on a pad.

But when she clicked on the Notifications button, there was evidence of recent activity. Lots of it. Immediately she began to feel better. But as she scrolled down, her momentary good humour dissolved, replaced by a growing sense of horror. All of the messages were from accounts she didn't recognize. And every one was abusive, pouring vitriol on pieces she'd written and even on Hannah herself.

The stalking piece in the Mail by @HHfreelance was the most shoddy piece of journalism I've ever read.

Hope @HHfreelance is an intern and isn't being PAID to turn out the drivel she writes.

And the one that made the blood in her veins ice over:

@HHfreelance wrecks people's lives.

An internet troll, surely, making a random attack? The thought didn't make her feel any better. The list went on and on. Someone had been very busy. Someone hated her enough to do all that.

Hannah sat back in her chair staring at the screen, her hand held up to her mouth to stopper the scream she could feel building in her throat. Her heart thudded so painfully against her ribcage she felt convinced, for one awful moment, that it might dislodge the baby inside her.

Someone hated her.

Someone really hated her.

For Hannah, who had spent her entire life in the pursuit of being liked, it was a sickening realization. All through her childhood, while Gemma would go barging into situations acting on impulse and not caring what people thought, Hannah had loitered behind, brokering and negotiating her way. It limited what you could get done, and it tended to dilute the passion in life, like the watery squash their mother made them, but at least she could go to bed knowing she hadn't made an enemy that day — and for her that was the most important thing.

'Because of an accident that wasn't even your fault, you feel like you have to be nice to everyone for the rest of your life,' Gemma had once said accusingly, angered because Hannah had insisted on inviting a couple of girls no one liked, and who clearly didn't like them either, to a party, just so they couldn't accuse her of leaving them out. Hannah knew she was right, but she couldn't help it. Teachers, cashiers at the supermarket till, neighbours, other dog walkers, people who had nothing to do with her life and who she'd never see again: she wanted them all to like her. It was a compulsion. She forced herself to go back through the list of notifications. They were all from brand-new accounts with few followers, and when she clicked to see who those followers were, they turned out to be carpet-cleaning companies and loan agencies — faceless computer-run accounts, on the whole. Those were the only people who'd see these malicious tweets, she told herself, trying to calm herself with logic. Hannah put her hand to her stomach, aware she was still trembling.

Someone had spent a long time doing this. Setting up new accounts wasn't hard, but it was time-consuming — selecting backgrounds, choosing monikers.

She was still staring at her screen when the doorbell sounded, startling her and causing Toby to erupt in a frenzy of barking.

The intercom was on the blink (again), so she left the door to her flat open while she crossed the communal hallway and drew back the heavy cast-iron catch on the main front door. Her eyes widened in shock when she saw the slight, hunched figure standing there.

Sasha looked terrible. In just a few days she seemed to have shrunk to nothing; her skin had a curious yellowish tinge and seemed to mould itself like wax over her nose and forehead. Though it was briskly cold — hard to believe it was already nearly Christmas — Sasha wasn't wearing a coat, just a gunmetal-grey top with long sleeves that flared slightly at the wrists. Hannah had been with her when she bought that top — the two of them on a rare shopping trip together, finishing off laden with bags (well, Sasha anyway) and sipping mojitos in a Regent Street hotel bar, crying with laughter just because they were out and child-free and feeling young. Could that really have been just a few months ago? Now the top was at least two sizes too big, hanging off Sasha's tiny frame like a scarecrow's clothes. Without even thinking, Hannah stepped forward and folded her arms around her friend.

After a while, she pulled away and half walked, half carried Sasha through to her flat. She was still too shocked to speak as she deposited her on the sofa.

'I look revolting, don't I?' Sasha's voice was gravelly, as if it hadn't been used for a while.

Hannah couldn't respond.

'What's happening to me? I feel I've gone completely mad. Sometimes I imagine people are outside the house watching me, waiting for me to spin totally off the edge. Everything I thought I knew about my life has turned out to be not true, or not there. Like it was built out of sand. Oh, you can't understand what I mean.'

'I think I probably can.'

Sasha glanced at her and Hannah saw a flash of the old Sasha — amusement and scorn mixed together.

'How could you understand, Hannah? You

have Josh, Lily, your home, your job, your new baby.' Was she imagining it or did Sasha's voice wobble on that last word? 'Everything is secure in your life. It's not going anywhere, whereas my whole world has disintegrated. You know Dan is trying to force me out of my home, don't you? He wants to live there with his slut and September and airbrush me out as if I never existed.'

Sasha was gesticulating in her anger, and the sleeve of her top shifted slightly back. Hannah felt her stomach twist at the sight of the scratches scored into her arm. She'd almost forgotten about them, and this sudden reminder made her feel queasy. What's more, she might be wrong, but they looked strangely fresh. The dried blood was red rather than brown and coagulated into raised welts. Sasha pulled down on her sleeve and Hannah tore her eyes away.

'You know he introduced September to her — to that bitch. After all those promises he made.'

Hannah clapped her hand over her mouth. 'But how? I thought you were only letting him see her with you there?'

Sasha's dull sunken eyes fixed on Hannah's. 'My lawyer convinced me to do it. She said it would show a judge that I've tried to be reasonable. He said he'd take her swimming. He didn't tell me that *she*'d be there too. So now September thinks the sun shines out of her fucking arse. Says she looks like a princess with lovely long hair and why don't I try to grow my

351

hair long and then maybe Daddy will love me again.'

Hannah felt her own eyes filming over with tears. 'Oh Sasha, that must be so hard. But surely a court won't let him get his own way? He can't just take your house and your daughter away from you.'

'My solicitor says there's a very good chance he'll get what he wants, thanks in part to Josh's email.'

'I'm so sorry.'

Sasha shrugged, then she shot Hannah another look that Hannah found hard to gauge. 'Actually it was quite interesting. Caroline, my solicitor, sent me the *whole* email that Josh's so-called testimony had been taken from.'

There was something about the way she stressed the word 'whole' that Hannah didn't like.

'Turns out it wasn't just my parenting skills Josh slagged off. He said some pretty choice things about your sex life, too. Or lack of it.'

'He wouldn't . . . '

The words came out before Hannah had even thought about them, but immediately she realized that of course he would. And he obviously had. She felt sick.

'Don't worry, I know he was exaggerating. If you'd been that frigid you wouldn't be up the duff right now!'

Hannah felt her face burning.

'Oh Hans, I didn't mean to upset you. I guess I want everyone to be as miserable as me. I've turned into the most horrible person. My

352

mother always used to tell me I was, when she . . . Oh Hannah, please forget I said anything.'

Hannah nodded, but they both knew there were some things that couldn't be forgotten.

'The truth is I'm jealous of you. That's a terrible thing to say, isn't it? But it's true. I want what you've got, what I used to have.'

Sitting on the other end of the sofa, Hannah couldn't find the words to tell Sasha how wrong she was about her so-called perfect life.

'Oh God,' she said, suddenly aware of the time. 'I've got to go. It's pick-up time. Is September at nursery?'

September hadn't been at nursery since the last time Hannah had seen Sasha. Hannah had assumed it was because Sasha didn't want to risk bumping into her and Josh. She felt guilty now at how relieved she'd been that Lily was having a break from her.

Sasha, who'd been staring off into the middle distance, nodded. 'It's OK. I've got the car. We'll make it.'

But on the way to nursery, Sasha seemed to sink further into herself. Inside the car, their breath came out in clouds and Hannah waited for her to put the heating on, but Sasha didn't seem to notice the cold, staring fixedly ahead with her strange, empty eyes. Once she shook her head fiercely as though categorically denying something to herself, but when Hannah asked her what she was thinking about she just shrugged.

At the nursery, September came running up to Hannah and flung her arms dramatically around her as if they'd been parted for months. 'Please can I come to your house to play? Please, please, please.' The little girl's grip around her waist was tight as a belt.

Lily appeared by her side, gazing at Hannah wordlessly, but she couldn't read the expression on her daughter's round, serious face.

'I'm not sure,' she wavered. September responded by tightening her hold. There was a sense of desperation about her that Hannah found unsettling. She glanced at Sasha for some sort of support, but Sasha was staring off into the distance as she had done in the car.

'*Please*,' September begged into Hannah's stomach.

Hannah didn't have the energy for a scene. Something told her that a tantrum from September at this point might just send Sasha — or her, for that matter — over the edge. And besides, there was something about September's naked need that worried her.

'OK,' she said weakly. 'You can come back with us. Both of you, of course,' she added looking at Sasha, who merely shrugged again, as if it was all the same to her where they went.

On the way to the car Hannah cursed herself for saying yes. From the rigid way Lily was holding herself Hannah could tell she wasn't happy, and Sasha didn't seem too delighted either. She kept clenching and unclenching her tiny, crab-like hands in a way Hannah found quite disconcerting. She tried to remember if there was anything in the fridge she could possibly knock up into a semblance of lunch, but her mind was blank. Shopping hadn't been at the top of her to-do list recently. She tried not to think about the work she wasn't doing, or those abusive tweets lined up one on top of the other in a scroll of bile.

September was gripping her hand tightly, as if scared she might run off.

Lily normally liked going in the back of Sasha's SUV. It was so high off the ground and you could tell from her shy smile that she felt a sense of grandeur driving around looking down on passers-by and people in other cars. Today, however, there was no trace of a smile as Hannah got her belted into the back seat. 'You OK, Liliput?' she murmured into the wisps of fine baby hair that still framed her daughter's face, much to Lily's distress. (The other day Hannah had come into the bathroom and found Lily arching backwards so that her hair touched her shoulder blades. 'Look, Mummy,' she'd said excitedly. 'I got long hair now!') But Lily didn't reply, just stared stonily ahead.

Sasha started the engine before Hannah even had a chance to get into the passenger seat. She kept revving on the accelerator rhythmically as Hannah buckled up her seatbelt, as if she was tapping her foot in time to a beat only she could hear.

'Are you sure you're OK, Sash?'

But Sasha seemed not to hear.

As they pulled off into the traffic, Sasha started drumming her hands insistently on the wheel. Hannah kept glancing over nervously. There was something disturbing about the rhythmic thud of Sasha's bitten fingers hitting the hard leather again and again. She wanted to tell her to stop.

'Well, this is fun, isn't it?' she said loudly to the girls in the back. 'Just like old times!' She was babbling just so there wouldn't be silence, but she knew immediately that it had been the wrong thing to say. It wasn't the slightest bit like old times.

'Sorry,' she mouthed at Sasha, then she stopped as a noise came involuntarily from her that was partly a gasp and partly a cry. Everything in her froze except the blood pounding insanely in her ears. Sasha turned to her and caught her expression and immediately tugged down the left sleeve of her too-baggy top that had slipped right back, exposing a frighteningly frail arm. But it was too late. Hannah had already seen it, and she knew it was an image that would be etched into her memory for ever.

Scored into the flesh of Sasha's arm in gobs of congealed blood, shocking against the sallow skin, was a word.

HELP.

'Oh my God, Sasha!'

Sasha shot her a look so full of silent appeal that Hannah felt as if little bits of her heart were splintering off and lodging like shrapnel inside her.

'I just can't,' Sasha whispered, and Hannah knew she was telling her something important, but she couldn't work out what. Everything seemed to be going round and round in her head

— the Twitter abuse, Josh, *frigid*, the horrible thing on Sasha's arm. Her brain was churning with unthinkable thoughts. She was so lost in them that at first she wasn't aware that Sasha was trembling all over, her fingers shaking on the wheel, the knuckles blue-white.

'Sasha?' she ventured when at last she noticed her friend's strange, fixed expression. 'Sasha!' she shouted as she glanced through the windscreen and saw the T-junction up ahead that they were approaching much too fast, the car veering across the road from left to right and back again. *Not again. Please God, not again.* The jolt of déjà vu from that earlier teenage accident was sharp and savage. She grabbed the wheel, but there was nothing she could do. She tried to twist round to look at Lily, but just got a flash of September's terrified face. Then there was a scream she only vaguely recognized as her own, and the gut-wrenching jolt of impact.

And then nothing.

27

Dan sounded almost euphoric. 'I told you she was dangerous — to herself and to other people!'

He'd jumped up from the grey chaise longue he'd briefly been sitting on and was pacing around the huge living room that he'd always claimed to dislike, insisting that Sasha had made all the design decisions and his only involvement was the signing of the cheques. Every now and then he stopped to pick up this ornament or that photograph, examining it intently then returning it and moving on. It was as if he was rediscovering his house, Josh decided, reclaiming his territory for his own.

'You don't know it was her fault.' Josh was weary, speaking almost without thinking. They'd been over this so many times during the course of that awful, endless day, it was as if they were stuck in a loop, doomed to repeat the same conversation over and over again until the meaning had all but drained out of the words.

'You saw her arm.' Sienna was curled up in the wide white armchair. She'd had a shower and was wearing a grey towelling dressing gown Josh guessed must belong to Dan, and her wet hair was combed back from her face. She looked tired, and terribly young. 'And Hannah said she was acting really strange. She needs help.'

'She couldn't have made that any clearer.' Dan shook his head.

'But the police guy did say he found a nail in the front tyre — the tyre that blew.'

'Yes, and he also said it was unusual for a nail to get embedded in a front tyre — usually it's the back tyres that it happens to. If there's a nail in the road, the front tyre will flick it upright and it's the back tyre that gets punctured when it rolls over it.' Dan sounded like a salesman reciting a carefully prepared spiel. 'And don't forget he also said it was strange for the nail to be embedded in the sidewall of the tyre rather than the tread.'

'You really think she'd have done that herself? It doesn't make sense,' said Josh.

'Another thing to blame on me!' This time the triumph in Dan's voice was clear. 'She probably wanted to claim I did it. You know she was about to accuse me of being addicted to hardcore porn, don't you? Her and that charlatan lawyer of hers.'

Sienna, probably aware how paranoid Dan sounded, chimed in, 'Whether or not she put the nail there herself, I think it's pretty obvious she could have controlled that car if she'd wanted to. They weren't even going that fast.'

Dan, who was now absently riffling through his vinyl collection, housed in custom-built shelves along the back wall of the living room, nodded his head vigorously. 'Thank God this will show everyone just how crazy she really is. She could have killed them all. It's a miracle no one was seriously hurt.'

'Dan!' Sienna warned.

'Oh fuck. Sorry, mate. I didn't mean . . . I forgot . . . '

He was waiting for Josh to absolve him, but he didn't oblige. Dan had hardly seemed to register the news that Hannah had lost the baby — no, how did the doctor put it? The baby had died in the womb. They'd all been at the hospital where Hannah and Sasha and the girls had been taken after the accident. When Hannah had whispered to him that she was bleeding, at first Josh had scanned her head anxiously for wounds, before realizing what she actually meant. Then the registrar with the sad eyes and cold-blocked nose had said it might be nothing but they should run a scan on Hannah while she was there, just to make sure everything was as it should be. Right from the start it had been obvious there was something very wrong. She kept passing the electronic thing over Hannah's belly, and then doing it again. And again. And all the time not saying anything at all, just staring intently at the monitor.

'I'm terribly sorry,' she'd said after a few long, silent minutes, and Hannah had made a noise that sounded as if it had been ripped from her, and Josh had held her hand uselessly and watched her tears form a damp patch on the hospital sheet. He felt nothing. Wrung out. Empty.

It had completely done for him — first the phone call from Dan to say there'd been an accident, while he and Sienna were out walking on the Heath. Then the mad dash to the hospital and the visceral relief of seeing Lily sitting up gazing with proud awe at the large plaster on her knee, and Hannah, pale and shadow-eyed but still managing to smile weakly at something a nurse was saying to her. For a short while he'd thought everything would be OK, that they'd survived unscathed. On the way to the hospital, he'd made all sorts of promises to all sorts of gods he didn't believe in. He'd never begrudge Hannah anything again. She could visit her mother whenever she liked, for however long she liked. They could set up camp in the bloody graveyard if that's what she wanted. And he'd tell her everything that had been going on at work. He'd be a better husband, better father, better provider, if only they were OK. And for that short period there in the hospital, he had believed his prayers had been answered.

Then came that scan, *just to be sure*, and that awful silence stretching on and on, and that 'I'm terribly sorry', and he realized he hadn't been listened to, after all. How could he ever have believed otherwise?

And now this. This curious emptiness.

Dan, on the other hand, seemed full to bursting, to the point where he just couldn't seem to stay still. He'd been in this same supercharged mood when Josh first saw him at the hospital. He'd appeared with September clinging to his arm as Josh and Lily were waiting for Hannah to have an X-ray on her wrist to make sure it wasn't broken. This was before the scan and the silence that came after it. Sasha was in a different ward, he told them. She might not be out for a couple of days. Psychological assessment, Josh learned later, when September and Lily wandered off to the vending machine to ogle the chocolate. The doctors were taking the wounds to Sasha's arm as a cry for help. Not to mention the circumstances of the accident, where Sasha had failed to slow down at a T-junction, ending up smashing into the car parked on the opposite side of the intersection. A blow-out, she insisted. She'd had no chance of controlling the car. And there was the nail and the burst tyre to prove it. The nail that might or might not have been hammered in there on purpose.

'You see?' Dan kept saying. 'You see how things are?'

With Sasha being detained on the general ward, ostensibly for a bump on her head, but really so that staff could find out whether she presented a threat to herself or anyone else, it was obvious that Dan should move back home to look after his traumatized daughter. September had pleaded for Sienna to come too and had spent the evening curled up on her lap in the same armchair Sienna was now sitting in. Now the two girls were asleep upstairs. Josh had been in such shock following the scan he hadn't had the energy to protest when Dan insisted he and Lily come back with them rather than stay by themselves, and he docilely strapped his quiet daughter into the back of the Golf and followed Dan's unmistakeable red car back to the very house he'd been lurking outside just the night before. Saying goodbye to Hannah at the hospital had been both a nightmare and — he hated himself for thinking it — a relief. After the scan, they'd been given the option of going home and letting the miscarriage happen naturally or Hannah staying overnight and having an ERPC procedure in the morning to eliminate what the sad-eyed registrar called 'the products of conception'. '*Products of conception?* She meant our baby,' Hannah had sobbed afterwards. The registrar had told them that the baby was smaller than they'd have expected at this stage, which could mean it had died up to ten days before, but Hannah had refused to listen. 'It was the crash,' she repeated stubbornly, and then, 'It was Sasha.'

Hannah was in a ward with three others, and had already taken a strong sleeping pill by this time. She'd hardly looked up when he bent over her to kiss her goodbye, so she didn't notice he was finally crying, fat round tears that bubbled up unbidden. Or maybe she noticed but didn't comment.

'Just go,' she'd said, closing her eyes. Her hair on the pillow was the colour of dried blood.

So now here they were, in this house where he and Hannah had spent so much time — Saturday nights staying up far too late playing poker for a tenner-a-head stake and drinking cocktails they took it in turns to invent; Sunday lunchtimes that bled softly into evenings, sitting so long around the white round retro table that they got hungry all over again and raided the fridge for leftovers.

Where had those people gone?

363

Now Josh sat in the black leather and chrome 1960s chair that Dan had bought for a small fortune at auction one drunken Saturday afternoon and insisted on putting in pride of place, despite Sasha's vehement objections, and felt like he was visiting the place for the first time. It was familiar, yet unfamiliar. Like something he'd seen on television.

'How are you feeling, Josh?' Sienna's voice — warm with concern — brought back the treacherous tears pricking his eyes.

'I'm OK. Dreading tomorrow. Not half as much as Hannah is, of course.'

'I'm so sorry.'

She'd said it a thousand times over the course of the afternoon. Josh was aware she meant well, but he wished she'd be quiet now. He didn't want to have to talk or think. What if he'd put the nail in Sasha's tyre himself? The thought came into his head before he had time to stop it, through the gap that Sienna's question had opened up. He'd been here last night, outside this house in his usual spot and all these thoughts had been crowding into his head, whirring around and around until it was like an explosion in his brain. And then nothing. One minute he'd been standing in the shadows outside Sasha's study window, and the next he was waking up back in his bed, with Hannah asleep next to him and a strange hungover feeling. On a rational, logical level, he knew he'd never have done anything like that — wouldn't even have known how to. But he hated this lapse in his memory, and how the things that were going on in his life were slowly stripping him from the self he'd always known.

He was conscious that Dan and Sienna were exchanging meaningful looks, and then Dan came and perched on the arm of his chair.

'Sorry, Josh. I've been a knob, haven't I? Going on and on about my stuff when you're going through . . . Well, you know.'

'Don't worry.' Josh's voice was unsteady. 'I'm used to you being a knob.'

But then Dan was off again, moving around the room, opening cupboards and reacquainting himself with all the possessions he hadn't seen for the last few weeks. He'd been furious when he first saw his study. 'Babe, come in here!' he'd called to Sienna. She and Josh had arrived in the upstairs room moments later, to be greeted by a scene of total devastation. Papers were strewn around the floor, many of them crumpled into balls; his prize-winning photographs, which had once been proudly displayed on the wall in heavy black frames, had been taken down and smashed, leaving discoloured rectangles of paint on the wall and glass all over the sofa. His hugely expensive photography books had been pulled off the shelves, their pages ripped to shreds. Everywhere there was carnage. Creepiest of all was that in the middle of all the destruction, a small space had been cleared in which there was a pillow and a duvet.

Sasha had been sleeping there.

Now Dan found something else to focus on.

'The Blake!' he exclaimed from the upstairs landing. 'I don't fucking believe it!'

When they got there he was squatting in front of a white Scandinavian-style sideboard whose doors he had just slid open. He reached in and withdrew a small, squarish picture in a dark wood frame. Josh knew, even before he opened his mouth, what Dan was going to say.

'It's the one she swore had been stolen. The one she said I'd broken in — *to my own house* — and stolen! The crazy, vindictive bitch!'

Josh felt a stab of pure, viscous pleasure. He'd been right then, about Sasha. She *was* dangerous. Evil even, when you thought of all the things she'd done, the lies she'd spread. Telling them Dan had tried to kill her — that he was violent, sadistic even. The phone calls to his headmaster (his stomach lurched involuntarily at the thought).

Then the doubts came again. But the nail . . . And just what did he do last night?

'At least now there'll be no more surprises,' said Sienna. 'At least everyone will know the truth.'

'I'm going up to check on September again,' said Dan. He looked suddenly pale and tired, as if the structure of his face, of which he was so proud, had partly caved in. Josh realized with a start that this couldn't be easy for Dan. Sasha was the mother of his child. They'd slept together in the same bed until a few months ago, waking up to each other every morning, using a bathroom still warm and damp with each other's smell, hearing the private noises they made in their sleep. And yet she'd done all this: faked robberies, lied, cut letters into her arm so deeply

366

that doctors doubted the scars would ever completely fade.

Not to mention what she might have done to her own daughter. When they'd first got back from the hospital, September had clung to her father as if she was velcroed there, following him from room to room as if she was frightened that if she let him out of her sight, he'd be gone like a leaf in the wind. 'I want to live with you, not Mummy,' she'd said several times.

A cursory tour of the house gave some indication why. There was no food in the fridge, just three bottles of white wine and an out-of-date packet of cheese strings. One cupboard held a couple of tins of coconut milk and one of black beans, all dusty as if they'd been there for a while. The bread bin was rank with various crusts of bread, all covered in powdery green mould. Only the cereal cupboard was well stocked, although the packets were all open, the contents mostly stale.

'The poor child must have been living on dry cereal!' Sienna had been horrified, her green eyes wet with pity.

The master bedroom had been in a state. When the thick curtains were pulled back to let in the light, they could see Dan's clothes were all over the place, many of them in pieces, jagged scraps of material lying in multicoloured heaps around the floor. There were also a couple of Dan's T-shirts in the bed. Sasha's underwear was strewn about too, as was her make-up here and in the ensuite bathroom, where there was a box of razor blades on the side of the basin that Josh had tried hard not to look at.

'When did Katia last come, princess?' Dan asked September, who was gazing around with blank, unperturbed eyes that had clearly stopped seeing the devastation as out of the ordinary.

The little girl shrugged. 'Katia stopped coming after Mummy hit her.'

A little muscle at the side of Dan's mouth twitched as if he was pressing his teeth together to stop any words coming out.

Only September's room was in some semblance of order, her clothes neatly put away, the duvet pulled up over the pillow.

'I tidy my room like Mrs Mackenzie says,' she explained proudly.

'I think she means when they have tidy-up time at school,' Josh hazarded.

Sienna had knelt down then, crushing September to her and burying her face in the little girl's hair.

Meanwhile Dan was puzzling over the cracks in the wood of the door and the dark marks around the bottom. 'What happened here?' he asked, running his hand over a patch where the wood had been chipped completely away.

September snuggled in closer to Sienna, and for a moment her eyes looked frightened, as if she was anticipating being told off. 'I don't like it when Mummy locks me in,' she said in a small voice. 'Sometimes I try to get out.'

No wonder Dan needed to go and check on her, even while she slept. Josh couldn't imagine the guilt he must be feeling at having left her in

368

Sasha's care all this time.

'He'll never get over it,' Sienna said now, as if she could read Josh's mind. She had resumed her position curled up in the white armchair in Dan's outsized dressing gown, her bare feet tucked under her. Josh felt a stab of pain as he watched her rubbing her belly in that automatic gesture Hannah did too. Or rather, Hannah used to do. He didn't want to talk any more. Didn't want to think or feel. Didn't want to look at Sienna's hand on her still non-existent bump. Didn't want to think about Hannah's voice saying, 'Just go.' Didn't want to think about the blank space in his memory where last night should have been.

'Aren't you worried about Hannah?' Sienna was staring at him fixedly, and Josh felt a rush of confusion.

'Of course I'm worried about her. She's lost the baby. We both have. God knows how she's going to get through tomorrow.'

Sienna frowned. 'Not because of that,' she said abruptly. Then she saw his face and immediately modified her voice. 'I know you're worried about her because of the baby. We all are, but what I meant is, aren't you worried about her being in the same hospital as Sasha? The woman nearly killed the lot of them.'

Again that sick feeling. The black hole in his memory.

'We don't know for sure she did it deliberately . . . '

Sienna wasn't having it. 'Josh, stop being so nice for once.'

'I'm not being nice. It just seems so far-fetched.'

'Oh, and claiming to be pushed down an escalator isn't?'

He dropped his head into his hands. 'You're right. It's just all so fucked up.'

All of a sudden, he was conscious that Sienna had moved and was standing next to his chair. He felt her hands gently stroking his hair.

'You'll be all right, Josh.'

He closed his eyes, willing himself to believe her.

'You'll be all right,' she said again.

The silk cushion he was clutching was soaked before he even realized he was crying.

★ ★ ★

Josh slept surprisingly well in the pale-grey-and-white guest room on the ground floor of Sasha and Dan's house. For the first time in weeks, he didn't lie awake worrying, or wake up after just one or two hours with violent dreams still crashing around his head.

The rest of the household was still asleep when he awoke, so he got dressed and showered as quietly as he could, grateful that Sasha's particular brand of crazed housekeeping hadn't made it as far as the guest bathroom, and then crept upstairs to find Lily. Pushing open the door of September's room, his eyes fell once again on the cracks in the wood and the horror of yesterday's discoveries returned. Sasha had locked her daughter in this room for long

370

enough that she had tried to kick her way out. He remembered Hannah's fear that there had been no babysitter the night she and Sasha had gone out. He'd never found out what happened, but he knew something had gone seriously awry that night. In the dim light he could make out the prints of a small hand on one of the door panels. His stomach clenched imagining Lily in that situation, the terror she would feel.

September had one of those high beds with a sofa underneath that opened up into a spare bed for sleepovers. In the past, both girls had insisted on sleeping together in that sofa bed, keeping each other awake for hours, squealing with pleasure when their toes tickled each other's legs. But now only September was down there. Lily lay in the top bed, her big eyes wide open.

'Hello, sleepyhead,' he whispered, out of habit, even though she looked far from sleepy.

She turned her face to him and his heart flooded with love at the quick blast of hot, sweet, small-child breath on his cheek as she put her still-chubby arms around his neck and pulled him in close.

'Daddy has to go to the hospital to see Mummy now,' he murmured.

She tightened her grip and shook her head.

For a few seconds, he buried his nose in her soft skin.

'I have to, Liliput. Mummy isn't very well. She needs me to cheer her up.'

He prayed she wouldn't ask about the baby.

Luckily Lily wasn't in the mood for asking questions. 'Don't want you to go,' she said.

'I know, sweetheart, but Sienna will be looking after you and September. Won't that be fun?'

Lily shook her head.

'She says she's going to make a gingerbread house with you this morning — for Christmas.'

'Please, Daddy.'

Josh felt a lump in his throat like a brick. Struggling to keep himself together, he pulled away gently. 'I'll be back before you know it.'

He tried to ignore the agonized 'Daddy!' that followed him out of the room. But minutes later, when he started the car, it was still ringing in his ears.

★ ★ ★

Hannah was awake and — the giddy relief — pleased to see him. Seeing the light go on in her eyes made Josh realize just how long it had been since that happened, since his arrival had produced any reaction other than apathy or mild irritation. The empty, echoey feeling that had dogged the last twenty-four hours was washed away in a sudden wave of love. This was his wife. This was Hannah. The woman he'd loved from their very first weekend together, when they lay in bed reading the papers in silence and there was no awkwardness at all, just a real sense of release — and relief that he'd found her.

'I'm sorry about the baby,' she said.

She looked so desolate, he dropped down next to the bed and folded his arms around her. 'Don't be daft, Hans,' he tried to say, although

372

the words struggled to get past the huge lump in his throat. 'It wasn't your fault.'

'But it was. I didn't want her enough. I thought she'd get in the way. I killed her, just like I nearly killed Gemma.' Her voice splintered into fragments on the last word.

'Shush, darling.' He stroked the hair back from her grief-smudged face as if she was a child — as if she was Lily. Of course, he knew — had known from the beginning — that this car crash would bring back to her that earlier accident, the night that still threaded itself snake-like through the shadows of her mind and dragged her screaming from her dreams.

'It's nothing like what happened with Gemma. It wasn't your fault. It wasn't even your fault back then, Hans. You know that.'

But now Hannah was pumped so full of guilt that it just had to escape, like gas through a valve.

'It was, though. Mum was so ill at that time, you've no idea. It was her worst episode ever. She was so down and so paranoid. Every time we set foot out of the door, she thought something would happen to us — we'd get knocked down by a bus or mugged or stabbed by a random crazy person. She wouldn't let us out of her sight. You can't imagine what it was like.'

It was as if she was trying to convince him, but Josh had heard this before, so he *could* imagine it. The two teenage girls going stir-crazy with boredom. The headstrong younger sister pacing the walls of the little terrace house like something caged.

'But it wasn't your idea. Gemma thought of it.'

'Yes, but it was me who was driving. I went along with it.'

Though Hannah was the older sister by thirteen months, she'd always been the appeaser, the one who tried to keep Gemma level. Josh, who'd first heard the story near the beginning of their relationship, when Hannah was spilling her secrets with the zealousness of a condemned man confessing his sins, could see exactly how it had gone. Hannah was seventeen and had been having driving lessons for three months. Gemma, desperate to go to a party in a village just a few miles away, full of pent-up hormones and resentment, somehow persuaded her that they should sneak out, take their mother's car. She was in bed — well, wasn't she always? She wouldn't even know they were gone. And anyway, she was such a bitch at the moment. Their lives were draining away in front of their eyes. And it was all quiet country roads, after all.

'Gemma can be very persuasive,' said Josh. 'No one could blame you.'

'But they did!' Hannah's pale eyes seemed to be dissolving in tears she had yet to shed. 'I blamed myself — of course I did. I'd never driven in the dark. I completely misjudged that bend. And Mum blamed me. You should have seen her face, Josh!'

This part of the story was new to him. Always in the past, Hannah had skimmed over her mother's reaction, so protective was she of her mum's memory, so determined that he should

374

think only the best of her.

'She arrived at the hospital just after we were brought in, and it was like she hated me, like she wasn't even my mother. I kept telling her I couldn't stop the car, but she was too angry to listen. She kept saying if Gemma died I'd have to live with it for the rest of my life. Then afterwards she went completely the other way, insisting it was all her fault for making our lives so miserable, slapping her own head again and again, asking, 'What have I done?' which was way worse than the anger. And now it's happened all over again.'

Hannah's voice had risen as if about to take off, and Josh instinctively put his arms around her again to tether her to the ground and to him.

'You did nothing wrong, Hans. Don't forget, Gemma's accident was what finally got your mum to seek help. And this wasn't your fault. You didn't make Sasha crash that car.'

At the mention of Sasha's name, Hannah's mouth hardened into a tight line. 'She did it on purpose, you know? She knew exactly what she was doing.'

The rest of the morning was a nightmare. By now Hannah's bleeding was much worse, and she lay in her bed with tears streaming down her face. The hospital was short-staffed and operating on a note of suppressed panic. At one point a senior doctor they'd never seen before bustled into the cubicle where Hannah lay still waiting to go down to surgery, took one look and called to someone else outside, 'No, can't come right now, I've got a bleeder.' Josh had never in his life wanted to hit someone so much.

Hannah was by turns angry and then, barely a minute later, convulsed with sorrow and self-reproach. She raged against Sasha, particularly when Josh explained what they'd found at the house.

'She's always been selfish,' she said. 'People go through tragedies. That's life. They don't have to drag everyone else down with them. They don't have to have such a public unravelling.' Then her whole face crumpled. 'Josh, she could have killed Lily, as well as the baby.'

At other moments, she was almost normal, like when another woman on the ward came out of the loo and remarked conversationally, 'You should see the size of the blood clots I'm passing. One just fell out on the floor and I thought it was my liver.' After she'd gone, Hannah and Josh looked at each other and burst out laughing, quite as if they weren't in a hospital going through one of the most heartbreaking events of their lives. As if, in fact, they might never stop.

Mostly, though, she was wracked with sorrow and guilt, lurching from blaming Sasha to blaming herself. 'I never made the baby feel loved,' she sobbed, and Josh stopped contradicting her and instead just held her and tried to absorb some of her pain, because that was all he could think of doing.

After she was finally taken down to surgery, Josh paced the paved area outside the hospital, breathing in great lungfuls of fresh, non-institutional-smelling air. Outside the main entrance with its desultory Christmas tree, patients in dressing gowns or anoraks over their pyjamas, their bare legs purple with cold, dragged desperately on silent, lonely cigarettes, and for the first time in his life, Josh wished he smoked. Just to give him something to do, some distraction. When he returned to the little waiting room off the ward, his mind heavy with thoughts of Hannah and what she was going through, he remembered the bargain he'd struck on the way to the hospital. He would have to tell her, it occurred to him suddenly. After weeks, even months of estrangement, the events of the last twenty-four hours had brought him and Hannah vividly, clashingly back together. And if they were to have any chance of staying that way, he needed to come clean about what had been going on at work. He would have to scrape out the contents of his mind, just as her body was even now being scraped clean. She needed to know.

Later, after it was all over, he pulled a padded chair with yellow sponge poking through a hole in the cushion up to the side of Hannah's bed and watched her while she slept, overwhelmed with tenderness for her and with grief for the baby they'd lost, and gratitude that at last they felt like a couple again.

When she awoke, he admitted finally, his heart swollen with dread, what had been going on at work — the accusations, the anonymous call he now knew with absolute certainty had been made by Sasha. 'But where have you been going all day?' Hannah asked him, too stunned by a

377

mixture of shock and the after-effects of the anaesthetic to react. Then, without waiting for a reply, she held him for a very long time.

It was tea time, while she was sitting up drinking a cup of tea so stewed it looked orange ('Your tea's been Tangoed,' Josh joked weakly, which set them off again, though it wasn't remotely funny), when she said, 'I want to see Sasha.'

As soon as she'd spoken the words, Josh realized he'd been waiting for them all along. Throughout that endless morning, awareness of Sasha's presence just a couple of floors away had been like a constant shadow in the room.

They looked into each other's eyes and then he nodded.

A text from Dan told them which ward Sasha was on, and after Hannah had been officially discharged they made their way to the lifts.

'Are you sure you're up to this?'

Hannah was as pale as Josh had ever seen her as she huddled in the lift, swaddled in an old hoodie of his and baggy sweatpants. She walked slowly and falteringly after the morning's traumas, holding on to his arm as they made their way towards the ward. At the entrance, the door was being held open by a woman in a pink dressing gown, her skinny legs plunged into outsized furry pink slippers complete with grubby rabbit ears, who was deep in conversation with an awkward-looking young man. 'You tell him, promise?' the woman was saying. Her hand, which still had the cannula for a drip taped to it, was clinging to his arm, holding him back. 'Promise me,' she repeated as Hannah and Josh shuffled past her.

The nurses' station was unmanned, but there was a whiteboard up on the wall behind it with a list of patients and corresponding bed numbers. Sasha Fisher, bed 14.

Josh stopped still. Now that they were here, he found his nerve failing him. Over the last few days and weeks, the Sasha of his imagination had passed from troubled, cast-off wife to the very incarnation of evil. He'd spent night after night lurking outside her house, incubating his hatred until he was so full of it, it hurt to breathe. He'd driven himself to the very brink of madness. But now that he was vindicated, he was finding it hard to hold on to that hatred — it turned to dust when he tried to grab on to it. Hannah, however, was as determined as he'd ever seen her, leading the way into the inner ward without hesitating.

'Oh!'

The sound escaped him before he had a chance to check it. Although he'd been told about the marks on Sasha's arm, he still wasn't prepared for this. The ugly weals of blood. The stark undisguisable letters scored into her flesh.

Sasha herself looked terrible. As if someone had opened a valve and let all the air out of her. Standing awkwardly by the side of the bed, Josh found himself thinking of a hologram, wondering whether, if he went just a little too far to the side, she might disappear altogether.

Her eyes filled with tears when she saw them. 'Oh fuck, I'm so happy to see you two. I've been

379

going crazy in here. Well, crazier anyway!'

She reached out a hand towards Hannah, but Hannah refused to take it.

'Hans, I'm so sorry. About the baby. Dan told me. There was nothing I could do. The car was out of my control.'

'You did it on purpose.' Hannah's voice was unemotional, flat, as if she was passing comment on the weather.

Sasha's face crumpled.

'We know, Sasha. OK?' Sasha's self-pity had infuriated Josh. 'We know what's been going on. We know it was you who did all that stuff — you staged the break-in at your house, you keyed Dan's car and smashed the window and made up lies about him being violent and into disgusting, sick pornography. That's your daughter's father! What were you thinking? And then when we wouldn't take your side against him, you turned on us, too. You could have ruined my career, you know?'

Sasha was staring at him, her eyes huge in her shrunken face. She was shaking her head slowly, tears silently flowing down her hollow cheeks. 'No. You're wrong. I wouldn't hurt you two. I'd never hurt you. You're my friends.'

'Exactly,' Hannah broke in. 'We're your friends. Or rather, we *were* your friends. Yet you nearly killed me — and Lily — and you did kill the baby. All to try to get back at Dan, to try to make him feel guilty.'

'Hannah.' Sasha tried to grab Hannah's hand, but she moved out of the way. 'This is me you're talking to — Sasha. I would never hurt Lily. I

380

love Lily, you know that. Look, I know I've been going off the rails these last few months. Dan leaving brought back everything from my childhood and I admit I've struggled to cope. I know I've done some really stupid things.' She winced as she swallowed, as if it was painful. 'You're right, I did that thing to Dan's car and smashed the window of that woman's flat. I couldn't stand it, don't you see? I could see the four of you in there laughing and it felt like I'd been completely erased, like I didn't exist. And Dan never hit me, or left porn on the computer. I shouldn't have said all that stuff. I've just been so crazy with grief.'

She looked at Josh, as if for sympathy, and he felt another twinge of anger.

'But I didn't do the other stuff, I swear. Someone *did* try to kill me, someone *did* break into the house. And I have no idea about the calls to your work, Josh. I promise.'

'I saw it, Sasha! I was at your house last night and I saw that painting you claimed had gone missing. It was in the sideboard.'

Now that the anger had finally arrived, he was almost enjoying it. There was something almost righteous about it. Finally, after all these weeks of being powerless to act against all the crap that had been going on, here was his chance to be heard.

'I don't understand.' Sasha was looking at him in total incomprehension.

'And I suppose you don't understand about the razor blades in your bathroom either, that September could easily have found, or the marks on her door where she tried to get out after you locked her in her bedroom — probably so you could go out, leaving her all on her own. She's not even five years old!'

Now Sasha collapsed entirely. 'Oh God,' she moaned, raising her hands to her face. 'Poor Temmy. I can't explain it. I was sick. I always waited until she was asleep.' Again that quick glance of appeal. 'Fuck, I'm a terrible mother. No wonder they've taken her away from me. Oh shit, shit, shit, shit.'

Josh clapped his hand to his mouth as Sasha began banging her head rhythmically backwards on the metal hospital bed.

'Shit, shit, shit,' she continued. Clang, clang, clang.

A nurse hurried over, her round face knotted in disapproval. 'What's all this noise about, Mrs Fisher?' she said, grasping Sasha roughly by the shoulders to stop her throwing herself backwards. 'We don't want to be upsetting all the other ladies, do we?'

She looked suspiciously at Hannah and Josh. 'I think Mrs Fisher needs to rest now. You'd better come back another time.'

As they turned and walked away, the soft thud of Sasha's pitiful body against the bedpost followed them across the room.

28

It was an unseasonably warm day, and Hannah raised her face greedily to the sky, soaking up that sense of wellbeing that always came with feeling the rays on her skin after a long, sun-starved winter.

The excited squeals of laughter coming from the giant trampoline in the corner of the garden mixed with the distant birdsong and the lazy buzzing of not-quite-awake bees, creating a Sounds of Summer soundtrack although it was still only late March. She took a long breath in, enjoying the sensation of filling her body with oxygen and flushing the toxins out of her system.

'Ta-da!'

Sienna plonked a huge bowl of salad down on the long, silvery teak table. Hannah recognized the bowl as one Sasha had picked out at a souk in Marrakech when the four of them had spent a weekend in a riad — Sasha and Dan's present for her thirty-second birthday. It seemed like a different life now.

'Please don't look too closely,' Sienna said of the eclectic mixture of leaves and vegetables heaped in the brightly patterned ceramic dish. 'I just threw everything in together. Douse it in dressing and it'll be fine.'

'All the ingredients are edible?' Dan poked the concoction dubiously with one of those wooden salad servers shaped like a hand. 'You sure that big thing in the middle isn't a pan scourer or something?'

'It's an avocado, idiot! At least, I think it's an avocado . . .'

Hannah looked up and smiled, thankful that she could finally look at Sienna's now visible baby bump without that answering painful lurch in her own abdomen. Now that she and Josh had decided to try for another baby, she felt much calmer about everything. There was an old song lyric that had been constantly lodged in her head in the days after the accident about not knowing what you had till it had gone. She mourned her lost baby with a desperation that shocked her. But she was starting to make peace with herself. 'It wasn't your fault,' Josh kept telling her with a touching insistence. 'It wasn't either of our faults.' Now, at last, she was starting to believe him.

'Can we eat on the trampoline?'

September's transparently fluttery-eyed appeal invoked the usual indulgent capitulation in her father.

'I think that might just be permissible.'

He'd have to start saying no to her eventually, but for the time being no one begrudged the little girl the chance to be spoilt. Not after what she'd been through. The trampoline had been the biggest gift, entailing the digging up of Sasha's prize decked Moroccan chill-out area, but there'd been a stream of others. Dan's way of trying to make it up to September for not having been around to protect her. Lily, as usual, was quieter than her friend.

'You OK, Liliput?' Hannah called.

Her daughter nodded slowly. 'Don't like salad,' she said, eyeing the heaped bowl in pride of place on the table.

Sienna breathed in slowly, and for a second Hannah thought she was offended. Then she smiled. 'Don't worry, you two can have fishfinger sarnies. How's that?'

Dan put his hand out and gave Sienna an affectionate pat on the bum and Hannah closed her eyes again. Now that she and Josh had started, very slowly, to rediscover each other sexually, she no longer felt that instinctive recoil at the sight of other people being intimate in public, but it was still a little odd to be sitting in the garden Sasha had designed (well, with the help of an expensive 'landscape architect'), while her husband, albeit soon-to-be-ex-husband, touched up his pregnant new girlfriend.

On the whole though, it was almost miraculous how fully Sasha had been expunged from their lives over the last three months. The police had examined the tyre but hadn't found any conclusive evidence that it had been deliberately tampered with, so there were no charges to bring. However, in view of the self-inflicted damage to her arm and her neglect of September, social workers had been involved, and it was agreed Dan should stay in the house to look after his daughter. In the meantime, Sasha had been admitted to an upmarket residential psychiatric clinic often in the headlines for treating celebrity addicts. The money had come from a trust fund her father

385

had set up for the express function, as far as Hannah could tell, of bailing his daughter out when things went disastrously wrong.

Hannah hadn't seen Sasha, of course. She doubted whether she would ever be able to see her again. So many times in the past she had forgiven her behaviour, made excuses for her, tried to see things from her perspective. But this last thing she found she couldn't forgive.

It had been a strange time, trying to claw her way out from the pit of her grief without the support of the people she'd normally turn to. Her mother (stupid how her heart still constricted at the thought of her being dead), Sasha. Even Gemma hadn't been around so much. She'd come to stay the first weekend after it happened, but there had been a stiffness there, an awkwardness that had never existed between them before. Hannah told herself it had nothing to do with the photograph of Josh or what Sasha had told her, nor the car crash that had brought that earlier accident rushing back into her head, but still she found it hard to be natural around her sister, and the next time Gemma had offered to come to stay, she'd found an excuse to say no.

But how weird it was that the woman she'd first perceived as nothing but a threat should turn out to be such a saviour. Since Hannah got back from the hospital, all but paralysed by guilt and grief, Sienna had been quietly and unobtrusively present — sorting out the mess of the flat, writing explanatory emails to features editors on her behalf, picking up Lily from school. Just sitting there listening when Hannah needed to vent about what had happened. Now she couldn't imagine life without her. Gemma hadn't liked Sienna, of course. But then Gemma hadn't liked Sasha either. Now Hannah wondered whether her sister might not just be jealous of her friendships. More worryingly, Lily wasn't too keen on her either, but then, as Josh said, Lily was used to having Hannah to herself. And maybe she and September had outgrown each other. It happened at that age. When she felt stronger, Hannah resolved to widen her social net. Well, big school was already helping with that. But for now, Hannah needed Sienna's support.

'How was your first week back at school?' Sienna was asking Josh now, peering over the top of her eccentric-looking salad.

'Oh, you know. Interesting.'

Josh liked Sienna — Hannah sometimes worried that he liked her a little too much, but she knew he wasn't about to go into details about how it really felt to go back to work after you'd had such a big question mark hanging over you. Kelly Kavanagh had withdrawn her allegation — Josh said the supply teacher who'd replaced him had actually given her worse marks than he had, which had led to a rapid change of heart. And when the head had been informed by social workers of what had gone on with Sasha and the likelihood of her being behind the anonymous calls, the governors had agreed there was no case to answer and Josh had been unanimously reinstated. But, as he'd said to Ian at that first meeting, mud sticks. Josh knew some of the kids called him Paedo behind his back, and Hannah could only imagine how awful that must feel. They still hadn't had a proper, honest discussion about that period when Josh was leaving the house in the morning and going God knows where, because he couldn't face telling her the truth about what had happened. She'd failed him then, she realized now. And while they were both enjoying their fragile, newly cemented accord, Hannah knew that until they'd really explored what had gone wrong during that time, they wouldn't completely be able to move on.

'I still can't get over being able to be here, with her,' Dan said, gazing at September as she and Lily ate their lunch cross-legged on the trampoline, their heads bent together. 'It's like being given a second chance, you know.'

'If you start counting your blessings, I might have to be sick into this most excellent salad,' said Josh.

'Oi, less of the sarcasm,' laughed Sienna, prodding Josh with one of the wooden salad-server hands.

Dan, though, was clearly intent on having a serious moment. 'I blame myself, you know.'

For a moment Hannah thought Dan might actually be about to take some responsibility for the chain of events he'd set in motion.

'I should have realized my leaving would set Sasha off. I was just too in love to see it.'

Sienna blew him a kiss across the table, while Josh shuffled awkwardly in his chair next to her.

'What exactly did happen to Sasha when she was little?' Hannah had never dared ask this question outright. Sasha's traumatic childhood was one of those mythical things that everyone knew existed, but not exactly what they were.

Dan glanced over at the trampoline, but September and Lily had now gone back to bouncing again, taking it in turns to perform silly mid-air jumps and grading each other out of ten.

'Sasha's mother was a cunt, basically.' Dan picked up a lettuce leaf from his plate and started tearing it to pieces. 'She never really got over Sasha's dad leaving and blamed Sasha, because she couldn't accept that he just couldn't stand being married to her. She hardly had anything to do with Sasha if she could help it, and then she married this complete arsehole who got off on little girls, and when Sasha told her mum what was going on, she ignored it. She told Sasha she was making it up to get attention. She accused her — a nine-year-old child — of being jealous of her. She said Sasha had driven her father away by fawning all over him and she wasn't going to let her drive his replacement away too.'

'She knew, and she did nothing?' Hannah felt sick. It was what she'd always suspected from the little snippets that Sasha had let slip over the years, but to hear it spelt out like that, so brutally, was a shock. For a moment all four of them watched the two girls on the trampoline and Hannah knew they were all thinking the same thing — Sasha would have been not much older than September and Lily when the abuse started.

Sienna got up from the table and went inside

the house. Hannah wondered whether being pregnant might make her especially sensitive. She was well aware of how the hormones could drive you from one emotional extreme to another. Hers had well and truly disappeared now, but the memory of them had lingered for quite a while after the miscarriage, tricking her trusting body into believing it was still growing something inside it, still expectant, still fruitful.

'What about her real father?' she asked Dan.

'He was a selfish bastard. He'd moved on to wife number two by then, and had another baby and moved to France. Having a child from his first marriage come to stay would have got in the way of his playing happy families.'

Dan seemed oblivious to any irony in what he was saying, to any links between the situation he was describing and his own.

'But surely he couldn't just ignore what Sasha was saying?'

'Yes, but she didn't say it, did she? Bear in mind she was just a child and she hardly ever saw her dad. They didn't have the kind of relationship where you just say, 'Oh Daddy, by the way, my mother's husband comes into my room at night and rapes me.' She hinted at it the few times she saw him, but he never picked up on it.'

'But you think he knew?'

'I think he wouldn't let himself know. It would have been too inconvenient for him. I'm sure that's why he set up the trust fund for her before he died, the one that's paying for the five-star nut house she's in now. It's guilt money.'

For the first time since the accident, Hannah allowed herself to feel pity for Sasha, for the child she'd once been. No wonder she was so totally screwed up. What chance did she have — had she ever had — to lead a normal life, with all that lurking in her past?

'How long did she put up with it?'

'Till she was sixteen. That's when she left home and came to London.'

Seven years. She'd lived with it for seven years. What did that kind of thing do to a child? How did it affect your ability to form relationships? To parent? How did you learn love when you'd never been shown it?

'Now,' said Sienna, emerging through the folding glass doors at the back of the house bearing a large cheesecake, 'it's time to stop talking and celebrate your fabulous new commission with cake. Double celebration, because I didn't make it myself!'

Hannah was embarrassed, but still pinkly pleased. The commission wasn't anything exciting in itself — just a straightforward case-study interview. But it was a newspaper she'd never written for before. And after the work famine she'd just been through, any commission was a bonus.

'I thank you all kindly,' she said as the girls scampered over to toast her with cake. 'And thanks for offering to look after Lil, too. I'd have been totally up the creek if you hadn't.'

It was only after she'd accepted the work and put the phone down to the commissioning editor, hoping she had managed not to sound too pathetically grateful, that she'd realized the day the interview had been set up was an inset day at school, so she had no childcare. If she closed her eyes, she could still feel that tight band of panic across her chest as she'd imagined phoning the editor back to say she couldn't do the job after all. Luckily she hadn't had to. Josh had convinced her that Sienna wouldn't mind looking after Lily and had even rung her himself to ask, reporting back that she'd be delighted to help. Lily herself wasn't so delighted, but Hannah would make it up to her when she got paid. Take her out somewhere special.

'Fiddlesticks!' Sienna was smiling, showing her perfect little teeth, white like Tic Tacs. 'I'm happy to do it.'

★　★　★

Later, when they were back at home and Lily was finally asleep, after a protracted bout of tears that seemed to come out of nowhere, Hannah brought up the subject of Sasha again. She was like a sore spot you just couldn't stop touching.

'No wonder she was so desperate for her and Dan to stay together. After what happened to her, it must have seemed like the end of the world for September to be part of a broken family. And it must have triggered so much stuff from her past.' They leaned back on the sofa and Josh put his arm around her, still tentatively, as if he was half expecting her to shrug it off or stiffen under his touch as she would have done not so long ago. They still had a long way to go to get

392

their relationship back to where it used to be. Sometimes, when Hannah was crying in the night and wouldn't let him comfort her, she felt the distance between them unfurling endlessly like a coil of rope and wondered if they'd ever find their way back to each other. But at other times, like now, she felt as if they might just make it. She found it helped to view the last few months as some sort of endurance test that they had been through, like one of those sadistic game shows where contestants have to eat live frogs and crawl through rat-infested sewers. She was proud of how they'd survived. Occasionally, she sought out statistics on how many marriages fail and felt quietly content that they were still here, still together.

They would come through this, she decided now as Josh picked up the remote and flicked his way through the channels in the way she was determined not to resent. Their marriage would be one of the successful ones. She realized how many threats lurked around the shady edges of their relationship, but they were wiser now, warier. If nothing else, the tragedy of Dan and Sasha had taught them not to rely on anyone else. They were the unit — the two of them, and Lily, of course. Everyone else was on the outside.

On y va, as Sienna would say.

She leaned back against Josh's arm, closed her eyes and allowed herself, finally, to relax.

Lucie/Sienna, aged twenty-four

Lucie is back, that petite cochonne. I think it's because of the baby. Until recently, I hadn't seen her for years. I wish she'd go away again. I'm worried what she'll do. I'm worried what she already has done. Gobble, gobble, gobble. When Lucie and Eloise were in the womb, Lucie ate Eloise. No, really, she did! There's a name for it. Vanishing Twin Syndrome, where one twin grows so big it totally absorbs the other. Pffff. Now you see it, now you don't. Mother never got over it. Imagine expecting two little babies and ending up with one giant, greedy one! No wonder she lost the plot. She couldn't get past what Lucie had done, couldn't stop thinking about poor fragile Eloise she failed to protect.

And now my baby needs protecting, too. Not from Sasha any more, now she's locked away merrily self-harming somewhere (that thing on her arm that so shocked them all — amateur time, baby!). It's Hannah and Josh who are the threat now. Lucie doesn't like how they stuck by Sasha and refused to write statements even when they knew she wasn't fit. Mothers should be fit to be mothers. It's a basic maternal requirement. Lucie made the call to Josh's work, and wrote the things on Hannah's Twitter. She popped that note into little Lily's bag. She doesn't like how much influence Hannah and Josh have over Dan. She doesn't like the history they all shared before, the way they keep telling in-jokes that only they understand. Some of us non-Jurassics were still at school when all these oh-so-amusing things (not!) happened. But you know what Lucie especially doesn't like? Those two little girls. They're sitting in the back of the car right now. I can see the tops of their heads. From where I'm sitting, here behind the wheel, they could almost be twins. Double trouble!

I love those two girls, really I do, but I'm scared Lucie doesn't understand.

She's been quite a bitch to them, setting one against the other, strongest against weakest. It's survival of the fittest, she says. But then she's insane. All that stuff she did to Sasha — the break-in, the escalator, the nail in the car tyre — I'm scared of what will happen when the baby comes. Lucie is such a greedy-guts. Gobble, gobble, gobble.

We're on our way to the seaside for the day — heading down to Sussex for a nice long walk near the cliffs on the South Downs. Me and the double-trouble girls. I offered. I'm happy to help out. They've all been through so much — Dan and Josh and Hannah — and I feel like it's my fault. If I hadn't fallen in love with Dan, none of it would have happened, so this is the least I can do. I just wish Lucie hadn't come too. Sitting there in the front seat as if she was invited. Cheeky cow! Maybe she'll leave soon. Now that would be a relief. Maybe she'll check her phone, and realize she's late for something, and unbuckle her belt and go. I'll see her in the rear-view mirror — a blur of motion at the edge of my vision. Here today, gone tomorrow.

Lickety-split.

Acknowledgements

Massive thanks to everyone who made this a better book — Felicity Blunt at Curtis Brown, and Jane Lawson, Kate Samano, Bella Whittington and Leanne Oliver at my wonderful publishers, Transworld.

Thanks also to Dr Roma Cartwright for her help with all things medical, and to Fiona Godfrey for advice on schools and disciplinary procedures. Any mistakes that remain are completely down to me.

I've been lucky enough to enjoy tremendous support from writer friends during the gestation of this book, particularly Louise Millar, Amanda Jennings and Lisa Jewell.

Other friends have also done their bit to keep me sane, notably Rikki Finegold, Juliet Brown, Mel Amos, Helen Bates and, of course, the Tuesday Club.

Writing days can be long and lonely — special thanks to Ben Clarke for cyber company and up-to-the-minute weather reports.

I owe a huge debt of gratitude to my lovely family — Gaynor Cohen, Sara Cohen, Simon Cohen, Emma Cohen, Colin Hall, Ed Hall and Alfie Hall, Margaret Fawcett and Paul Fawcett.

And love, as always, to Michael, Otis, Jake and Billie.

We do hope that you have enjoyed reading this large print book.

Did you know that all of our titles are available for purchase?

We publish a wide range of high quality large print books including:
Romances, Mysteries, Classics
General Fiction
Non Fiction and Westerns

Special interest titles available in large print are:
The Little Oxford Dictionary
Music Book
Song Book
Hymn Book
Service Book

Also available from us courtesy of Oxford University Press:
Young Readers' Dictionary
(large print edition)
Young Readers' Thesaurus
(large print edition)

For further information or a free brochure, please contact us at:
Ulverscroft Large Print Books Ltd.,
The Green, Bradgate Road, Anstey,
Leicester, LE7 7FU, England.
Tel: (00 44) **0116 236 4325**
Fax: (00 44) **0116 234 0205**

Other titles published by Ulverscroft:

SOMEONE ELSE'S WEDDING

Tamar Cohen

Mr and Mrs Max Irving request the company of: Mrs Fran Friedman, mourning her empty nest, the galloping years and a disastrous haircut. Mr Saul Friedman, runner of marathons, and increasingly distant husband. The two Misses Friedman, Pip and Katy — one pining over the man she can't have, the other shaking off the man she no longer wants. At the marriage of their son, James Irving, forbidden object of troubling desire. For thirty-six hours of secrets and lies, painted-on smiles and potential ruin. And drinks, plenty of drinks . . . There's nothing like a wedding for stirring up the past. As Fran negotiates her way from Saturday morning to Sunday evening, she is forced to confront long-buried memories, and to make decisions that will have far-reaching consequences for them all.

THE WAR OF THE WIVES

Tamar Cohen

Imagine being happily married for twenty-eight years. You have three children, a lovely house and a husband who travels a lot — but even after all this time, you still love each other. Or imagine being happily married for seventeen years. You have a young daughter, a lovely home and a husband who travels a lot — but you really love each other. Then one day you get a call that turns your world upside down: your husband is dead. You are devastated. You go to the funeral . . . and come face to face with his other widow. Another wife, another family. They never knew you existed, you never knew they existed. It can't be true. It must be a mistake. It has to be her fault — all of it. Or is it?